TREACHERY ON TENTH STREET

Also available by Kate Belli

Gilded Gotham Mysteries
Betrayal on the Bowery
Deception by Gaslight

TREACHERY ON TENTH STREET

A GILDED GOTHAM MYSTERY

Kate Belli

CROOKED
LANE

NEW YORK

Published in the United States by Crooked Lane Books, an imprint of The Quick Brown Fox & Company LLC.

Crooked Lane Books and its logo are trademarks of The Quick Brown Fox & Company LLC.

Library of Congress Catalog-in-Publication data available upon request.

ISBN (hardcover): 978-1-63910-092-7
ISBN (ebook): 978-1-63910-093-4

Cover design by Nicole Lecht

Printed in the United States.

www.crookedlanebooks.com

Crooked Lane Books
34 West 27th St., 10th Floor
New York, NY 10001

First Edition: October 2022

10 9 8 7 6 5 4 3 2 1

For the women in the pictures

CHAPTER 1

Newport, Rhode Island

July 1889

The relentless crashing of the waves suited Daniel's tumultuous mood.

He stared at the black, churning water, leaning on the balustrade of the veranda of the Otts' grand summer cottage. The massive, shingled house loomed at his back, all twisting, pointed towers and thrusting balconies. It was a pleasant enough house during the day, cool and shady with impressive views of the bay, but at night something about its misshapen silhouette disturbed him.

At least, tonight it did.

Daniel swirled the very good whiskey in its cut crystal tumbler and took a sip, appreciating the mellow burn of the amber liquid as it traveled down his throat. Clarence Ott kept a well-stocked liquor cabinet, but then so did all the summer denizens of Newport. He couldn't hear the sounds of the ball transpiring inside over the roar of the ocean, and frankly that suited him fine.

They blended together, these events. He'd been in Newport only a week and was already tired of it, already longing to get back to Manhattan, despite how relentless the July heat had become. He knew, from the long years of his childhood, the city would be sweltering, barely habitable, but from this vantage point it sounded like heaven.

The city in the summer was an *empty* city.

Secrets that were hidden among the typical press of bodies, the endless rounds of parties and obligations due to the social season and work, might be laid bare in the summer, exposed by those hot, vacant streets.

Daniel sighed and returned his attention to the waves. The long stretch of beach he contemplated was bright with moonlight, almost as if theater lights illuminated it. The desire to descend the wooden staircase that led from the veranda to the beach was nearly overwhelming. He could visualize his shoes neatly lined up at the foot of those stairs, feel the sand under his feet, between his toes.

It was bright enough he could take a swim, if he wanted to.

Suddenly his muscles yearned to be moving through the water, finding joy in the resistance and effort of the motions, in the sting of salt water. He'd already swum that morning, already enjoyed the weightlessness of it, of finding a moment of peace floating on his back, with nothing clouding his vision but the surrounding water and the endless expanse of summer blue sky. Swimming was his preferred method of exercise; whether in a natatorium, the ocean, or a clear lake, he relished the intensity and primacy of it.

Never in the Hudson, though. That river was off-limits to him, for reasons far more personal than its filth.

Daniel knocked back the remainder of his whiskey and glanced over his shoulder at the brightly lit interior visible through the French doors. The ballroom was on the opposite end of the corridor, and while a few guests milled in the hallway, the vast majority were still in that grand room, doubtless eating and drinking and dancing and laughing and doing all the things one typically did at a ball.

Genevieve was nowhere in sight.

The unceasing sound of the waves drew his attention back to the beach.

He knew the source of his restlessness, and she was somewhere in that ballroom wearing a dusty-pink gown. The same color, he realized with a start, as the first time he'd seen her in a ballroom, a year and a half ago now. When he had figured out that she wasn't a girl playacting at being a reporter, trying to make it in the big city, but that she was, like him, one of New York's elite Astor 400.

He'd be leaving the day after tomorrow, Daniel reminded himself.

You can make it another two days.

Daniel rubbed his hand across his jaw, thinking. It was less about the time he had to spend in Newport, which was pleasant enough—more than pleasant, really. He hadn't spent many summers in this enclave of upper-tier society, but there was no denying the refreshing quality of the place. The salty air, the wild ocean, the sailing, the less restrictive schedule, all suited him well. No, it wasn't Newport itself that had him anxious; it was the two unpleasant tasks he had to undertake before he could leave.

First, he had to inform his best friends and hosts, Rupert and Esmie Milton, that he would be leaving.

He hated to do it. It was their first season here as a married couple, newlyweds as their honeymoon had been postponed, and so far, they were a grand success. Rupert was typical Rupert, the same incorrigible charmer, but marriage had softened him somewhat, smoothed out some of his rougher edges. No, not just marriage. Esmie had done that.

And Esmie was coming more and more out of her shell, her confidence building with each passing day. She and Rupert had even talked of hosting a party at the season's end, the prospect of which would have caused the Esmie of a year ago such stress she would have turned a violent shade a pink and not been able to utter a syllable. But she was blossoming, right before their eyes. Somehow Rupert's innate confidence gave her confidence as well.

They were a good match. Better than anyone, including themselves, could have anticipated.

And they would be sorely disappointed by his abrupt departure. Though, once he explained, he hoped they would understand the necessity.

That was the first unpleasant task.

The second was informing Genevieve he would be returning to Manhattan with her.

He could already anticipate her bristling reaction and the argument that would ensue. Her protests that she was perfectly capable of handling herself, that she was a grown woman, that she didn't need a minder.

All of which were true. None of which would dissuade him.

Genevieve was returning to New York to investigate a potential murder, and despite her tremendous capabilities, he wasn't going to let her do so alone.

Not after what they'd been through together a mere few weeks prior.

And just like that, he was there again. His mind had been doing this of late. Sending him when he least expected it back to that moment deep in the bowels of the city's gas-works, barely conscious and bloody, staring down the cold, deadly barrel of Tommy Meade's gun. It was so real that, for a moment, the noise of the waves, the brine-scented breeze, the moonlit beach all disappeared, and he felt again the pain in his head from where it had been hit, the same in his gut from being kicked, the nausea of contusion. He could see the dim, distant stars shining indifferently behind Tommy's head, feel how wet his shirt was from his own blood.

He could see, clear as if he were looking at a photograph, the mental picture of Genevieve he had clutched in his mind, of her recovering after their treacherous swim through the East River, fleeing gunrunners.

It was the image by which he'd chosen to take his last breath, as he truly had believed he was on the verge of dying.

It was the moment he'd realized how complete his love was for her.

But he wasn't ready to risk telling her, not yet. Genevieve had become distant again. Not quite as cold and unreachable as the stars he'd seen that night he was sure he would die, but close. It had been this way ever since her friend Callie Maple had appeared in Genevieve's dining room last week, after having disappeared for months while trying to forge a new life for herself following the loss of her fortune.

Daniel's heart sank to his stomach at the memory, the same as it had as soon as he'd seen Callie's face that bright summer morning. As happy as he had been for Genevieve to be reunited with her friend, he had known, instantly, that Callie was in trouble.

Trouble. They couldn't seem to shake it, he and Genevieve.

No, now was not the time to air his feelings. He was willing to be patient a bit longer, while this situation with Callie played out. Maybe, once the dust had settled, he could broach the topic.

A small, glowing ember of hope burned in the center of his chest at the thought. He tamped it, but not all the way, allowing a spark to remain. It was enough for now.

It would have to be.

Sighing, Daniel straightened. It was time to return to the ball. Perhaps he could dance with Genevieve again.

The thought made him smile. They had already danced twice tonight, and a third might raise a few brows, but both of them were old enough not to care.

Genevieve was an excellent dance partner.

As he turned to go, a flash of something white flickered in the periphery of his vision, stopping him in his tracks.

Someone was on the beach.

Daniel leaned against the balustrade again and squinted, trying to make out what he had seen. The strip of beach was long and thin, tapering into rocky outcroppings at either end, which rose into impenetrable walls of granite and black shale studded with hardy wildflowers. The only way to access the sand was from one of the few houses that sat atop these rocks and had, like the Otts', a wooden staircase leading to the beach.

Had someone come out before him? Some other attendee of the ball anxious for a few minutes' peace, desirous of the sound of the ocean filling their ears?

The specter moved more quickly, and Daniel straightened, a frown forming on his forehead. The figure in white was running. And another, more shadowy form appeared, harder to see against the background of the rocks, but it seemed to be someone dressed in black.

A man and a woman. Her in a pale dress, him in evening clothes.

Daniel's concern morphed into alarm as the woman ran straight toward and then into the surf, not pausing even as a wave crashed against her shins. The man was behind her and the forms merged, locked together and swaying, knee-deep in the water. Daniel found his hands were gripping the balustrade, and he forced his fingers to relax.

The sound of applause echoed from within the cottage, loud enough to be heard over the waves. A quick glance over his shoulder into the lit interior confirmed something of interest must be happening in the ballroom itself, as the corridor was now devoid of people.

He turned back. Another wave crashed into the figures, nearly knocking them down. Was it his imagination, or were they deeper now?

Who were they, tangled in the ocean? Lovers sharing an embrace?

Something about the way they moved, about how the woman had run into the water, told him this wasn't the case.

And if they weren't embracing, then . . . what?

Nothing good.

His body was moving, fast, even as his mind tried to talk him out of it.

Don't jump to conclusions. Just because you almost died a few weeks ago doesn't mean every situation is sinister, doesn't mean everyone is in danger.

The logical part of his brain knew this and understood it to be true, but the illogical side—his gut, for lack of a better word—didn't believe a word of it.

His gut knew there was trouble happening on that narrow strip of sand.

The wooden stairs were slick and unstable as he pounded down them in his dress shoes. Daniel held tight to the rough banister for fear of slipping, ignoring the sharp pain of a splinter embedding itself in his palm. The beach disappeared from sight as he descended, the staircase encased by the low, rocky cliff on either side, then reappeared as he leapt over the bottom three steps and landed in the damp sand.

Panting, Daniel ran in the direction he had seen the couple, straining his eyes to find them again in the dark.

There was no one.

He ran the length of the beach, alternately scanning the waves to his right and the rocks to his left, searching for any sign of the couple. But despite the luminosity of the moon, he saw nothing. When he reached the spot where the sand ended, hemmed in by rocks and water, he stopped and turned, taking in the route he'd just traversed.

Foreboding settled over his shoulders. The waves continued to crash, only now the noise was troubling, transforming his earlier restlessness into disquiet. Daniel placed his hands on his hips and stared at the water for a few minutes, waiting for his heart to slow.

Where did they go?

His mind recoiled from the obvious answer.

Daniel retraced his steps back to the Otts' house, slowly this time, continuing to look for some trace of the people he'd seen from the grand veranda. The sea yielded nothing, offering only its continuous roar. He followed his own footprints in the sand, hoping against hope he wouldn't have to disrupt the ball and call the authorities.

What if you didn't see anyone? What if your mind is playing tricks, new ones now, making you see things and people that aren't there?

Daniel ignored the voice, despite its insistence, and stubbornly let his eyes continue to rove every inch of sand he could.

There.

Something he'd missed earlier, in his haste to find the couple. Footprints in the sand, fresh ones. Two sets, it looked like, jumbled and confused in some spots but clearly walking side by side in others. They crossed his own set in a perpendicular line, moving from the rocky bluff to the water rather than down the length of the beach.

The water was, obviously, one end point. Daniel gazed thoughtfully at the rocks that constituted the other end point, then followed the scuffed marks in the sand in that direction. As he approached, a staircase, similar to the one he had descended at the Otts' house, appeared.

Daniel paused, indecisive. This obviously led to someone's private residence. For a moment he pictured himself climbing the stairs and knocking on a stranger's door, asking if anything was amiss.

He glanced back at the ocean again.

No, whatever had transpired, whatever he had witnessed, was private. The footprints suggested that as soon as he had run for the Otts' stairs, the couple had pulled themselves from the ocean and walked the short distance to this staircase.

The alternative was unthinkable.

Reluctantly, Daniel walked the rest of the way back to the Otts'. There was no way he could rejoin the ball now, no way he could have that last dance with Genevieve. His shoes were filled with sand, his socks and the cuffs of his trousers soaked. He would have to send a footman in to find Rupert and Esmie so he could explain.

Once back on the veranda, Daniel leaned his hands against the railing and stared into the night. A few clouds were drifting by now, not many, not enough to suggest rain, but enough to occasionally dim the moon with their passing, throwing the beach into shadow. Now that he was on higher ground, he tried in vain to make out the other houses that dotted this section of the bluff, but it was no use. The grand estates were too far apart, and it was too dark. Not a single light shone from another structure that he could see, save that of the distant lighthouse.

Whose houses were on this particular bluff? Genevieve would know.

Genevieve.

The very thought of her pulled his attention away from the dark and turbulent ocean and toward the bright, warm corridor just on the inside of the glass doors he faced.

Maybe it was time to get the second of the unpleasant tasks he had to face out of the way. He pushed the couple on the beach out of his mind for now, knowing he would return to it later.

It was time to leave, both the ball and Newport.

But first, he would have to tell Genevieve he would be joining her investigation.

CHAPTER 2

Genevieve had just taken a large bite of a lemon tartlet when someone tapped on her shoulder. She turned, surprised to find one of the Otts' footmen discreetly hovering behind her.

"Yes?" she said, swallowing hastily. Esmie watched them with curious eyes over her own plate, piled high with delectable sweets, as the footman leaned over and whispered in Genevieve's ear.

Another surprise.

"Daniel wants me to meet him on the veranda," she said to Esmie as the footman walked away. Genevieve frowned after the footman's departing back, puzzled. Why on earth would Daniel summon her to meet him outside? Why didn't he simply come inside to find them? She and Esmie had been enjoying sampling the dessert buffet.

Esmie looked longingly at her plate.

Genevieve sighed and handed her own plate to a different passing footman with a tray, surreptitiously brushing the crumbs from her fingertips. "You don't have to come," she said. "I'll go see what he wants and find you later."

"No, let me find Rupert and join you," Esmie said. "I just want to try the Neapolitan cake first."

Genevieve smiled. Esmie adored sweets, even more than she did.

"Though," Esmie continued, a slight flush staining her cheeks, "perhaps Daniel wants to speak with you privately?"

The thought brought Genevieve up short, and she felt her own face heat in response. There was no denying she and Daniel had grown closer this summer, when they had joined forces to save a young society woman, Nora Westwood. Daniel had nearly been killed by his longtime nemesis, Tommy Meade, but luckily, she had shot Tommy in the nick of time.

Genevieve had been keeping a slight distance from Daniel ever since. The shock and anguish she'd felt when she had believed he'd been about to die still reverberated through her body at times and, combined with the trauma of having taken someone's life, had culminated in a miasma of emotion she found herself ill equipped to handle.

Added to all that was the fact that she had turned down his marriage proposal the year prior. She hadn't been ready to accept any such thing at the time, but the rush of feeling brought about by Daniel's near death left her scraped raw and vulnerable, now questioning what exactly she *did* want from him.

She needed time to think, to sort through her feelings.

What if she had accepted that proposal, for example? Would he expect her to cease her work, to stop being a journalist, to stay home and be a good society wife?

Genevieve shook her head slightly, trying to clear her thoughts. Esmie was watching her expectantly, her mouth full of Neapolitan cake.

"If Daniel wants to speak to me in full privacy, he may come visit me at home, not call me to a secret midnight meeting on a veranda in the middle of the Otts' ball," Genevieve said, suddenly cross. "When you're ready, find Rupert and come join us."

With that, Genevieve lifted her skirts slightly and made her way in the direction the footman had indicated, though a kernel of doubt still plagued her mind. What if Daniel was asking to speak privately to express some emotion, some sentiment that was similar to the ones she harbored?

Her heart began to beat faster.

It was dark on the veranda, the moon obscured by a cloud. A strong ocean breeze ruffled her skirts, and she crossed her arms over her chest against the slight chill in the night air.

"Daniel?" Genevieve called softly. "Are you here?"

He stepped out of the shadows and into the light streaming in from the interior. It was hard to stop her breath from catching. Daniel McCaffrey, with his strong jaw and piercing dark-blue eyes, was still one of the most handsome men she'd ever laid eyes on. His black curls had been tousled by the wind and the moisture in the air, springing up out of their previous neatly combed style, but that only added to his appeal.

"Thank you for meeting me," he said. Genevieve nodded, but the slight anticipatory butterflies she had felt upon crossing the threshold outdoors now shifted to concern. It wasn't just his hair that had become disheveled, she noticed, but his jacket was undone, tie loosened, and the top two buttons of his shirt were open.

"What's happening?" she asked, suddenly wary. "You look a bit . . ." Genevieve paused, unsure of how to address his newly rumpled appearance. An abrupt, unwelcome thought struck her, and she was glad the low light hid the heat rushing to her face.

Had he been out here with a lady?

Daniel grimaced. "I know, it's why I couldn't go back inside. My shoes are soaked as well, likely ruined." She looked down and saw a crust of sand encasing his cuffs, coating his shoes.

"You were on the beach?" she said, confused.

"Come over here," Daniel said, gesturing for her to join him against the railing of the veranda. Puzzled, Genevieve complied, leaning against the balustrade and taking a deep breath of sea air. Daniel pointed down the beach. "Do you know who else has a home on these bluffs?"

"There are only two," Genevieve said. Where was Daniel going with this? "Matthew Shipman's house is next, and the Rutherford family is farther down, right where the bluff comes to a point."

Daniel gazed into the darkness. She could just make out his contemplative expression. "Do the Rutherfords have access to this beach?"

"I'm not sure," she said. "I don't think so, as the house faces the other direction. Daniel, what's going on?"

Genevieve's concern grew as Daniel explained why he had been running on the beach. She tried to envision the scene he described: a ghostly figure in a white dress, another in dark evening clothes, struggling in the surf by the light of the moon.

"And the footprints led back to a set of stairs leading up the bluff?" she asked. Genevieve peered into the darkness. She knew the Shipman cottage was there, even though it was too far away to see.

"They did," Daniel said. A stronger gust blew in from the ocean, and Genevieve shivered. She rubbed her upper arms, bare from the elbows up in her sleeveless ballgown. The warmth of light wool suddenly settled on her shoulders as Daniel draped his jacket across her back.

"Nobody else is out here," he murmured in the wind with his familiar, wry half smile. "Your reputation is quite safe."

Genevieve huffed a small laugh. "I think there is little I could do to truly shock society at this stage," she said, though she knew this to be untrue. There were several activities she had undertaken with Daniel that would make her an instant social pariah were they to be made public: spending time with him in a hotel room the year prior, even though they had only done so to have a private place to talk, and then sharing a room—and a bed, no less—with him in a brothel only a few weeks ago. Again, this had happened due to necessity, and Daniel had remained the perfect gentleman, but still. She knew they had been extremely lucky, both times, that these incidents had remained private.

Daniel's smile widened a bit before fading. He, too, turned his attention back to the distant homes. "So the stairs in the rocks must lead to Matt Shipman's house."

Genevieve shivered slightly again, despite the warmth of Daniel's jacket. She pulled it a little tighter around her chest. "Do you know him?"

He bobbed his head side to side in an indecisive motion. "Not well. Enough, I suppose. I think every man in society knows Matt a little."

"I've heard stories." Now it was her turn to be wry.

"Of course. Why wouldn't you have heard tales of the wildest parties in the city?"

"*Now* you're worried about my modesty?"

"What goes on at those events makes even me blush."

Genevieve felt her eyes widening. "Well, now you must tell me more."

"I will do no such thing," Daniel said, sounding affronted.

"Oh, come on. I know enough, I just need details."

"If you've heard even a fraction, you've heard plenty. I know you're no delicate miss, Genevieve, but honestly, some of it borders on debauchery. Maybe you can tell me something instead," he said, as if he could sense she was about to argue with him.

Which she had been. Genevieve knew he was trying to divert her from the subject of Matthew Shipman's famously sordid parties but allowed herself to be redirected, letting the matter rest. For now.

At her questioning look, he continued. "Do you know if Mr. Shipman is here?"

"Here in Newport? Yes. He was at the Cambridge lawn party two days ago." Genevieve leaned against the railing, trying without success to see deeper down the beach.

"Alone?"

She shrugged. "I don't know. Probably. He doesn't usually bring his mistresses to society events." At Daniel's continued apparent incredulity, Genevieve offered another shrug. "What? It's common knowledge the man keeps a string of young actresses. One after the other, they say."

"Who is they?"

She twirled her hand lazily in the night air. "Everyone."

Daniel stared at her briefly, then shook his head. Exasperation welled within her.

"Daniel, I'm twenty-seven, and a journalist to boot. Quit acting like I'm a schoolgirl with no knowledge of what goes on between men and women."

Genevieve's annoyance softened as Daniel held his hands up as if surrendering. "You're right, you're right. I simply . . ." He turned his gaze back to the beach. "The parties I'm referring to go beyond mere knowledge of what transpires behind closed doors between a couple. Some of the girls he procures for entertainment are quite young. Almost children."

She drew in a sharp breath; this was shocking. "Children? Surely that isn't right. How young do you mean? And what kind of entertainment?"

"Thirteen, fifteen?" Daniel said with a sigh. "I doubt they've anyone to register a complaint with the authorities on their behalf; indeed, many of these young girls are sent to parties such as Shipman's through talent agencies or their own guardians. To dance." He turned a thoughtful gaze to the ocean.

Genevieve digested this, troubled. She knew that men formed sociable clubs and had male-only parties in their homes or in the private rooms of their brick-and-mortar clubs or restaurants. Women were strictly forbidden, or more accurately, *wives* were strictly forbidden. Apparently other women were allowed, as cooks or servers or, as Daniel put it, "entertainment." She knew that young girls often turned to the streets if they came from impoverished circumstances and had few options, had even seen these poor girls during her and Daniel's forays into the Bowery earlier this summer. But for a wealthy gentleman, a member of elite society and the Larchmont Yacht Club, to be engaging in something untoward with young teenagers shook her more than she wanted to admit.

Every time she thought herself worldly, a new fact upended that idea. Daniel was constantly trying to protect her from this type of information, but she had been protected her whole life. If she wanted to do her job correctly, and if she wanted to help people in the process, she needed to know the way of things, no matter how troubling.

"What are the two of you doing out here in this wind?" Rupert's voice demanded as he and Esmie joined them on the deck. "Come back inside. We've been having a jolly time." He made a show of shoving his hands into his trouser pockets and shivering dramatically.

Esmie cast a subtly inquiring look at Genevieve. She shook her head in response.

"Calm down, Rupert, it's not that cold," Daniel said, rolling his eyes at his friend. But with affection.

"Cold enough you gave Genevieve your jacket," Rupert pointed out.

"As you should give yours to Esmie," Daniel retorted.

"I feel quite comfortable," Esmie said.

"Isn't she marvelous?" Rupert beamed at his wife for a moment, a look that warmed Genevieve's heart. It was easy to forget, after all they had been through, that the couple were still newlyweds. "But let us simply go back in, and everyone can wear their own clothing." He took Esmie's hand and turned toward the house.

"I can't go back in, I'm afraid," Daniel said, stopping Rupert in his tracks. "In fact, I'll need to go back to the house, if I may use your carriage. I'll send it back for you if you'd like to stay." He was staying with the Miltons, as he had no Newport home of his own.

"Of course," Esmie said with a worried expression. "Is something amiss?"

"No. Well, I don't think so. I ventured to the beach, and I'm afraid I'm quite sodden now." Daniel gestured at his sandy trousers and shoes.

"What are you running about on the beach for during a ball?" Rupert demanded, eyeing Daniel's lower body with distaste. "Not you too?" he asked Genevieve. "Is this why you're in Daniel's jacket? Did you get wet out there?"

"I didn't go to the beach; I was simply cold," Genevieve said. Impatience was beginning to well within her. She wanted to continue talking with Daniel about what he had seen on the beach but wasn't sure whether to bring it up in front of Rupert and Esmie.

But Daniel surprised her. "Can you stand it another few minutes, Genevieve? As we're all together, I have something I need to tell you. All of you."

Genevieve quickly looked to Rupert and Esmie, wanting to gauge their reactions. She expected her expression matched theirs: concern mixed with wariness. She knew that Rupert and Esmie, like her, had been worried for Daniel since his ordeal earlier that summer.

"Rupert and Esmie, I'm sorry to do this to you, but I must return to the city for a while," Daniel said, the regret in his voice obvious.

Genevieve had a sinking suspicion she knew why he wanted to return to the city. She crossed her arms under Daniel's coat and waited.

"That is too bad," Rupert said cautiously. "This past week has been some of the most fun I've had in Newport in ages. It's wonderful having you in the house. How long is a while?"

Daniel hesitated but cast a guilty look in Genevieve's direction. She could feel her lips purse and willed them to relax.

"You're going back because I am, aren't you?" Genevieve said. A mix of emotion rose within her. A familiar annoyance at his presumption, but also unexpected relief. It was a surprising sensation; she hadn't realized how much she'd been hoping he would help her with the coming task until now.

Esmie looked between them, confused. "But I thought you had to return to New York to help Callie get settled," she said. "I still can't believe she's back. You will give her my very best, will you not?" Genevieve managed a smile; Esmie had asked her this already several times since she had broken the news that Callie, who had disappeared for several months, had shown up on her doorstep out of the blue the week prior.

Daniel shrugged slightly at her, a mix of repentance and expectance.

Genevieve swallowed. She supposed she would have to tell Rupert and Esmie the truth at some point.

"In truth, I fear Callie might have stayed away forever had not something occurred. One of her friends has died, and she was hoping I could assist."

Esmie's brow puckered in confusion. "I'm so sorry to hear that. She wants your help with the arrangements, I take it?"

"No," Daniel said. He cast a swift look at Genevieve, silently asking if he could tell the story. She gestured for him to go ahead, suddenly feeling insurmountably tired. "Callie fears her friend was murdered and is asking Genevieve—and myself, if I am willing—to look into the matter."

Rupert looked at his friend sharply in the dim light. "And it seems you are willing. Daniel, are you sure it's a good idea to get involved in something like this so soon? It's only been a few weeks since you nearly died." His tone was uncharacteristically sharp.

Genevieve folded her arms tighter but kept silent. She had worried about this exact same thing; it was why she had initially planned on taking on the task alone.

Daniel opened his mouth as if to speak, then shut it again.

"Surely this is a matter for the police?" Esmie said. Her voice was gentle, but Genevieve could hear its undercurrent of fear.

"The police have ruled the death as accidental," Daniel said.

"Perhaps you ought to trust the police, in this instance," Rupert said, though he sounded doubtful. Rupert's being falsely imprisoned for a murder he didn't commit earlier in the year, and in the notorious Tombs no less, made them all a bit wary of the force.

"One cannot accidentally cut one's own throat," Genevieve said with more force than she intended. A wave of regret and shame immediately washed over her as she saw Esmie's face drain of color. Esmie's mother, Elmira Bradley, had been murdered in the exact same manner the year before.

"Esmie, I'm so sorry," she said miserably, reaching over to take her friend's hand. Esmie nodded. "How unbelievably careless and cruel of me. I've been quite distraught over this and I didn't think. Please accept my apology." Esmie nodded, her eyes shiny with sudden tears.

"I understand," she said, wiping her eyes delicately with a handkerchief Rupert handed her. "But in case it is not clear, I agree with Rupert. I think it is too soon for either of you to be chasing killers again. Neither of you have been yourselves since the incident at the gasworks." She gave the handkerchief back to Rupert and folded her hands in front of her chest, favoring them both with a stern look.

Genevieve and Daniel exchanged a glance. She had been thinking this of him; had he the same opinion of her? If so, he'd be correct. She was still grappling with the reality of having killed a man.

But that didn't change the current reality. Callie needed help, and there was no one else to give it.

"And what of your job, Genevieve?" Esmie tried a different tactic. "You were already late getting to Newport, and you did say Mr. Horace was not happy about it. How do you plan to cover the social season from New York?"

Esmie wasn't wrong; Genevieve was already on thin ice with her editor at the *New York Globe*, where she covered the society pages. He had relented somewhat after she had exposed the circle of gunrunners using an old mansion in the Bronx to supply arms to Cuban revolutionaries, but after a short period Arthur had insisted she resume her duties reporting on the summer season in Newport.

"I think I have a plan for that," Genevieve said. She didn't want to fully explain her idea just yet, as she knew it was a risky endeavor and her friends would try to talk her out of it. "And I was always planning to go back to New York for a brief period, as my brother Gavin returns from Egypt soon. I may just stay a bit longer than I had thought," she admitted.

"Why on earth would the authorities classify a woman's death as accidental when it was obviously not?" Rupert asked.

"We don't know," Daniel said. "Callie wasn't able to stay long, and Genevieve was due in Newport right away."

"Which is why I promised to return to the city as soon as I could," Genevieve interjected. The breeze had intensified while they'd been talking, and she shivered despite the warmth of Daniel's coat on her shoulders. "Esmie, you must be chilled to the bone."

"Yes, let's go," Rupert said. He looked despondent, and worried. "Daniel, head straight to the front; I'll bring the carriage around for us. Genevieve, will you stay?"

"No, I'll take our carriage home and send it back for Charles, if he's not ready to leave," she said. She and her brother Charles had opened the Stewart family's Newport home in advance of their parents, who would come after Gavin's long-awaited return.

Rupert nodded. "When are you leaving? Day after tomorrow?" At Genevieve's nod, he sighed. "Well, keep us apprised of your progress. And if you need help, you'll know where to find us." He blew out another breath and looked at the sea. "And here I thought we would finally have a proper summer."

"Maybe we still can, in a few weeks' time," Daniel suggested as they gathered at the door heading back into the house. "It's only the middle of July. Maybe this will all turn out to be nothing."

Genevieve smiled at him as they passed through the doors. She appreciated Daniel's facade of optimism, but she knew in her heart that whatever had happened to Callie's friend was not nothing.

Somehow she knew, even then, that the young woman's death was quite the opposite. That instead it was part of something more horrifying than they could yet comprehend.

CHAPTER 3

The townhouse was nothing like she had expected.

High, airy ceilings gave the parlor an open, expansive feel, compounded by large windows letting in streams of bright late-morning sun. It was expensively decorated, with tasteful, subtly striped wallpaper and some truly impressive paintings: a landscape Genevieve recalled having seen at the National Academy show some years ago, featuring an explosively orange-and-pink sunset over a mountain-studded vista; a luscious portrait of a pink-cheeked child crafted in brushy, airy strokes. A five-foot-tall marble sculpture of a female nude glowed in one corner of the room, surveying them impassively.

Daniel gazed at it for a beat, then raised a brow in her direction. Genevieve smiled; he seemed as startled by their plush surroundings as she was.

"You're here! Forgive my being delayed a few moments. Were you offered coffee? Tea?" Callie bustled in, rushing straight into Genevieve's arms.

A fierce rush of feeling swept through Genevieve as she embraced her friend. Along with Eliza Lindsay, Callie was her oldest, dearest friend in the world, and Genevieve had missed her terribly in the months since Callie had removed herself from their lives.

It was a bit of a shock to find Callie had removed herself only to East Fifteenth Street.

"Oh, I've missed you so." Callie beamed as she released her, enfolding Genevieve's hands within her own, echoing her thoughts almost exactly. "Sit, both of you. And Mr. McCaffrey, thank you for coming."

Daniel turned the full power of his smile on Callie, causing her to twinkle her bright-green eyes in Genevieve's direction. Callie had always adored men, the handsomer the better.

"Callie, this room is quite beautiful," Genevieve ventured as she settled on the damask-covered sofa. She was pleased when Callie sat right next to her, continuing to hold her hand as a maid came in.

"Shall we have lemonade? Or champagne? It's never too early for champagne, is it? Besides, it's a reunion, a reason to celebrate."

"Lemonade is fine," Genevieve interjected. If they were to discuss what had happened to Callie's friend, she wanted a clear head.

"Oh, pish. Bring both," Callie ordered the maid. "And yes, isn't it pretty?" she continued after the maid had left, gesturing around the parlor. "The whole house is quite nice. I'll give you a tour after we've talked a while."

"I hate to broach the obvious, but . . ." Genevieve began, then paused, not wanting to cause offense.

"How can I afford it?" Callie guessed. She smiled gently at them both.

Genevieve blushed but nodded. It was no secret Callie's grandmother's death the year prior had left her friend quite impoverished. The once-enormous Maple family fortune had vanished, mostly squandered by corrupt investors her grandmother had mistakenly trusted, and Callie had been left with nothing. Though her curvy, petite figure, dark-haired beauty, and general air of gaiety had earned Callie several offers of marriage, she had refused to settle for a love-less union. Following her grandmother's death and the pub-lic revelation that the Maple wealth was gone, the marriage offers had disappeared, leaving Callie alone and penniless.

But she didn't appear penniless any longer. Callie was wearing a lovely day dress cut in the latest style, cream colored, adorned with bright robin's-egg-blue flowers and delicate lace trim.

The dress, like the townhouse and its trappings, would have cost quite a bit.

"This townhouse belongs to a friend," Callie said care-fully. "He is allowing me to live here as long as I like."

Understanding settled over Genevieve uncomfortably. She swallowed.

Daniel was regarding her with a sympathetic expres-sion. He, of course, must have realized the arrangement immediately.

Callie had become someone's mistress.

"Is this friend someone I know?" Genevieve asked, feel-ing tentative. "I can't believe you were right here this whole time." The townhouse was directly across from Stuyvesant Square, only about ten blocks uptown and a few east from her own house on Washington Square Park.

The maid returned bearing a silver tray with both lem-onade and champagne. Genevieve relented and joined Callie in a glass of champagne. Daniel raised a brow at her but said nothing, choosing lemonade for himself.

"Well, I haven't been here that long. Just since March. Before that, I was living at the Mildred Penny House."

"The YWCA?" Daniel asked, looking interested. "That's not far from here."

Callie smiled, taking a sip of champagne. "No, it's not. It was a pleasant place to land after grandmother's house was sold. The rooms were clean and bright, very modern furnishings." She gazed out the big windows that looked toward the bright-green trees gracing Stuyvesant Square Park, her smile fading. "They were kind to me there, and I met some wonderful girls. It's where I met Beatrice. Bea, we called her."

Genevieve assumed Bea was the deceased. She stayed silent, allowing Callie to collect her thoughts.

"But the House also imposed an eleven PM curfew, quite strict, and after a time it became simply untenable. So Walter offered me the use of this house," Callie concluded brightly.

"Walter . . . ?" Genevieve prodded.

"Walter Wilson."

"The architect?" Daniel asked, sitting a bit straighter in his armchair. Genevieve understood the reaction. Walter Wilson was a well-known figure in town.

"The very same," Callie said, finishing her glass and pouring herself more. "He'll be coming by later; he's as anxious for you to get to the bottom of what happened to Bea as I am. More champagne?" She tried to splash more of the wine into Genevieve's nearly full glass.

"No, thank you," Genevieve said, pulling her glass away and setting it down on a side table out of Callie's reach. The few sips she'd had weren't sitting well, and her head was spinning from trying to follow what Callie was saying. "Callie, can you go back to the beginning? How have you been making a living? The Mildred Penny House is for working women, is it not? I must admit I looked for you every time I went to Ladies' Mile, hoping to see you selling gloves or scent . . ."

Callie's smile returned. "I understand. Being a shopgirl does seem like it would have been the most suitable job for me, as I have no other significant education or skills. But no, I have been making my living another way." She poured herself a splash more champagne, and Genevieve had to make a conscious effort to keep a frown from marring her forehead.

"You used to accompany Eliza and me to the Tenth Street Studios sometimes, remember?" Callie asked.

Genevieve nodded; of course she remembered. It was a diverting way to spend a winter evening, walking from artist's studio to artist's studio, admiring their latest work, running into friends. Sometimes her parents went to the open studio evenings and purchased a piece, though they didn't patronize anyone in particular.

"One day last winter, Eliza and I went—you were at some function for work, I believe. I admit I was feeling rather low; it was right before the house was sold, and I was indeed on the cusp of heading to Lord & Taylor to inquire about a position there. Eliza was caught up discussing something very technical with Mr. Chase—you know, with whom she is studying this summer? You remember how she gets in those moments."

Genevieve did know, and could picture the scene perfectly, having visited Mr. Chase's studio many times. Eliza was also an artist and could easily lose hours talking with her colleagues and teachers about the intricacies of her craft, none of which was particularly interesting to her or Callie.

"I left Eliza to her devices and visited a few studios on my own and eventually noticed someone was following me," Callie continued.

Daniel's brow furrowed, and he set down his glass of lemonade. "Mr. Wilson?" he asked in a dangerous tone.

"No, not Walter. A man called Benjamin Rathvon. He explained he was a photographer and asked if he could take my picture. He worked with all the artists and with some theatrical agents."

"That sounds fairly predatory," Daniel said. His voice sounded easy, but Genevieve knew him well enough to hear the undercurrent of anger lacing his words.

Callie sipped more champagne and tilted her head to one side, considering. "Perhaps it was. I'm sure he noticed my dress was worn at the hem and two seasons out of date. But I was desperate, so I contacted him the following week and arranged a meeting. He paid me for the pictures, and then I had money for the Mildred Penny House. Mr. Rathvon then showed the pictures to some artist friends. And, well, everyone will find out next fall when the next National Academy show opens—I began working as an artist's model."

Genevieve's mouth dropped, and she snapped it shut quickly again. "We would have given you any—" she began, but Callie cut her off.

"I know, and I know you and Eliza meant well. But I couldn't accept your help. I'm proud of the work I do. I've become the most sought-after model this season; I suspect you'll be seeing rather a lot of me in the fall exhibitions."

Callie raised her chin slightly and looked at Genevieve defiantly, as if she expected a scolding. Genevieve blinked, trying to envision what such a position might entail. She herself had never studied art and hadn't given much thought to the figures who appeared in paintings or modeled for sculptures. The sunlight gleamed off the bright-white marble of the nude in the corner, and Genevieve felt heat rise to her face.

Callie followed her gaze to the sculpture and straightened in her seat a bit more, though a coy smile danced around her mouth. "Yes, I do pose in the altogether at times," she said, using the colloquialism for posing in the nude. "For both painters and sculptors. Indeed, Walter is working on a new marble of me right now, posing as Persephone. But that"—she pointed to the figure—"is not me."

"That is *Clytie*," a male voice declared, followed instantly by the speaker himself.

Daniel stood as Walter Wilson entered. The new-comer shook Genevieve's hand. "Miss Stewart," he said. Genevieve was unsurprised by the melodious nature of his voice; it seemed to match the elegance of the house and the urbane appearance of its owner. He was impeccably dressed in the aesthetic style, in a relaxed dark-blue morning coat with burgundy velvet trim, over a soft white linen shirt and a loosely knotted silk tie. His dark-brown hair was worn longer than fashionable, swept back from his forehead and curling slightly as it approached his collar, but it suited his tapered jaw and wide, welcoming smile. "I know your brother Charles, of course. Bested me out of the Smythe Bank commission last spring, but he is a worthy competitor; his work of late has been most impressive. And you and I have been introduced, though we haven't spoken in some time."

"It is lovely to see you again," Genevieve said politely. She knew Walter by sight and was sure they *had* been introduced at some point, though she couldn't recall when.

"And Mr. McCaffrey. Thank you so much for agreeing to help." The men shook hands. Genevieve watched Daniel carefully during the interaction. She wasn't sure yet if she trusted this Mr. Wilson, who seemed to have taken over Callie's life so completely.

Daniel gave no outward sign of being troubled by Mr. Wilson's presence, though, as he smiled an easy smile and accepted the handshake with civility.

"You were admiring *Clytie*," Walter said, as he sat on Callie's other side and pressed a kiss into her presented cheek. Genevieve felt the flush return to her cheeks; it was startling to see Callie so openly intimate with a man. "Oh, champagne," he said with pleasure, pouring himself a glass. "What a wonderful idea, darling."

"From Ovid, if memory serves?" Daniel asked, referring to the sculpture.

Walter raised his glass in appreciation. "Good memory, Mr. McCaffrey."

"I don't recall that part," Genevieve said, frowning. "I only remember Narcissus, pining away in front of his own reflection."

"Clytie is another story of pining," Walter said, brushing back a stray lock of hair that had fallen forward with an elegant hand. "A water nymph in love with the sun god Apollo, who abandoned her, as Apollo was wont to do. For nine days she stared at the sun, inconsolable, refusing food or drink, until that fickle deity finally took pity on her and transformed her into a sunflower. Then her face followed him always."

Genevieve wasn't sure she had ever heard the story. It sent prickles down her spine. The idea of a lovelorn woman staring at the sun for nine days, blinding herself over a faithless man, only to be turned into a blossom that could never look away, appalled her. She turned her attention away from the sculpture, whose lustrous white marble now appeared cold and heartless, and back to the live flesh of her friend.

Her friend, whom only a few weeks ago she'd despaired of laying eyes on ever again.

"The sunflower on the base is a nice touch," Daniel remarked, taking a sip of his lemonade. "It's your work, I take it?"

Walter smiled expansively, leaning back on the sofa and stretching an arm along its back length, behind Callie's shoulders. "It is. I've been fortunate to be able to pursue my two main passions in life, sculpture and architecture. People always ask if I paint, too, but I'm afraid not. I strictly work in three dimensions." He chuckled a bit, and Daniel smiled in response.

There. Now Genevieve saw it, visible only to someone who knew Daniel well. A slight shuttering around the eyes, an underlying stiffness to his smile.

Daniel wasn't sure he trusted Walter either.

"Perhaps you could tell us more about your friend," Genevieve said to Callie. She wanted to soak in Callie, hear every detail of what her life was like, but not in front of Walter. There would be time for that later; now that Callie had reappeared, Genevieve didn't plan on letting her go again. "Bea, you said her name was?"

"Beatrice Holler," Walter answered. He leaned forward, placing his glass down. "Lovely girl. Everyone adored her. We really do hope you can help; the police have been useless."

"You knew her too?" Daniel asked in a guarded tone.

Walter's brows rose in surprise. "Of course," he said. "I'm sorry, I thought you knew. That's Bea, right there."

Genevieve followed the line of his finger. The marble sculpture of Clytie, staring upward for eternity, paid her no notice in return. The prickles turned to a shudder.

"The deceased modeled for your sculpture?" she asked Walter, wanting to make sure she understood.

"Yes," Walter said. "Bea was a popular model. Has been for years. Or had been, I suppose. Dash it all, it's still hard to take in."

"But I thought you met her at the YWCA, Callie?" Genevieve asked. She wasn't sure she was following the threads of this story.

"I did," Callie said. "We were introduced there by some of the other girls. But the following week I saw her coming out of Mr. Paxton's studio as I was going in and realized she was a model as well. I had just started, and Bea was a wonderful guide. She recommended me to a whole host of artists, helped me get even more work."

"It's through Bea that we met," Walter chimed in, once again settling his arm behind Callie's shoulders. "Elbert Paxton is a close friend of mine; was a sound mentor to me when I was a young buck, trying to impress the Academy. Bea really was the most lovely girl. Hair the color of new hay, giant blue eyes."

Genevieve's gaze strayed back to the sculpture in the corner of the room. The nude figure—this dead girl's figure—was standing in a classical contrapposto stance, weight resting on one leg, the other bent. She did have a beautiful shape, slender but strong, captured in stone forever by Walter's chisel. Genevieve admitted to herself he was talented, but the sculpture still imbued her with anxiety.

"Who found her?" she asked quietly. There was no need to elaborate on which moment she meant.

"Her . . . companion," Walter said.

"Bea had recently moved out of Mildred Penny House into rooms of her own," Callie added. "Much like I moved in here."

"We understand," Daniel said. Genevieve understood too. Bea Holler also, then, had recently become somebody's mistress. "And we understand the need for discretion, but if we're going to help, we need to know the name of Miss Holler's benefactor."

Callie and Walter exchanged a look. "It was Matthew Shipman," Walter said, brushing a speck of nonexistent lint off of his trouser leg.

A quick look of shock flitted across Daniel's face, there and gone so fast Genevieve wasn't certain she saw it, even though it echoed her own feelings perfectly. But Callie must have observed the same, for she rushed to fill the sudden, weighted silence that settled over the room.

"I know his reputation, but he really is a very nice man, and very kind to those under his protection," Callie added. "Bea had a beautiful set of rooms, up in the East 40s. Their arrangement was quite new, but Bea seemed happy. And Matthew was devastated, stunned by what he found."

"Mr. Shipman came to her apartment and found Miss Holler murdered?" Daniel asked. He had resumed a neutral expression, but Genevieve could hear the disbelief in his voice.

"Indeed," Walter answered in a surprisingly firm tone. "The police have ruled him out as a suspect. Bea had been dead for several hours before Matthew found her; he'd been at Whitaker Carson's stag party upstairs at Sherry's all night. Ironclad alibi; countless others were with him the whole time. Myself included."

"The manner in which she died, though . . ." Genevieve couldn't bring herself to say the words *cut throat* aloud again, not after her gaffe in front of Esmie. Callie was already looking quite pale. "Do you have any idea as to why they are calling her death self-imposed?"

Callie shook her head. "It's the most baffling thing. But we were visited by the police and warned very strictly to keep it quiet, that the case was closed."

Daniel looked to Walter. "You as well?"

"That's correct," he confirmed. "Most of our crowd had already left town for the summer, gone upstate, so just a few of us were formally warned, I believe. But news spreads, people talk."

"Do you know who else was told by the police not to discuss the crime?" Daniel asked.

Callie and Walter exchanged another look, and in response, Daniel slid his eyes Genevieve's way for a brief moment. She nodded back as imperceptibly as she could; she'd noticed it too. Walter and Callie were checking with each other, trying to decide how much to say.

What were they trying to hide?

"William Chase," Walter finally said. Genevieve put down her barely touched glass and sat a little straighter in concern. Mr. Chase was the artist their friend Eliza was studying with this summer, out on Long Island. "And Elbert Paxton."

She knew Paxton's name, too, and not just because Callie and Walter had mentioned it earlier. The elderly Hudson River School painter was a fixture in the New York art world. Genevieve's family owned three of his pieces: one large oil that hung over their fireplace in their drawing room, a lovely view of the White Mountains in New Hampshire; another smaller painting of a waterfall in the same region; and a nice little pastel.

"Why them?" she asked.

"Bea was a popular model," Callie said. "She posed for both artists quite frequently. And they were both in town when she died."

"Both were dismissed as suspects by the police?" Genevieve asked. She couldn't fathom why the authorities wouldn't make the death public. She suspected whoever was behind that had had conversations with all the newspaper editors in town, too. Including her own.

Walter shrugged. "Apparently. Paxton was with some clients in his studio, and Chase was with his family, including his mother-in-law. They both originally returned to town for a funeral."

"Who, specifically, made this determination? Who was in charge of the case?" Daniel asked, leaning forward. "Did you get a name?"

"I have a card around here somewhere," Walter said. "Wait one moment."

As Walter left to find the officer's card, Genevieve grabbed Callie's hand again and offered her friend a reassuring smile. "We'll do what we can to find out what happened," she promised, though out of the corner of her eye, she caught a slightly doubtful expression cross Daniel's face. He was right to be concerned. That the police were trying to suppress the true nature of Bea's death, for whatever reason, was going to make their job significantly harder.

"Found it," Walter said, displaying the card to Daniel with a small flourish. "One Detective Aloysius Longstreet."

Genevieve's insides sank. The detective was no friend to her or Daniel. In fact, with Longstreet at the helm, she now feared the task could prove impossible.

CHAPTER 4

"That can't possibly be all you want to eat."

Daniel looked at his plate in surprise. It was loaded with scrambled eggs, bacon, a toasted muffin, and toasted bread, plus a side dish of peaches and blackberries. Added to the coffee at his elbow, it was far more than he normally consumed at breakfast.

"Mrs. Stewart, I assure you this is plenty of food."

"Breakfast must sustain you throughout the day," Anna Stewart, Genevieve's mother, protested, frowning at Daniel's plate. "Wilbur, make sure Mr. McCaffrey gets more eggs when Nellie returns with the dish."

"If Mr. McCaffrey feels his plate is full, then we must respect his wishes, my dear," Genevieve's father answered mildly, spearing a piece of sausage with his fork. "Though I would dearly enjoy some more cocoa."

Anna summoned the maid Nellie back in for a second pot of cocoa, and Daniel blinked as he found more eggs piled onto his plate.

"You just learn to accept it after a while." Genevieve grinned at him from behind her coffee cup. "You don't have to eat everything if it's too much."

This was the second meal Daniel had taken with the Stewart family since his and Genevieve's return from Newport. He was fond of all of them, particularly her parents, both of whom exuded warmth and intelligence. A few weeks ago, a meal would have included the younger of Genevieve's two brothers, Charles, but he was absent at present, having settled in Newport for the summer. After a slightly rocky start, Daniel felt he and Charles were now on good terms. The elder Stewarts were waiting on tenterhooks for the arrival of Genevieve's oldest brother, Gavin, whose ship from Egypt was meant to dock today. None of the Stewarts had seen Gavin in nearly three years, and the excitement in the household was infectious.

"I wish you could be here when Gavin arrives, Genevieve," complained Anna, though her desire was not expressed very forcibly.

"I'll be here tonight, and I'll see Gavin all summer," Genevieve answered, selecting another piece of toast from the silver rack on the table. "Is there any strawberry jam? Besides, we don't know what time his ship will dock, nor how long it will take him to get all his effects in order after the long journey. Today was the most convenient day for Callie to meet."

"Glad to know Callie Maple's schedule outranks your brother's homecoming," a wry voice interrupted. "Some things never change, it seems."

Daniel stood as Genevieve squealed and jumped out of her chair, rushing to throw her arms around a tall, handsome man with thick, nut-brown hair and a matching pair of laughing eyes. This, Daniel assumed, was Gavin, finally home from abroad. Anna and Wilbur crowded their son, Anna freely crying joyful tears. Daniel noticed Wilbur discreetly wiping his eyes with a handkerchief.

He knew he should leave. This was an intimate family moment, and as fond as he was of the Stewarts, Daniel was not family. But as he edged toward the dining room door, fully prepared to slip out and send his regrets later, his name was called, stopping him in his tracks.

"Mr. McCaffrey, I presume?" Gavin strode toward him, hand outstretched, with a polite smile on his face but steel in his eyes.

Daniel winced internally; surely Gavin had heard something of him from Charles. Genevieve's brothers were obviously very protective of her. The previous summer, Charles had cornered him at an event in Newport—quite literally—and made it clear he was on the cusp of rounding up the entire crew of the *Anna Charlene* and making sure Daniel wouldn't be able to walk for a week. Charles had still been seething over the dangerous position Genevieve had found herself in during her and Daniel's first investigation, that of the Robin Hood of the Lower East Side, a jewel thief suspected of several brutal murders. And had a further hair been harmed on his sister's head, Daniel was sure Charles would have made good on his threat. Said crew of Charles's award-winning racing yacht were also in attendance at this particular gathering, and Daniel had thought it prudent to leave at once, not liking the half-lidded looks being thrown his way over beer bottles and highballs. He could hold his own in a fight, but had he taken on all seven robust-looking crew members with only Rupert for backup, he very well might not have walked for a long time indeed.

Besides, he didn't blame Charles a bit.

"Mr. Stewart. It's a pleasure to make your acquaintance."

Gavin's handshake was a firm, no-nonsense grip. "We have been introduced, but it was some years ago. Before you went abroad for so long. And then I was abroad myself."

Gavin eyed him curiously. "I confess I probably recall the meeting better than you, as you had newly come into your fortune and were still the object of much speculation. I never considered then that you'd become so close with my sister."

The words were friendly enough, but Daniel heard a warning tone in them all the same. As predicted, Gavin was making clear he wasn't yet sure if he approved of Daniel's relationship with Genevieve.

"Leave Mr. McCaffrey alone, you rascal, and let me have a look at you," Anna said, pulling Gavin back and hugging him again, before holding him away from her at arm's length. "You've become nearly as brown as an Egyptian yourself. Now you will cut a striking figure on the shore this summer. Won't he, Wilbur?" she asked, beaming.

"He cuts a striking figure anywhere, land or sea," Wilbur replied, his eyes twinkling warmly. "How was the journey? Have you eaten?"

Everyone but Daniel began to talk at once, moving toward their seats. Daniel caught Genevieve's eye and inclined his head at the door, indicating he was going to leave. He had no business at a family reunion. She rolled her eyes in response, grabbed him by the wrist, and guided him back to his chair. A smile rose to his face, both at the firmness of her grip and at her inclusion of him in the moment.

It was a good sign.

"Of course, the bathing costumes for both men and women are ridiculous," Anna was saying, once he'd settled back at the table. "How is one to swim in a healthful way when encumbered by so much clothing? We should be engaging in water sports in our natural states, though I would get drummed out of Bailey's Beach were I to pull such a stunt." She waved her butter knife, thankfully devoid of butter, in the vague direction of the men seated around the table. "You gentlemen have your swimming holes where you undress completely, I know you do. It is far riskier for us ladies. Another example of unfair expectations between the sexes." Anna emphasized her displeasure over this state of affairs by viciously plunging her knife into a small porcelain dish of butter and attacking a piece of toast.

Another memory, a better one than nearly getting thrashed by a group of half-drunken yachtsmen, arose in Daniel's mind, this one of Genevieve undressing as she prepared for a treacherous swim in the East River. The bright moonlight had shone on her body, rendering her flimsy underclothes nearly transparent.

He swallowed at the thought.

Anna caught whatever emotion was playing across his face and apparently mistook it for discomfort. "Do not be embarrassed, Mr. McCaffrey. The human body is nothing to be ashamed of." An eye roll passed between Genevieve and Gavin; apparently this was an oft-repeated phrase in the Stewart household. "Though you also may feel free to keep your shirt on. While there is no denying you are a fine specimen of the male species, you are also of direct Irish descent, and I fear your bare chest in the sunlight might cause a glare strong enough to blind anyone in the vicinity."

Daniel choked on his coffee.

"Mother," snapped Genevieve in an aggrieved tone, patches of color blooming in her cheeks.

He waved away Gavin's solicitous offer of a glass of water but hid a smile under his slowly subsiding coughs, wondering if Genevieve was also thinking of their time on that narrow strip of rocky beach called Duck Island, when she had seen him bare chested.

"We will be late if we don't leave now," Genevieve said, rising and glaring at her mother and emphasizing the word *now.* "I'm sorry to leave so soon after your arrival, Gavin, but I'll be back this afternoon. I think Mother and Cook have quite a feast planned for you tonight."

Daniel rose, following her lead, and prepared to make his good-byes.

"Where are you going?" Gavin asked, taking more bacon from the platter on the table. "Something to do with Callie? I thought she'd vanished."

"She's returned," Genevieve responded shortly, folding her arms over her chest.

Gavin put his fork down on the side of his plate. "Is this something untoward again? Charles filled me in on what's been going on here the last few years. I'm not entirely sure I approve of any new ventures between the two of you." He flicked his finger between Daniel and Genevieve, his gaze hard.

If anything, Genevieve's color rose more. "Now see here, Gavin . . ."

Anna spoke at the same time, her words overlapping her daughter's. "Gavin! I don't know what you're referring to, but I can assure you that Mr. McCaffrey and Genevieve have never engaged in anything improper. Why, they're heroes. I've sent you Genevieve's clippings from the *Globe.* She's made quite a name for herself at the paper."

"And that's all that matters? What of her safety, her reputation? Has everyone in this family gone daft since I went abroad?" Gavin's eyes were hard, and though he was staring at his sister, Daniel knew much of this anger was directed at him.

Anna uttered a slight gasp, and now Genevieve cut in. "You have no right," she started, clearly furious, but her brother interrupted.

"Someone has to look out for you. You're unmarried, Genevieve, and while your exploits with McCaffrey here have resulted in some good, I admit, surely it cannot outweigh the social damage you must have experienced. Charles has written to me of the gossip. Do you want to remain an old maid forever?"

"*Enough*." The single word silenced the table. Wilbur stood, his normally genial manner replaced by uncharacteristic severity. "Gavin, you are being intolerably rude. Apologize to your sister and to Mr. McCaffrey."

Gavin stared at his father for a few beats. Daniel tensed, now wishing very much that he'd left when the urge had struck. His presence was an obvious sore point for Genevieve's brother, but, as when Charles had threatened him last summer, he couldn't blame the man.

"I'm sorry," Gavin finally said in a stiff voice. He looked at his plate of bacon rather than at Genevieve or Daniel. "I worry about you, Genevieve. That is all."

Daniel could feel Genevieve soften an inch beside him. "I'm perfectly safe. And more importantly, I'm happy."

Gavin did return his gaze to his sister then, the force of his chestnut eyes as piercing as Genevieve's amber ones could be. "Are you?" he asked softly.

Another moment passed, and a fleeting look of bewilderment passed over Genevieve's face, causing Daniel's heart to constrict painfully.

"We will be late," she repeated, leaning to deposit a quick kiss on Gavin's cheek. Her color was still high, but her voice was steady now. "I'll see you all in a few hours." She left the room without looking back, and Daniel ducked his head apologetically as he followed.

★ ★ ★

"Of all the heavy-handed, insulting, rude, *boorish* things to say. He stepped off a boat from *Egypt* not an hour prior, hasn't seen me in three *years*, and yet believes he can dictate how I live my life because he received a few *letters*? And from *Charles*?"

Genevieve had begun ranting in this fashion the moment they turned up Fifth Avenue, ostensibly to find a cab uptown. This running diatribe was not directed at him, Daniel knew. It was meant for Gavin, and for society as a whole.

"*Charles*," Genevieve repeated, stopping on the sidewalk and whirling at Daniel, shaking a finger at his chest. He jerked back a bit in alarm. "Is he going to get a piece of my mind." She turned on her heel and began to stalk up the sidewalk again, muttering under her breath.

Daniel jogged a few steps to catch up.

"Filling Gavin's head with nonsense about gossip," Genevieve continued, staring murderously up the street. "What do I care for *gossip*? For what the society ladies and matrons with nothing but time on their hands have to say about *me*, about *my* life?" Genevieve stopped and turned to him again. He stared back warily. "I meant what I said. I'm *happy*."

She didn't look happy. There were smudges of color under her eyes, circles that had been there since she had killed a man.

For him. To save his life.

It was on the tip of his tongue to repeat Gavin's question, *Are you?* But before he could, Genevieve turned again, this time waving a hand to hail a carriage to carry them the rest of the way uptown.

She was silent in the cab, and Daniel thought it best to let her gather her thoughts in peace. He had offered several times to talk with her about how she must be feeling after Tommy Meade's death, but so far Genevieve hadn't been willing to have that conversation. He watched the buildings shift to grander, larger houses the farther uptown they drove, though they turned east on Fortieth Street before they passed the truly giant mansions that characterized the few blocks between them and Central Park's south side.

"Here we are," was all he said once the cab stopped at the right address, halfway between Lexington and Third Avenue. Genevieve, who had been staring out the opposite window, seemingly lost in thought, started at the sound of his voice. She nodded, and they disembarked.

Once he had paid the driver and the carriage clattered away, they stood on the sidewalk, taking in the handsome, four-story brick building in front of them. It looked like a perfectly ordinary, perfectly pleasant structure.

Not a place where a woman had been brutally killed a few weeks prior.

Walter's head suddenly popped out from the front door.

"Oh good, you're here. We're on the third floor. Come on up."

Callie met them at the apartment door, pale but composed. Genevieve put her arm around her friend's shoulders once they were inside.

"Is it too difficult to be here?" Genevieve asked.

"It's hard, but I'll manage," Callie said, grasping Genevieve's hands in hers. "Let me show you around."

The late Beatrice Holler's apartment occupied the entire third floor. It was a handsome, open set of rooms, with dark wood moldings around the doors and windows and highly polished floors covered by thick patterned rugs. The kitchen was small but serviceable and had a decently sized dining room attached, with a table large enough to seat eight and a grand china cupboard occupying one wall, perfect for an intimate dinner party. The sitting room was large and airy, with windows that overlooked the street. A red damask sofa and two matching low armchairs were arranged in front of a large fireplace.

Tangible evidence of Bea's life, one that had been filled with friends and a lover and work, was everywhere: a magazine open to a spread of fashion plates and a newspaper with a lurid headline resting near the sofa; a glass of wine that might have been full two weeks ago, now evaporated to a dark stain on the crystal, still sitting on a small side table.

The apartment contained two bedrooms, one large, which had clearly been Bea's, dominated by a big pink-covered four-poster bed, and one small, perhaps meant for a maid or a child, which contained a small writing desk and a Singer sewing machine.

The rug in the latter room had been rolled up and pushed against the far wall.

"She was awfully clever at making clothes," Callie said. Her voice sounded high and thin. "Her mother had been a seamstress. Bea learned from her."

"She made costumes for lots of the models," Walter added. He was in a soft linen jacket of deep purple today, paired with a pale-yellow shirt. "If you needed an Ophelia or a Lady of Shalott or an Artemis, Bea would whip up something suitable."

Daniel hadn't thought of this before, that of course artists and their models would often need access to appropriate outfits. It felt airless in the sewing room with the four of them pressed into the small space.

Dots of dark-brown dried blood splattered a partially unrolled bolt of pale-green fabric resting on a low shelf.

"This is where Matthew found her?" he asked, glancing Walter's way. The other man crossed his arms over his chest and nodded. Callie swallowed, then quietly excused herself, stepping back into the hallway.

"Where was she from?" Daniel asked. There was a faded red velvet armchair in the corner, near the room's one small window—this bedroom was at the back of the building and offered a view of a small slice of sky, the rest blocked by the taller structure at the building's rear. Poignant remnants of Bea's life were here, too: an old stuffed toy rabbit sat melancholily on the chair; a few unopened letters rested on the desk.

Dust was beginning to accumulate on the surfaces.

"Kansas?" Walter answered with a small shrug. "Or Ohio? A farming community."

"You don't know?" Daniel didn't mean for the question to come out as harshly as it did but couldn't help himself.

Walter had the grace to flush slightly. "I don't care for my models to speak much during our work. It can be quite distracting when one is trying to create. It's important to let the muse do her work, you know. Bea understood that."

Daniel stared at him for a beat or two, thinking of the cold marble sculpture of Clytie. How could you stare at another human for that long, chisel the image of their flesh from stone, and not know something as simple as where they were from?

"Callie would know," Walter continued in a half-placating, half-defensive tone. "Or Matthew. I didn't have that kind of relationship with Bea. Paxton did, though. She truly was his muse, if she was anyone's; he created some of his best work with her as his model. His heart was breaking that she wouldn't sit for him any longer."

Genevieve shot Daniel a wry look as she gingerly ran a finger over a pair of spectacles folded on the chair's thick arm.

"His muse?"

"Given your knowledge of Ovid, surely you are familiar with the concept of muses, Mr. McCaffrey. We artists need them to create."

"This was a real woman, Mr. Wilson." Daniel strove for a measured tone, though judging by the admonishing glance from Genevieve, he was unsuccessful. "A living, breathing person, not an abstract idea to inspire Mr. Paxton, or anyone." Daniel turned a slow circle, trying to take in as much of the room as he could. Plus, he couldn't abide looking at Walter Wilson just now.

"Of course." Walter sounded surprised. "That is the beauty of muses. I've been lucky enough to have been so stricken myself, in the past."

"Priscilla Langston?" Genevieve said, raising her brows gently.

"You followed the story then, Miss Stewart?" Walter smiled. Daniel frowned at them both, disliking not knowing what they were discussing.

"The *Athena* sculpture? On the post office?" Genevieve prompted, seeing Daniel's confused expression.

Daniel shook his head. He knew the building, of course. It was hard to miss, having so many tiers and stories it resembled a wedding cake. "I think that was erected when I was still abroad. It's yours?" he asked Walter.

The architect ducked his head in modest assent. "Originally it was topped with a gilded sculpture of Athena, but the tastes of this town proved too provincial."

"The sculpture was removed," Genevieve added. "It was quite the story, oh, ten years ago? I wasn't working yet, but I recall it clearly. The model was called Priscilla Langston."

"Yes," Walter confirmed. "Priscilla was my, erm, companion." He glanced at the door, seeming to not want

Callie to overhear him speak of a former mistress. "A great muse. I accomplished some of my best work with her as my model."

"What happened to her? Is she still modeling?" Daniel asked.

Walter looked surprised. "She returned to Pittsburgh," he said. "Couldn't stand the publicity. I used to hear from her quite regularly, but it has been some time now. My guess is she married." His smile turned a little sad. "It took some time before I was able to regain my focus after her departure. Creative people need muses. Who is yours, Mr. McCaffrey?"

Daniel ignored the question. He had studied the classics rigorously, both at British boarding school and Harvard, and he wasn't about to engage in an intellectual debate with an aesthete Bohemian like Walter, not when a woman's blood stained the interior of that rolled-up carpet. He shifted the conversation back to the matter at hand.

"And Bea's throat was cut?" Daniel asked quietly. He hoped Callie, who might still be within earshot, couldn't hear him. "There was no forced entry?"

There was something here, some piece of information that could help them, somewhere in this apartment. It was like a word on the tip of his tongue, niggling at him with insistence, but he couldn't quite place it.

What am I missing?

"The door was probably unlocked." Callie was back, leaning in the doorway of the sewing room. "There would have been little reason to lock it, as she was home. This is a very safe neighborhood, and she was expecting Matthew after his party ended, which she knew would run quite late. Of course, he had a key, though."

"Who else had a key?" Genevieve asked. She folded her hands in front of her waist and gazed around the room sadly.

"Me, obviously," Callie said. "The landlord, I suppose. I'm not sure who else."

"The police didn't collect the keys?" Daniel asked. That seemed odd. "They let you come and go?"

Callie shrugged. "Once they claimed the death was self-inflicted, they turned the key back over to me. I believe Bea had no next of kin. She was an orphan. Her whole world was her circle of friends, the artists and the other models. Matthew is arranging for her effects to be packed and given to charity, but he said I and a few other girls could come sometime and take what we liked, if we wanted a keepsake or memento of her."

Genevieve squeezed past Daniel and Walter to stand by Callie at the door. "Have you?"

Callie shook her head and sighed. "No. It's too unbearably sad."

"It's so strange the police don't want to investigate," Genevieve said, obviously frustrated. "I hate to sound like my mother, but I can't help to think if Bea had been wealthy, had family to agitate on her behalf, they would be doing more."

Walter drew himself up, affronted. "Bea had family. We were her family."

Daniel had to keep himself from catching Genevieve's eye, knowing she was thinking the same thing he was. Walter didn't even know which state Bea hailed from, hardly the definition of family.

"We've been trying," Callie said. "But this is why we need your help. The police are a dead end."

What Callie and Walter were claiming did not add up with what Daniel knew of Detective Aloysius Longstreet. The man had risen quickly in the ranks of the New York City Police Department, largely as a result of his well-earned reputation for fierce tenacity and an often-overzealous sense of justice.

The Detective Longstreet Daniel knew wouldn't let an obvious murder go unsolved.

"I'm not convinced they're *not* investigating," he said slowly, looking around the room again.

What is it? What am I missing?

"What do you mean?" Genevieve puzzled at him. "You heard Mr. Wilson and Callie. Longstreet told them the case was closed."

"Or he wants people to *think* it is closed," Daniel answered, pushing out of the room and into the bedroom. The thing he couldn't put his finger on continued to gnaw at him.

It was something in these rooms.

The others followed.

"Are you suggesting this detective was paid off by the killer, something like that?" Walter asked, his voice troubled. "That this is a conspiracy? I hope you're not insinuating Matthew had anything—"

Daniel shook his head, less from negation and more as if to shoo an irksome thought. His gaze traveled across the bedroom, taking in the partially opened wardrobe bursting with colors and textures: bright-red silks, deep-peacock velvets, apricot-sprigged cotton. The dressing table was littered with perfumes, powders, and cheek stain, and a black silky negligee lay on the neatly made bed.

A quick peek in the bathroom revealed nothing of interest: a tin of tooth powder, a tub of face cream, a vial of bath salts.

"Daniel, what are you looking for?" Genevieve's frustration was directed at him, now, as he made his way to the sitting room, the others trailing in his wake.

He shook his head again, unable to answer.

What is it?

"Remember how Longstreet tailed us earlier this summer?" he asked instead, picking up a book and leafing through it briefly.

Nothing.

"You know this Longstreet fellow?" Walter asked, placing his hands on his hips.

"Unfortunately, yes," Daniel said, running a hand through his hair as he checked the titles of the few other books stacked on the mantel. He had refrained from mentioning the association earlier, wanting to know more facts first. "Remember, Genevieve, Longstreet arrested Rupert when he was really following us, hoping we would lead him to the gunrunners. We know he's not above using a red herring, obscuring his true intentions."

"The gunrunners, right. I read your story in the *Globe*," Walter said admiringly. "Couldn't believe it when Callie said Polly Palmer was her best friend," he added, referring to the pseudonym Genevieve used when writing for the paper. "That was quite a story."

Story.

That was it.

Daniel quickly crossed to where the folded newspaper lay on a side table. He opened it wide, revealing the salacious headline:

RIPPER HYSTERIA HITS NEW YORK!
HAS JACK CROSSED THE ATLANTIC?

CHAPTER 5

A ripple of something, not quite fear but its close cousin, traveled down Genevieve's spine.

"Don't be ridiculous, Daniel," she snapped, covering her sudden feeling of foreboding by snatching the paper out of Daniel's hand. She held it at arm's length and read the headline with distaste, noting the byline. "The *World* is the least reputable paper in the city. It's utter garbage. And that Jim Crawford is a predator, haunting crime scenes like a ghoul."

"Jack the Ripper?" Callie asked, crowding in behind Genevieve. She sounded bewildered. "But what does he have to do with Bea?"

"Nothing, surely," Walter interjected, wrapping an arm around Callie's shoulders. "Whatever are you suggesting, McCaffrey?"

Genevieve raised a brow at Daniel. She had the same question.

"These types of papers," Daniel began, raising a brow back at Genevieve in response to the small snort she had involuntarily emitted, "have been drumming up wild stories for weeks that Jack the Ripper may have traveled to New York."

"Pure poppycock," Walter declared stoutly, though he threw a troubled glance in the direction of the sewing room, where Bea's body had been found. "As Miss Stewart—Polly Palmer, no less—said, the *World* is trash. Sensational stories designed to cause outrage and stir up trouble. You should see what they print about me, for example, or Matthew."

Genevieve recalled what Daniel had told her about Matthew Shipman's parties with young girls and wondered if the *World* was terribly off the mark in that instance, but held her tongue.

"Daniel, you can't seriously believe these rags are correct. Jack the Ripper is not in New York, and he had nothing to do with Bea's death," Genevieve said instead, trying to signal with her eyes that he was upsetting Callie, who had paled considerably.

"*I* don't believe it," Daniel said. "But I wonder if Longstreet is keeping Bea's death quiet because of stories like this." He tapped the paper Genevieve was holding. "If a paper like the *World* got hold of the story that a young woman's throat had been cut, they would instantly proclaim that the Ripper was indeed on our shores."

"And cause a public panic," Callie murmured.

"But the Ripper's victims were—if the ladies will pardon my language—streetwalkers," Walter protested. "Bea was killed in her own home."

Genevieve's temper rose. The previous fall, she had closely followed the story of the notorious London killer and had been consistently irritated by the insistence of the press—including her own paper—on characterizing the victims as prostitutes. "As far as we know, many of the victims were simply impoverished and not necessarily of ill repute," she said in a deliberately acidic tone.

"Regardless," said Daniel, flashing her a warning look that only annoyed her further, "the police may want to avoid any such connection. This is just a theory, mind."

Silence settled over the group as they pondered Daniel's words. Genevieve debated pursuing the unjust treatment of the Ripper victims in the press with Walter but decided against it, certain her argument would fall on deaf ears.

"It is a sound theory," she finally said. "It could be what is holding Longstreet back from being more aggressive with Bea's case. But we don't know that, and until we do, we should continue to pursue the matter ourselves." She locked eyes with Daniel, sending him a questioning look.

Do you agree, it asked?

Daniel hesitated for a beat or two, indecision playing across his face. She could tell he was wrestling with a whole host of factors: the odd behavior of the police, a reluctance to tangle with Aloysius Longstreet again, and most certainly, his own recent near-death experience.

A sudden, urgent thought struck Genevieve.

Don't do it. Say no.

It was so strong her breath caught.

Was the thought for her, or for Daniel?

Or for them both?

"Yes, we should," Daniel said. He continued to hold her eyes, and something that could be regret pooled in his gaze before he blinked it away, his manner becoming business-like and brisk.

They made plans to keep in close contact with Callie and Walter about next steps and parted on the sidewalk in front of the stately brick building.

"We'll leave you to it, then," Walter said, shaking first Daniel's hand, then hers. "Despite this heat, I believe Callie and I may take a restful stroll over the East River Bridge,

allow its beauty to take our mind off this horrid business."
He gave a slight shudder under his purple jacket and flicked
a lock of hair out of his face. "I envy the Roebling family
their talent but am glad their masterpiece graces our fair
city. It is truly the most spectacular feat of modern engi-
neering, is it not? It brings me great comfort."

Callie smiled sadly at Walter and patted his back, nodding her good-byes to Genevieve and Daniel. Genevieve
watched her friend's lace-trimmed grass-green summer
frock recede as she drifted down the street, her arm linked
through Walter's. He leaned in close to say something into
her ear, a lock of his long dark hair obscuring his face, and
she nodded in response.

They made a striking pair.

"You don't like him, do you?" Daniel said. He was
following her gaze. Callie and Walter turned south on
Lexington, disappearing from sight.

A sigh wrested itself from her chest.

"Not really," Genevieve admitted. She wrinkled her
nose. "Though I admit I have no real basis for my dislike. He appears to care for Callie deeply and is certainly
taking good care of her. I suppose I simply want more for
her."

Daniel was silent but regarded her with sympathy.

She took a deep breath, hoping to clear her head, and
opened her parasol against the climbing sun. The temperatures were climbing along with it, and she suspected by
afternoon the heat would be unbearable. "Walk with me
toward my next appointment?" Genevieve asked.

A familiar half smile curved the side of Daniel's mouth,
and he offered her his arm. Genevieve smiled to herself as
she slid her hand into the crook of his elbow, enjoying the
physical contact.

It was grounding, after their time in the depressing apartment upstairs.

She steered Daniel toward Third Avenue, in the direction opposite the route Callie and Walter had taken. It was still challenging to reconcile the laughing, optimistic girl Genevieve had known with the slightly jaded, sophisticated young woman Callie seemed to have become. One who was kept by a man. One who took off her clothes as part of her employment.

"I confess I'm not sure what our next step here should be," Genevieve said, tearing her mind away from Callie. "Do you think we should try to talk to Mr. Shipman?"

Daniel looked pensive as they slowly strolled. They passed a grime-stained laborer carrying a shovel over his shoulder, a tired-looking mother pulling two heat-wilted, bedraggled children in her wake. The temperature was such that nobody was in much of a hurry.

"Not yet," he said. "If Walter is to be believed, Matthew's alibi is as solid as they come. I am curious what he was doing on that beach in Newport, though."

"We don't even know it was Shipman on the beach," Genevieve said in a distracted voice. "I wonder if we should start with the artists Walter and Callie mentioned." She gestured with her head to the opposite side of the street, where there were more shade trees. They waited for a break in traffic before crossing. Her dress, though a light cotton, felt as though it were plastered to her back, and they had only walked two blocks at a leisurely pace. "Hear what they have to say before we pursue Mr. Shipman."

"Elbert Paxton and William Chase," Daniel said, once they were on the north side of the street. He took off his hat and briefly fanned his face with it before replacing it on his head. "Do you know them?"

"We've been introduced," she said, stopping under a large maple. "Would you please hold this?" Genevieve shoved her parasol at Daniel, who took it with a surprised expression. Though her gloves were thin, she couldn't bear to have them on her hands another moment. She stripped them off and shoved them into her reticule. "My friend Eliza Lindsay knows Mr. Chase quite well," she continued, holding her hand out for her parasol. Daniel handed it over wordlessly. "In fact, she is studying with him on Long Island at present. Odd that he was in town when he is meant to be in Shinnecock."

"It was for a funeral, recall. I believe Walter said he was with his family the night of the murder. Perhaps he left them here while he teaches?" Daniel suggested.

Genevieve couldn't believe that anyone who had the means to leave the city during the summer would dream of staying. The heat seemed to rise off the very sidewalk and become humidly trapped between the buildings, weighing upon her in an almost physical manner.

Truth be told, she had come to the startling realization earlier in the week that she'd never spent the summer in the city before. Like clockwork, her family packed their belongings and left their Washington Square residence at the end of every June. They went to the Newport family house, and come September, they returned to New York.

She had no idea what the city was like during the summer months but was coming to realize, more than anything, it was *hot*.

There was no way she would admit this to Daniel.

"Whatever Mr. Chase's arrangement, he's back in Long Island now," she said instead, turning to continue east. "I've had a letter from Eliza just yesterday."

"Mr. Paxton, then?" Daniel asked.

"I'll inquire with Callie," Genevieve agreed. "She may know if he's still in town. Or Walter will, I suppose." Like it or not, it seemed Callie's gentleman was a part of their investigation.

At the corner of First Avenue, Genevieve paused again. "I'll catch a cab from here," she said, looking up the street for one.

"Allow me." Daniel stepped into the street to hail a carriage as it approached. "Where are you heading?"

"Work," she sighed. Normally Genevieve relished spending time at the office. She loved the hustle and the pace of it, the large, airy windows and high ceilings of the open space containing all the journalists' desks. She realized again, though, that she didn't know what it would be like during the summer. In her previous role at the paper covering ladies' interests, her editor had allowed her to send in her columns from Rhode Island.

In her current role at the society pages, of course, being in Newport during the summer was essential.

Which was why she was dreading going to her office. Her editor was going to be furious with her.

Daniel nodded as he helped her into the carriage, then leaned on the open window. The sun glinted off a few stray curls peeking out from under his hat, his dark hair appearing almost red in the bright late-morning light. "Do you have a plan to keep your job?"

"I do."

"Will you tell me what it is?"

"Only if it works," she replied, before rapping smartly on the carriage's roof to signal the driver to begin.

★　★　★

"Well look who it is. Didn't think you swells spent the summer in town." Luther Franklin's amiable face grinned down at her. Genevieve put down the correspondence she had been riffling through at her desk and looked at her friend with real pleasure.

"We don't."

"And yet here you are."

"Here I am."

He laughed, a low mellow sound, and perched on the edge of her desk.

It was good to see Luther. Genevieve was genuinely fond of him, which was not something she could say about everyone she worked with. There had been some difficult moments between them in the past, mostly when it became apparent that Luther hoped for more from her than friendship. He had been horribly jealous of Daniel, but finally understood that Genevieve's relationship with Daniel was purely professional.

Or she had convinced him it was.

As Genevieve indulged Luther's recounting of recent office gossip, she pondered whether or not to ask if he had heard anything about Bea's death. Luther covered homicide for the paper, and even though Longstreet seemed to be doing his best to keep the murder quiet, she knew word generally got out.

Police officers were also prone to gossip.

It was on the tip of her tongue to ask when the elevator doors pinged open and the paper's editor, Arthur Horace, bustled into the office, his nose buried in a telegram. One of the assistant editors jumped up to follow him.

Physically, Arthur did not cut the most imposing figure. He was short of stature and slightly portly, a pair of wire-rimmed spectacles perched on his nose under an impressive set of bushy eyebrows, all topped by a balding pate surrounded by tufts of thick gray hair worn a trifle too long.

If one didn't know better, one might assume he was an absent-minded schoolteacher, or the aging, harried clerk of a Wall Street broker.

But Genevieve, like most of New York, did know better. Arthur was a force to be reckoned with, editor of one of the largest newspapers in the whole city and, by extension, the country. He knew well the full extent of his power and wielded it with precision. He was an exacting boss who held his employees to high standards and had taken a chance on Genevieve when she was young and recently jilted but determined to prove herself.

She would be forever grateful for Arthur's trust in her then, and hoped he would trust her again now.

Without breaking stride or even glancing in their direction, Arthur called her name.

"Miss Stewart! To my office. Now."

Genevieve jumped herself and scrambled after him.

"Close the door on your way out, please," Arthur said to the assistant once she was there, handing over the telegram to the young man and picking up a draft of something from his desk.

Genevieve drew a breath to speak, but he held up his hand and presented her with what sounded, at first, like a math riddle.

"Tell me, Miss Stewart, if a train leaves from Newport to New York thrice daily, including carrying the bulk of its post, and it takes five hours to reach our fair city, how is it you were able to report on Mitzy Taylor's garden luncheon in Rhode Island yesterday, when you were spotted at Delmonico's here in Manhattan that very same afternoon?"

Her mouth dried. Dammit, she'd known it had been a bad idea to socialize before explaining herself to Arthur.

"The only reasonable explanation, Miss Stewart," Arthur continued, setting down the document and fixing her with a devastatingly angry expression, "is that you flew. Because there is no earthly way, even in a German horseless carriage, you could make it from Mrs. Taylor's Newport cottage at one o'clock to Delmonico's near Madison Square by four o'clock by any other conceivable method."

Genevieve's shoulders had begun to creep up to her ears, and she willed them back down with effort. She opened her mouth to explain, but Arthur kept talking.

"And yet I have a very detailed, and quite well-written, account of said garden luncheon. As a newlywed, Mrs. Taylor was certainly anxious to make a good impression for her first society luncheon, wasn't she?" He picked up the papers again and peered at them through his spectacles. "I know what the flowers were like—white roses; a classic choice, don't you agree? I know who was in attendance, that Mrs. Schermerhorn left early—that must have upset the hostess a bit, but at least she made an appearance— and that Katharine Bellew was sporting a hat of the new Parisian style not yet thought to be available in the United States. I thought the cross-reference to the fashion pages a nice touch, which," he said, fixing his harsh gaze back on Genevieve, under which she felt herself wither, all her excuses drying on her tongue, "should have tipped me off."

"I know that terrapin was served—rather costly for a garden luncheon; young Mrs. Taylor might have done better to save that for her first formal dinner, don't you think? And that the Neapolitan ice cream dessert did not suffer overly from the unusually high temperatures. Yes, the piece was succinct yet informative, descriptive without being tedious, had just the right hint of snobbishness to keep those not in the upper classes intrigued yet those in the upper classes assured of their place in the world; in short, it had everything I tend to want from a society piece."

He threw the papers down on his desk and leaned back in his chair. Genevieve folded her hands in front of her waist and, with difficulty, kept silent, knowing the scolding wasn't over yet. It was deserved, but if he would just let her *explain*, perhaps she would still have a job afterward.

"Except, of course," Arthur continued, his voice rising, "that it was not written by the person I assigned to write the society column. Namely, *you*. Genevieve, did you really think I wouldn't catch this, or that I would allow a piece by an unknown author to be published in my paper? I'm shocked at many things around this treachery, but firstly that you'd allow someone else to write under your name."

Now she did try to speak, but Arthur cut her off once again, his voice thunderous.

"It has taken you years, Genevieve, to build your reputation as a journalist. To gain my trust, and that of your fellow reporters. Not to mention that of the public. And to throw it all away in a childish stunt such as this has seriously undermined all of that, or would, if I allowed this to become public knowledge. What on earth could be so important that you would abdicate your responsibilities to our paper, to me, and come racing back to Manhattan in the middle of the summer social season?" Arthur finished his diatribe by standing, pounding his fist on his desk on his last word.

"Jack the Ripper, sir," Genevieve said. It gave her only the smallest amount of satisfaction to watch shock cross her editor's face. Whatever he had been expecting to hear, it wasn't that. "It is possible the killer may be in New York."

CHAPTER 6

Arthur stared at her, his eyebrows dancing furiously above his glasses. Genevieve held her breath. She hadn't planned to blurt out Daniel's theory around Jack the Ripper, but the more she thought about it, the more plausible it seemed. Not necessarily that the dreaded murderer had crossed the Atlantic, but that the police might be keeping a murder quiet so as not to stir up the public.

Though Bea's throat *had* been cut, same as the Ripper victims'.

"Sit," Arthur ordered, pointing at a hard wooden chair opposite his desk. "And explain."

Genevieve released her breath and sat. She explained about the murder, about Detective Longstreet's insistence the death was self-inflicted and his refusal to publicly investigate, and how she and Daniel had become involved through Callie. Arthur listened, his brows giving the occasional twitch.

"What if Longstreet is correct, though?" Genevieve said. "Even if he is keeping Beatrice Holler's death quiet to avoid inciting a panic, Jack the Ripper really could be here. You know there's been speculation about this ever since the murders stopped; it's one of the theories of British law enforcement, isn't it? That the killings ceased because he left London and came here." A chill passed through Genevieve at the thought.

"Other papers have been spreading this rumor, Genevieve. Disreputable papers. I don't know if the *Globe* should be engaging in such speculation," Arthur said. He looked troubled, though, and Genevieve noticed he didn't contradict her.

"Either way, there's a story here. Even if Beatrice Holler's murder is unrelated to the Ripper—and I agree that it probably is—the police are covering up the violent death of a prominent artist's model, mistress to a wealthy man known for his debauched parties."

Arthur's brows shot nearly to his hairline. "What do you know of Matthew Shipman's parties?"

Genevieve bristled. Why did every man think it necessary to protect her from such knowledge? "Enough to know that it seems suspicious his mistress should wind up dead and the authorities will not investigate it," she replied tartly. Something told her not to mention the incident Daniel had seen in Newport, as they had no solid proof it had even been Shipman on that beach, let alone that anything nefarious had occurred.

Though the fact that he, or someone aligned with his household, was with a woman—struggling? embracing?—in the surf mere weeks after his mistress's death was something she hoped to get to the bottom of.

Arthur drummed his fingers on the surface of his desk, once, and frowned at her. He stood abruptly and walked to his office door, sticking out his head and calling for Luther.

"What's up, boss?" Luther said, panting as he hustled in. He glanced between Genevieve and Arthur.

"What do you know about the murder of Beatrice Holler?" Arthur asked, folding his hands over his stomach as he leaned back.

Luther appeared baffled. "Um . . . nothing? The name doesn't ring a bell." He pulled a pad from his front jacket pocket and began to furiously flip through it.

Arthur slid his eyes to Genevieve and inclined his head toward Luther, indicating she should tell him what she knew.

Genevieve launched into the tale again, watching as Luther's eyes grew rounder. He found a clean page in his notebook and jotted down a few notes as she spoke.

"I haven't heard a peep about this," he muttered, shaking his head. "Want me to shake a few trees, boss?"

Arthur regarded both of them over the tops of his spectacles for a few beats. Genevieve bit her lower lip.

Arthur's answer might well decide her future.

"Yes, but quietly. Share with Genevieve here anything you find out." It took an immense amount of effort for her not to sag in relief. Apparently, she still had a job. "If Luther hasn't heard about this unfortunate death, it does seem we have a cover-up on our hands. Anything further," he added with a significant look, and Genevieve understood he meant any Jack the Ripper connection, "remains to be seen."

Luther scurried out, casting one final, amazed look in Genevieve's direction.

"I came in today to speak with you about my leaving Newport," Genevieve said hurriedly, wanting to explain herself before her editor could change his mind. "I never meant for you to get the article draft directly; it was supposed to come to me first."

"Is that supposed to make this better, Genevieve? I think you'll agree I have been extraordinarily lenient with you in the past. *Extraordinarily.*"

Genevieve swallowed miserably. It was true.

"Who wrote this?" he demanded, tapping the article in question.

"Suzanne Anwyll."

Arthur's brow furrowed. "The youngest Anwyll daughter? The one who came out early? She can't be more than, what, nineteen?"

"Yes, nineteen," Genevieve said. "I met her at her debut two years ago. We talked for some time. Her parents had her come out early, as they wanted her to circulate in society as soon as possible."

"Something she does not want to do, I take it?" Arthur guessed.

"Exactly. I must say, I find in Miss Anwyll something of a kindred spirit. She longs to write, Arthur, and as you have seen, she's quite good. She's miserable in Newport, miserable in society, but I had a feeling—and this piece proves it—that she'd be quite good at observing it."

Arthur blinked at her, and again, to the uninitiated, his look would appear lazy.

Again, Genevieve knew better.

"You planned this," he said. "Before you knew about Beatrice Holler's murder, you thought to bring Miss Anwyll on board. I know you, Genevieve, and you would never recommend someone untried. You had her write some practice pieces, I take it?"

She could feel the heat rise to her cheeks. "I did. I wanted to see if she was worthy of the paper before I proposed the idea to you. But Arthur, one person writing the society column is not enough. It is exhausting attending every single event. And after my success with the story on Robin Hood, and on Thomas Meade and the gunrunners, I had thought you would allow me to pursue more investigative stories."

"Then you speak to me, Genevieve. You don't bring in other writers without my knowledge or consent."

"I did speak to you. Repeatedly." The blush remained on her cheeks, but Genevieve sat straighter in her chair.

Arthur sighed and removed his glasses, rubbing them on his jacket lapel. "That you did." He replaced the glasses and regarded her through their lenses.

"Fine," he finally said, and a surge of triumph shot through her. "You look into the police cover-up here. Miss Anwyll can write about Newport until you're finished. Leave me her address, as I'll be needing to correspond with her myself. I'll consider this a trial run, see how she does. And I want you back on the society pages when this wraps up. Then we'll see about other stories."

This was, Genevieve knew, as good an offer as she was going to get right now. She stood, flushed with excitement, and shook Arthur's hand. "Thank you, Arthur. For believing in me. I won't let you down."

Arthur returned her handshake but looked at her so gravely Genevieve faltered.

"Be careful, Genevieve," was all he said.

★ ★ ★

"I've never seen it so empty," Genevieve murmured as she and Callie stepped into the halls of the Tenth Street Studio Building. She breathed a sigh of relief at finding the interior of the vast, labyrinthine building far cooler than it had been outside; the temperatures continued to rise, day by day, and the city had become unbearably stifling.

"It's better to wait inside, is it not? Daniel should be able to find us if we linger in the hallway," Callie said. "Oh!" she exclaimed, jumping aside and shaking at her yellow skirts. A robust ginger cat appeared from under the fabric, twining itself around Callie's booted ankles. "Where did you come from?" she murmured, leaning over to pet the creature.

Callie's question was immediately answered as several more cats of varying colors and sizes bounded into the hallway from a door that stood slightly ajar at the opposite end of the building. The noise of their mewing was sudden and intense, almost overwhelming.

"Isn't that Mr. Chase's studio?" Genevieve asked as she, too, reached down to stroke the head of a black-and-white cat who had perched at her feet. It leaned its head into her hand and mewed, loudly and repeatedly. "I've no milk—or anything else—for you," she told the cat firmly. It butted its head more insistently.

"It is," Callie said, wrinkling her nose, as no fewer than four cats were now circling her feet. "I don't recall him keeping the cats."

"I believe they are nobody's in particular and belong to the building itself," Daniel's voice chimed in. Genevieve had been so distracted by the multitude of cats she hadn't noticed him enter. He crouched down to scratch a small black fellow with bright-yellow eyes under the chin.

Genevieve was thankful the three of them would be alone for this appointment, as Walter was, according to Callie, tying up some loose ends around a large project.

Upon hearing this, Genevieve had made a mental note to ask her brother Charles about Walter, as the two men were professional colleagues and had even vied for some of the same commissions. Try as she might, the two days since they had toured Bea Holler's unsettlingly still apartment had done nothing to ease Genevieve's disquiet around Callie's lover. She knew she was being unreasonable, perhaps even prudish, but there was no harm in checking on his reputation.

"How do they survive in the summer months?" Genevieve asked, gently nudging a particularly insistent gray striped cat away from the lace at the hem of her dress. She liked cats fine but didn't want her dress used as a batting toy.

The Tenth Street Studio Building was a hive of activity from November to April, when the artists who rented the twenty-five studios comprising the building were in residence. They held three open studio evenings each winter, when potential buyers roamed from room to room, viewing the various work for sale. Genevieve had attended these evenings, though not with the regularity of Eliza or Callie. But in the summer the artists, like everyone else, it seemed, fled the steamy city for cooler locales, sketching and drawing in preparation for their larger canvases.

"I don't know," Daniel said, rising and taking in the shuttered doors and empty hallway. The studios, she knew, contained large windows, but the entryway was windowless and quite dark. "Perhaps the building's owner feeds them, or some of the artists who occasionally stop by, like Paxton."

"He's waiting for us," Callie said. "His studio is on the second floor." Callie had arranged the meeting with the elderly painter, who was still in town following the funeral of his compatriot Sturgis Sawyer, a fellow Hudson River School painter who had recently passed. "Walter's is on the third, but he's not been using it much lately."

As they moved up the wide staircase with its thick mahogany banisters, the cats accompanied them, weaving around their collective ankles. Genevieve moved with care, lest she trip over one of the animals, and thought of all the artists who labored behind the closed doors in the fall and winter months. She also thought of their models, young women like Callie and Bea, who labored alongside them, sitting or standing still for hours at a time.

How odd it must be, to have someone stare at your body for so long.

She leaned in close to Callie. "How is the sitting with Walter going? Are you enjoying being Persephone?"

Even in the dim light of the staircase, Genevieve could make out Callie's blush. "Oh, it's fine. We're still in the sketching phases, so we haven't moved to the studio yet, where he'll work with the marble. He has me in a rather difficult pose to hold for long periods, but we manage. It's hard work, being a model," she said, in a somewhat defensive tone. "He is sketching me from all angles."

"I don't doubt it." Genevieve longed to ask Callie what it was like to pose in the nude but didn't want to do so within earshot of Daniel, his broad back advancing a few steps ahead of them up the stairs. Genevieve blushed herself at the thought of his gaze swiftly traveling across her own nearly nude body on Duck Island. It had been the briefest of moments, before he caught himself and turned his back, but that look had made her skin tingle unbearably, causing a heightened awareness of her own flesh she had never felt before.

Genevieve's breath caught, ever so slightly, at the memory.

Would it be like that? Did Callie feel that way, all those hours Walter's eyes were on her, or was it more clinical?

Somehow, she suspected the latter.

"Here is Paxton's studio," Callie said as they reached the top of the stairs, pointing to the third door on the left.

"Have you posed for him?" Genevieve asked in a quiet voice as they made their way toward the door.

"Not yet, and I doubt I will. Once Bea stopped sitting for him, he began to move away from figural work, focusing on landscapes again."

"Back to his roots," said Daniel in a thoughtful tone.

Genevieve regarded him in surprise. "Have you been here before, then? Come to the open studios?" They stopped a few feet from the studio door, talking in quiet tones.

Daniel offered his half smile. "Of course. And then some."

"Ah, you've attended some of the infamous parties here, with Lord Umberland, no doubt," Callie said with an arch, knowing look, referring to Rupert by his title.

Daniel's smile broadened. "You know us too well, Miss Maple."

"What parties?" Genevieve was mystified.

Callie and Daniel exchanged a look, making Genevieve feel like a child, as when her brothers shared a secret they didn't want to tell her. She resisted the urge to stamp her foot.

"Have you attended these parties?" she asked Callie. "But you've only been . . ."

"Out of polite society a few months?" Callie finished Genevieve's sentence wryly. "I know. But when I began modeling this past winter, it was the height of the social season for this set too. It really has become quite tropical in town, hasn't it? I can't wait to leave."

"You're leaving too?" Genevieve asked, surprised. And, truth be told, disappointed. She had assumed Callie would remain in the city throughout the summer with her.

Callie looked surprised in turn. "Yes, we are also going to Long Island. Walter has a house there. When he's wrapped up the details with his client, that is. And if you feel you no longer need us. There's not much beyond these interviews we can add to the case."

Genevieve digested this, and caught Daniel's slanted sideways look of inquiry tinged with concern.

Are you sure you want to do this? the look implied.

She frowned back at him, unable to answer.

"Tell me about the party," she urged instead.

"It was quite a to-do," Daniel said. "Some years ago—
'77, '78, something like that? Right before I went abroad.
Rupert had wrangled an invitation to the writer Oliver
Crenshaw's birthday dinner, and it was filled with artists
and other writers. Someone had the idea to come here, and
we brought all the leftover food and bottles and tromped
through the snow, where it turned into a spontaneous masquerade party."

"A masquerade?" Callie asked, a smile playing about her
lips.

"Oh yes, I remember it well," came a creaky voice from
behind them. Genevieve turned to see Elbert Paxton leaning in the doorway of his studio, regarding them with a
thoughtful expression. "You wild young men roamed from
studio to studio, grabbing whatever outfits you could find,
and your set and the young ladies present began dancing in
the corridors, costumed in all manner of garb."

"Rupert somehow jammed himself into a set of medi-
eval armor," Daniel said, grinning.

"That was from Leutze's studio," Elbert said, pointing
down the hall. "And someone found a Native headdress
in Bierstadt's place, and Puritan dress in Weir's, combin-
ing them for a most unusual ensemble. The ladies tended
toward the cloths and draperies from the East, but quite
little of it, if memory serves." Now the elderly artist smiled
himself, a bit wickedly.

Daniel inclined his head. "I recall that as well."

Genevieve was astonished. By "ladies," she assumed
they meant either models and mistresses like Callie or paid
companions. Between this and the happenings at Matthew
Shipman's parties, there was apparently a whole world of

debauchery out there she had known nothing about. How had she made it to almost twenty-eight years of age and never before heard the details of the demimonde?

Elbert opened his door wider, inviting them in. "Sawyer returned from the theater and was shocked to find the hallways filled with capering figures," he said. "He seized this very table"—Elbert rapped his white, shaking knuckles on a small but sturdy ornate round table covered with mosaic tile—"hoisted himself atop it, and recited poetry in his perfect Arabic, his voice carrying as an accompaniment to the guitar music being played."

The group paused in the center of the studio. The cats had followed them in and were busy darting behind stacked canvases and pouncing onto precariously loaded credenzas. There were paintings and drawings on every available surface and piles of photographs haphazardly placed on chair seats; at least three easels, one containing a large, half-finished canvas, the other two empty; a massive brocade settee and two matching armchairs; an antique mahogany table surrounded by mismatched dining chairs; and bric-a-brac everywhere. Venetian glassware, various pieces of old armor, Egyptian pots, jars of paintbrushes, musty books, and even an old sword littered the walls, spilled out of a Renaissance cabinet, and balanced on table tops.

"Normally it's a bit neater in here, particularly when I entertain. You must forgive me, I didn't prepare anything today; my sister Eloise takes care of all that now that my Gertie has passed. Besides, it's far too hot to host a luncheon or the like, don't you agree?"

"We don't expect to be hosted, Mr. Paxton," Callie said. "I'm so grateful to have caught you before you return to New Hampshire. And I was so sorry to hear about Mr. Sawyer's passing," she said.

The older man let his eyes roam his studio walls, perhaps trying to understand how it looked to his young visitors. "Not many of us left from my generation now. Chase came, though. Awfully kind of him. Get down, you," he said to a cat, perhaps the same ginger one who had originally accosted Callie's ankles—frankly, there were so many cats they were starting to all look the same. Elbert shooed the creature off the narrow strip of wood on the front of his easel. "Wretched creatures. Some of that paint is still wet; don't want animal hair stuck to my canvas. Their noise kept me up all last night, the infernal things."

"You slept here?" Daniel asked.

"Oh yes, oh yes. My house here in town is closed for the season. It's easier to stay here rather than go through the trouble of opening it up just for a short time. Come, I'll show you." Toward the back of the space was a small, spiral, wrought-iron staircase Genevieve hadn't noticed before. She followed Elbert and Daniel up, Callie trailing behind. The stairs deposited them into a small, tidy sitting room, and Genevieve could see the foot of a neatly made bed in the attached room to her right.

A sound between a gasp and a cry whirled her around. Callie stood at the top of the staircase, tears pooling in her green eyes, hand covering her mouth.

Genevieve rushed to her side. "Callie? What it is?"

"It's Bea," said Callie, pointing.

Looking in the direction her friend indicated, Genevieve let out a gasp as well. Deeper in the bedroom were dozens of pictures—from quick sketches to finely finished paintings—of the same face. Beatrice Holler's face, caught in almost every emotion or expression humanly possible, lined the walls and appeared in stacks along the floor, over and over and over.

CHAPTER 7

Daniel refrained from gasping himself, but it was a close thing.

He had never met Beatrice Holler in life, but he still might have recognized her from the sculpture of Clytie in Callie's house.

Or Walter's house, he supposed, in which Callie currently resided.

The long, straight, aquiline nose, the round eyes, the slight curve to the chin—they all matched the sculpture. Of course, Bea-as-Clytie was pure, dazzling white marble, while many of these images were full of color: the warm peach of the deceased girl's flesh, the stain of pink on her cheeks, the bright blond of her hair.

Bea's eyes, a startling cornflower blue, gazed back at him from every corner of the bedroom.

"Ah, my Beatrice. My angel, my muse. Such a tragedy," sighed Elbert.

"Did you and she have an arrangement?" Daniel asked quietly.

Elbert gave him a sharp look. "Of course not. She was a proper young lady. Merely a comfort to me after my Gertie passed. Inspired me to accomplish some of my best work, I believe."

"I wasn't aware you did figural studies, Mr. Paxton," Genevieve said, sounding a trifle faint. Callie had sat on the top step and was staring at the repeated image of her dead friend's face in horror. "My parents own several of your landscapes."

"Do they now? And remind me of your name, my dear. Miss Maple here told me who was coming, but I confess I've forgotten."

"Genevieve Stewart. My parents are Anna and Wilbur Stewart," Genevieve said, shaking Elbert's hand. She still appeared slightly nonplussed as she glanced at the abundance of pictures with barely concealed distaste.

"Of course, of course. They own *Franconia Notch at Sunset*, from 1866, do they not?"

"And two others," Genevieve confirmed.

"I always liked that one. Well, you're a proper young lady too. Like Miss Maple here. So unlike those others, the ones we were speaking of earlier." At Genevieve's puzzled look, Elbert continued. "From the party," he explained. "That your gentleman friend attended."

"Daniel McCaffrey," Daniel said, also shaking the artist's hand, which was sweaty and unpleasantly limp in his. It was hard not to pull his hand back immediately.

"Quite, quite. Yes, Mr. McCaffrey remembers. The girls in their—if you'll forgive me—half-dressed states that night. Shocking, shocking. My Gertie was a proper, modest woman, God rest her soul. And lovely young Beatrice was as well."

Several of the pictures crowding the room featured "lovely young Beatrice" fully unclothed: a charcoal of her seated on a stool, back to the viewer, peering solemnly over her shoulder; a full-length oil of her nude, stretched on a grassy bank with a slim red cord trailing in front of her, possibly posed as Ariadne; a few others. Elbert followed Daniel's gaze with rheumy eyes.

"In the service of *art*, my dear boy, female nudity is not depraved. Some of these giddy young creatures who come to the open studios are fearful of entering my space without a chaperone, which is nonsense. Art is not lewd or wicked, nor is the creation of it, nor the discussion of it between the sexes. What I'm saying is that Miss Holler—Beatrice, as I called her," Elbert said, giving the name an Italian pronunciation, "was an unassuming young woman. She lived quietly in a woman's boarding house. Not one to take up with some of the younger set of artists here, as some models do, and debase herself."

Daniel shot a curious look at Callie and Genevieve, both still at the top of the stairs. Was it possible Elbert didn't know that Bea had become Matthew Shipman's mistress in the months before she died? "When did Bea last pose for you, Mr. Paxton?"

"Oh, nearly a year ago now." Elbert fussed with a drawing on a small side table near the bed, smoothing corners that had begun to curl. "When I returned from the mountains last fall, she told me she was too busy with other projects, other commitments." He sighed deeply and frowned at the drawing. "Such a shame."

"We've taken enough of your time," Daniel said. Callie eagerly stood at the suggestion of leaving, and Daniel couldn't blame her. There was something deeply unsettling about the endlessly repeated dead woman's face, laughing, frowning, looking pensive, wistful, playful, coy, and on and on.

"Mind those felines," Elbert murmured as the group slowly made their way down the wrought-iron stairs. A few of the cats had ventured up with them, and a small gray one now raced down the steps and sat by the door to the hallway, mewing loudly.

They made their good-byes, and by unspoken mutual agreement, nobody spoke until they were back down the grand staircase and in the front hallway. The cats clustered around them, several dashing back into Chase's studio.

Daniel stared after them.

"That was terribly odd, in Mr. Paxton's studio," Genevieve said, yanking his attention away from the cats.

"Odd is one way to put it," Daniel agreed grimly.

"He didn't realize about Bea and Matthew, I suppose," Callie said. "It was kind of nobody to tell him, in a way."

Daniel removed his hat and ran a hand through his hair, thinking. "I don't care for how he put this young woman on a pedestal, one from which he surely would have knocked her, had he known about her arrangement with Shipman. She must have sensed this, as she kept the true nature of her personal life from him—didn't reveal she'd left the Mildred Penny House, for example. He obviously would have been quite displeased if he'd known."

"Are you suggesting Mr. Paxton had something to do with her death? He too had an alibi, apparently," Genevieve said, looking troubled.

Daniel replaced his hat and rested his hands on his hips. "I don't know. No, probably not. He's quite elderly—did you notice his hands were shaking? I'm surprised he can hold a brush steady. But to have an illusion like the one he had of Bea shattered . . . well, I'm sure he would have reacted quite poorly. For all we know, violently. And for all his talk of his precious departed Gertie, I'm sure that bedroom had other purposes back when Paxton was young."

Genevieve's eyes opened wide. "Oh," she said. "Callie, do most of the artists' studios here have that kind of arrangement? A bedroom or someplace to sleep?"

"Many do, yes," Callie said. "Walter's certainly does. And as Daniel is suggesting, it is a convenient way for many of the artists to hide their, ahem, extramarital activities from their wives. Mr. Chase has almost a whole apartment in there. It's the largest studio in the building, though I've never heard of him consorting with anyone. He's quite faithful to his wife, I believe. I swear, these are the *loudest* cats I've ever heard," she said, leaning down and patting a handsome calico even as she made a face at the animals' collective noise.

Callie was right, the din of the cats was becoming worse. If anything, more had emerged from Chase's studio, and many were darting excitedly from the slightly opened door, out to their group, and back again. It was no wonder Paxton had had trouble sleeping.

"Are they always like this?" Daniel asked, taking a few steps toward the open door. He didn't recall seeing quite so many the times he had visited the building in the past.

"No," Callie replied, her brow furrowing. "There's always a pack, and they mill about during the winter months, sleeping here or there, but I've never seen them act like this."

"I thought you said Mr. Chase was back in Long Island," he said to Genevieve.

Something about that open door didn't sit right with him. It wasn't open enough that he could see inward, but the black sliver of emptiness between the door and the jamb gleamed ill-naturedly, like the slit of an opening eye.

"He is, or was, according to Eliza," said Genevieve.

"So why is his studio open?" Daniel took another few steps in that direction.

"Perhaps it's the cats' main residence?" Callie suggested, offering a shrug. "Maybe someone leaves food for them there."

Daniel nudged the already partially open door a bit wider. "Hello?" he called. "Mr. Chase?"

There was no answer.

The majority of the cats scrambled over his feet, back into the studio. Several stayed close, twining themselves around his ankles and continuing their loud complaints.

Genevieve and Callie crowded close to his shoulders. "I posed for Mr. Chase earlier this spring, I don't think he would mind if we entered," Callie said quietly.

Daniel glanced over his shoulder at the women. Genevieve still looked troubled, Callie anxious. They sensed it too. Something wasn't right here.

Daniel opened the door wider and walked into the studio's main space. He had visited William Merritt Chase's rooms years before, and they were largely unchanged. If anything, they were more elaborate, and more curio filled, than Elbert Paxton's were. The main room had originally been constructed as a gallery for use by any of the artists in residence but had been taken over by Chase a decade or so earlier, if memory served.

Inside, rear skylights offered enough illumination that turning on the mounted gas lamps was unnecessary, even though shadows gathered in the corners. There was enough light to make out the rich tapestries that hung on the high walls, over which the artist had placed many of his own works. Where there was no art, the walls were festooned with antique arms and weapons and a variety of musical instruments. A large, carved Renaissance chest held a coffee set of Middle Eastern origin, a silver lamp, piles of books, and various jugs and pots from all over the world.

Japanese umbrellas stood in a glazed green stand in the corner, and a pile of women's footwear nestled to its side. Turning around, Daniel spied the mounted head of a polar bear over the door through which they had entered and a pair of stuffed cockatoos in the opposite corner.

"The living areas are through here," Callie whispered. They hadn't agreed to speak quietly, but Daniel was glad she was doing so. It felt appropriate, somehow.

Genevieve stuck close to his shoulder as he followed Callie through the main studio and past multiple easels mounted with work and an open portfolio of drawings and sketches haphazardly placed on an old table—unwisely, he felt—next to a Persian incense lamp.

The herd of cats accompanied them on their short journey, mewing incessantly, running ahead of Callie into the back rooms, then bounding back out again. Was it his imagination, or had their numbers increased?

Callie's scream yanked his attention away from the cats.

He rushed past her into what turned out to be a sitting room, though the details of it barely registered.

All his attention was focused on the dead woman lying in the center of the floor.

★　★　★

"Mr. McCaffrey. Miss Stewart. Why am I not surprised?" Detective Aloysius Longstreet's lip curled under his impressively large moustache. He obviously was not happy to see them, and the feeling was mutual.

As soon as Daniel had seen the body, he'd hustled Callie, pale and shocked, out of the room. Genevieve had settled her in an elaborately carved wooden armchair.

"Oh God. Another one. Another one." Callie turned her tearstained face to Genevieve. "Am I next, Genevieve?"

"What are you saying?" Daniel knelt by Callie's chair, the horror and dismay he'd felt at seeing the body morphing into dread. "Do you know that woman?"

She looked at him with wide, terrified eyes. "It's Violet Templeton. I can't see her . . . face, but I'd know that hair anywhere. She's a model too. Like Bea. Like me. Genevieve, what is happening?" Callie buried her face in her hands and began to cry.

Daniel met Genevieve's eyes, sure his face was as stunned as her own. Two models, both dead with cut throats. He would never say so aloud, but privately he thought Calle had reason to be concerned.

"Callie, listen to me. We must call the authorities. But in case they attempt to quash this case as they did Bea's, publicly at least, I need to take another look at Violet. Will you be all right waiting here with Genevieve?"

Callie had removed a yellow linen handkerchief from her reticule. She dabbed at her eyes and nodded. "You go too, Genevieve. The more eyes on this, the better."

Genevieve gave her friend a concerned look. "Are you sure?"

Callie waved her handkerchief in the direction of the sitting room. "Yes, go. I'll be fine. It was the shock of seeing her, I suppose. I was momentarily overcome."

"Anyone would be. I'm overcome myself," Daniel said.

After hearing another assurance from Callie that she would be fine by herself while they conducted a quick investigation, Daniel and Genevieve returned to the sitting room and stared at the corpse on the floor.

The dead woman called Violet was nude, lying on her side in a near-fetal position, one arm tucked under her head, the other crossed over her face in an almost gentle gesture. Her knees were bent and stacked, pulled about halfway to her chest, with the bottom foot inserted behind the top knee, toes peeking out. Daniel understood immediately why Callie had been able to identify her without seeing her face, Violet's hair was a most unusual color, an almost brick red. It was neatly bound at the nape of her neck.

Even though her face was turned toward the floor, it was obvious her throat had been cut.

"Daniel," came Genevieve's strangled voice.

He hadn't noticed her move away, but now he saw Genevieve standing in the open doorway of yet another room. It was a small bedroom holding a single, rumpled bed. The was an immense pool of blood drying on the Middle Eastern rug, and a gruesome, halfheartedly wiped trail led from the rug and out of the bedroom to the deceased.

The area around the body, though, was spotless, save for a small puddle of blood underneath her neck, staining the rich, flower-patterned gray silk cloth on which she was arranged.

As Daniel followed the trail of blood to the corpse with his eyes, it struck him, all at once: the body was just that. Arranged. *Posed*. It was a careful, deliberate placement of the dead woman's form.

"She was killed in here, left to bleed out, and then dragged or carried to the next room," he said under his breath, hoping Callie wouldn't overhear.

Genevieve was pale but continued to bear her singular resolute expression. "What does it mean?" she asked, looking from room to room. One hand fluttered to her mouth and stayed there.

Daniel shook his head. "I don't know. Don't touch anything. We have to alert the authorities. Paxton may have heard Callie scream and done just that already."

"The blood looks fairly fresh," Genevieve said, matching his quiet tone.

"It does," he agreed. "I would think she's been here for no more than a day. Perhaps only a few hours." The cats had continued to cry plaintively and circle, and a faint wave of nausea had passed through him as he noticed bloody paw prints in varying hues, depending on their freshness, throughout the bedroom, dotting the furniture.

Now Detective Longstreet shooed away a white cat with his foot with more force than necessary. As they were only a few short blocks from Genevieve's house on Washington Square North, Daniel had stayed with the body while the women rushed to the Stewart home, using the telephone to call the police. Genevieve had left Callie in the capable hands of her housekeeper and returned to the Tenth Street Studio Building at once.

He felt Genevieve flinch at the loud pop of a flash emanating from the sitting room, where the police photographer, Dagmar Hansen, had set up his equipment. He knew Dagmar from around the neighborhood of Five Points, where he had grown up and where he still had friends. Dagmar wasn't a bad sort, and Daniel had heard rumors he was hoping to use his photographs of slums in the service of reform, a cause near to Daniel's heart.

The man surely had enough material. Crime was rampant in his old neighborhood. Daniel reminded himself to have a conversation with Dagmar at a more suitable time.

"You were here for no reason other than to visit Mr. Paxton?" Longstreet asked, narrowing his eyes at both of them. The police had roused Elbert from his own studio upstairs, interrupting the artist's preparation to return north, and brought him into the main room of Chase's studio for questioning. At the sound of his name, the elderly man looked sharply in their direction.

Nothing wrong with Paxton's hearing, then.

Longstreet was overdressed for the weather, as he had been earlier in the summer, sporting a heavy tweed jacket and a hearty black bowler hat. It was cool enough in Chase's studio, but Daniel thought he must broil outside.

Longstreet pushed another cat away with his foot.

"That's correct," Daniel replied, casually putting his hands in his pockets and drawing his shoulders back.

There was no need for Longstreet to know they were pursuing Bea's death.

And now Violet's as well, he assumed.

"Miss Callie Maple informed me Mr. Paxton was in town, and I was of a mind to perhaps buy something. So we arranged a visit." Daniel hoped Elbert overheard him and played along.

"My parents own several of Mr. Paxton's pieces," Genevieve chimed in. "They're always ready to consider growing their collection, so when I heard Mr. McCaffrey was coming, I decided to come along."

Longstreet seemed to bristle under his hat, and Daniel suppressed a grim smile. Genevieve was playing it perfectly; the detective had a loathing of elite society, and irritating him by reminding him of their upper-class status—she by family and wealth, he by the pure chance of an inherited fortune—sometimes threw Longstreet off his game and worked to their advantage.

"Aren't you supposed to be in Newport, Miss Palmer?" the detective asked, his voice making his opinion of those who summered in Newport perfectly clear.

"My eldest brother has just returned from Egypt," Genevieve replied. "He's been abroad for three years. We're in the midst of a family reunion, and then yes, back to Newport I go." She smiled sunnily.

"Perhaps your parents will make a decision before that time, Miss Stewart." Elbert's voice floated in their direction. "I know they were having a challenging time making up their minds. Of course, I am happy to let them borrow the pieces in question, to see if they would suit. Sometimes one does need to lay eyes on the painting in one's own home before making a selection."

Longstreet flashed a disgusted look the artist's way. "Surely you all can save the sale of *art*"—he veritably sneered the word—"until we are finished with you. This is a police matter now."

"I'm so glad to hear that, Detective," Genevieve piped in. "I was distraught to hear you were declining to investigate the murder of Beatrice Holler."

Over Longstreet's shoulder, Elbert's head snapped up like that of a deer sensing danger.

"How the New York City police authority conducts its business is no affair of yours," Longstreet ground out.

"Perhaps not," Daniel agreed. "But Miss Stewart, er, Miss Palmer, as you noted, does work for a newspaper, one that would be most interested to question exactly why you were ruling an obvious murder as self-inflicted."

"What's this? What?" Elbert pushed his way past the officer who had been questioning him and shook his finger in Longstreet's face. "Beatrice Holler's death self-inflicted? Nonsense! You should be ashamed of yourself."

Longstreet cut his eyes to the officer, who pulled Elbert back roughly.

"Now see here," Daniel began, reaching for the older man, just as Genevieve cried, "Hey, stop that!"

At Longstreet's nod, the officer released Elbert, who rubbed at his arm and favored both policemen with a mutinous expression. The detective glared at the three of them, his moustache twitching.

"Miss Stewart, we have made an agreement before," he finally said. Daniel knew he was referring to earlier that summer, when Genevieve had agreed not to pursue Longstreet's deliberate false arrest of Rupert in exchange for him serving as a quoted source in her story about gang-related gunrunning. She hadn't wanted to do so, but Rupert and Daniel had convinced her it was best for all parties.

Genevieve nodded, narrowing her eyes. Daniel had no doubt that making the compromise still rankled.

"Then I offer another one. You keep quiet about the deaths of these models, and I'll give you first access to any information when we do find something. That goes for the rest of you, and Miss Maple too," Longstreet said, his gaze sweeping the room to include Daniel and Elbert. "Because between us—and *just us*; if word about this gets out, I'll have you all arrested for interfering with police business—we are treating Miss Holler's death as suspicious. Surely you can understand why I don't want the public to know about a young woman, two young women now, found with their throats cut. Particularly not after that nasty business in London last year, and with what many papers are insinuating now."

A small, satisfactory surge of internal triumph shot through Daniel; he had been right. The police *were* keeping Bea's death quiet to avoid unnecessarily worrying the public and so as not to feed into the burgeoning theories around the Ripper's possible location.

He shared a glance with Genevieve. She tilted her head at him. It was a silent question. *What do you think?*

Another surge, this one of warmth, ballooned in his chest. He loved these intimate, unspoken exchanges with her. There had been too few in recent weeks.

Honestly, he thought Longstreet's offer was as good as they were going to get. He gave a slight incline of his head in return. *Let's do it.*

"That will work, Detective," Genevieve said. "That will work."

CHAPTER 8

The gentle rocking of the railroad lulled Genevieve in and out of sleep. Transportation often had this effect on her, and it was inelegant, she knew, to sleep on a train. But she couldn't help it. They had quickly passed from the brick buildings of Brooklyn into the picturesque, sleepy towns of Long Island, and the swaying of the rail cars combined with the comfort of her plush seat all conspired to put her to sleep at once.

"Genevieve." It was Callie's voice, accompanied by a soft shaking of the shoulder. "We're almost there."

Genevieve yawned and tried to stretch as surreptitiously as possible. The view out the window had turned to low, undulating hills, and she could smell the briny tang of salt water in the air.

Daniel smiled lazily at her from his own plush seat across from her and Callie's, then turned his attention back to the window. "Next stop is Shinnecock Hills," he said, gesturing out the window with his straw hat.

Excitement coursed through her, pushing aside any residual sleepiness. They were on the Long Island Rail Road, on their way to visit Eliza—and to speak to her teacher, William Merritt Chase—at the informal art colony Chase had begun with the help of several interested patrons. Five days had passed since she, Callie, and Daniel had made the horrific discovery of Violet Templeton's body in Chase's studio. She had exchanged a flurry of letters with Eliza, as Eliza had no access to a telephone, in which Genevieve had explained about Bea's and Violet's murders and her and Daniel's investigations. Eliza had written back quickly, noting that rumors of Violet's body being found in Chase's Tenth Street studio had reached the budding art colony, causing shock and dismay among the students and, so she'd heard, several of the benefactors as well.

The manner of poor Miss Templeton's death is unknown here, Eliza had written, *but it is generally thought she died of natural causes and it was simply poor luck she was staying at Chase's studio at the time. Knowing otherwise, as you have written me about the horrible true circumstances, I have kept an eye out and observed the police visiting not once but twice. Mr. Chase's movements are well accounted for, though, so I believe he is not considered a suspect.*

Genevieve wondered if Eliza's theory was true. How long could the real cause of Violet's death be kept a secret? She was surprised another news outlet in the city hadn't gotten wind of the murder and connected the dots between Bea Holler's and Violet Templeton's deaths, and once again she suspected the long arm of Detective Longstreet.

Indeed, she and Daniel had had a lengthy discussion about whether or not to keep investigating the case following their encounter with the detective. The evening after they'd found Violet's disturbingly arranged corpse, they had met for cold pints of Würzburger pilsner at the beer garden behind Lüchow's. Earlier that summer Genevieve had discovered, much to her surprise, that she enjoyed beer.

It was particularly refreshing in the early evening, just as the day's intense heat was starting to break.

"The police have all but admitted, to us at least, that the deaths of Beatrice and Violet are connected somehow," she mused, taking a sip and tearing off a piece of the large pretzel they were sharing. "If they are undertaking a proper investigation, should we continue this work? Or trust them to do their jobs?"

Daniel slanted her a look over his glass.

"I know." She answered the unspoken statement. "I don't trust Longstreet either."

"The question remains," Daniel mused, "are the police *really* keeping the murders quiet because they don't want to stoke Ripper fears, or are they covering something up for one or more of the city's elite? There is, of course, a long history of corruption within the New York City Police Department—that of subverting any real justice to appease the wealthy and powerful." He helped himself to a piece of the pretzel and chased it with the remaining beer in this glass. "I may order a herring salad. Would you like one?"

"Oh yes, please," she said. Daniel signaled for one of the impeccably dressed waiters. "I thought you believed Longstreet was incorruptible, wholly committed to the rule of law."

"I think most men, and I suppose women, are susceptible to corruption if the price is right," he said, tapping the edge of his empty glass with a finger. "But who would he be covering for? Matthew Shipman? He's certainly powerful enough to command the police department's attention."

"We don't know yet whether Violet had a similarly well-connected lover," Genevieve said. "Callie had no idea. She swears Violet and Mr. Chase were not attached, and regardless, I cannot envision the police burying such a story to protect an artist."

Daniel huffed a small breath of frustration. "You're right. Whatever is going on, though, stinks to high heaven. Two murdered young women, and no public knowledge or outcry?" He leaned back to allow the waiter to deliver their salads as well as fresh glasses of beer for both of them.

"I stand by my assertion that if they were young women of wealth, the story would be different," Genevieve fumed. She speared a piece of herring with more vigor than necessary. "The police believe that these women, because many of them are mistresses of wealthy men, are expendable."

"You're correct about that as well, I fear," Daniel said, eating his own salad with a bit more care. "So, do we keep investigating? If Longstreet gets wind of it, he'll be displeased, to say the least."

Genevieve chewed thoughtfully and considered. Whatever the real reason behind Longstreet's reticence, the mere fact of it made her feel these women's deaths might not receive the attention they deserved.

In her mind's eye, she saw Callie in Violet's place, curled on the studio floor, terrifyingly pale, dried blood adhering her severed neck to a piece of Japanese-embroidered silk.

"We do," she said firmly, shoving the image away. "Yes, we do."

They had decided the next best course of action was to speak to Mr. Chase, in whose studio the dead Violet had been found. Her mind roved back to the dim, shuttered Tenth Street Studio Building, the gruesome, bloody footprints of the cats around Violet's body, and she crossed her arms over her chest, overcome with a sudden chill. What else was hidden behind the closed doors of those studios?

Callie seemed to sense her discomfort and laid a comforting hand on her arm. Genevieve willed herself to relax and offered her friend a smile. She couldn't wait to see Eliza. The three of them—her, Callie, and Eliza—would soon be together again. Losing Callie, even for a few months, had been like losing a part of herself. She knew Eliza was equally overjoyed at the impending reunion.

The train slowly churned to a stop, and Daniel stood to gather their few parcels and bags. She and Callie had brought a picnic to share as well as some foodstuffs to leave with Eliza.

A cool ocean breeze greeted them as they stepped off the train, along with sweeping views of the area's famed hills, Shinnecock Bay, and the Atlantic Ocean. Genevieve sighed in satisfaction. The city remained deep in the clutches of its awful late-summer heat, and she feared there was no end in sight. Being back at the seaside, even if only for the day, was a blessed relief.

The railroad station was a charming little structure, featuring a circular stone tower and a terra-cotta tiled roof. They transferred to a hired carriage to take them to Mr. Chase's homestead, rolling alongside undulating dunes topped with waving beach grass. Puffy white clouds floated harmlessly across an azure sky, and the scent of the ocean increased with every passing mile.

"This is not a formal art school, then?" Daniel asked.

"Not yet," she replied, glancing across at Daniel, who was again in the seat opposite her and Callie. "Mr. Chase has gathered some of his best students here for the summer, and for a small price is instructing them in the French plein-air style. I do believe there are plans to formalize the arrangement in the coming years, should enough funds be available."

"Eliza has been having a whale of a time," Callie remarked. "It's been so good to hear from her."

Genevieve refrained from pointing out that it was Callie who had kept her and Eliza at bay for many months and chose instead to revel in the fact that they would all be together again within moments.

"She jumped at the chance to go," Genevieve added.

"I wonder if she was looking forward to living away from her father for a bit," Callie mused, watching the scenery pass. Genevieve felt Callie was probably correct; Eliza's father, a merchant who had made his fortune in garment manufacturing, was still shunned by much of New York's elite society but had been hoping his only daughter's beauty and large fortune would result in a successful match within those realms. Eliza, however, had proven resistant to the idea of marrying anyone, despite multiple sincere offers for her hand. She remained convinced a husband would interfere with her chosen profession and require her to give it up.

"Is her art a career or a hobby?" Daniel asked, after Genevieve relayed a little of Eliza's situation. "I do not mean to sound impertinent or dismissive; this is a genuine question."

Genevieve and Callie exchanged a look. "I believe we can call it a career," Genevieve finally said. "It is certainly her life's passion. She's meant to have her own exhibition this fall and has received some minor commissions in recent months. I do think that, combined with her age, is why her father has been less insistent of late about marriage."

"I'm sure he simply wants to see her taken care of," Daniel ventured.

"Daily happiness creating her work *does* take care of her," Genevieve returned, her temper rising somewhat. It was unlike Daniel to take such a conventional stance.

"Yes. As she needn't worry about funds, she has the freedom to do as she pleases," Callie added in a wistful voice. "Making art is what pleases her most. It always has."

Genevieve shot an annoyed look at Daniel and nudged his ankle with her foot. *Don't pursue this any further*, the gesture meant. The last thing she wanted to do was remind Callie of her own misfortune, her reduced circumstances that had led to her current situation. Genevieve crossed her arms again and glared out the window.

The mood in the carriage turned sour.

"It is very lovely here," Daniel said, gazing out the window himself, perhaps trying to lighten the atmosphere. "A fitting place for artists to gather."

"Yes." Callie sighed. "Walter and I were meant to be in Southampton by now, but I'm not sure we'll make it this summer after all. Walter's commission has become quite consuming for him." She toyed with the woven straw bag in her lap. "It's easier, here, for us to be together. Newport is too restricting."

Genevieve felt a further pang. Of course, as a previous member of the Astor 400, Callie would not want to be seen by her former friends, most of whom, infuriatingly to Genevieve, had distanced themselves from Callie the moment it was clear she had been left bankrupt—on the arm of her lover. The scandal would be overwhelming.

The carriage rolled to a stop in front of a large, rectangular shingled house, topped by a Dutch gambrel roof dotted with dormer windows. A balcony with a low, diamond-patterned balustrade encircled the length of the second floor, wrapping around the corners of the house, and a similar veranda graced the lower level. The house sat majestically at the edge of a long, wild lawn featuring a small pond, and faced the ocean rather the road. As they disembarked and walked up the path to the front door, the dunes, beach, and sea rose into view. Genevieve could just make out figures dotting the shoreline and the hills, sitting at easels under umbrellas.

"You're here!" Eliza was suddenly standing on the veranda, waving enthusiastically. Callie and Genevieve took the last few steps up the path and the stairs at a near run. Genevieve dropped her basket and flung herself into her friend's waiting arms, pulling Callie into their circle.

It had been a long, hard winter and a trying spring. Genevieve had missed her friend so much it ached. All three of them were, in some ways, misfits within the strict codes that defined upper-class New York society, Eliza and Genevieve by pursuing careers over marriage and Callie by her fall from respectability with her loss of wealth.

They *needed* each other, Genevieve thought as she hugged her friends closer.

"We've brought food," Callie said, pulling away and beaming at both of them. "And drinks. Bottles of lemonade, and I believe Mr. McCaffrey added some wine, didn't you?"

"I have," Daniel said, smiling. "And some ginger beer." He was standing a few feet away from them, kindly giving Genevieve and her friends a little space.

"So good to see you again, Mr. McCaffrey," Eliza said, returning Daniel's smile.

"And you."

"The sea air agrees with you," Genevieve said, admiring her friend. Eliza was always beautiful, tall and graceful, with gleaming chestnut hair and bright-blue eyes, but at present her eyes held a particularly happy sparkle and her cheeks were flushed with healthy color. She wore a jaunty blue-and-white-striped day dress and a wide-brimmed straw hat.

"I believe it does," Eliza agreed, smiling even more broadly. "Come, let's take this marvelous picnic to the hills where we can view the ocean, and I'll tell you all about it. And I want to hear more about these unfortunate circumstances that brought you here. Though, unfortunate or not, I am simply glad you're here. Mr. Chase will join us in a bit. He is instructing some of the others but is expecting you."

They followed Eliza down a sandy path that led away from the house and toward the water, through low hills studded with tall grass, shrubbery, and purple wildflowers. At one crest, Eliza trooped off the path and led them to a small clearing within the grass.

"What do you think?" she asked, flinging her arms open.

"It's perfect," Genevieve answered. And it was. The hill gave a stunning view of the beach and ocean, and they were much closer now to several of the art students, who perched at their easels, capturing what was in front of them. Waves billowed onto the shore and streamed out again; the green grass, blue sky, golden sand, and wild ocean were glorious fodder for the painters, male and female, who bent assiduously to their respective tasks. She could just make out the figure of an older man with a trim white beard standing over one of the young male students. The older man was pointing and gesturing, while the young man, who like Eliza was also clad in stripes, though his were on a jacket, nodded vigorously.

Daniel helped Genevieve and her friends spread a red picnic blanket over the patchy grass, and they set out a feast prepared by Daniel's admirable cook, consisting of thick beef sandwiches, several cold salads, and lemon cookies.

"Is that Mr. Chase I spy?" Genevieve asked, pointing out the older man in the distance to Eliza.

"It is indeed." Eliza waved both arms over her head, catching her teacher's attention. He waved back. "He should come to us shortly," she said.

"Eliza, where do you live? Surely not at Mr. Chase's house," Callie said as they settled themselves around the blanket. Daniel passed around the sandwiches and asked what they would like to drink.

"I would love some of that ginger beer, please," Eliza replied. "No, Mr. Chase resides there with his wife, Alice, and their two children. Alice is expecting a third, I believe. I board with the Hendersons, a couple who are quite invested in turning the area into a resort. They are building a golf course next summer, they say. They want to see Mr. Chase open a proper school full-time. I am not alone; several of the lady students are staying there."

Genevieve had already heard of Eliza's arrangements and helped herself to some lemonade. "Tell Callie what you told me, Eliza."

"Well, I confess it's been quite illuminating, staying here this summer. There's a freedom here, a license for us students to do as we like, come and go as we please. We stay up late, discussing art and philosophy."

"The men too?" Callie asked, biting into a lemon cookie. "These are divine, Daniel."

He smiled. "Mrs. Rafferty is an excellent cook. I'll pass along your compliments."

Eliza nodded. "Oh yes. There is no separation of the sexes here, except in lodging. Last week some of us fitted out one of the area barns for a dance. We hung examples of our work, strung up dozens of Chinese lanterns. There was a piano, some banjo players, and a guitar, and it was amazing fun. Nobody counting whether you'd danced too often with a particular partner, some ladies choosing to dance with each other or alone . . ." She trailed off, sipping her ginger beer and gazing for a while at the ocean, before shrugging in what might have been embarrassment. "I've never been so happy," she finished quietly.

Genevieve tried to catch Callie's eye, but her friend kept her gaze fixed on Eliza's face, a mischievous half smile playing about her lips. Genevieve guessed Callie had the same thought she did: Eliza sounded as though she were in love.

Has Eliza taken a lover?

Gracious, did everyone have a lover except her?

Genevieve found her eyes sliding to Daniel.

He was not watching Eliza. He was staring, instead, at her, with an intensity to his dark-blue gaze that sent an instant tingling to her middle.

Genevieve flushed deeply and swallowed, quickly busying herself with offering salad to Callie, who shook her head and reached for another cookie.

"Especially now that you have come back, Callie," Eliza continued. She leaned over and wrapped an arm around Callie, pulling her close for a moment. "Please don't leave like that again."

Callie broke her cookie in half. "I will do my best," she said enigmatically.

"I can't believe you've been working all winter with artists I consider my associates and our paths never crossed," Eliza said, a touch of bitterness in her voice. "Of course, they don't allow women to rent studios at Tenth Street. I've not yet hired a model, and the Art Students League still doesn't allow women to study the full male nude from life, just casts. And you're posing for Walter Wilson, no less."

"I'll pose for you anytime you like, darling. Free of charge." Callie grinned.

"Oh no, I'd insist on paying you. This is your livelihood now."

"I'd make a lovely Cleopatra, don't you think?" Callie turned her head and raised her face, adopting a regal expression.

"You're rather too pale to serve as the model for an Egyptian, Callie," Genevieve chimed in. "What do you all think? Should we open the wine?"

"Oh, let's do," Callie agreed. "Speaking of Egypt, how is Gavin enjoying being back?"

Daniel poured them all wine in squat, stout glasses.

"Is there any of that for me?" a voice asked.

William Merritt Chase was standing above their group, the sun illuminating his pristine white jacket. Daniel stood and shook his hand, then handed him a glass as the artist folded his legs to join them on a corner of their blanket. Shaking his head at their offers of food, Chase sipped his wine, his face somber under a straw boater, his eyes shadowed. Eliza introduced Genevieve, and Callie, who had modeled for Chase previously, said hello.

"Miss Maple, lovely to see you. You're creating quite the stir among my fellows. I hear Wilson is using you for his *Persephone*?"

"That's right," Callie said.

"And Miss Lindsay, what is your next sculptural project? I know that medium is where your true heart lies, and you are partially indulging my whims this summer in trying your hand at oil," he said, smiling gently in Eliza's direction.

"You know I am delighted to be here, though oil does not come naturally to me. I do think I will return to marble in the autumn, yes. I am considering embarking on a piece featuring the Biblical Judith, holding aloft the head of Holofernes," Eliza said.

Callie perked up at this. "Now that is a subject I would adore modeling," she enthused. "I would make an excellent Judith."

"Are you sure you won't at least take a cookie?" Eliza offered the tin to her teacher. "They're good and tart."

"No, no," Chase said. "My appetite has been quite gone these past few days. I am so distraught over Violet's death." The artist took a deep drink of his wine and sighed. "Eliza tells me you have questions about this. I've spoken to the police already, but she tells me you are performing a separate investigation?"

Genevieve and Daniel exchanged a look. "We are hoping to offer additional assistance," Daniel said, clearly choosing his words with care. "You knew Miss Templeton well, then?"

Chase looked surprised. "Oh yes, quite well. For some years now. She was my favorite model, you see."

CHAPTER 9

The lovely afternoon by the ocean turned dark, even as the sun continued to shine, as Chase told them of his relationship with Violet Templeton.

"She was a vibrant, intelligent woman," he said, staring moodily at the water. "She enjoyed modeling, but her real desire was to become a nurse, trained in the manner and principles of Florence Nightingale. Last month, when I was in town for Sturgis Sawyer's funeral, we met, and she told me she had finally saved enough and had been accepted to study at the school in New Haven. She was planning to leave later this summer. I would have been most sad to see her go, of course, but was also pleased she was fulfilling her dream. Violet had so much potential." He sighed unhappily.

"Do you know why she wouldn't have enrolled in the school at Bellevue?" Genevieve asked, puzzled. "There was no need to travel to Connecticut to studying nursing."

Chase hesitated, taking a deep drink of his wine. "I hesitate to say this, but I did tell the police as well. I believe there was a man, one from whom she may have wanted some distance. This was merely an impression I had; she did not confide such things in me. But based on what she did say, this was my suspicion. I know she suddenly did not have a permanent home and was moving from friend's house to friend's house. I thought perhaps there had been a falling-out with a lover, and offered her use of the studio while I was away for the summer."

Daniel put his glass of wine aside, having lost the taste for it. The sea breeze had momentarily stilled, and the sun was suddenly as hot and oppressive as it would have felt on Fifth Avenue. "Who else had access to your studio?"

"I'm afraid a great many people. Several of the other artists who keep studios in the building, a few other trusted friends and models . . . anyone could have loaned their key and I would have no idea."

"And you have no idea who this gentleman might be? The one involved with Miss Templeton?" Eliza asked, looking troubled.

Chase shook his head. "Not a clue. As I said, we discussed many things, and I admired and respected Violet, but we did not discuss her private life. I felt it was just that, private. I assumed he was some dashing young laborer. I never saw her about with another artist."

Daniel caught Genevieve's eye. She, too, had put down her wine and replaced it with lemonade. Callie, on the other hand, poured herself more, pulling her knees into her chest and wrapping an arm about them, despite the heat.

We need to find Violet's lover.

Genevieve nodded back infinitesimally.

"And Violet was your favorite model?" she asked Chase gently. "How often did you paint her?"

"Well, my favorite after Alice, of course," Chase said, draining his glass and handing it back to Daniel with a nod of thanks. "Though in the years before I met my wife, I painted Violet often. The contrast of that dark-red hair on her pale skin . . . well, it was something Titian might have captured. And she had great stamina, no trouble holding still for long periods of time. I must have made dozens of images with her as the subject, usually in domestic motifs."

The afternoon never regained its original, lighthearted mood, even after Chase made his excuses and left. They watched him weave his way across the low dunes toward another student, this time a woman about Genevieve's age in a pale-pink dress.

"He is not himself," Eliza murmured, her eyes on her teacher's back. "He seems to have aged a decade over the course of less than a week."

"What did his wife think of Violet staying at his studio?" Daniel asked, beginning to pack up the picnic things.

Eliza turned her attention back to their group, a surprised look on her face. "She was fine with it, as far as I know. But I admit I am not in Alice's confidence."

They spent the remainder of their time in Long Island walking the beach and touring the area. A few clouds rolled in and a light wind resumed, returning the temperature to its previous pleasant state. Eliza showed them her accommodations and the barn where the dance had been held, which was also where they painted on days the weather was foul. The friends embraced, promising to see each other again within the next few weeks.

★　★　★

"Do you think he killed her?" Daniel leaned closer to Genevieve and whispered the question, not wanting to alarm the other passengers on the train. She smelled of salt air and lemon.

"I do not," she replied, dropping her head toward his conspiratorially. Now it was Callie who had fallen asleep on their return trip to Manhattan, undoubtedly made drowsy by the wine, sun, and sugar. "How on earth shall we find Violet's young man?" Genevieve leaned her head back against her seat. Her body swayed slightly with the movement of the train. "It would be like hunting a needle in a haystack."

"Do you think Callie might know who Violet's intimates were? Her friends?" Daniel asked.

Genevieve glanced at her sleeping friend. "She said she didn't know Violet very well, not like she knew Bea. But I wonder if Walter knows."

Daniel hesitated before asking his next question, hating to even plant the seed of suspicion in her mind. "Do you know if Violet ever posed for Walter, like Bea did?"

"I do not," she said, frowning. "But it is worth finding out."

The train pulled into Hunter's Point, its wheels noisily grinding to a halt. Genevieve roused Callie, who blinked and yawned mightily, and the trio gathered their things and made their way to the ferry to cross into Manhattan.

Despite his enjoyment of boats in general and ferries in particular, Daniel was ready to be done with conveyances for the day. The visit to Long Island had left them with more questions than answers, and he was itching to have a quiet night in his study with a good book and a glass of something cold. Genevieve and Callie looked as wilted and dispirited as he felt.

It was already ten degrees hotter in the city, even on the river.

After the hired carriage had deposited Genevieve and Callie at their respective homes, Daniel sighed in anticipation of returning to his own. It hadn't always been his home, of course; he had inherited the Gramercy Park mansion from Jacob Van Joost, his former employer, then benefactor.

It was a beautiful, stately place, and while he enjoyed its location on the private park, the privilege of it—of having access to a park designated only for its surrounding residents in the middle of a crowded city—didn't sit well with him.

Up until the year prior, Daniel hadn't spent much time in the mansion. He'd kept more modest bachelor quarters during his time at Harvard and in his years apprenticing at law in New York, and then he'd moved abroad for a decade. It wasn't until he returned to town in late 1887 that he'd set up residence in the old Van Joost place.

He was going to sell it, and soon. It was where he'd come to live as an orphaned child and was the site of his sister's death. It had never felt like his, even though he was now a thirty-five-year-old man with a fortune of his own to manage.

But for now, the house was still in his name, and he would enjoy the peace of it.

An invitation waiting on his desk shattered that peace and sent his thoughts spinning in a thousand directions.

Matthew Shipman had invited him to a party.

★   ★   ★

"A party? What type of a party?" Genevieve demanded, putting down her iced tea and crossing her arms over her chest. It was just past breakfast at the Stewarts' home on Washington Square again. Daniel had not dined with the family today but chosen to call early.

It was damned hot in town, and the morning hours were the most comfortable for traversing about, even in a good carriage.

"A birthday party for Eugene Goodyear. His fortieth, I believe." Daniel sipped some of his own iced tea, having declined an offer of coffee.

The thought of a warm drink was unbearable, even in the Stewarts' relatively cool and comfortable front parlor.

"Eugene Goodyear? The financier?" Her brow furrowed. "What is he doing having a birthday party in town on a Thursday evening when his family relocated to Newport months ago? I haven't heard a thing about this."

"It's a gentlemen's party, Genevieve," he said. "You know men like Goodyear stay in town during the week to work and see their families on weekends."

"Chasing the almighty dollar." Gavin, Genevieve's brother, had come into the room with a folded paper. "Someone's got to keep the cogs turning. You were invited too, then?" Gavin sat in one of the room's comfortable armchairs and opened his paper, but he kept his polite gaze on Daniel.

"Yes," Daniel said. He didn't know why he should be surprised Gavin had been invited, but he was. "Are you friendly with Shipman, or Goodyear?"

"Neither, really. Or not anymore," Gavin admitted. "I knew Matthew back in school, and we were friendly in the years following, but we'd rather fallen out of touch since I've been abroad. Perhaps my inclusion is a way of welcoming me home. Do you plan on attending?" he asked Daniel.

"I think I shall," Daniel said, casting a look at Genevieve. He didn't want to say exactly why in front of Gavin, but he hoped that if he could talk to Shipman, he could get to the bottom of what he had seen on that Newport beach two weeks ago.

The memory of what he had witnessed that night, the *off*-ness of it, still sent a prickle across the back of his neck. What did it mean that a man had chased a woman through the surf on a pitch-black beach when his mistress had been murdered only a short time prior? Whether or not that shadowy event was actually connected to the death of Bea Holler, he had no idea, but a night with Matthew Shipman might provide some answers.

"So you're both going to this debauched evening where scantily clad young women will parade about for gentlemen's pleasure?" Genevieve asked, uncrossing her arms with what appeared to be effort. She picked up her tea instead but then replaced it on the side table, her hands curling into fists in her lap. "Gavin, Mother would be furious if she knew. And Daniel, I thought you had better sense than that."

Gavin's jaw dropped. "What do you know of scantily clad young women?" He shot an accusing look at Daniel.

"Enough to know desperation likely drives them to engage in such work," she snapped. "But as it happens, Daniel and I have an interest in Mr. Shipman. He was attached to the young woman whose death we are investigating. Attending this party may be useful for you," she said to Daniel, her tone reluctant.

Daniel was unsurprised to hear Genevieve echo his own thoughts almost exactly, but he wished she hadn't voiced them in front of her brother, who had made it clear he disapproved of their informal partnership.

Indeed, Gavin folded his paper with a snap, then stood and left the room without another word.

Genevieve watched him leave, her gaze murderous. "I've had about all I can take of his judgmental high-handedness," she muttered. "To think, he's planning on attending this so-called *gentlemen's* event, yet lecturing me about propriety. I can't wait until he leaves for Newport with Mother and Father next week."

"You'll be fine staying here by yourself?"

"One or two of the servants will stay with me. I won't be entirely alone. And frankly, I am looking forward to the solitude, yes. I am rarely by myself in this house. It will be a refreshing novelty."

Daniel considered this statement. He lived alone and had for many years. There were times it suited him, but mostly it just felt lonely. He had grown up with a pack of siblings, and the ache of their loss was what he imagined living with a phantom limb felt like.

Genevieve sighed and picked up her glass again. "I wish I could attend this party with you."

"No, you don't. Truly."

"I feel as though we are at a bit of a dead end with these murders. Two artists' models brutally killed, no overt assistance from the authorities, and anyone with a motive or connection to them seems to have been dismissed as the killer . . . Daniel, what if the *World* is correct?"

An unease gathered between his shoulder blades.

"What if Jack the Ripper really has crossed the Atlantic?" Genevieve pressed. "What if he is in New York?"

The image of Violet Templeton's oddly posed, mutilated form lodged in his brain and wouldn't leave. The way the blood had congealed under her neck. The bluish tint to her cold skin. The way her glassy eyes stared sightlessly.

"I doubt it," he said slowly, willing the picture to dissipate. "I think the British authorities—and newspapers—are hypothesizing that theory as they can't explain why the Ripper ceased his killings in London. It gives them an easy out to say Jack's fled the country."

She nodded reluctantly. "It calms their populace while inflaming ours. But what *if*, Daniel? What if the person we are searching for is capable of that kind of violence and brutality? Whoever it is, they clearly target vulnerable women, just as the London killer did."

Despite his efforts, Violet's body refused to vacate his mind's eye. "Women alone," he said, mulling over the circumstances of each death. "In homes or rooms they believed to be safe. Not necessarily vulnerable." It struck him with a force like a blow to the gut: Genevieve would be home on her own soon. He filed that away for later discussion, but it crowded his brain regardless, alongside the preternaturally still Violet.

"The method of killing is different also. The victims in London were further disfigured," he continued.

"But perhaps this is someone who was inspired by those actions," Genevieve said softly.

The idea was shocking yet forceful in its simplicity and did nothing to ease Daniel's mind about Genevieve's soon-to-be solitary state.

"Shipman is our best lead for now," he said. "I'll see what I can find out at this birthday party."

★ ★ ★

The gathering started out exactly as Daniel had imagined it would.

Thirty or so men in evening dress were assembled in one of the private dining rooms at Sherry's. There were both married men and bachelors, but all were from the highest echelon of society, and all knew the code they were expected to keep.

What went on at parties such as this was private, for men's eyes and ears only. And not just any men, *these* men, or those like them. Leaders of industry, bankers, railroad tycoons, financiers, scions of Wall Street, they were among the wealthiest and most powerful men in the country, or they were those men's sons; they all had unbelievable sums at their fingertips. There were no women present, not yet, and Daniel knew that any who did appear would be strictly for entertainment.

The party had started informally, with gin cocktails and congenial handshakes; a few early cigars were lit, pleasantries exchanged. The air hummed with anticipation of what was to come. After perhaps thirty minutes of greetings, the men were urged to their seats and served a cold cucumber soup paired with an excellent white wine by Louis Sherry's impeccably trained, white-jacketed army of waiters, whose job it was to anticipate guests' needs before they themselves did.

Daniel sipped at his wine but declined a second glass. He knew it would be a long night and wanted to keep his wits about him. He asked instead for a bourbon, planning to nurse it for the remainder of the evening.

His goal for the night was to speak to Shipman and find out what, if anything, he could about their gregarious host's knowledge of Beatrice Holler's death. Daniel swirled his bourbon in his glass and kept an eye on Shipman, who was conveniently seated within easy eyesight at the next table. His host had consumed three gin cocktails and was well into his wine, gesturing to a waiter for more.

The two long, rectangular tables were lined perpendicular to the stage, with no one seated at the head, so everyone would have an excellent view of the entertainment. As soon as the soup was cleared away and a course of broiled, chilled salmon was served, the onstage festivities started. A fairly mild vaudevillian act started things off, a man and a woman trading jokes that became increasingly off-color, centering around the topic of birthday guest of honor Goodyear's virility.

The raucous laughter of the group swelled, and a slight headache began to pulse behind Daniel's right eye.

He had also been a little perturbed to find that Gavin was not only at his table but had chosen a seat next to him.

"I don't recall many of these types of parties before I left," Gavin confessed into Daniel's left ear. It was hard to hear him over the din of the other men. Daniel had to lean in closer.

"Yes, they've become more popular in recent years, I understand. I don't attend many myself," he replied.

Gavin speared some salmon and looked at the assembled men, growing drunker and louder and more red-faced by the moment. "It's not so bad," he said.

Daniel refrained from commenting. Gavin was right, it wasn't so bad, not yet. But he knew from experience it could *get* bad. Of course, this depended on how you defined what was distasteful. He had never seen the appeal of hiring young men, typically of African descent, to fight each other until one was unconscious and bloody. Or of animal baiting. Or, for that matter, of ogling the parades of scantily clad, or sometimes unclad, young women Genevieve had accused him of being eager to view. But he knew any of these spectacles and more could happen as the hour grew later.

Sure enough, as the salmon was cleared and the porterhouse steaks were brought in to resounding applause, a trio of young women in flimsy Middle Eastern garb took the stage, introduced by the male vaudevillian performer as "The Jewels of Egypt." Each wore a tiny bolero vest with nothing underneath, loose, gauzy trousers that gathered at the ankles, black stockings, and velvet slippers.

The applause doubled, accompanied by appreciative hoots. A deep red wine was poured to accompany the steaks, and many of the party guests had glasses of Scotch or whiskey as well. The girls began an undulating dance, shaking their hips in circles, and when they raised their arms, the jackets rose as well.

The crowd roared its appreciation.

Gavin looked appalled. "Is this what they think goes on in Egypt?" He shook his head and stabbed at his steak. "How soon can we politely leave?" he asked, cutting a piece. "The steak is divine, but I don't know how much of this I can stomach. Don't get me wrong, I appreciate a pretty girl as much as the next man, but this . . ." He gestured with his empty fork to the stage, then to the raucous men pouring liquor down their throats. "This feels tawdry," he finished, so quietly Daniel could barely hear him.

Daniel agreed with Gavin, though. *Tawdry* was the perfect word to describe the scene. Grown men with teenage daughters the same age as the dancers were undoing their ties, unbuttoning top buttons, making lewd gestures and yelling for the bolero jackets, which covered precious little as the girls danced, to be removed entirely.

Daniel sipped his whiskey and pushed his plate aside. Gavin was correct, the steak was excellent. But he had lost his appetite.

For appearance' sake, he kept one eye on the stage, and with the other he held Matthew Shipman in close watch. Their host was standing, twirling his napkin in the air, and yelling, "Take it off!"

The girl closest to Mr. Shipman, a petite blonde who looked no more than sixteen, flashed the man a nervous smile but kept dancing.

Daniel released his glass and pressed his fingertips onto the table, readying his body to jump if need be.

He would not stand to see one of these girls molested.

Gavin, who had assiduously kept his attention on his steak for several minutes, leaned close again. "I hear my brother Charles threatened you bodily harm should any injury occur to my sister." The words were delivered mildly, as if Gavin were commenting on the weather.

Daniel nodded in response. He swirled his bourbon again but didn't drink it. Instead, he continued to keep his gaze on Shipman, who was now laughing uproariously, his arms slung around Peter Stuyvesant Jr. and Martin Webb, the former of whom sneaked the occasional terrified look in Daniel's direction.

Stuyvesant should look afraid, Daniel thought grimly. He had been part of the ring that had been profiting off slum construction, so much so that some members of their group had committed murder rather than be discovered. A scheme Daniel and Genevieve had exposed.

"You know I'm far tougher than Charles," Gavin continued in the same casual tone, leaning back to allow a waiter to remove his steak and replace it with a portion of sliced roasted quail. "He'd round up his sailor friends and beat you to a pulp, true. But if one hair on my sister's head is harmed in her dealings with you, I'll make sure what's left of your body is never found."

Daniel jerked his gaze away from Shipman and stared at Genevieve's brother instead. Gavin stared back, his chestnut-colored eyes hard as steel in his sun-browned face.

The man was serious as death.

They held eyes for a few beats.

"If you dislike me so greatly, why are you sitting next to me, nattering on?" Daniel finally asked, irritated. "Go sit elsewhere."

Gavin looked away, then considered this as he sampled his quail. "In an odd way, I feel I have more in common with you than I do with most of these others, now. Maybe I've been abroad too long, but this"—again the gesture with the fork—"holds no appeal for me. I sense you are also a bit of a fish out of water, despite that massive fortune you control."

Daniel took a sip of his drink. It burned slightly going down but then mellowed and softened.

Like all the other food and drink served tonight, it was excellent.

"Genevieve is a grown woman, who has come into her own money, and who makes her own choices," he finally said. "I cannot control what she chooses to do with her time any more than you can. We are friends who work together occasionally, nothing more."

The lies slipped from his throat easily.

Gavin put down his fork. "I don't think I could eat another bite, yet I know there's a cheese and sweet course still to come." He fixed Daniel with a beady eye. "What you say about my sister might be true. Still, I'm not going to Newport and leaving her alone. I will stay as long as she insists on continuing this nonsense and keep an eye on her." He raised his chin at Daniel, clearly expecting to be challenged. The gesture was so like Genevieve that Daniel almost laughed. Instead, he raised his glass toward Gavin, feeling almost overwhelmed with relief that Genevieve wouldn't be alone after all.

Genevieve's brother looked momentarily startled, but then raised his own wineglass in return.

Daniel drank deeply. He hoped Gavin wouldn't try to interfere with their investigation but was willing to tolerate his presence while he and Genevieve continued their work if it meant she would not be left home unaccompanied. A part of him knew he was being irrational; Genevieve was not an artist's model, and other than her friends at the paper, she didn't associate with the more Bohemian world to which the victims belonged.

Regardless, he was glad Gavin would be staying.

The dancers seemed to be winding up to a big finale; the small band was reaching a crescendo. In unison, the girls twirled in a wild circle, their unbound hair swinging, their hips gyrating. The men were equally wild, stamping their feet in approval, giving long whistles, standing, and yelling their encouragement.

Daniel sought where Shipman had been and uttered a low curse when he saw the spot between Stuyvesant and Webb was now vacant. He stood, trying to see through the crowd of jeering, whooping men, looking for the face of their host, the one man he was enduring this ridiculous spectacle for to speak with.

But Matthew Shipman was gone.

Chapter 10

"Gavin, do you see Shipman anywhere?" There was no keeping the urgency from his voice. *Dammit, dammit, dammit.*

Gavin's gaze immediately sharpened, the transition again so like Genevieve that Daniel started slightly. Gavin also stood and began to scan the room. He shook his head, frustrated.

The dancers finished, at long last, by removing their jackets, holding them aloft as they spun to the last few frenzied notes. The men roared their approval. It seemed the entire crowd, apart from Daniel and Gavin, was very drunk indeed.

As the Jewels of Egypt shimmied their way off the stage, the guests took their seats, laughing and pounding one another on the back. More drinks were poured, and waiters brought around a cheese course. Daniel and Gavin remained standing for a few moments, searching the faces for that of Matthew Shipman.

He seemed to have vanished.

"How did you like our version of Egypt, then, Stewart?"

And then suddenly there he was, leaning on Gavin like a drunken sailor.

Daniel hid a frown of confusion. Where had Shipman been? Visiting the water closet? Backstage? It seemed odd that the host would disappear during the Egyptian Jewels' big finale.

"Hardly an accurate representation," Gavin muttered, staring in the direction the Jewels had disappeared.

"Ha! Accurate representation." Shipman guffawed. "Only you, Stewart. Say, what's next for you? Never say you're heading abroad again; you just returned."

Gavin resumed his seat and leaned back in his chair, seeming to force himself to relax. "Not abroad, no. But I am heading to Chicago at the end of the summer to accept a position at the University of Chicago."

"Really?" Shipman appeared flabbergasted. "Why would you want to do a thing like that? Fine town, Chicago, but it's not New York."

Gavin smiled. "No, it's not. But they have other scholars of Egyptian history there and are beginning to take it seriously as an area of study."

Daniel took his seat as well and watched this exchange silently, taking another appreciative sip of his whiskey. He wondered if Chicago not being New York was, in fact, the point.

"And you, McCaffrey." Shipman turned his large, florid face in Daniel's direction. "You're helping, aren't you? You're helping with my Bea's death."

Every sense was instantly awake at this abrupt turn in conversation. Daniel worked to maintain a casual posture, leaning forward on his elbows, one hand casually wrapped around his glass.

"Who told you that?" he asked in a nonchalant tone. But he knew, even as the words left his mouth.

Walter. One of Shipman's intimate friends. Daniel allowed his eyes to roam the room as Gavin helped Shipman mop up wine the latter had jostled with his elbow.

Where *was* Walter? Why wasn't he here?

"Thank you, Stewart. Good man," Shipman said, signaling a waiter for another glass of wine despite Gavin's protests that he didn't care for one. "I got some beautiful butterflies for tonight, didn't I?" he asked slyly, referring to the dancers who had vacated the stage.

"Very," Daniel replied. This was the moment to keep Shipman talking, by whatever means.

"Bea was one too, you know. What a butterfly she was, caught before her time." The man was turning morose. "But I have one more surprise left for the birthday boy," Shipman said, turning jolly again. His moods were swinging like a pendulum, and it was hard to follow his train of thought. "The most glorious butterfly of the night is yet to come. Just you wait." He guffawed again and smacked Gavin on the back.

Daniel and Gavin both looked toward the stage, though the curtain was still drawn.

He had to get Shipman talking about Bea again.

"Matt, what do you think happened?" Daniel began, but Shipman cut him off.

"There are ancient curses in Egypt, aren't there, Gavin?" their host asked. The noise from the crowd had quieted as the guests tucked into their cheese and waited for the next act to appear, and Shipman dropped his gravelly voice as well.

Daniel paused, struck by the oddness of the question and the sudden, stark hopelessness in Shipman's tone.

Gavin must have heard something troubling in Shipman's voice as well. He regarded his old acquaintance with concern. "That's mostly a superstition," Gavin started, but Shipman interrupted.

"How can someone tell if they've been cursed? I think I am. It's the only explanation."

The band began playing a jaunty tune, and the stage curtains opened. An enormous cake, tall as a side table, had been centered in the middle of the stage. It was covered with whipped cream and decorated with chocolate rosettes. A laughing, balding man was pushed onto the stage, his shirt undone almost halfway down his chest, his tie hanging loose about his neck. This was presumably the guest of honor, Eugene Goodyear.

Daniel didn't give a fig about cakes or birthdays or the once-again swelling noise of the crowd and the music. He was singularly focused on Shipman.

"What do you mean, Matt? Why might you be cursed?" he asked urgently, resisting the impulse to shake the man's shoulder. There was a leaden, sunken feeling in his gut, a dread pooling around what he feared he would hear.

Matthew Shipman blinked at him with bleary eyes. He was so intoxicated Daniel was surprised he was still upright.

"I found her, you know. Bea. But you found Violet," Shipman said, the sadness in his voice apparent even in the midst of the ever-increasing din. The music continued to build, and the assembled men were cheering and clapping in anticipation of whatever had to do with that cake, but now Daniel did grab Matt by the shoulder.

"What did you say?"

"You found her," he said again, then looked at Daniel with unbearable heartache on his face. "I must be cursed, mustn't I?" Matthew Shipman was not a particularly handsome man, with a nose too large for his face and prematurely heavy jowls, but he normally exuded a boisterousness that could be infectious, if one was in the proper mood. Rupert possessed a similar quality, but while Rupert was a joyful prankster, full of harmless innuendo, Shipman teetered on the edge of propriety, even decency, in his pursuit of pleasure.

It was jarring to witness the anguish on Shipman's normally jolly face.

"Did you know her, then? You knew Violet Templeton?" Daniel leaned his face as close to the other man's as he dared, smelling the liquor on Shipman's breath, his musky aftershave mixed with the scent of heavy perspiration.

Daniel's blood was thrumming loudly in his ears, and his fingers tightened on Shipman's shoulders unwittingly.

"Knew her?" Matthew Shipman bore the look of someone with nothing left to lose, desperate and hopeless and reckless all at once. "I loved her."

Daniel's blood ceased its thrumming and froze, chilling him to the marrow.

Shipman jerked out of Daniel's grasp and leapt onto the stage, holding Goodyear's hand aloft as he led the crowd in a chant to the rhythm of the band.

"*Three, two, one!*" the men cried on Shipman's cue, and as one they roared in appreciation when the top of the cake popped off and an exceedingly beautiful girl clad in tights, topped by what could only be described as a tiny loincloth with petal shapes on it, gossamer-thin butterfly wings, and a bow and arrow, sprang forth. She pushed the remainder of the cake aside, it being only a thin paper shell covered with cream, and playfully shot a fabric arrow at Goodyear before leaning forward and nuzzling his neck, to the crowd's obvious approval. Goodyear blushed and laughed, reaching for her waist as she twirled away. The band started a new song as the girl stepped forward, clearly readying herself to dance as workers hastily cleared the remainder of the mock cake away.

Daniel was in the unfamiliar position of being so shocked he was momentarily incapable of moving, dimly aware that his mouth was hanging agape but wholly unable to help himself.

The girl in the cake was none other than Callie Maple.

Gavin seemed to have no such qualms, though, as he swiftly jumped onto the stage just as Callie was about to perform, wrapped his jacket around her shoulders, and hustled her off the stage.

All hell broke loose. The guests protested vociferously, breaking into a noisy chorus of boos and aggrieved cries. Someone even threw a glass, which exploded against the back wall in a shower of shards. Several other men rushed the stage, protesting and trying to prevent Gavin from leading Callie backstage, one even grabbing at Gavin's jacket and trying to rip it from her body.

Daniel's momentary paralysis fled. He leapt over the chair recently vacated by Gavin and onto the stage, forcibly pulling the person manhandling Callie—Martin Webb, as it turned out—from her and casting him to the ground. He raised his fist as Webb made a move to stand, causing the other man to sink back to the ground warily. Webb looked to his fellows for support, but none of them seemed willing to take Daniel on, instead backing away and muttering.

The public knowledge that he had begun his life as a street tough in notorious Five Points came in handy sometimes.

Once they were backstage, Callie rounded on Gavin.

"Genevieve complained to me of your high-handedness, Gavin," she began in a furious voice, "but she is your sister. I am of no relation to you, and you had no right to ruin my act." Callie tore his jacket off and flung it to the ground.

"I was meant to sit there and watch you debase yourself?" Gavin answered, his voice tight. "Watch you *undress*? Callie, you grew up across the Square from me; I've known you since you were born. Several of the men in that room made you proposals of marriage, if memory serves. How *any* of them could watch is beyond me. What on earth were you thinking of?"

"Money," she snapped. "That I used to be high society is part of the appeal. It's part of my price. I get *paid* to do this, Gavin. This is my livelihood now, and you've cheated me out of fifty dollars tonight."

"I'll give you fifty dollars."

"You will not. I will *earn* my money. I can't go back out now; the illusion is ruined. I may not get hired for this sort of act again," she said, stamping a foot. "Now every theatrical manager is going to worry there's a potential Gavin Stewart in the audience, ready to play at being a white knight and stop the show lest my nonexistent modesty be tainted."

"It's not nonexistent," Gavin nearly roared in return. "Not to me."

"You are immaterial here," she shot back. "If my reputation mattered so much to you, you would never have gone to Egypt."

Gavin reeled back as if he'd been slapped.

A line of girls, none of them a day older than seventeen, wearing matching tights and form-fitting sleeveless dresses that stopped at the upper thigh, were hustled past them down the hallway and entered the stage area one by one. There had been a steady refrain of booing from the private dining room that now transitioned to exuberant cheers.

A clean-shaven man wearing a bright plaid jacket but slouching under a disreputable-looking bowler hat brought up the rear, keeping an eye on the young women from backstage. Daniel started at the sight of him.

It was one of the gangster John Boyle's men. Daniel recognized him from earlier this summer, when he and Genevieve had been at Boyle's Suicide Tavern on the Bowery several times.

"I don't . . . Callie. We were kids; you were only fifteen. It was a summer flirtation, nothing more. You can't possibly . . ." Gavin's voice expressed bewilderment.

There was obviously some history here to which Daniel wasn't privy, but he had little time for whatever personal drama was unfolding.

He moved next to Boyle's man, looking past the now-topless dancing girls from backstage to scan the audience.

Shipman had known Bea and Violet. Moreover, he claimed to have loved Violet. Had she been his mistress also? The artist Chase had intimated Violet was leaving town partially to untangle herself from a relationship and give herself distance from a man.

Was Shipman that man?

As before, their host for the evening seemed to have disappeared. He was nowhere in the dining room. Daniel cursed under his breath. Boyle's man shot an aggressive look in his direction, and Daniel met it with one of his own.

"Your boss running girls instead of guns these days?" he asked the man. John Boyle was one of the gang leaders behind the gunrunning scheme he and Genevieve had upended earlier that summer.

The man in plaid regarded him mildly enough, but Daniel saw a flicker of recognition in his eye. He knew who Daniel was.

"We are a talent recruitment and management agency, nothing more or less," the man replied in a thick downtown accent. "No matter who's in charge." He spit a thick stream of saliva at the floor near Daniel's feet, then shoved his hands in his pockets and looked back at the girls onstage.

Daniel turned away, unsurprised. Boyle had his hand in a bit of everything that had to do with vice in this town—girls, guns, drugs, booze, gambling; you name it, Boyle was involved in it. It made a sick sort of sense that the gangster was using a talent agency as a front for what likely amounted to prostitution.

He stepped back toward Gavin and Callie. "Why are you doing this if you have attached yourself to Walter Wilson?" Gavin was saying. "You model for respectable artists; you're not one of these types of girls." He gestured at the stage.

Callie crossed her arms in front of her chest and gave a short, harsh laugh. "Of course I am. Models, actresses, any girl of marriageable age . . . we're all just interchangeable butterflies. Lots of models perform on the stage and vice versa. I do this because I like to have my own money. Money Walter doesn't know about."

Gavin's eyebrows shot up in alarm. "Callie, is Walter . . . does he treat you well?"

"Yes," she said irritably. "Yes, Walter is nothing but considerate and kind. But you enjoy having your own money too, don't you?"

Gavin blinked at the comparison. He didn't seem to have thought about how a woman might come by money before.

"Callie, where is Walter?" Daniel interrupted. "Isn't he good friends with Shipman?"

"He's gone upstate to meet with clients," Callie admitted. "It's why I accepted this job. He wouldn't like . . ." She let her voice trail off, looking down.

Daniel and Gavin exchanged a look. Walter wouldn't like his mistress dancing at another man's birthday party, it seemed.

"Did you know Matthew Shipman knew Violet Templeton? Maybe had a relationship with her? Or admired her in any way? Has Walter ever said anything about that?"

Callie shook her head. "No, never." She sounded surprised. "Why? Do you think there is a connection?"

Daniel hesitated. The thug who worked for Boyle was nearby, and his gut told him discretion was of the utmost importance.

Callie followed his gaze. "Come to the dressing room," she said quietly. "It's the adjacent dining room. The other girls will be onstage a while."

There was one remaining dancer in the makeshift dressing room, a girl with her foot propped up on a dining chair. She was startled to see another show girl entering with two men but buried her head back into a section of newspaper, signaling she wasn't paying them any attention.

Daniel pulled Callie and Gavin to a far corner of the room and relayed what Shipman had said.

"Loved her?" Callie frowned. "Matt said he loved Violet? Perhaps it was one-sided or very secret. I can ask Walter when he returns."

"Callie, please. Can you put something on?" Gavin asked. "Let me take you home."

"I can make my own way, thank you," she informed him icily. "Or Mr. McCaffrey can see me home. In fact, I think you ought to leave now."

Daniel watched a series of emotions play across Gavin's face, frustration and hurt and anger and regret, before the man turned on his heel and left.

Callie watched him go, her head held high and her shoulders back, until the door shut, at which point she wilted slightly and excused herself to change behind a large Japanese screen.

Daniel moved to wait in the hallway.

"Excuse me? Sir?" It was the injured show girl.

"Do you need assistance?" he asked politely. Perhaps she couldn't stand or wasn't able to reach something because of her ankle, which was very clearly swollen. She ought to have ice on it.

"No. But did I hear you say Violet? Did you mean Violet Templeton, the one who just died?"

"Yes," Daniel said, taking a cautious step forward. The girl had large hazel eyes in a pretty, freckled face. "How did you hear of her passing?" As far as he knew, the death was still unreported publicly.

"We all heard. All us girls. Something like that—word gets out."

"Did you know her?" he asked.

She tucked her head toward her chest. "Yeah. A while ago, she danced with some of us. You don't forget hair like that. I figured she'd do more on the stage, but instead she went to work with them artists. Stopped dancing. I was real sad to hear she'd died."

Daniel glanced curiously at the closed door separating this room from the hallway that led to the stage entrance. He thought of the man in the plaid jacket. Boyle's thug, ferrying girls to and from their engagements.

At some point, Violet had been one of those girls.

Violet had worked for Boyle, even if indirectly.

Which meant Daniel was going to have to see the gangster, the very man who had tried twice to have him killed only a few short weeks ago, face-to-face.

CHAPTER 11

It had been only a few weeks since Genevieve had last been on the Bowery at night, and she had distinctly hoped she'd never have to return to that place ever, much less after dark. It was exactly as she remembered, the stuff of nightmares. Gruesome shadows cast from barrel fires danced on the walls of adjacent buildings, resembling capering goblins, while local gang members stumbled and drank or, worse, silently strode in grim, purposeful groups, their hands shoved in their pockets, their sharp eyes missing nothing. Women advertised for potential clients, and a few joined the groups of men drinking around the fires, the crowds and flames making the hot night feel hotter.

Perspiration trickled between her shoulder blades as she swallowed and wove her way through the crowd, wearing a plain shirtwaist and skirt. She could feel strands of hair escaping her simple chignon and sticking to the sides of her face. Between the throngs of people, the oppressive temperature, and the ceiling of the elevated train tracks overhead, the atmosphere was near unbearable. But she knew the best way through was to look purposeful herself, and to show as little fear as possible.

All the same, she had her trusty derringer in her pocket.

Despite her efforts, some of the local toughs seemed to have sniffed her out. The hair on the back of her neck stood up as she skirted a particularly large group bellowing a sea shanty. Out of the corner of her eye, the shadowy forms of two men behind her loomed.

She was being followed.

Genevieve didn't dare turn around to confront her pursuers. It was better to keep walking briskly and try to lose them in the crowd.

She picked up her pace slightly, allowing her right hand to rest in the deep pocket of her skirt, feeling the comforting weight of her small gun resting there. She would use it only if she had to, but knowing it was an option helped her keep her shoulders relaxed and her expression stern rather than fearful.

Even though she was afraid, very much so, and becoming more so with every passing step.

They were getting closer.

Genevieve's breath became shallower, and she felt goose bumps prickle her arms despite the warm temperatures. She was reaching a section of the Bowery that was moving from commercial to more residential buildings.

The crowds were thinning, but this didn't make her feel safer. On the contrary, she felt more exposed.

More vulnerable.

She quickened her steps. Those behind matched her pace, the sound of their rough footfalls echoing through the emptying streets.

She finally reached a block that was mostly dark and shuttered. It was now or never.

In one smooth motion, Genevieve drew her derringer and whirled around, ready to face whoever was chasing her.

"Put the gun down, miss," said Paddy, his hands held high. His compatriot Billy's hands were raised also, an almost comical expression of surprise on his face.

"It's just us," Billy said, sounding aggrieved.

Genevieve lowered the gun slightly but didn't pocket it. Paddy and Billy were . . . well, she wasn't sure what characterized their relationship with Daniel. Not quite friends, but not *not* friends. They had all been part of the Bayard Toughs when they were young, one of Five Points' most notorious street gangs. Daniel was no longer officially associated with the Toughs, but he wasn't *un*associated either. He had once explained to her that gang ties ran deep and were nearly impossible to break.

Paddy and Billy, though, were still entirely active in gang life. Indeed, Genevieve had often wondered if Paddy was the gang's leader. She hadn't quite dared ask.

She knew these men, but she didn't exactly trust them, not when Daniel wasn't around. They were loyal to Daniel, though, and she thought that loyalty extended to her.

At least, she hoped it did. The men had helped her and Daniel several times.

But what did they want with her now?

"Why are you following me?" she asked. "You could have announced yourselves. You scared me half to death."

"Billy here saw you," Paddy said, jerking his thumb at his partner, who still had his hands raised. "Out the window of the Barking Seal. What are you doing here, miss?"

"It's not safe," Billy chimed in, finally lowering his hands.

Genevieve pursed her lips and considered how much to tell them. They would surely get word to Daniel if she told them her intentions.

"It's a personal matter," was what she finally settled on. "None of your affair."

The men exchanged a look.

"Told you," Billy muttered, nudging a pile of ashes with his toe.

Paddy ignored him and kept Genevieve in his hard, birdlike stare. "You're not thinking of paying John Boyle a visit now, are you, miss?"

Annoyance flared within Genevieve, and her teeth involuntarily clenched. She raised the gun an inch, just to be contrary, and was glad to see Paddy go still.

But what was she going to do, stand here all night pointing a derringer at Daniel's associates? She sighed and dropped the gun, all the way this time, and shoved it into her pocket.

"Where is he?" she asked, crossing her arms.

There was no need to say who *he* was.

"He was meant to meet us at the Seal, but then we saw you. He's probably there by now." Billy sent a longing glance over his shoulder, undoubtedly thinking of whatever drink he had left behind at the establishment.

Paddy cocked his head at her. "Come see for yourself."

Genevieve huffed a breath but walked, flanked by Paddy and Billy, back through the several hellish blocks she'd just traversed: past the sea shanty men, past the women beckoning to Billy, who eyed them with appreciation, and past the men who took a respectful step back when they saw the Toughs come by, until they reached a glass storefront with the words OYSTERS and LAGER emblazoned on its front window in chipped gold paint.

At the front end of the bar near the window sat Daniel, a glass of whiskey in his hand.

She stood before him and placed her hands on her hips.

"Sicced your dogs on me, did you?"

Billy shot her a wounded look at being referred to as a dog.

Daniel placed his glass on the bar and raised his hands defensively. "I merely asked them to keep an eye out. I had a feeling you'd come this way, and I was right."

"I can go where I please."

"Of course you can, but Genevieve, think. Do you really believe it would be wise to head to Boyle's Suicide Tavern on your own? You remember what happened the last time we were there."

"I remember John Boyle was prepared to let you die," she shot back. All the rage and fear she'd felt that night, the night she had seen Daniel's limp, unresponsive form being carried into the dark back alley behind the tavern and shoved into a carriage, rushed to the surface of her mind, her skin.

She'd been terrified. Not for herself, but for him. Terrified she had been too late, that she would never get the chance to tell him how she felt.

Terrified he was lost to her forever.

"And yet you would go back without me, I knew," she continued. "So yes, after Callie told me Violet had been a dancer with the talent agency Boyle manages, I decided to come see him myself. I was hoping to get there before you."

Daniel ran both hands through his hair, making it nearly stand on end. His eyes were so dark in the dim bar they appeared almost as black as his hair, yet she could read the worry and frustration there all the same. "And what would happen to you, a society woman alone at Boyle's? You know he is not someone to be trifled with, Genevieve. If you even made it there in one piece." He shook his head. "I knew Callie overheard me talking to that show girl," he muttered.

"Callie is much smarter than many give her credit for. She already knew of Boyle's connection to that particular agency; it's well known among that set. She hadn't, though, been aware that Violet had once worked there. Let's go together, Daniel. Now that Shipman has disappeared, Boyle is our next best lead."

Daniel had called her on the telephone earlier that day and filled her in on some of the details of the evening at Sherry's the night before, namely what Shipman had said about Violet Templeton. He hadn't mentioned Callie jumping from a cake or referred to her presence at all, but later that morning, Callie had arrived at her doorstep and told her the whole story over tall glasses of lemonade in the Stewarts' cool front parlor. At one point, Gavin had walked in, seen Callie on the settee, and stalked right back out.

Neither Callie nor Gavin had been willing to explain. She guessed that Gavin, like her, was more than a little troubled by Callie's willingness to dance at Eugene Goodyear's birthday party. But she also understood why Callie had made that choice.

Callie had said she had no idea where Matthew Shipman might have gone.

"I've sent a telegram to Suzanne Anwyll in Newport," Genevieve told Daniel. "She replied quickly, saying she hasn't seen Shipman yet but will keep an eye out."

"Your replacement at the paper?" Daniel asked.

"Associate," she replied. She had finally revealed her scheme of using Miss Anwyll to cover the society pages while working on the potential Jack the Ripper story after her meeting with Arthur. "Miss Anwyll is an excellent writer. Shipman will turn up eventually; men like him always do. But in the meantime, we must talk to Boyle."

Daniel downed the rest of his drink and eyed her with a resigned expression. "There is nothing I can say to convince you it is foolish for you to go with me, is there?"

In truth, Genevieve was very afraid of returning to Boyle's. The last time she had been inside the tavern, they had been chased out by a former prizefighter firing a gun at them; she and Daniel had barely escaped with their lives. And then there was the night of waiting in the alley behind the bar with Rupert, knowing Daniel was inside somewhere, trying to rescue a young girl, culminating in Genevieve killing Tommy Meade.

It had been the longest, darkest night of her life, except that Daniel had survived.

That also made it the brightest night of her life.

Now she thrust her shoulders back and raised her chin. "There is not," she said. "So we might as well get on with it."

Behind Daniel, Paddy gave a small shrug. Billy had already applied himself to his new drink and was gesturing to the bartender for another.

"All right, let's go," Daniel said, reaching for his hat. It was clear by his tone he still thought her accompanying him was a bad idea, but he didn't seem prepared to argue it further.

A few blocks later, they once again passed under the sign above the tavern's entrance that read *Better Dead*, and as always, the motto sent a shiver down Genevieve's spine. They walked through the deserted tiny front room, through a dingy door, and into the main space of the bar. There was a different man behind the bar than there had been during their last visits, which was to be expected. The previous bartender and bouncer, Edward Murray, also known as Knockout Eddie, was currently serving a life sentence at Sing Sing, having pleaded guilty to multiple murders on his boss John Boyle's behalf.

Like the Bowery itself, the inside of Boyle's was as she remembered, and not a place she had wanted to return to. It was packed with customers, rough men and women drinking and openly cavorting, and sure enough, a fight between four men and a woman broke out in the far corner of the barroom, the sound of crashing glass resonating.

The bartender pointed in that direction, and two other men Genevieve hadn't noticed rushed over to contain the fight.

"It's the man from Sherry's," Daniel said, so quietly only she could hear.

The bartender looked both unsurprised and unhappy to see them.

"He's been expecting you. Or you, at least." The man thrust his chin toward Daniel. "Said to send you back if you came. Don't know about her."

"She goes where I go," Daniel said. Genevieve heard a subtle shift in Daniel's language, just as she had the other times they had visited Boyle's—a return to the rhythms of speech of his youth.

The bartender shrugged. "You'll find out pretty quick if he don't want her here, I guess. Go ahead." He gestured again with his head, this time toward a door set to the right of the stage in the back of the room. As they worked their way through the crowd to the door, two of the men who had been fighting were hustled past them on their way to being ejected from the bar. One yelled in outrage about his treatment, which earned him a vicious blow to one ear from Boyle's employee, hard enough it left him looking dazed.

"Stop here." A simply enormous man halted their progress just before the door. Like Knockout Eddie and Daniel's secretary, Asher, he had the look of a boxer, with a scarred face and giant, meaty hands.

After a look toward the bar, the big man grunted and patted Daniel's sides, removing a gun from wherever Daniel had stashed it in the back of his jacket, then led them into what turned out to be a large and surprisingly ordinary-looking office.

A shelf of ledgers lined one wall, and behind a plain, wide wooden desk sat John Boyle, his broad face and slicked-back brown hair also more ordinary than one might expect from one of the most feared gangsters in New York.

"Did you check her for weapons too?" Boyle asked the man Genevieve assumed was a bodyguard. The thug gave a slight snigger, but Boyle raised a brow at him.

"This is the little lady who took out Thomas Meade. I've no intention of following in his footsteps."

Chastened, the bodyguard approached Genevieve, but she removed her derringer and handed it to him before he could run his hands over her body. At Boyle's nod, the big man left the room, closing the door behind him.

Boyle did not invite them to sit.

"I don't know why you're here; our business finished last month. But when Dickie out there said Danny was asking him questions last night, I thought I might see you soon. Let me be clear: this is a one-time courtesy meeting, not that I owe either of you any courtesy." He eyed them coldly. "I didn't expect you'd come back." This he directed at Genevieve before turning his attention back to Daniel. "You here on behalf of the Toughs, Danny? They want me to stop edging in on Meade's old territory?" A wintry smile lifted the corners of the gangster's mouth.

"I'm not involved with any of that anymore, John, you know that. Any disputes with the Toughs are between you and Paddy," Daniel said.

Genevieve mentally filed away that information, pleased she'd been right.

"This is a different matter, nothing to do with territory," Daniel continued. "We want information about one of the girls that used to dance for your agency."

"Chasing little girls again? That didn't end so well for you last time."

"This one's already dead. We just want to know more about her, maybe find out who killed her. Violet Templeton."

John's brows raised slightly. "Violet, huh? I remember her, mostly because of that hair. Most unusual color I'd ever seen. She stopped working with the agency one, two years ago, something like that. Tried to go more legit, I think. Got naked for painters instead of onstage. She's dead?"

Daniel nodded. "Throat cut."

Boyle's face remained impassive. "That's too bad." He didn't sound like he thought it was too bad. "What's it to me?"

"She have any enemies you know of? Or anyone who maybe wanted to do her harm?"

Boyle stared at Daniel coldly. "I don't keep up with all those girls, Danny. You should know that. They're meat to me. Pretty meat, but meat all the same. They come in, they go out, sometimes they get caught in the cross fire."

Genevieve had been silent through this exchange, but at Boyle's words, her temper spiked uncontrollably. These were *people* he was talking about. "She's not the only one."

Boyle turned his snake eyes to her, a look that chilled her to the core.

"Not the only one dead," Genevieve clarified. It was taking every ounce of her courage to hold Boyle's gaze. "Another girl's throat was cut as well. Also a model. Do you know anything about that?"

"I don't know anything about dead girls. Bad for business."

Genevieve and Daniel exchanged a quick look. The bar was called Boyle's Suicide Tavern because so many young women had taken their lives there in desperation. Boyle capitalized on the bar's grim reputation, to the point that it was a badge of honor to have spent the night in one of the rooms upstairs and survived.

Boyle caught their look and interpreted it correctly. "The bar name is different," he said. "Good for business." The bodyguard peeked his head in, and Boyle gave him a restless nod.

"The police think it might be Jack the Ripper," Genevieve said quickly, sensing their time might almost be up.

Boyle stilled. "The Ripper ain't here. That's your kind"— he thrust his head toward Genevieve, referring to her status as a journalist—"spreading rumors. Selling papers."

The shift in his eyes told Genevieve that Boyle was holding something back. "So you've not heard anything about a killer cutting the throats of young women? No chatter, no whispers?" she pressed.

Boyle's eyes moved between the two of them. "Maybe," he finally said. "But just that: whispers. If that monster is in this town, he'd better stay the hell outa my territory, if he knows what's good for him."

Genevieve drew breath to ask him another question— what were these whispers?—but Boyle stopped her with a look. "I don't know about how or why Violet got killed. And I don't know about no Jack the Ripper. You've used up your courtesy visit, and now we're done. Don't let me see either of you in this bar again."

The bouncer, who had slipped inside, now opened the door and jerked his head, signaling that they should exit.

Daniel nodded his thanks at Boyle, who stared back expressionlessly. The bouncer escorted them through the crowd and past the bartender, through the abandoned front room, and to the door that led to the street. Only then did he return their weapons.

"You heard the man. Don't come back." These were the first words the bouncer had spoken, and though his deep, rough voice was so low it was barely above a whisper, the menace in his tone caused Genevieve to swallow in fear.

It wouldn't be a hard directive to follow. She never wanted to return to Boyle's Suicide Tavern again.

CHAPTER 12

The heat settled over the city like a damp cloak, oppressive in its weight.

Genevieve hadn't thought the temperatures could climb much higher than they'd been but had been sorely mistaken. A week after her and Daniel's visit to Boyle's Suicide Tavern, the thermometer shot upwards of ninety-eight degrees in the shade. There was nary a breeze nor a thunderstorm to break its clutch on the city, and the stale air grew fetid and suffocating with nowhere to go. The smell of garbage was so thick in some areas it was almost overpowering, and Genevieve spent the majority of her days confined to the Stewarts' front sitting room, drinking iced beverages and cooling herself as best she could with a Japanese fan. Daniel, and sometimes Callie, often joined her, the three of them reviewing what they knew about the murders of the two models.

Unfortunately, they were at an impasse.

Walter had returned from visiting his clients upstate, where he was designing a large lake house in the Swiss chalet style for a wealthy family. "I haven't heard from Matt and don't know where he could be," Callie's lover had told

Genevieve and Daniel when they questioned him, sounding genuinely distressed. "And I had no idea he was involved with Violet Templeton. Are you sure Chase doesn't have any further information? It was in his studio the poor girl was found, after all."

"The police have questioned Mr. Chase thoroughly, and he was seen by over a dozen people in Long Island the night Violet was killed," Daniel said. "His daughter had a summer cold, and the maid recalls waking and seeing Mr. Chase holding the girl on the veranda in the middle of the night in an attempt to soothe her. There doesn't seem to be a way he could have made it to town and back; the timing doesn't work."

Walter nodded slowly, but his features remained troubled. "Violet was the model he used most often, you know. She inspired him to create the most splendid of his paintings. I do hope his work doesn't suffer."

Daniel shot a look at Genevieve, who suppressed an angry utterance. Walter's being more concerned about how Violet's death would affect Chase's painting, rather than about the dead girl herself, was so deeply offensive she couldn't put her outrage into words.

Walter's response was also dishearteningly typical of how many men seemed to be reacting to these women's murders. The general consensus seemed to be that the deaths were tragic, but in some ways inevitable, and that the women's roles in important men's lives could easily be replaced.

She knew this assessment wasn't entirely fair. Boyle was a street thug who valued no human life; Walter was a dreamer with his head in the clouds—and he and Callie, after all, had been the ones to get her and Daniel involved. The police claimed they were trying to do what they could. But it seemed nobody felt a sense of urgency around these murders anymore.

Perhaps it was the heat, which was making even the most lively and energetic of individuals droop.

Whether the heat or a general dismissal of women was to blame, the lack of action on the case was both discouraging and infuriating.

And now Genevieve and Gavin were alone in the Washington Square townhouse, suffering in the high temperatures.

"I will never understand why the two of you won't come to Newport," Anna had fretted to her two children as she oversaw one of the maids packing the last of her things. "It's so dreadful here."

"Mother, you know I'm in the middle of an investigation."

"Yes, but these poor women are already gone. Surely you can solve their murders in a more agreeable location?"

"*Mother.*" Genevieve was shocked. If there was one person who would understand how the lives and deaths of these women mattered, she would have thought it would be her mother.

Anna sat on the edge of her bed and smoothed her hand over its surface. "I'm being selfish, aren't I? Well, do as you must, dear. But Gavin, you won't come? We've barely seen you for years, and the city in August is no type of homecoming." Tears stood in her mother's eyes, and Genevieve felt a pang of sympathy.

It was her fault Gavin was staying in town, though she'd urged him to leave with their parents.

"I'm used to being hot," Gavin said in a gentle voice. "We'll be fine. And I'm sure with Genevieve and Mr. McCaffrey doing the sleuthing, the case will be wrapped up shortly. We'll join you then."

Genevieve had been surprised at her brother's generosity, after he'd been so critical of her working with Daniel, but was grateful for his support, as it appeased their mother.

Dabbing at her eyes with a handkerchief, Anna stood purposefully and then tucked the rectangle of cloth away. "They are a rather formidable pair. Very well. But make sure it's sooner rather than later. Your brother is counting on seeing you."

"I'll see him very soon," Gavin had promised.

Now, in the stifling heat of her bedroom, Genevieve wondered if perhaps her mother had been correct. It had been two weeks and nobody else had died, Longstreet swore the police were working the case, and she and Daniel were entirely out of leads.

While Beatrice Holler had enjoyed a wide circle of friends, they could find no one who wished her ill, and the few key individuals who'd had the opportunity to harm her had all been accounted for that evening. Violet Templeton, on the other hand, had led a life so private they had been able to uncover little about her. Yet what they did know did not suggest an obvious—or not-so-obvious, for that matter—suspect in her death.

Maybe the two murders had simply been a random coincidence and there was little to investigate. The killer or killers had struck, then melted back into the fabric of the city.

Maybe it really was Jack the Ripper, having come to New York; maybe not.

Maybe Bea and Violet had simply been unlucky.

Perhaps she should let the police handle the matter and return to the delicious ocean winds of Newport.

Genevieve shifted slightly in her bed, trying to find a cooler spot. All the windows in the house were open in a futile attempt to allow the air to circulate. She was lying atop her sheets wearing only a thin cotton chemise and was tempted to peel it off and sleep in the altogether.

Try as she might, she couldn't believe that the tale she'd spun for herself was the reality of the situation. The murders were connected, one way or another.

Both women had some involvement with Matthew Shipman, who still remained at large. Daniel had discovered the police were searching for him as well.

The subtle tightening around John Boyle's mouth when she'd asked if he knew anything was another clue. And there was something so deliberate, so odd, about the way Violet's body had been left.

As if the killer was trying to tell them something.

The grandfather clock at the foot of the stairs chimed midnight. It was so hot it was almost challenging to breathe, and between the still air and the puzzle whirling in her brain, Genevieve felt sure she wouldn't be able to sleep, but she finally dozed off.

Later, she wouldn't remember what woke her. Maybe it was a gentle shift in the air around her sleeping body. Maybe an unfamiliar scent worked its way into her dreams. Something, though, caused her to consciousness to rouse.

There was a tickling sensation on her cheek. Mostly asleep, she lazily brushed at it, expecting a bug to have made its way into the room.

Her hand encountered hard flesh.

Genevieve's eyes snapped open.

A man was half in, half out of her bed, with his feet on the floor and his upper body draped on the mattress next to her. The tickling she had felt was his thin moustache as he deposited a kiss on her cheek.

The man stared at her intently.

A scream ripped from her throat.

The man sprang back as Genevieve scrambled to the opposite side of the bed, fumbling at the drawer in her night table for her derringer. She couldn't stop screaming, and her hands were shaking so hard it was a challenge to find purchase on the drawer handle.

The stranger danced away, almost catlike in his movements, and skirted the edge of the bed toward her open window. She yanked the drawer open and pulled out the gun just as heavy footsteps sounded down the hall.

"Genevieve!" Gavin cried, flinging open her bedroom door, his bare chest and white undershorts glowing brightly in the dark night, before launching himself at the silhouetted figure in the window.

Still shaking uncontrollably, Genevieve raised the derringer and pointed it.

They were both too late. The man had leapt, nimble as a forest creature, out the window and into the night.

★   ★   ★

Detective Aloysius Longstreet drew his head back in from Genevieve's window.

"Looks like he jumped to one of the roofs on the Mews back there," he said. "Must have come in through a downstairs window. You shouldn't have your windows open at night." He had arrived with two other officers after Gavin's call to the police department. "I recognized the address," Longstreet had said wryly on entering, "and figured it'd be best if I came as well."

Gavin, who had quickly donned a shirt and trousers, stood near the detective with his hands on his hips and made an impatient noise. "You can't expect us to close ourselves in during this type of heat."

Longstreet gave Gavin an assessing look over his moustache. "Then you risk intruders. It is why the wealthy typically leave the city during the summer and the impoverished sleep on their rooftops."

Genevieve wrinkled her nose. She knew the detective carried ill feeling toward her class, though she wasn't sure why.

He didn't seem to like those of lesser means either.

"For your own safety, Miss Stewart, you may wish to leave the city," Longstreet continued. "It would serve the added bonus of getting you out of this infernal heat."

Her forehead prickled. "Do you think I was targeted? I assumed this was a random incident."

"Yes and no," one of the officers answered. Genevieve had been displeased to recognize him as Officer Jackson, with whom she had had less-than-pleasant dealings before. "There have been a spate of peeping incidents of late. Jack the Peeper, as we've taken to calling him, has a fondness for handsome women." He gave her a look that could only be described as a leer.

Genevieve drew her thin summer wrapper closer around her body. Gavin stepped between Officer Jackson and his sister.

"You're saying there is a man spying on women in the neighborhood and there's been no warning from the police?" he asked incredulously.

Detective Longstreet and Officer Jackson exchanged a glance—Longstreet's fierce, Jackson's abashed. So the officer hadn't been supposed to spill that particular detail.

"It hasn't happened before in this part of town," Longstreet said, clearly choosing his words with care. "We were seeing it in Brooklyn, even as far as New Jersey. The perpetrator has harmed nobody, but he has been taking advantage of open windows and climbing into private homes."

"Hasn't harmed anybody *yet*," Genevieve said, affronted. "He kissed my cheek. If my brother hadn't been home, he might have tried more."

Officer Jackson slid his eyes toward the detective. "He's kissed other women," he said, after receiving a nod from Longstreet that he could speak. "But mostly he simply stands over them. Nothing has been stolen from any of the residences," he added in a helpful tone.

"What do I care if an intruder takes the silver?" Genevieve cried. "I'd far prefer that than a threat to my person."

"That you've known this man was a potential cause for alarm and concern, to the point of giving him a *nickname*—and a highly distasteful one, I might add—yet done nothing to warn the public is a travesty," said Gavin angrily.

Longstreet's eyes skittered to Genevieve and back again. "As your sister is aware, Mr. Stewart, the police have no wish to cause a public panic. This man's behavior, while troubling, has not shown itself to be dangerous. To warn citizens of a mere peeper when there is existing fear that a killer may be amongst us—which is unproven, of course—would cause a stir that, combined with the current temperatures, could have devastating consequences."

Genevieve could hardly believe her ears. A man who sneaked into people's homes and stared at or fondled sleeping women was not considered dangerous? "How would you like it if someone kissed you in the night, with neither your knowledge nor consent?" she asked, outrage making her voice shake.

"Depends on who's doing the kissing, I guess." Officer Jackson smirked.

Gavin took a threatening step in the officer's direction, his fingers curled into a fist. The second officer, who had remained silent so far, stepped between the two men. "Easy now," the officer said, casting a warning look at his colleague. Longstreet sighed and wiped the sweat from his brow with a handkerchief.

"Jackson, wait outside, please," he said in a weary voice. "I understand your concern, Mr. Stewart," Longstreet continued after the other man had left. "And it does you credit. We will file a report. You have no clear description of the perpetrator, Miss Stewart?"

Genevieve bit her lower lip and shook her head in frustration. "Only what I already told you. He was young, no more than thirty. And slender, and fit. He had a thin moustache, dark in color, as was his hair. But it all happened so fast, I can't recall any other particulars."

"That matches what others have said," the unnamed officer confirmed. "It's very probably the same man. We'll catch him eventually."

"How?" Gavin demanded. "If he does this all over town and even into New Jersey, how will you catch him? And how can you be sure it isn't the same man who murdered those two models, now come after my sister?" There was a slight flush to his face that Genevieve knew had nothing to do with the heat. Gavin had a terrific temper, and she felt sure the only thing holding him back from taking a swing at one or the other of the men was their status as police officers.

"It's police business I can't discuss," Longstreet said, his voice curt. "But I do believe this incident is unrelated to the murders. We'll see ourselves out. Miss Stewart, I assume I'll be seeing some version of these events in the *Globe*?" He eyed her with displeasure.

"If you won't alert the public, I certainly will," she snapped in response. "Despite your fears of some kind of mass hysteria, which I believe are rather overblown, people deserve to know."

Longstreet uttered a small sigh. "Do what you must. But I do think you would be safer if you left town. That is my official recommendation."

"Is that a threat?" Gavin asked in a dangerous voice, the flush on his neck rising to his cheeks.

"Merely a piece of advice," Longstreet replied coldly. With that, he and the officer departed, Longstreet giving Genevieve a final warning glance she wasn't sure how to interpret.

She flinched at the sound of the front door slamming. Gavin scowled harder and followed the noise down the stairs. The sound of the front door being locked floated to her ears, before he began moving throughout the house, noisily closing and locking the downstairs windows.

Genevieve's thoughts were in turmoil. Was this peeper fellow the same man who had killed the models? Was she in greater danger than she'd thought?

"This is ridiculous," Gavin growled at Genevieve as he stalked back into her bedroom, closing the windows with a jerk and angrily turning the locks. The temperature instantly rose. "We're leaving for Newport tomorrow."

"Gavin, I can't leave now," Genevieve said, irritation replacing her fear. "I have a story to write, and I'm not finished with my investigations. This peeper fellow can't get to the upstairs windows, so we'll simply lock those downstairs at night. Surely this heat can't go on for much longer." She moved to unlock her window.

He whirled at her, the angry flush now suffusing his entire face. "You don't have a choice, Genevieve. It is not safe for you here. That Longstreet fellow was an officious prick, but he was right. You can't risk yourself like this."

Irritation blossomed to indignation. "I absolutely have a choice, as it is my life and my person we are discussing.

My choice is to stay. If you wish to head to the shore, you should do so. I can ask Callie to stay with me."

"Callie can't protect herself, let alone you," Gavin yelled. "You are my sister, and I will not see you jeopardize yourself."

"Your sister I may be, but I am also a grown woman with my own money. Neither you, nor Father, nor Mother, nor Charles, nor anyone, has any say over how I conduct my life." She was so angry she was yelling too, surprised to find tears of rage pricking her eyes. Genevieve crossed her arms over her chest and blinked rapidly, hoping the tears wouldn't fall.

"I should move out," she said miserably, "if you insist on staying. I like living here, love being with Mother and Father. But they leave me to my own affairs. I'll be twenty-eight this fall; I suppose it's time I find an arrangement of my own." The idea saddened her. Unmarried women of her class typically stayed with their parents until they passed away, but it wasn't unheard of for ladies like her to live on their own.

Maybe she'd enjoy it.

"Well, now you're being stupid," Gavin said sulkily, the fight seeming to leave him all at once.

"Are we children again?" she asked. "It's not stupid. Perhaps it's just time."

Gavin wiped a weary hand across his face. "It's late. We're not thinking clearly. Let's go back to bed, and we can discuss this in the morning."

Genevieve's anger, too, dissipated like smoke. Suddenly she was simply hot, and exhausted, and most of all, sad. Gavin had always been the more outgoing and outrageous of her two older brothers, Charles tending toward quiet and introspection. Gavin had treated her like one of the boys when they were children, never daring to suggest she couldn't do what they could. He had been the first person to voice the opinion it was a good thing her engagement to Ted Beekman seven years ago had ended, forcibly stating that Beekman wasn't man enough for a woman like Genevieve, even as the rest of society whispered behind their hands, wondering what she had done to cause Beekman to leave. He had helped her convince their parents a career in journalism would be perfect for his intrepid sister, cajoling them to use their significant influence and connections to help her find a position. Something had changed in him during his years abroad, hardened him, burying his carefree, exuberant spirit so deep she wasn't sure it would ever resurface. Genevieve had noticed it ever since he'd returned, but it was apparent primarily in his attitude toward her.

"What happened to you, Gavin?" she asked, unable to keep the sorrow out of her voice. "You used to be the first to laugh in the face of authority, to dare me to climb higher in the big sycamore tree in the park, to brag I could outrun your friends in a race. Why are you now so worried I can't handle myself?"

A lock of chestnut hair fell over his brow, and her brother's eyes glistened. For a shocked moment, Genevieve was sure he was about to cry himself. But instead he blinked fast, then shook his head in an angry gesture.

"I've seen how the world can treat women who have nobody to look out for them," he said quietly. "Look at what happened to Callie."

And without another word, he turned from her and trudged out the door, moving like a man carrying a deep, heavy burden.

CHAPTER 13

"Let's go see the elephant."

Genevieve paused in the midst of bringing a coffee cup to her lips and stared at Daniel, looking flabbergasted. "What did you say?"

Daniel smiled. It was an odd way to start a conversation, he supposed.

"The elephant. At Coney Island. We should get out of town for the day, have some fun."

A tentative, returning smile began to creep across her face. It lightened Daniel's heart to see it. "Today?"

"We could go today, sure. It's early enough we could spend the afternoon and stay well into the evening."

Genevieve drummed her fingers on the side of her cup for a moment, her nails on the porcelain making a clinking sound. "I was going to begin work on my article about this peeping tom," she mused, then gazed out the window. "But it does seem a fine day to see the ocean."

"Your own paper is saying we may get thunderstorms late tonight, and a break in the heat afterwards," Daniel said quickly. "It may be rainy tomorrow."

A mischievous gleam entered Genevieve's eye. "Perhaps I could play hooky," she said. "Arthur is anxious for the story, but he did give me a few days. And the beach sounds delightful."

"You've a bathing costume, I assume?"

"I have," she nodded, putting down her cup. "Let's do it. May Callie join us?"

Daniel took a taste of his own coffee. Despite its heat, today he welcomed the strong flavor. "If you like, of course." Visiting Coney Island had been an impromptu suggestion, and for the briefest of moments he had fantasized about the two of them there alone, holding hands and laughing while the Atlantic rushed over their bare toes.

But Genevieve's smile had widened, and a slight glow returned to her previously wan cheeks in anticipation of the outing. It was a sight Daniel would have paid most of his fortune to witness, and if Callie Maple joining them was part of that pleasure, then they would be a party of three.

The rage that had consumed him upon hearing of her midnight intruder had been so overwhelming it had taken every ounce of self-control he possessed to not run from the Stewart drawing room and start physically tearing apart the neighboring buildings, searching for the man who had dared enter Genevieve's bedroom while she slept. Gavin, who had been in the room as Genevieve told the tale, had seemed to recognize Daniel's wrath. The two men made eye contact, sharing a silent pact that they would do whatever it took to keep Genevieve from harm.

"I've never been to Coney Island, you know," Genevieve confessed. "As the weather turns fine, we're typically in Europe, and then once home, we head to Newport. It will be an adventure. Shall I have the carriage readied?"

"Yes, but only to take us to the terminus of the elevated at Whitehall. If we're going to go, let's do it properly and take the steamboat and train," Daniel suggested. Her excitement was infectious, and now he longed to feel the sea breezes on his face. They planned to reconvene at one o'clock, and he left the house feeling buoyed, despite his lingering fury at Genevieve's unknown intruder.

Before they left, he would have a word with Paddy about this Jack the Peeper and ask the Toughs to keep an eye out.

When Daniel returned at one, ready to shepherd Genevieve and Callie downtown to catch the ferry, he was surprised to find they were joined by two other young ladies as well as Gavin.

"This is Ida Gouse and Maude Pratt, friends of Callie's," Genevieve said, then introduced him. "Ida and Maude and Callie were meant to have a different outing today but decided a day at the shore sounded so much better." They were a striking pair of friends, Ida tall and lithe, with sleek dark-brown hair and an open, enthusiastic expression, Maude petite and plump, with a mass of dark-blond curls piled on her head, but so shy she could barely look his way.

Slightly bemused at finding out that what he had initially envisioned as a party of two had grown to a group of six, Daniel shrugged mentally and directed everyone into two carriages, his and one of the Stewarts', to take them to the foot of Whitehall Street. Once there, it was only a short wait until the next steamboat to the Sea Beach Line railroad departed.

The four women made a happy, chatty party, and Daniel was content to lean his forearms on the railing at the bow of the steamboat and listen to the rise and fall of their voices as they exclaimed over the passing scenery. He removed his hat to let the wind tease his hair and cool his brow and was unable to hold back his smile as they glided past familiar landmarks: the smooth, rounded walls of the old fortress turned prison to his left, the newer, imposing form of Bartholdi's impressive Statue of Liberty on his right. He had made this journey several times the previous summer, restless during those long, hot months when he and Genevieve hadn't been in each other's lives.

But he had always kept her in his thoughts.

Gavin joined him at the railing, and they watched the undulating greens of the Brooklyn shoreline pass in companionable silence. The women's light cotton dresses in various pale hues fluttered gaily in the wind, as did the ribbons of their summer hats. Their easy conversation washed over Daniel, and he learned that Ida and Maude had both worked as artists' models also but that Ida was recently engaged to a young clerk at a bank and had ceased modeling. Maude modeled only occasionally, and had steadier employment at B. Altman selling millinery. The other women marveled at the cleverness of her bonnet.

"Here already," Daniel said, rousing himself and pointing out the handsome ferry landing as they approached Bay Ridge. He and Gavin gathered the various bags and satchels as they all departed the gently rocking steamboat and transferred to the open cars of the Sea Beach railroad. The ladies shared one bench, and he and Gavin sat behind them.

"How far is it?" asked Genevieve, placing a hand on her straw bonnet as the train started with a slight lurch.

"Only fifteen minutes," Ida replied. "Is the route new to you?" There were several other railways or boats one could take to the amusements at Coney Island, and the Sea Beach Line was among the most recent.

"I've never been at all," Genevieve said, flashing a quick smile at Daniel, seemingly aware she was repeating herself from earlier that morning.

"Nor I," Callie cried, clasping Genevieve's hand on her right and Ida's on her left. "I cannot wait. Shall we ride the Switchback?"

"There's a newer ride, Shaw's Channel Chute, that circles the Elephantine Colossus," Maude chimed in, grinning. "It had just opened when I was here a few weeks ago."

"I had thought you and Walter might have visited Coney, Callie," Genevieve said.

"No, he says it's not his style," Callie replied. "I'll tell him all about it when he returns. He had to go back to the Adirondacks. The chalet people were most insistent."

"And you didn't go as well? Get upstate, away from the heat?" Ida asked.

"No, I wanted to stay in town," Callie said, sending a small smile Genevieve's way. Daniel understood: Callie was staying in town in case he and Genevieve needed help investigating Bea's and Violet's deaths.

"And how is the sculpture coming?" Ida asked Callie, who wrinkled her nose in response.

"It isn't," she said. "Between this chalet upstate Walter's working on and my helping Genevieve and Daniel here, poor *Persephone* has languished. I'm not sure she'll ever be finished."

Daniel noted Callie didn't explain what he and Genevieve were doing. Interesting. It seemed the other models knew about their investigation.

"You know I was Walter's *Columbia*, the one he did for the Centennial," Ida said. "He is rather exacting to work for, as I recall."

"The Centennial?" Genevieve frowned. "But you must have only been a child."

"I was thirteen," Ida said. "My first big job. And I was meant to represent young Columbia, awakening into maturity. It was an appropriate age." She shrugged nonchalantly. "My mother was there."

"I was thirteen for my first job too," Maude said.

"In the altogether?" Genevieve said. Daniel could tell she was trying and failing to keep the shock from her voice. "That seems awfully young."

"Not that one, no," Maude said. "But I was a live model at the National Academy of Design when I was fifteen, and that was in the altogether." A light blush rose in Maude's cheeks.

Daniel kept his eyes on the lush scenery that appeared past Gavin, who was seated on the outside of their row, as he internally frowned at the thought of both these women posing in the nude at such young ages. Gavin was staring intensely at the back of Callie's head, watching her black curls bob as she talked. He caught Daniel looking at him and shifted slightly in his seat, crossing his arms.

The women's talk shifted to Maude's sweetheart, who also worked at B. Altman's. Her blush deepened when Ida teased her about her beau's attractiveness.

"His lashes would be the envy of any girl, truly," Ida said, laughing when Maude swatted at her shoulder.

"I can smell the sea," Callie sighed. The words had no sooner left her mouth than a collective happy gasp rose from the patrons of the train as the top of Coney Island's famed iron tower rose into view, dramatically silhouetted in lone splendor against the bright-blue sky, soon followed by the sloping roofs of the Sea Beach Palace and then a large gray humped structure the same height as the tallest roof.

"The elephant!" called out a little boy no more than six wearing a jaunty sailor-collared shirt. He began to clap, and a smattering of other children joined in the applause, twisting in their seats in joy at the sight.

"Oh my goodness," Genevieve breathed, laughing herself. She turned to Daniel over her shoulder. "I had no idea it was so large."

He leaned forward, catching a whiff of her unique scent, blended with salt air and the greased metal of the train's wheels. "One hundred seventy-five feet high."

"It's remarkable." The light in her eyes was back, and Daniel sat into his bench again, catching Gavin's eye and grinning. Gavin inclined his head slightly, silently acknowledging that the excursion had been a good idea.

The pendulum of emotions Daniel had been riding began to slow. He was still incensed over the peeping tom having violated Genevieve's home, still troubled over Matthew Shipman's disappearance, and the worry that Bea and Violet's deaths might go unsolved—or worse, that another murder could occur—gnawed at his chest incessantly. But all of these worries, their jostling voices fighting for dominance in his mind, receded somewhat as the train pulled into the Sea Beach Palace terminal. How could they not? The bright, flapping flags that topped the Palace snapped in the wind, the happy din of crowds watching a roller-skating demonstration surged, the off-key music of the closest merry-go-round orchestra tinkled.

He would spend the day at the shore with Genevieve. Dimes would flow from his pockets freely, and he would buy her and her friends whatever beverage or trinket or meal they desired. He would laugh, and enjoy the hot sun on his face, and the cooling effects of the fresh ocean air.

And perhaps, when their group went bathing, he could still stand by Genevieve's side, revel in the feel of the water on his feet, and marvel at the pleasure in her face.

Genevieve deserved a day of respite, of amusement, a day to erase the smudges that seemed to lodge permanently under her amber eyes.

Nothing untoward would happen to her here. He wouldn't allow it.

★ ★ ★

There was so much to see, Genevieve didn't know where to look first.

A riot of colors and sounds and smells invaded her senses before they even disembarked from the train and only furthered once they emerged into the Sea Beach Palace, the terminal for their line. Bright sunlight poured in from the windows that lined the entire upper story of the steel-and-glass structure, which was topped with a giant glass dome. Within the Palace itself, multitudes of people milled, some heading toward one of the attached restaurants for a fine dining experience, some sampling from piles of what Maude informed her was free food, sandwiches and salads and cakes stacked on gleaming white plates and continually replenished, set out on a long table. An involuntary exclamation of wonder sprang from her mouth at the sight of dozens of roller skaters gliding over a vast, smooth floor in bright costumes, some performing astonishing jumps and leaps.

"Would you like to rent a pair of skates, try it out?" Gavin asked the ladies as they paused to watch. "It's probably not that much different from ice skating."

"No, it's too hot," Ida said decisively, answering for the group. "Come on." She grabbed Callie's hand and pulled her toward one of the sets of double doors leading to the outside.

On Surf Avenue, Genevieve felt like a child again, trying to look in every direction at once and take in as much as she could. One would think she had never seen the amusements of London or toured the wonders of Paris and Greece. Or even the splendors of her own city, just over the river.

But despite her worldliness, nothing had prepared her for this. Her realm was the stately trees and dignified brick row houses of Washington Square, the mansions and ballrooms of Fifth Avenue, the genteel rolling hills of Central Park. In the service of her journalism career and her work with Daniel, she had ventured into other parts of New York: dive bars in Five Points and the Bowery, the dripping, horrible interior of the Tombs prison, she'd even spent the night in one of the city's most exclusive brothels. She was well used to the variety of people and classes and cultures that crowded the city's streets, the array of languages one might hear as one traversed city blocks. But here, citizens from the entire metropolitan area—all of them, it seemed, save those of her own class—were at their absolute leisure. Married couples with faces of various hues, from sun pinked to dark brown, linked arms and strolled, laughing, while young men purchased tall glasses of a purple liquid for their sweethearts; several mothers, clearly impoverished but smiling broadly, laid out elaborate packed lunches for their thin-faced but also beaming children, taking advantage of tables arranged under a pavilion.

It was as if all the normal cares and woes of an entire populace had been collectively shed, and those assembled were devoted to nothing other than their own pleasure from the moment they left the boat or train that had brought them here to the moment they reboarded that conveyance and made their way home.

The boardwalk was lined with innumerable businesses and vendors of all stripes: there were camera obscuras, photography booths, hot sausages for sale, drink dispensaries, a replica of a German beer garden, and at least three merry-go-rounds. The tall slide of what turned out to be the Switchback Railway undulated from a dizzying height, and Genevieve stopped to watch a small car make its surprisingly gentle descent, its inhabitants whooping and shrieking as they glided over the metal tracks. Two iron piers stretched out into the sea, each swarming with people and lined with yet more impressive buildings containing amusements of all kinds—carnival games, food stalls, any type of drink one wished—all topped with an array of brightly waving flags.

The entire strip, of course, was lined by a wide stretch of gorgeous yellow beach, not rocky like some of the New England beaches but comprising pure golden sand, welcoming the ever-present fluxes of the Atlantic Ocean.

Callie seemed equally stunned.

"What shall we do first?" Daniel asked the group, grinning. With his hands shoved in his pockets and his hat thrust back on his head, he almost resembled one of the young mashers roaming the avenue. "Is anyone hungry?"

"Might we start at the ocean?" Genevieve asked. "It's so much less frightfully hot here, but a swim would still feel wonderful." The lovely beach, dotted with other bathers, beckoned enticingly.

"You don't want to visit the elephant?" Daniel teased.

"Later, absolutely," she grinned back. The giant structure loomed over the Palace, over the entirety of Surf Avenue. Tiny dots of figures were visible high up in the animal's howdah, transformed to an observatory.

"The beach it is, then," Daniel said, the others nodding enthusiastically.

Once they had changed in the various bathing houses scattered across the shore, they reassembled on the hot sand. Small children dug with shovels and pails; older children and adults splashed in the water. Maude and Ida, in rented bathing ensembles, clasped hands with Callie and ran to the tide line, giggling as the water rushed forward and submerged their ankles, running out of the surf and back into it again and again as if they were children themselves. Gavin waded up to his chest and dove underwater, swimming in sure, steady strokes.

The salty water was deliciously cool as it soaked into Genevieve's dark-blue bathing costume, plastering the wet fabric against her skin. She was a good swimmer and delighted in bobbing against the waves as they crashed into her chest, then in the feel of the currents as they gently pulled at her once she was beyond the waves. She closed her eyes and floated on her back, allowing her body to bob and drift for a few precious, quiet moments.

Sensing another presence beside her, Genevieve righted herself and stood, toes grazing sand. Daniel had swum up next to her and was turning in lazy circles.

"The one thing I've missed about Newport," he said, spreading his arms wide in the water. "I do love the ocean."

Genevieve thought of the whirl of society events and activities they were missing this summer: the elaborate lunches on trim, speedy yachts, watching a lawn tennis match at the Casino, the polite paddling at Bailey's Beach, the sumptuous balls in residents' giant cottages. She could be there now, writing about all of those happenings, rather than spending her summer in Manhattan, drooping in the excessive heat, being spied on by a peeper, and chasing her own tail in a pair of murder investigations that were producing neither stories for her editor nor satisfaction for the victims.

Did Daniel wish he had stayed in Rhode Island?

Did she?

Genevieve floated again, water filling her ears and muffling her senses, watching a few white, puffy clouds float by high above her. The salty water lapped at the sides of her face, stinging pleasantly.

"Are you regretful you're not there?" She couldn't bear to face him as she voiced the question, instead riding the gentle swells of the ocean, keeping her face turned to the sky. "Do you think we're wasting our time?"

"No." The reply was swift and forceful. "Not at all. You did the right thing agreeing to help Callie, Genevieve. *We're* doing the right thing."

Genevieve knew Daniel was correct. It *had* been the right thing to do. The question was, was it still the right thing? The feel of the peeper's moustache tickling her cheek came on as suddenly and clearly as if he were in the ocean with her, and Genevieve flinched wildly, floundering momentarily in the water before going under.

Her feet found purchase on the sandy ocean floor and she stood, gasping, furiously wiping the streaming salt water from her face.

"*Genevieve.* Genevieve, are you all right? What happened?" Daniel's concerned face was inches from hers; his hands hovered near her shoulders but didn't quite touch.

"I'm fine," she said, taking a deep breath to control the sudden pounding of her heart. "Just fine."

She wasn't fine, though. A killer was on the loose and had possibly been inside her house, despite what the police said about the man's harmlessness. Genevieve was made of strong stuff, but images from the past few weeks kept flashing in her mind: the intruder's shuttered face in the darkness of her bedroom, the tangle of cats tracking Violet's congealed blood across the floor of Chase's studio. A shudder ripped through her, despite the hot sunshine.

She looked toward the shore, at the relentlessly cheerful flags, at the flocks of people crowding the beach and the avenue. The giant elephant loomed over it all, casting its shadow long and wide. Suppressing another shudder, Genevieve followed the waves and began to swim toward the shimmering, golden sand.

CHAPTER 14

"You're heading in? I was coming out to meet you." Ida halted Genevieve's progress back to shore, standing stomach high in the foamy brown water.

"Too much sun," Genevieve lied.

"Oh," said Ida, obviously disappointed. Maude waved at them from the beach, where she and Callie remained wading up to their ankles. "Maude is fearful of jellyfish. I was hoping to splash around a bit with you two. Or would you rather be alone?" Ida peered at Daniel, who was standing nearby but not quite within earshot. "Did you have a row with your beau?" she asked, dropping her voice.

A blush stained Genevieve's cheeks, which she hoped Ida would mistake for sun. "He's not my beau," she said, glancing in Daniel's direction. "Just a friend."

"Really?" Ida swam in a small circle. "I don't think it would be possible to be *just friends* with a man that handsome." She grinned wickedly. "You must be quite strong willed."

Genevieve laughed despite herself. It was exactly the kind of thing Callie would say, and she told Ida so.

"A fondness for attractive men is a trait Callie and I share," Ida laughed. "I understand what she sees in your brother." She looked in the direction Gavin had swum.

The comment was unsettling. Ida knew about Callie's relationship with Walter and therefore must know that Callie and Gavin were not a couple. Women had always flocked to Gavin, and historically, he had been an incorrigible flirt. She hoped her brother wasn't toying with Callie's affections. "And your fiancé?" she asked, steering the conversation onto more comfortable ground. "Does he fall into that category?"

"Very much so." Ida beamed. "My Mikey is a good man, who only wants to take care of me. He may not be as adventuresome as I'd like, but I've had my fair share of adventures. It's time to settle down." She swirled once more in the water, then began to walk in the direction of the beach. "You're right, we should go in. I'll be a bride in two weeks, and it wouldn't do to freckle now."

After changing out of her wet bathing costume and back into her light day dress, Genevieve still felt a bit sticky and was sure the condition of her hair was unspeakable.

"There are many wonderful restaurants," Daniel offered, once they had all gathered again at the foot of one of the iron piers. "Shall we try one?"

"I don't think I'm in any state for fine dining," Callie laughed, patting her hair, though Genevieve noted with envy it retained its neat style.

Gavin smiled at her. "You look perfect," he said, "but follow me."

He led them to a German vendor selling hot sausages in rolls.

"How do you know about this?" Genevieve asked.

"I've been here a time or two before," he said with an enigmatic smile. "This stall is a must when visiting."

The man behind the counter handed over the sausage rolls, which were topped with a smear of hot mustard and some fragrant pickled cabbage. "They come with mustard and sauerkraut," Daniel explained. "Wienerwurst, though the locals call them weenies."

"We have to get drinks from the Inexhaustible Cow," Maude exclaimed, leading the group with their sausage rolls to a small circular kiosk. Inside was a large sculpture of a cow, and from its udders one could purchase milk, beer, sarsaparilla, and even champagne. Children crowded around its counters, drinking milk dispensed by young, pretty servers dressed as milkmaids.

It was ridiculous. It was wonderful. Genevieve accepted a glass of beer and sat at one of the nearby benches with her friends and brother.

The sun was slowly starting to descend, and a cooling breeze had picked up, even though it wouldn't be fully dark for at least two hours. The food and drink, combined with the general jolly atmosphere of people watching on Surf Avenue, soothed Genevieve until she found herself laughing with abandon at Ida's recounting of the last time she and Maude had gone sea bathing (when the pair actually had encountered a jellyfish), and the troubling visions she'd had in the water gradually receded.

Over the next hour, Genevieve allowed those images to continue to subside. For a short time, she forgot about the murders, about Jack the Ripper and Jack the Peeper, forgot about Violet's cut throat. Forgot about Daniel's bloody, dazed face in the gasworks. About what it had felt like to pull the trigger of a gun aimed squarely at Tommy Meade's head. Instead, she lost herself in the absurdity of riding a painted zebra in a carousel and laughing at Gavin, similarly situated on a hippogriff. She thrilled in being hoisted to

a dizzying height in a basket beneath a balloon, all courtesy of a small crane, which lifted her and Daniel far above
the avenue. Maude refused the ride, so Daniel repeated
the adventure with Ida, followed by Callie and Gavin. She
had a second glass of beer and a small, delicious fried cake
dipped in icing sugar, and was persuaded to ride Shaw's
Channel Chute by Ida, decidedly the less timid of her two
new friends.

Twilight was descending, and both electric lights and
gaslights were beginning to sparkle along the boardwalk,
along with jaunty strings of Chinese lanterns. Orchestras
were taking their place in large, open-air ballrooms, tuning
their instruments, as people began to gather in anticipation of dancing. Genevieve saw with delight that one of the
orchestras consisted entirely of women, all dressed in white.

"They're from Vienna," Daniel said, following her gaze.
"As competent as any band you've heard."

"We've yet to visit the elephant," Callie cried, walking so fast and happily she was nearly skipping. Genevieve
was glad to see Coney Island was having an ameliorative
effect on Callie as well; her friend seemed more like her
old self than she had at any point since she had returned to
Genevieve's life a few weeks prior.

Daniel led them to the entrance of the colossal structure,
which was located in a toe of the creature's left front leg,
and paid everyone's admission fee, a dime each. Genevieve
hesitated for a moment, letting the others go first.

"Do you not wish to climb?" Daniel asked, pausing as
he waited for her to accompany him.

The behemoth loomed above them. Despite the illumination from artificial light up and down the boardwalk, the
area under the giant structure was in shadow. Genevieve
peered in and gazed at the spiral staircase that wound its

way up the front leg, the footsteps and laughter of the others echoing down the hollow space.

There was something about the colossal elephant that unnerved her, now that darkness was approaching, though she couldn't put her finger on what. Perhaps it was its sheer bulk, combined with its zoological design. To her mind, it strove for but contained none of the whimsy of its smaller cousin the Inexhaustible Cow.

Instead, the elephantine colossus was perturbing, as if it could suddenly come to life and begin moving down the boardwalk with heavy, booming treads, smashing stalls and booths, scattering those visiting Coney Island and chasing them screaming into the night.

Genevieve shook her head sharply to clear it of the gruesome vision, then managed a smile for Daniel, who had begun to sport a worried look again, as he had when they were in the ocean. "Let's go," she said.

Up the spiral staircase they walked, the rounded walls of the leg's interior feeling as though they were pressing in on her, despite the various windows punctuating the structure's exterior. The climb seemed to go on forever. Genevieve paused at one of the windows and marveled at how high they'd already ascended.

"It's at least twelve stories tall, altogether," Daniel remarked. "I'd say we're about the equivalent of four flights up right now. We're almost to the top of the staircase; let's keep going."

They emerged into an open cavernous space, painted to resemble the interior of the beast's stomach. There were patrons seated at a restaurant, there was a bar, and Daniel pointed out meeting rooms down the hall, which could be rented if one desired.

"There's also sleeping accommodations for rent on the upper floors," he remarked. "Though I've begun to hear tell that they are often used for, um, unsavory purposes."

Genevieve's eyes flew to the ceiling, opening wide. She knew what Daniel meant: that women who sold their bodies for trade sometimes utilized the elephant for their business.

"But the public areas are respectable, for the most part." He grinned. "Families tour the elephant regularly. It's a great hit with children."

Indeed, several children were running in circles, shrieking with joy at being inside the elephant's stomach, as their parents sipped glasses of cider and smiled indulgently from the bar. But the somewhat graphic paintings of internal organs did nothing to ease Genevieve's discomfort about the building; if anything, they made the entire affair even more macabre and odd.

Which, she supposed, was meant to be part of its appeal.

It was not appealing to her.

Daniel led her through several other rooms meant to represent the animal's innards, including a museum located in the left lung, where they ran into Ida and Maude, who greeted them merrily before moving on, and into a cheek room, from which they could look out of windows in the location of the elephant's eyes. The railings of the Channel Chute, located directly outside the structure, blocked a portion of the view.

"The best views are from the howdah," Daniel said. "Are you up for one last climb?"

She was, and up another staircase they went, finally arriving at an observation deck under a painted wooden canopy.

Even in the dwindling light, the view was nothing short of remarkable. The glittering ocean stretched on in an endless, nearly black sweep, the sky above it just a few shades lighter as the sun fully dipped below the horizon line. Marshes, the bay, and farmland were laid out before them, and the dazzling lights of the boardwalk, the ballrooms, the vendors, and other amusements glowed in the night air.

From here, Genevieve forgot she was 175 feet in the air on a wooden-and-tin building shaped like an elephant. With a gentle sea wind caressing her face and teasing strands of her hair and no walls to constrain the panorama spread before them, being in the howdah was almost akin to flying.

She leaned against the balustrade of the railing and stared at the ocean.

"Isn't it breathtaking?" Ida's happy voice turned her head. The tall, pretty woman was at the opposite balustrade, her arms stretched wide.

"Do back away, Ida." Maude sat at the top of the stairs.

"She's afraid of heights," Ida said, smiling kindly at her friend. "Just stay there, Maude; I'll come down in a minute. Maybe we can figure out a way to slide down the trunk." She winked at Genevieve.

Maude rolled her eyes in turn, but even under the electric lights fitted within the howdah, Genevieve thought she looked pale and noted how she gripped the iron banister of the staircase. Her fear of heights appeared quite serious.

"I'll wait in the stomach, Ida," Maude said, slowly making her way down the stairs.

"Never mind, I'm coming." Ida sighed. "Have you seen Callie?" she asked Genevieve on her way down the steps.

Genevieve shook her head. "You all went up before us, so I'm not sure where they are."

"This elephant is quite large; it could be easy to get lost," Ida said. "Particularly if two people wanted to be alone." She winked again, then disappeared.

Genevieve started slightly. Was Ida referring to Callie and Gavin? Or her and Daniel?

He continued to lean on the railing, looking into the night, but smiled her way once she rejoined him there.

They were not alone, of course. Plenty of other visitors came and went from the howdah, but many didn't stay long, as the view was diminishing in the increasing darkness.

They watched the night rise in silence, the exclamations of the other visitors swirling around them.

"Do we keep going?" The question burst from her before she could help it. Though they had discussed the matter briefly while swimming, a kernel of doubt plagued her, and she found herself needing further confirmation that continuing the investigation was the right thing to do.

It was unlike her to be so indecisive.

Daniel's eyes slid to hers, thoughtful. He knew what she meant.

"Let's see what the next few days bring," he finally said. "If Shipman doesn't appear and nothing new presents itself, perhaps we should return to Newport and take a break. Rupert and Esmie would be glad of it, as would your family."

Genevieve turned this over in her mind. The relief at having some kind of plan after days of feeling stalled, thin as the plan was, acted as a balm.

"You can stay with me, you know," Daniel continued, quietly enough to avoid being overheard by the few others on the observation deck. "If your own home doesn't feel secure at present. Gavin, too, for propriety's sake. It's likely no cooler than your townhouse, but Asher would be there.

I could even install a few of the Toughs, if it would make you feel better."

Slight embarrassment washed over Genevieve; was her lingering fear from the intruder's presence in her bedroom really so transparent? But a stronger emotion was a surprising gratitude at Daniel's thoughtfulness. Though she really shouldn't be surprised; she had learned how observant Daniel was during their acquaintance.

"Thank you," she said, and meant it sincerely. "Let me think on it. I'm not sure I'd be able to convince Gavin." She tried to picture Gavin and Paddy sharing a breakfast table and failed utterly.

"I believe your brother would move mountains to make you feel safe," Daniel said, his tone serious. "As would I."

She met his dark-blue eyes. The wind tousled his hair, already riotously curling from the salt water and sea air. Genevieve longed to reach out and smooth those untamed locks, to run her fingers through their thickness.

Something of her thoughts must have shown in her face, for Daniel's eyes shifted in response to whatever he read there, and his lips parted slightly. His fingers closed over hers, and he took a step closer, the distance between them narrowing to the barest of inches. Genevieve was suddenly, deeply aware of several things at once: Of the way the wind on her skin made it tingle. Of the rapid shallowness of her own breath.

Of the fact that they were now alone on the howdah, the other guests having departed, with all of Brooklyn and the Atlantic Ocean spread at their feet like a visual feast laid out for them and them alone.

"Oh good, you're still here. I was hoping to find you. Oh!"

Genevieve and Daniel flinched away from each other.

Maude was standing at the top of the stairs again, her hand pressed against her mouth, her eyes wide. She turned to descend, but Genevieve called after her.

"Maude, wait. Is everything all right?"

Maude paused a few steps down. She glanced at them and then away quickly. "I didn't mean to interrupt. It's just that I can't find Ida. Can you help?"

★   ★   ★

Genevieve followed Maude down the stairs and into the stomach room, Daniel behind them. From there, they poked their heads into both lungs and the heart. Ida was nowhere.

"Do you mind checking the cheek?" Maude asked. "Even that room is too high for me, with the view of the Chute. Gives me the willies." She crossed her arms across her chest and mock shivered, though it was obvious from her earlier behavior that her anxiety around high places was genuine.

"Of course," Genevieve said. "I'm surprised you came inside the elephant at all, given your fear."

Maude shrugged. "Ida often talks me into adventures that are more comfortable for her than me," she said. "I believe marriage may calm her some."

"How did you and Ida become parted?" Daniel asked.

"I needed to freshen up," Maude said. "Ida said she would wait for me, but when I came out, she was gone."

"And how long ago was that?"

"Maybe a half hour? I waited for a bit, thinking maybe she had gone to freshen up too, in the end, and we'd some-how just missed each other, but then I checked the WC, and she wasn't there. I assumed she'd found one of our gang and have been wandering around looking ever since."

"I'm sure you're correct and she is with Callie and Gavin, wherever they are. Why don't you wait here," Genevieve suggested, gesturing toward the bar. Maude agreed and perched on the edge of a stool, peering after them as they made their way toward the front of the structure to the cheek observation room.

Inside, the crowds hadn't thinned with the fall of night, but their character was shifting as the families with children departed for home and a slightly seedier element started to emerge. She quietly remarked upon it to Daniel on their way.

"You remember what I told you earlier, about the rooms upstairs," he said wryly.

She glanced back at the bar in concern. "Will Maude be safe?"

"Of course. Coney Island isn't dangerous, though it can get colorful. Well, it's not overly dangerous here."

"What do you mean?"

Daniel lowered his voice. "There are other parts of the island that have given over to gang life. Police have long since stopped trying to control it, and now they simply cordon the area off and try to keep any unsavory characters from the resort areas."

The hairs on her arms stood up, and Genevieve suddenly felt cold, despite the warm, closed air inside the elephant. Daniel saw her discomfort.

"Don't worry. We'll look in the observation room and be right back. Maude will be fine."

"And then, perhaps, we should gather the others and make our way home," Genevieve said. Worry about their current predicament, which had ebbed and flowed throughout the day like the tide itself, was now creeping back in.

And now there was the moment with Daniel in the howdah to add to her concerns. Unless she was sorely mistaken, she believed they had been about to kiss.

A faint blush rose to her face as she contemplated the moment.

Yes. They would have kissed, had Maude not appeared at the top of the stairs.

Or at least, Daniel would have kissed her.

And she knew, without having to think about it at all, that she would have kissed him back.

Poor Maude, to have walked in on such a scene. She had seemed more embarrassed than either Genevieve or Daniel.

A mere moment later, Genevieve found herself in exactly Maude's shoes as she and Daniel entered the elephant's cheek and Callie and Gavin guiltily jumped away from each other.

CHAPTER 15

It was hard to say who was more flabbergasted, Genevieve or, judging by their almost comically shocked expressions, Callie and Gavin.

"Callie?" Genevieve reached for her friend, but Callie sped past her, her face buried in her hands. Gavin stared after her, looking stunned, gripping his hat with white knuckles.

"Gavin, what on earth are you thinking?" Genevieve cried, before spinning on her heel and chasing after Callie.

She caught up with Callie at the entrance to the stomach room, Maude's waiting and Ida's temporary disappearance forgotten.

"*Callie.*" Genevieve grabbed her friend's arm to stop her progress. "What was that? Callie, come on, stop and talk to me."

Tears were streaming down Callie's face as she turned, and Genevieve and Callie were starting to attract concerned glances from the other patrons of the elephant. Genevieve led Callie into the nearby lung museum, which was blessedly empty.

She pulled a handkerchief from her bag and handed it to Callie, who dabbed at her face. Genevieve's emotions were ricocheting between confusion, concern, and a tiny, bright glow of joy. "What is going on between you and Gavin, Callie?"

Callie's face reflected her own wild array of feelings: embarrassment, defiance, heartache but also hope.

"I always wondered if you knew," Callie said, twisting the handkerchief between her fingers.

"Knew what?"

"That I love Gavin. I always have, ever since we were young."

Genevieve's heart plunged, then soared, as she tried to wrap her head around this astonishing piece of news.

Callie must have interpreted her stunned expression. "You know we had a flirtation when we were young, Genevieve."

"All my friends had a flirtation with Gavin!"

Callie slanted her a look. "Perhaps ours was more than a flirtation. At least, it felt that way to me. But he was a young bachelor, and I was barely out of the proverbial schoolroom—I knew it wasn't serious on his part, but I couldn't help it. I fell in love, and part of me has loved him ever since."

"You were still *in* the schoolroom, if I have my timing correct. This occurred when you were what, sixteen? Exactly what kind of relationship are we talking about here?" Images she didn't want blazed bright in her mind before she snuffed them out. Genevieve wasn't a prude but still found her hand had made its way up to her mouth.

Had her brother compromised her best friend?

"Fifteen," Callie corrected her. "Oh, don't be dramatic. And it was a few stolen kisses, nothing more."

"I hardly think I'm the one being dramatic. You've kissed plenty of men; you know that kissing does not equate to love." Even as she said the words, Genevieve knew she was being unfair.

One knew when one was in love.

Callie looked at her with big green eyes full of shimmering tears. "I was only three years from making my debut, Genevieve. Some small, secret part of me hoped he'd actually offer for me. But it soon became clear that wasn't going to happen. Then he made his plans to head abroad, and I knew that was that. And yes, I kissed other men. If I was going to marry one, I ought to find out if I liked kissing him first, oughtn't I?"

Over the years Callie had had plenty of proposals of marriage. A dreadful feeling sank over Genevieve. "Callie, did you never accept any proposals because you were holding out for Gavin?"

Callie scoffed at this. "Of course not! I knew he was gone to me. But maybe . . . maybe I never found anyone I liked kissing as well," she finished sadly.

"Oh, Callie." Genevieve felt sad as well. His whole life, Gavin had acted like a will-o'-the-wisp, never content to stay put. The thought of Callie pining away for him for years made her ache.

Though, could Gavin be ready to change? He was taking that position in Chicago, after all, and was so altered since his return from Africa.

Perhaps he was ready to settle now?

A new thought struck her: What about Walter?

"I don't love Walter, nor do I think he loves me," Callie sighed when Genevieve posed the question. "We are fond of each other, but it is more a business relationship than anything. He is a convenience."

"Does he know you feel this way?" Genevieve asked. Privately, she thought it was doubtful. She had seen the way Walter looked at Callie.

"Well, he must, mustn't he? This is what girls in my position do. We align ourselves with wealthy men so as not to become shopgirls like poor Maude, toiling away for meager wages, hoping some man will marry us. I share Walter's bed, he lets me live in style. I happen to model for him as well. He's so sentimental, he's taken to calling me his muse." She snorted a small laugh and dabbed her eyes again. "Oh, Genevieve. I feel I've made a mess of everything."

Genevieve wrapped her arms around her friend, pulling the smaller woman close. She smelled of salt water and lavender. "We'll figure it all out, I promise. And you've made no mess; you're just trying to survive."

Underneath her ricocheting emotions was another: anger, again, at Callie's situation; at the fact that because of unscrupulous investors and society's limitations, she was forced into her current role.

Once Callie's eyes were dry, she and Genevieve began to make their way back toward the stomach room, but Daniel found them in the corridor first.

"I couldn't find you," he said, a frown marring his brow. "I was getting worried."

At the sight of Daniel, thoughts of Maude waiting at the bar and Ida's disappearance rushed back in. It was past time to leave, now, and Genevieve said as much. "Callie, are you up for seeing Gavin, or would you prefer he make his way home without us?"

"No, I can see him. We'll figure it out, as you said." She offered a tremulous smile at them both.

"Have you seen Ida?" Genevieve asked Callie as they approached Maude, who jumped from her stool anxiously at their arrival. "Maude lost track of her."

"No, not since we came up the stairs," Callie said, looking from face to face. "She and Maude scampered away, and Gavin and I . . ."

Maude didn't let Callie finish her unspoken thought. "I've been asking folks here," she said, wringing her hands. "The bartender said he saw a woman of Ida's description leave with a man."

Genevieve frowned. A man? What man? "Daniel was with me, and Gavin was . . ." She faltered, not sure how much to reveal about whatever was happening between Callie and Gavin.

Gavin walked up. "With Callie," he said firmly. "We haven't seen Ida anywhere." One had to know him to know he was blushing slightly under his tanned skin. Genevieve narrowed her eyes at her brother, signaling they would have words on the matter later, even as he affected an innocent look under his blush.

Daniel called the bartender over. "This young lady says you saw our friend? Tall, slender, brown hair, in a pink-and-white-striped dress?"

The barkeep, a wiry fellow with a balding head and a shifty look about him, nodded. "Yeah, she was here earlier. Hard to miss a looker like that."

"And she left with a man? Did you see what he looked like?"

"Nah, didn't get a good look at him. He had his hat pulled low and coat collar pulled up. I didn't pay that much attention, but I did think he was awfully bundled up for this weather. They went thataway." The bartender jerked his head toward where the stairs from the entrance emerged.

"That's the way in, though," Genevieve mused to nobody in particular. "Where is the way out?"

Daniel pointed in the opposite direction. "Down a different leg over there, near the lung museum."

Maude crossed her arms around her chest as though she were chilled.

Daniel turned his attention back to the barkeep, snagging the man's sleeve to get his attention. "They went that way and didn't come back?"

The bartender shrugged. "Maybe they did and I didn't see them. Busy tonight."

The crowds were still thick within the elephant's innards; people were coming and going, drinking and laughing, but not so many that a tall, striking girl like Ida would be hard to see. *Where is she?* Though Genevieve told herself Ida could be anywhere within the giant structure and surely it was only that their paths had not converged, a new fear began to ripple in her stomach.

★ ★ ★

Daniel poked his head through the door that led to the entrance stairs, the others crowding behind him. The wrought-iron spiral staircase disappeared from view after a turn or two.

Could Ida and this mysterious man have left the elephant and gone down the wrong staircase? It was possible.

Other, more worrisome scenarios, though, raced through his brain. The gang violence he had mentioned to Genevieve was quite real, and a little more serious than he had let on. While the area was mainly safe, unsavory characters were known to slip in to where the amusements were and try to take advantage of unwary visitors.

The sound of a pair of voices, male and female, echoed up the staircase. Daniel leaned over the railing until he saw two heads appear, both varying shades of red. He shook his head at the group, and they backed out of the entryway to allow the couple, who glanced at them curiously, to enter the stomach.

"Should we divide into groups and continue searching?" Genevieve asked. "I only met Ida today. Would she go off with a strange man?" She directed this query to Callie and Maude, who knew Ida better.

Callie and Maude exchanged a look. "What?" Genevieve asked. "I thought she was happy to be getting married."

Callie sighed. "She is, but I'm not sure it's a true love match. Well, perhaps it is on Mikey's part, but for Ida . . ."

"She wants security," Maude said quietly. She met Callie's eye quickly and looked away fast. "Ida likes Mike, we all do; he's a treat. But mostly she wants to know she'll be taken care of."

Daniel didn't judge this an iota, though Maude looked embarrassed for her friend. Gavin shoved his hands in his pockets and frowned, turning away from the group and scanning the crowd.

"But would she go off with a stranger?" Genevieve pressed. "So soon to securing her goal?"

Maude and Callie exchanged another glance.

"I did tell you she liked adventure," said Maude.

"She's probably just waiting on the boardwalk," Callie said. "We should go outside and check."

"She might have gone poking about more in here, though," Maude said, her face pinched with worry. "With this fellow."

"She wanted to slide down the trunk," Genevieve added. Daniel heard the first traces of panic in her voice, and it was hard for his own anxiety not to respond in kind.

He ruthlessly tamped the feeling down, needing to keep a clear head in the face of everyone else's mounting apprehension. "She's probably just canoodling in a corner somewhere," he said quietly, though he wasn't sure he believed it. Was Ida in actual danger, or was she chasing a last-minute adventure, heady with the sun and carefree ways of Coney Island before she settled into the role of a wife? "We should split up eventually, yes," he added. "But first let's take another look at where she was last seen."

He returned to the staircase and looked down, listening hard. No voices or footfalls carried up. Daniel put his hands on his hips and slowly circled the small entryway, spotting something he had missed before: a door labeled STAFF ONLY.

The knob turned easily. The room was larger than the entryway but with none of the finished walls and ceilings. Here the skeleton of the building was exposed, the beams and bare metal that constituted the elephant's frame. He was in the vicinity of the creature's neck, he surmised. The plain metal walls and exposed support pilings gave the room an industrial feel, so different from the playfulness the architect had attempted in the interior.

"Ida?" he called. His voice echoed through the hollow space.

Nothing.

The others had followed him in.

"You think she might have wanted to explore?" he asked Maude. There was another door across the room, presumably leading to the opposite leg.

"Look." Gavin pointed, and they all looked up. A ladder in the center of the wall to their left led to what appeared to be the mouth of a tunnel. Daniel puzzled at it for a moment, until it hit him all at once: they were looking at the start of the elephant's trunk.

Maude gasped and shoved her hands against her mouth, her face draining of color.

A small piece of bright-pink-and-white-striped fabric was caught in the head of a screw at the opening of the tunnel.

Daniel leapt forward, closely followed by Gavin, and scrambled up the ladder. Gavin waited at its base, one hand on a rung, ready to climb if needed. "Stay back," he ordered the others as they started to crowd.

The tunnel's interior was swallowed by blackness only a few feet in, but there was just enough light that he could see it sharply descended. Daniel pulled the piece of fabric loose and considered it.

Presuming Ida had indeed slid down the trunk, rather than having simply climbed the ladder to look down, could the fabric have caught because her skirts or sleeves were in the way of her descent?

Or did it suggest something more sinister? That perhaps she hadn't slid of her own free will but had somehow been pushed or forced down the slide, and her dress had become caught in the scuffle?

He glanced at the wall opposite the ladder, which seemed to separate these interior workings from the vast stomach room. The cheek room with the observatory through the eyes was nearby too. The walls didn't appear to be that thick; if Ida had been in trouble, surely someone would have heard her scream?

As if his thought had summoned the sound, a chorus of screams ebbed through the exterior walls, filling the room and raising the hair on the back of his neck. Callie and Maude clutched at each other, and Genevieve took a few steps toward him with wide eyes.

"It's the Chute," Gavin said, though he had noticeably paled as well. "One of the main drops is right outside. You can hear the wheels on the rails. Listen."

Callie breathed an audible, shaky sigh of relief, but otherwise everyone remained silent, listening as the clacking of the Chute's wheels lessened and the happy screams grew fainter, signaling that the amusement car was circling to the other side of the elephant.

"Ida?" Daniel yelled into the tunnel once the Chute was quiet. "Ida, are you down there?" What if she had become stuck?

Only quiet answered.

He turned to the group from his perch atop the ladder, seeing the same emotions he felt echoed in their faces: concern, worry, helplessness.

"Where does the trunk lead?" Gavin asked.

Daniel climbed down. "Callie, wait at the bar with Maude. I don't think we should split up after all. It's possible Ida slid down and climbed back up the stairs and will be looking for you there. And if she's not below, we'll come back for you and begin a more organized search." He wondered if by that time they would need to alert the authorities. The last trains from Coney Island left at ten o'clock, and surely that hour was drawing near.

"Genevieve, Gavin, come with me."

The group scattered, exchanging not another word, Callie pulling an increasingly stricken Maude out toward the main room of the elephant while Daniel thundered down the stairs, Genevieve and Gavin close on his heels.

The moment was so eerily reminiscent of what he had experienced a few weeks prior, running down the slippery stairs outside the Otts' cottage, that his vision tilted slightly and he paused, for the barest of moments, to get his bearings.

"Daniel," Genevieve said, the urgency in her voice clear as she was forced to pause behind him, directly at his left shoulder.

"I know." He started running again.

"*Hurry.*"

"I know."

Once again, voices drifted up the stairs as another couple ascended, likely not Ida and the mystery man, as they were speaking in a different language. Greek, Daniel thought.

"Coming through," he yelled down, nearly upon the couple as he rounded the next corner. The man pulled the woman against the wall in alarm as they pounded past, a look of complete affront on his heavily bearded face.

Curses in Greek rained down on their heads as they continued.

They were almost to the bottom. The sound of Daniel's own harsh breath consumed him, followed by the cold glare of stars in an inky night sky as he burst from the staircase, past the startled attendant, and onto the boardwalk. The same stars that had shone on the beach at Newport, the same that had twinkled indifferently behind Tommy Meade's gun.

Daniel whirled, yanking his focus back to the present moment, trying to find where the elephant's trunk terminated.

"There," Genevieve said, grabbing his arm and pulling him toward a small shed at the base of the trunk.

Gavin got to the door first and tugged the handle, but it was locked. He pounded on the door. "Ida? Ida, are you in there?"

Daniel pushed Gavin aside and pulled at the recalcitrant door, then turned, ramming his shoulder against it. Gavin joined him. Somewhere in the recesses of his mind he heard the aggrieved cries of the elephant's attendant and Genevieve's frantic response, but he tuned them out and focused his awareness solely on the wood at his shoulder, willing it to give.

Come on. *Come on.*

As if he had commanded it, the door burst open under their combined pressure, and Daniel and Gavin stumbled into the tiny room.

There was a moment of complete, utter stillness when he was simply unable to move, barely able to breathe, as his overworked mind processed the grisly scene before him.

They were too late.

Ida was dead, left nude, her cheerful pink-and-white frock bunched in a corner. Like the others, her neck had been slashed, so recently that bright-red blood still pulsed from her wound, the shiny, gruesome puddle underneath her growing ever wider.

She was posed on the floor of the shed with her legs curled into her chest, one hand reaching long.

Her sightless gaze looked to her outstretched arm.

"No," came Genevieve's anguished shout from behind him. It broke through his temporary stupor, and he turned to take her in his arms.

Then a scream shattered the night air, and the whole world spun into motion.

CHAPTER 16

Detective Longstreet looked shaken. Even as he marched through the scene purposefully, barking orders at his men, forcing the remaining gawking crowds even farther back to create a wider perimeter, Daniel recognized the extreme unease playing around the detective's features.

Throughout his tasks, Longstreet glared at Daniel and Genevieve as though Ida's dead body were their fault.

The scream had come from Maude, who had followed them down the stairs, too sick with worry to wait in the bar. She collapsed in Callie's arms at the sight of Ida's fresh corpse, hysterical. Callie had looked about to collapse herself, and in three quick strides Gavin was at her side, supporting both women just outside the door to the shed. Strollers along the boardwalk, vendors, people enjoying the dances, had come running at the sound of Maude's cries, and dozens of horrified onlookers had clustered at the door, men shouting and women gasping and crying. The local authorities had arrived quickly, but Daniel was able to survey the scene before he, too, was pushed back into the throngs.

"We must have missed him by minutes," Genevieve had said in those few moments before the police arrived, her voice strangled.

He knew who she meant.

The killer. Whoever was cutting the throats of these beautiful young women had been in that shed, with Ida, mere moments before they arrived.

Had been strolling through the stomach room upstairs, targeting his prey.

Daniel's stomach lurched.

Had they, in fact, been followed from Manhattan?

Ida's body was still warm, her skin glowing, a faint blush still on her cheeks, but she had died within seconds of having her carotid artery cut.

Shoving the thought that the body he was examining had been living and breathing no less than ten minutes prior, Daniel had crouched down and tried to memorize exactly how she had been left. He knew he had precious little time before the local police were on the scene. Alarm bells were already clanging in the distance.

Her knees were not stacked, he saw, but the top one was pulled into her chest, the same arm lying atop it, and the bottom knee pointing down. There was something about her extended bottom arm that troubled him, particularly married with how her sightless eyes were fixed on that hand.

As if she were reaching for something just out of her grasp.

It was deliberate. This was not an accidental way for a body to fall.

That, combined with her disrobing, was disturbingly similar to how Violet's body had been arranged.

One bloody footprint pointed toward a small back window in the shed.

It was the only window open.

"Come, now, move out of here, we've got to secure this area. Detectives from Manhattan are on their way." The police had arrived, hustling Daniel and Genevieve out of the shed and into the night.

They were allowed to stay in close proximity, within the ring of the officers, claiming their association with the deceased. Gavin had taken Callie and Maude to rest on a nearby bench. When Daniel looked over to check on them, Callie appeared to be in a state of shock, white about the lips, staring down at her fingers as they twisted continually in her lap. Maude laid her head on Gavin's shoulder, her screams subsiding into low, choked sobs.

News of the murder spread like wildfire. Over the course of the next hour, the crowds ebbed and flowed, trying to catch a glimpse of the macabre sight. The local police formed a resolute barrier around the shed, but Daniel caught them exchanging uneasy glances with each other or staring into the gathered onlookers as if trying to spot the killer in their midst.

Daniel knew the man was long gone.

"Why am I unsurprised to see the two of you here?" Longstreet approached him and Genevieve, his eyes narrowing over his moustache. "Miss Stewart, I see you didn't heed my warning to leave town. And now here we are."

Genevieve's brows shot to her hairline. "You're not suggesting my presence had something to do with Miss Gouse's murder?" she hissed quietly. "You've obviously a dangerous killer on the loose, who is targeting a specific population, yet are doing nothing to secure these women's safety."

"But how is it that *you* happened to be at the scene of the crime for Miss Templeton's death, and now Miss Gouse's?"

Longstreet snapped back, his voice tight with anger. "Do you know something you're not telling me? There will be severe consequences, Miss Stewart, if you are withholding information for a *story*"—he fairly sneered the word—"or obstructing police business."

Genevieve gasped.

"Miss Stewart knows nothing of these crimes beyond what you do, Longstreet," Daniel interrupted angrily. "She is guilty of no more than being friends with the very women who are dying while supposedly under *your* protection."

Longstreet's nostrils flared in rage, and he turned from them abruptly, shouting at the crowd to move aside to allow the police photographer, Dagmar Hansen, into the shed. As when Dagmar had photographed Violet's body, Daniel felt Genevieve flinch at each sound of the photographer's loud, popping flash.

"Genevieve," a voice called. Luther Franklin was at the forefront of the onlookers, pressing against the solid arm of an officer.

Daniel's jaw clenched; he didn't like Luther, and the feeling was mutual.

"What's happening?" Luther asked as Genevieve edged closer. "We got word there was a murder. What are you doing here?"

"It's another model," she said, keeping her voice low so the other bystanders wouldn't overhear. The circles under her eyes had deepened, and no wonder. They'd been at Coney Island for hours now, the last trains having long since departed. "We were with her before she disappeared."

Luther's eyes flicked to Daniel, who met them coldly. "You okay, toots?" Luther asked.

Daniel bristled, both at the suggestion that Genevieve wasn't okay with him and at the familiar nickname.

She nodded, but crossed her arms over her chest and looked over her shoulder at the shed. "That's three now, along with Bea and Violet."

Luther emitted a low whistle and pushed his sweat-stained hat farther back on his head. The press of bodies around the shed, though diminishing due to the late hour, had pushed the temperature up regardless of the night ocean breezes wafting across the boardwalk.

"We got quite a story here," Luther said quietly. "Cops can't keep this under wraps much longer."

As if on cue, a tall blond man, so thin his face was almost cadaverous, shouted over the murmur of the crowd. "Detective Longstreet! Jim Crawford of the *World*. Can you comment on the rumors that a girl's throat was cut? Has Jack the Ripper started murdering women in New York?"

At the mention of the Ripper, the murmurs of those gathered turned into a low rumble.

Genevieve wasted no time but strode close to Longstreet, her hands planted on her hips. Daniel stayed close at her back, keeping a wary eye on the crowd, who were growing more restless with the mention of the notorious killer. The police were having a hard time holding them back.

Longstreet favored them both with a cold stare. He glanced at the man from the *World*, who was desperately waving to get his attention, then back at Genevieve, seeming to wrestle with a decision.

Daniel followed Genevieve's lead and waited.

"Fine," the detective finally spat. "Write your story, Miss Stewart. You will have the department's assistance if, and *only* if, you firmly state that Jack the Ripper had no part in these murders and is not in New York City. I'll send notice to Mr. Horace of these requirements as well."

Genevieve extended her hand, and after regarding it for a moment with extreme distaste, Longstreet shook it.

"I'll be working with my colleague Luther Franklin on this," she said. "He will abide by the same rules."

Longstreet nodded shortly. "We know Luther. I'll send Dagmar to you once he's finished. I assume you'll want access to the photographs."

"That we will." Daniel could hear the faint exhilaration in her voice under her exhaustion.

"You owe me, Miss Stewart," Longstreet said. Daniel tensed; he didn't like the undercurrent of threat he heard in the other man's voice. "Remember that."

It was all he could do to not tackle Longstreet as he moved away.

But when Genevieve turned to him, his anger at Longstreet turned to sheer concern for her. She looked as though she was about to drop.

"You need to rest," he urged. "Let's get back. You can meet with Dagmar and Luther tomorrow."

Genevieve hesitated, biting her lower lip, a gesture he had learned signaled indecisiveness. "A few minutes more," she finally said. Longstreet had signaled to the officer that Luther could come forward, and Genevieve moved to confer with him, their heads bowed together.

Daniel had long since removed his hat, leaving it on the bench where the others sat, and ran his hand through his hair. He moved toward that bench now; Maude had fallen asleep, her head in Callie's lap, and Gavin had left to find them some sort of conveyance home.

Callie still appeared stunned, sitting rigid and terrified, running her hand down Maude's arm in a soothing gesture.

He crouched next to the bench. "How are you faring?"

"I just want to go home," she said. "Though with Walter still upstate, I'm going to stay at the Stewarts'. Gavin invited me." A faint spot of color flushed her cheeks, which was heartening. "Oh, there he is." Callie sat up a bit straighter and shook Maude's shoulder.

"I've found a cab to take us," Gavin said, slightly breathless. "It's waiting down the block, and we'll all fit." He, too, looked drained by the events of the night.

"Good," Daniel said, standing up. Maude had awakened and instantly began to weakly cry. Gavin helped Callie gather her up as Daniel signaled he would be back momentarily with Genevieve.

There were only a few hearty bystanders left, mostly locals, waiting behind the officers, hoping to catch another glimpse of the body. The reporter from the *World* had a beady eye fixed on Genevieve as she spoke with Dagmar Hansen and watched her progress as she joined Daniel on the way to the waiting carriage. Daniel turned over his shoulder and glared at the man, hardening his eyes in clear warning.

Crawford stared back but eventually looked away, moodily returning his attention to the shed.

The remaining spectators went quiet as the police bore a blanket-covered stretcher from the shed, carrying it toward a waiting carriage, where presumably Ida's body would be taken to the morgue.

Daniel's skin prickled at the sight. He turned forward quickly, not wanting to draw Genevieve's attention to the sad spectacle, and moved resolutely toward their own waiting conveyance.

★　★　★

"You've outdone yourself." Arthur folded his hands across his stomach and regarded Genevieve over the rims of his spectacles. The *Globe*'s morning edition with her front-page story on "Jack the Peeper" lay on his desk, balanced atop stacks of papers and at least one stained teacup.

He moved the cup from under the paper and tapped the article. "We're already seeing a very positive response from readers. I've had dozens of telegrams in the past hour alone. Very well done, Genevieve."

Genevieve sighed in relief. She was proud of her work on that story. Once she'd gotten Longstreet's blessing to write about the models' murders, the police had become cooperative in sharing information about the peeper, and with Luther's help, Genevieve had interviewed several other victims of the man's break-ins. One of the paper's artists had even been able to produce a very lifelike sketch of the suspect.

Hearing the other women's stories had twisted Genevieve's stomach, as they were so similar to what she had experienced. She hoped the increased publicity around the matter would scare the peeper into ceasing his activity, or at least convince people to lock their windows at night.

The question lingered, though . . . were the peeper and the killer one and the same? She wasn't treating them as such in her articles, but the unknown remained, crowding her thoughts.

She barely had time to bask in her editor's infrequent praise before he moved on. "And the story on the models?"

"Should be finished by tomorrow at the latest," Genevieve said quickly.

Arthur nodded. "That will do. We can run it in Saturday's edition. It's a lot at once, but I have confidence in you. You and Luther make a good team," he said, tilting his head slightly, as if to gauge her reaction.

"We do," she acknowledged. As much as she craved her own bylines, she had to admit that she wouldn't have been able to complete two such complex articles back to back without Luther's assistance.

It had still taken intensive effort. Three days of near endless work—a whirlwind of interviews, fact checking, meetings with officers, writing up her notes, cross-referencing the paper's archives for similar crimes—had left her feeling like a husk of her usual self. Yet at the same time she was full of restless energy, fueled by endless cups of coffee and the occasional sandwich.

Daniel was helping in any way he could, running errands, arranging meetings, accompanying her to interviews when Luther could not. She didn't like the narrow way the two men often looked at each other but shoved it from her mind. Their petty male disputes were not her problem to solve. After seeing Ida's body, even Gavin had grudgingly become more supportive, sending food to her office and waiting up each night for her return, though some nights she wasn't home until two in the morning or later.

Callie would sometimes be awake with him, having temporarily moved into the Stewart household. Walter remained upstate, continuing to work with his difficult clients and, Genevieve suspected, enjoying the cooler mountain air. Callie had not informed him of Ida's death, saying it would only upset him and distract him from his work, though Genevieve thought he must know by now, given how fast news of the murder had spread through the scattered New York art community. Eliza had written to ask about the rumors the very next day.

Genevieve wondered why Walter didn't come home, but remembered Callie's comment that in many ways their relationship was a business partnership, not a love match.

Still, it annoyed her on behalf of her friend. Callie deserved someone who would rush to her side at the slightest glimmer of danger.

She also wondered what Callie and Gavin did in the house all day together, by themselves.

Daniel was sticking to her like glue.

Genevieve didn't have time to unpack the ramifications of any of these entanglements at present—Callie and Walter, Gavin and Callie, her and Daniel. She had a deadline, and she meant to keep it.

To her chagrin, nasty Jim Crawford at the *World* had beaten her to the punch about Ida's murder by a day. True to form, the tabloid had blared salacious half-truths about the state of the body and had openly suggested the murder was the work of Jack the Ripper. Genevieve was outraged, but Arthur told her not to worry.

"Once your and Luther's story is published, the *World* will look like the incompetent rag it is," he assured her. "There will always be that small but vocal segment of readership who prefers entertainment over fact, but the majority of readers, ours included, want the truth. This Crawford fellow knows nothing about the ties with the other deaths. Your wider coverage and context will give our story greater heft and far more credibility."

"And sell more papers," Genevieve smiled faintly.

"That too. Now go finish up." Arthur stood, and Genevieve followed. "I look forward to another resounding success."

Genevieve returned to her desk, preparing for her final meeting of the day, one she would take alone, as Luther was conducting a final interview with the Coney Island police. She was meeting with Dagmar Hansen, the police photographer, who was meant to furnish his pictures of the crime scenes. Her empty stomach recoiled slightly at the thought of seeing the naked women's bodies laid out in black and white, but she steeled herself as Hansen made his way across the open space of the *Globe*'s main office, heading toward her desk.

He removed his hat after shaking her hand and accepting a seat, revealing light-blond hair plastered to his forehead with sweat. It was mid-August now, and the dreadful heat that had held the city in its clutches for weeks showed no signs of abating. The late-summer blooms in townhouse gardens and window boxes were wilting miserably, drying up and turning brown, as was the grass in the city's parks.

Storm clouds gathered every afternoon, and the entire city held its breath and eyed the sky as one, hoping, but they always dissipated. It hadn't rained for weeks now.

After some pleasantries and the usual complaints about the weather, Dagmar removed a folder from his satchel and carefully arrayed a series of photographs across her desk. Genevieve's stomach, acidic from too much coffee, roiled again, but she took a deep breath.

You owe it to these women. Their stories should be told.

The thought was fierce and direct, acting as a coolant upon her own sweaty brow. Genevieve forced herself to sit up straighter and picked up the nearest picture.

It was of Violet. The image caused her chest to constrict painfully, the horror of finding the dead woman as fresh as it had been the day it happened. She made herself focus on the photograph's details, trying to look at the scene with fresh eyes, blocking out the memory of the cats' incessant mewing that automatically arose in her brain.

A nearby photograph of Ida's body caught her eye, and she picked that one up as well, comparing the two.

"They're both on their sides," she murmured, struck by the similarity of the women's poses.

Dagmar peered at the photographs. "I noticed that," he said in his slightly accented but impeccable English. "Except this victim has her arm outstretched"—he tapped the photograph of Ida—"while this one has her arm tucked underneath her, and her head is turned away."

Genevieve looked between the two photographs, frowning. There was something so uncanny about the way the women were arranged.

Was the killer trying to tell them something?

Several of the Ripper's victims in London had been mutilated, their organs removed. None of these bodies had been so disfigured, but there was still a pattern to this killer's method. She just hadn't yet figured out what it was.

She wished Daniel were there to ask, but he had a rare appointment of his own that afternoon.

When she posed the question to Dagmar, he nodded. "It looks very calculated on the part of whoever this monster is," he said softly. "It is hard to fathom the mind that could do this. Yet this victim is quite different."

He slid a photograph of another body across the desk to her. Genevieve was pleased to note her fingers shook only slightly when she picked it up.

She hadn't seen an image of Bea's dead body yet, as hers was the death that had put this whole affair into motion, so far as she knew. The one that had brought her and Daniel into the case.

Genevieve swallowed and studied the image closely. Even though she had never seen Bea in person, dead or alive, she felt she knew the lines of the woman's face and body well after seeing her repeatedly depicted in Paxton's studio.

Paxton's studio.

It was suddenly hard to breathe.

Photographs scattered to the ground as Genevieve abruptly stood.

"Excuse me," she said to Dagmar, barely able to choke out the words. He gaped at her as he bent to collect the images. "I have to use the telephone."

She needed Daniel.

Now.

CHAPTER 17

At the sight of the photograph of Bea's body, Daniel's blood ran cold.

"Do you see it?" Genevieve asked. She was biting her lower lip and kept glancing between his face and the photograph.

Dagmar still sat at her desk, watching their conversation unfold sharply.

It had taken a frantic telephone call to Daniel's house, the dispatching of Asher to Five Points, the ferreting out of Daniel from a meeting with Paddy, whom he'd been helping with a local family's eviction fight, and a cab ride at breakneck speed to get him to the *Globe*'s offices, but upon seeing the picture, Daniel was glad of their haste.

He nodded in response to Genevieve's question, not yet trusting his ability to speak.

"We saw this, didn't we? A painting of Bea posed like this, in Elbert Paxton's studio," she continued, her finger hovering over the image. "It's the same."

"The *Ariadne*," he said, all the breath leaving his body in a quiet gush. He sucked a great lungful of air back in again, relief and horror and confusion all rising with it.

Genevieve was absolutely correct. Though Bea was stretched out on the carpet of her tiny sewing room rather than the rolling green hills in the painting, her body was positioned in the exact same manner.

She lay on her side, her legs mostly extended, one knee slightly bent. Her arms were lengthened over her head, one curled behind her neck. It was a position of languidness, of sensuality, of pure idleness.

"It was difficult to take that photograph," Dagmar murmured, looking between the two of them. "There was so little space. I had to stand on a chair."

Daniel stared at him for a beat.

"We need to find Paxton," he finally said. "We have to talk to him and see that painting again."

"I don't think he's in town anymore," Genevieve said. "He said he was returning to New Hampshire, and that was some weeks ago. Surely he's still there."

Daniel swore, causing Dagmar to raise his brows. "If he's out of state, I suppose we'll have to leave that part to Longstreet. But maybe we can still see the painting."

"And Daniel . . ." Genevieve pulled two other photographs from the small piles on her desk and laid them side by side. Her finger moved just above the surface of each, wordlessly pointing to the arrangement of the bodies.

He flinched slightly at the images of Ida's and Violet's naked, mutilated corpses, captured in photographic emulsion forever, and again briefly wondered how Dagmar could perform his job. But he saw it, exactly what Genevieve was trying to impart.

"We need to see all of Paxton's paintings," she concluded gravely.

★　★　★

Daniel had been right on both counts. After they informed Longstreet of their discovery about the body matching the painting, he had instantly gotten in touch with authorities in New Hampshire to track down the elderly painter and send him to New York for further questioning. Longstreet had, though, allowed them to search through the inventory at Paxton's Tenth Street studio in the meantime.

"My men don't know art," he said, the word rolling out of his mouth as though it tasted bad. "You come to me the minute you find what you're looking for."

"We want this killer found as much as you," Genevieve said in a patient tone, though Daniel could hear the irritation hovering underneath it. Longstreet didn't reply but eyed her appraisingly. Daniel began to leisurely flick through a stack of charcoals on a tabletop in the main room of Paxton's studio, one hand in his pocket.

"As you know, Miss Stewart's parents are collectors," he drawled, playing the part of the dissolute playboy he knew Longstreet loathed. "I've acquired a few choice pieces myself recently. We know this world well, and we'll keep you apprised of our progress." He turned a deliberate shoulder to the detective, suppressing a smile at Longstreet's bristling while ignoring Genevieve's incredulous stare.

He couldn't help it. While Daniel normally took pride in his self-control, there was something about Longstreet that made him act devilish.

Besides, it was often helpful to be underestimated, though he knew he might pay for it later.

"I don't see why you go on antagonizing him like that," Genevieve complained once she shut the door behind the officers. There seemed to be fewer cats roaming the building than before, and she firmly shooed those that remained out of the studio. They cried plaintively outside the heavy oak door, begging to be let in.

Daniel rolled his shoulders. "I don't like the man," he muttered.

Genevieve shook her head at him in exasperation but paired it with a fond look. "You are not helping our cause. And speaking of our cause, how should we tackle this? Are we looking for pictures of Violet and Ida, or any picture where the painted figures resemble how their bodies were posed?" She eyed the canvases stacked against the walls and the piles of drawings on surfaces and stuffed into cabinets with a resolute expression.

"I don't know," he said, looking at the charcoals with greater intent now that Longstreet had departed. "Either, I think. As we only have the one connection thus far, it could be any of the above. Bea was the first victim, and we know her body was posed as a painting of her, so trying to find poses that match those of the other bodies might be a good place to start."

"First that we know of," Genevieve said in a thoughtful, quiet voice. She knelt on the floor and began to move a stack of stretched but unframed canvases to one side, carefully laying out the paintings. They were mostly landscapes.

An internal start jolted him. Of course, Bea was the first that they *knew* of, but that didn't preclude unknown others who might have come first. He hadn't thought of that. "Yes," he amended. "The first that we know of."

The idea that other dead girls might be out there somewhere, their bodies unfound and unknown but perhaps also posed in some way obscenely meaningful to the killer, was so horrific he had to forcibly shift his thoughts.

Daniel moved on to a portfolio brimming with drawings. He flipped them over one at a time: a striking waterfall, dozens of studies of rocky outcroppings in the mountains, a few lively sketches of an older woman he assumed was Paxton's late wife. None of the figures matched any of the deceased models' poses.

Hours passed. Daniel lost himself in the search, shifting painting after painting aside, glancing at each briefly or studying it closely before moving on to the next one. He looked at what must have been hundreds of drawings and charcoals and watercolors, until the trees and waterfalls and sunsets and boulders (Paxton had an overt fondness for capturing rocks, it seemed) all began to bleed together.

Other than several lovely portraits of Paxton's wife, Gertie, and a few of rather patrician old men, the vast majority of the images featuring a sitter were of Bea.

None of them showed her in a pose that matched Ida's or Violet's, and there were no other images of her as Ariadne.

"Maybe it's a coincidence," Genevieve finally said, sitting back on her heels and brushing a stray lock of hair out of her face.

Daniel leaned against the massive carved cabinet he had just spent an hour cleaning out. It had been stuffed with sketch pads, dozens of them.

"It's not," he said. "I'm sure of it." They had exchanged only a few sentences while they pored over their respective piles, sometimes showing one another a piece they had found or commenting on an unusual painting but mostly working in companiable silence. Genevieve's mere presence was soothing, even as his frustration mounted while he flipped through the innumerable sketch pads.

"Of course, these aren't all of Paxton's pieces," she said. "He's had a long career, since the 1840s, and his art is in dozens of collections, perhaps all over the country."

Daniel was unable to suppress a groan. "Would he keep an account of who owns what?"

Genevieve tilted her head, thinking. "Probably," she finally said. "He knew which piece my parents owned." She brushed her hands on her skirt, sending up a cloud of dust and emitting a delicate sneeze.

Indeed, the whole studio was filled with dust, stirred up by their efforts. Motes danced in a strong shaft of sunlight streaming in through a high window, illuminating Genevieve where she sat: dirt streaked, tired, but still achingly beautiful.

She caught his eye and held it, a small, inquisitive smile rising to her lips at his regard. The dizzying feeling of being with Genevieve on the howdah rushed back, directly into this filthy, crowded studio, and he cursed—not for the first time—Maude's abrupt intrusion on that moment.

He recalled it with perfect clarity. How the velvety night air had seemed to caress them both. How the glow of the electric lights had emanated from the boardwalk, illuminating the delicate line of Genevieve's jaw from below. The sharp crescent moon was just rising, punctuating the purple sky, and the stars had just begun to twinkle into existence.

Before they'd found Ida's body. Before the stars turned cold.

Mostly, he remembered the delicate feel of Genevieve's fingers under his hand as they stood at the railing, 175 feet high. How they'd twitched slightly at the pressure of his palm, then curled upward and lightly grasped him.

How he'd ached to pull her close.

"Maybe it is finally time to take a break." Genevieve's voice was soft, almost as if she knew what he was thinking and was hesitant to interrupt the spell.

He pulled out of the memory as though he were hoisting himself from a warm lake, reality hitting like a rush of cold air. "Yes," Daniel said, straightening. He brushed off his shirtfront for something to do, having discarded his jacket and rolled up his shirt sleeves long ago. "It's far past time. Coffee? Or something cold?"

Genevieve's smile widened, but there was some hesitancy around it as well. "Something cold, for now. But I meant a larger break."

She explained she was going to Newport for the weekend. "Mother is insisting on throwing a welcome-home party for Gavin, though I think it's really a ploy to get us to come to Rhode Island and stay for what's left of summer. You're invited, of course. It's going to be quite casual, a luncheon on the lawn with sailing and games, not a formal ball or the like. Mother very much wants you there."

Daniel hesitated himself. The idea of attending a lawn party at the Stewart Newport home was incredibly appealing, and he knew Anna's offer was sincere.

Did Genevieve want him there too?

"And there's not much more we can do here, not until Paxton is back in the city," she continued, seeming to mistake his lack of answer for reluctance.

"Well, we could," Daniel said. "We could see if we can find Paxton's records, start tracking down his other paintings . . ."

"Oh, if you don't want to come, that's fine too." Genevieve stood abruptly, flushing. "I thought perhaps you'd at least like to see Rupert and Esmie again; they're invited too, of course." A crestfallen expression flitted across her face, quickly masked but for a second clear as day. Daniel's heart lurched in response, and he took an involuntary step in her direction.

"I do want to come. Very much. A break would be wonderful."

And it did sound wonderful. Maybe a few days in Rhode Island would have the ameliorative effects he had hoped Coney Island would provide.

Relief and happiness lit her, and Daniel's own mood immediately lightened in response. "I'll cable your mother today, telling her I accept."

"Excellent." She moved to gather her things, a light summer jacket that matched her pale-yellow skirt and her straw hat and flowered bag, smoothing her hair. "Now, let's see if we can navigate our way around those infernal cats out there and find something cold. I'm far too great a wreck for Delmonico's, I'm afraid."

"The beer garden again?" Daniel put on his own jacket and offered Genevieve his arm. There mere thought of getting out of the hot, stinking city, if only for a few days, made him almost giddy.

"Perfect."

★ ★ ★

A slight ocean breeze lifted Daniel's hair and ruffled it, cooling his brow. Delicious. The breeze carried the scents of peonies and daylilies, delighting his nostrils, and soft strains of music wafted over the sweeping green lawn of the Stewart family house.

Even the waves sounded gentler than usual.

Being out of the city was as relaxing as he had imagined it.

"I've missed you," said Rupert. His best friend stood by his side at the edge of the lawn. Shoulder to shoulder, they gazed upon the endless spread of the Atlantic Ocean, the happy laughter of Anna and Wilbur Stewart's guests floating in the air behind them. *Thwock* came the sound of a croquet ball, followed by a woman's excited shriek. Callie's, maybe. Rich smoke filled his mouth, then exited smoothly, a puff of white dissipating out to sea.

The midday cigar was a rare indulgence, and also a gesture of goodwill toward Rupert, who had furnished one for each of them.

It was quite enjoyable.

"I've missed you too."

"Not enough to come back for good."

Another smoke cloud left his mouth and sailed upward. "Not yet, no."

Rupert squinted at the horizon line and changed the subject. "I'm a bit surprised to see Callie here," he said in a quieter voice. "Well, not Callie, but to see her with that architect fellow."

Daniel had been surprised, too, though he had tried to keep it from his hostess. He glanced over his shoulder. Walter had wrapped his arms around Callie from behind, ostensibly to show her how to better guide her croquet mallet, earning the couple a few shocked looks.

"Genevieve said they weren't invited as a couple. Charles invited Walter, and her mother invited Callie, but they came together."

Anna Stewart, watching the croquet game from the patio that graced the back of the large Queen Anne mansion, appeared oblivious to the raised eyebrows sent her way as she laughed and cheered Gavin's team on. Daniel suspected she would not care even if she did notice the censorious looks; Anna was keenly protective of her daughter's friend and would likely dismiss any gossip about Callie and the architect with a firm "Horsefeathers." Besides, the Stewarts had weathered far worse gossip than hosting an artist and his mistress, even if the mistress was an heiress fallen from grace. Between Anna's ardent views on universal suffrage and birth control and Wilbur's passionate legal defense of issues society considered lost causes, much of New York's elite had grown used to the family's somewhat eccentric ways.

"I'm sure she's happy to be out of the city for a few days," Daniel continued, turning his attention back to the ocean. "We all are."

"Sure I can't convince you to stay any longer than tomorrow?" The question was phrased mildly enough, but Daniel heard the undercurrent of hope in Rupert's voice.

Smoke from Rupert's cigar drifted upward and joined his own.

"I'm afraid not, as wonderful as it would be. Paxton will be back in New York in two days, and Longstreet has said he will allow me to sit in on the questioning."

Rupert's eyes snapped from the Atlantic to Daniel, an expression of extreme doubt on his face. "The same Longstreet who threw me into the Tombs, knowing I was innocent? That Longstreet?" He shook his head in disbelief.

Daniel grimaced. "Enemy of my enemy, for the time being."

"Watch your back."

It was good advice.

Rupert shook his head again. "I can't get over this whole business. Some ghoul killing these models and then posing them like their pictures?"

"Just the one, so far, that we know was deliberately posed. We haven't found pictures that match the other two bodies yet."

"Grim work, mate. Come, why don't you take a week off and stay here. Enjoy the summertime." Rupert gestured with his cigar to the ocean, the lawns, the genteel people dressed in white drinking champagne gathered on the lawn at their backs.

"You know I can't. Not while this is ongoing."

"The police are handling it," his friend pressed. "You've already done their work for them once this summer, catching those gunrunners. And nearly getting yourself killed for your efforts."

Daniel allowed his silence to answer. It was difficult to see the worry on Rupert's face and not assuage it, so instead he watched the waves, admiring how the light danced on the water, and enjoyed how the sun felt, for once pleasant rather than oppressive.

The smoke entered his mouth and left it, even and rhythmic.

A gusty sigh sounded to his right. "Are you ever going to tell her how you feel?" Rupert finally asked, his voice quiet.

A smile tugged one corner of Daniel's mouth. "Yes."

"For god's sake, make it soon so you can both come back to Newport before we run out of champagne."

A raw chuckle at the thought rumbled from his chest. Rupert could always make him laugh, no matter the circumstances.

"Really, though," Rupert continued, slanting him a sideways look. "Tell her."

"You're being awfully insistent today."

"You're being more stubborn than usual. Tell her."

"When the time is right."

Another sigh, followed by another small cloud of smoke. "Esmie is not going to be happy about this," Rupert said.

"What am I not going to be happy about?" Esmie joined her husband's other side and linked her arm though his, looking summery and cool in a light-periwinkle dress. "My, would you look at that view. I confess I never tire of it."

"I'm going back to New York, love," Rupert said regretfully.

Daniel whipped his head in surprise. "What?"

"Oh, that is too bad," she said, though Daniel thought she didn't look particularly surprised. "We're having the most wonderful summer, aren't we?"

"We are," Rupert agreed. "But these two will never figure out this mess if I don't assist. Can't do anything without me."

"Rupert, you should stay here," Daniel said. As much as he enjoyed his friend's company—and though it pained him to admit it, as much as he and Genevieve could do with a fresh set of eyes—the thought of involving anyone else he cared about in their current investigation sent a wary chill across his shoulder blades, despite the sun. "Esmie needs you."

"I'll be coming too," Esmie said brightly. "I'm not letting Rupert molder about the house alone with Father; they might come to blows in the drawing room, and I don't want to attempt to get blood out of Mother's damask curtains." Esmie's father, Amos Bradley, stayed in New York during the summer running his copper empire, traveling to Newport only occasionally.

"High time we got our own house," Rupert muttered.

"What is going on with you conspirators?" Genevieve demanded, marching up to join their party.

Two days in Newport had done wonders for her. Her face had lost its wan cast, and her eyes once again sparkled with vitality. She held a glass of champagne in one hand and used the other to press down her suddenly fluttering white skirts as the light breeze intensified for a moment.

"Rupert and I are coming back to New York to help with this investigation, and that is that," Esmie said, tightening her hold on Rupert's arm.

"Oh, you'll hate New York right now, it's so hot and dreadful," Genevieve said. Daniel was unsurprised to see that she, too, appeared wary of the idea. "Plus this matter . . . it's not going well."

"Which is why you need our help," Rupert said. He caught the eye of a footman with a tray of glasses across the lawn and waved him over. "What did I say, darling? Hopeless without us. There's no use in arguing, you two; you won't change our minds. Now, who wants to play croquet?"

Champagne flew from Genevieve's glass and into the blue sky as she was bumped by yet another person joining their group, this one a young lady Daniel didn't know, who came at them at a pace just slower than a run.

"Oof," said the newcomer, nearly stumbling as Daniel caught her arm to steady her. "Oh Genevieve, I am sorry. I didn't mean to spill your drink."

The girl was lovely, with light-brown hair and wide gray eyes behind a pair of spectacles, but brimming with a frenetic energy that seemed out of place on the lazy day. Her pale-green-and-white flowered day dress looked quite fashionable, even to his less-than-trained eye, and he noticed Esmie studying it with appreciation.

"It's fine, Suzanne, I can get more," Genevieve said, offering the girl a genuine smile. "Do you know Mr. McCaffrey, and the Earl and Countess of Umberland, Rupert and Esmie Milton? I'm so glad you were able to make it. I want to have a nice long talk with you and strategize. Mr. Horace says you're doing wonderfully; we'll get you hired full-time yet."

Ah, this was Suzanne Anwyll, then. Genevieve's temporary replacement at the paper. She was positively vibrating, grasping at Genevieve's arm. Daniel readied himself against another spill, though there wasn't much liquid left in the glass.

"So nice to meet you all," she gasped. "Well, I know the Miltons. But nice to meet you, Mr. McCaffrey." The words rushed together. "Genevieve, you wanted to know when I saw Matthew Shipman."

The beautiful, calm day shattered. Daniel tensed, every sense suddenly on alert.

"Yes, you were to cable me right away." Genevieve looked alarmed. "Where was this? We have to speak to him immediately."

"But he's here."

Suzanne pointed across the grass. and four pairs of eyes followed the line of her finger. Blood rushed to Daniel's head. There, across the wide lawn and milling easily among the guests as if he hadn't a care in the world, was the man they most suspected of murder.

CHAPTER 18

Matthew Shipman, a canape in one hand and a drink in the other, smiled broadly as Genevieve approached, his white suit gleaming in the sun. The scene was so normal— one guest among many, all bedecked in their summer finery talking and laughing, set against the backdrop of her family's mushroom-hued stone house—that for a moment time contracted. Was it really August, or was it twelve weeks prior? Had all the horrific events of those past weeks happened, or was it still June and this a normal garden party, one where everyone she cared about was safe? For the barest of moments, she could have sworn on her mother's life, on her career, that it was actually that earlier time and she had no concerns save whether or not it might rain, and there was no trail of dead girls littering Manhattan.

An automatic, answering smile rose to her lips, then faltered.

It wasn't early summer, not anymore.

Since June, she had taken a man's life.

And now three women were dead, and the man in front of her with the clean suit and caviar-stained lips might be responsible.

"Hello, Miss Stewart. How nice to see you again. So lovely of your family to invite me." Matthew reached for her hand, wiping his mouth first with a linen napkin before handing it to a circulating footman. She accepted the outstretched hand out of habit, nonplussed to find his handshake distressingly benign. Shouldn't a man suspected of having cut the throats of three women squeeze her hand too hard, or have an inappropriately sweaty grasp?

Shipman looked refreshed and cool, his perhaps overly hearty smile the only sign he knew that she knew he was a wanted man.

Gooseflesh tingled her arms, and one small shiver assailed her shoulder blades. She clasped her hands firmly at her waist in an attempt to hide the motion.

Daniel was a firm presence just to her left, and she was dimly aware that Esmie and Rupert were close too. Suzanne hovered farther back.

"I didn't realize you were on the guest list, Mr. Shipman," she said. "It is a happy surprise, though." Her pleasant hostess voice, the same she would use with any guest, sounded tinny to her ears, but she knew it would pass muster for those nearby. The last thing she wanted was to cause a panic.

Though nobody, it seemed, was giving them a second glance. She passed a curious gaze over the few guests within earshot. Did New York's elite have no idea Matthew Shipman was wanted by the police in relation to not one but two murders?

That appeared to be the case.

The realization was startling, though it shouldn't be. The sordid world in which she and Daniel had been immersed didn't touch the fair, privileged denizens of this resort. Aside from the recent press about the murders—horrid

Jim Crawford's piece in the *World* and also her own well-received article—how would they know anything about the crimes? Neither she nor Crawford had mentioned Shipman's connection to either girl in their stories. Crawford, she assumed, hadn't known, and Longstreet had asked her to refrain from mentioning it.

They had argued over this, bitterly. Genevieve had insisted that the greater the number of people who knew about Shipman's connection, the sooner they would find him. Longstreet had put his foot down.

"The last thing we want is for him to get spooked and hop a steamer abroad or a train to Canada," he had said. "I will not budge on this, Miss Stewart. Mention Shipman's name and I will revoke all access to our investigation, including Dagmar's photographs."

She would have defied the detective, but Arthur, to her surprise, agreed with the police, and her hands had been tied.

Genevieve didn't know if Matthew Shipman had killed any of the women. But she knew he had some relation to their deaths, enough that, now that she was speaking to him, a spiral of fear swirled deep in her belly.

She needed him off her patio, away from her friends and family, and under police custody until the truth could be sorted.

"Gavin sent round an invitation," Shipman said, finishing the remainder of his drink in one quick swallow. "Awfully nice of him." Genevieve kept her brows from rising, though internally, she was impressed. That was smart of Gavin, to pretend as though nothing were wrong and send an invite to Shipman's house like normal, see if he'd bite.

And bitten he had, for here the man was. Gavin was nowhere in sight.

Genevieve hesitated, unsure of how to remove Shipman from the party without ruining the whole event.

"Thought I might see you here, McCaffrey." Shipman slid his eyes toward Daniel, the smile faltering for a second before he slapped it back on.

"Did you hope to see me?" Daniel asked carefully.

"I did, that I did. I know some other gentlemen were also hoping to have a word, but I wondered if we could do so first. Man-to-man. Then I'll be happy to speak with those others, if they're still interested."

Genevieve shot a quick look at Daniel, who kept his own eyes fixed on Shipman. If she interpreted Shipman correctly, he wanted to speak with Daniel before talking to the police.

"I believe that could be arranged," Daniel said, still choosing his words with precision.

The smile seemed more natural now. "Excellent. Why don't you come to my cottage later, when all this winds down." He gestured with his empty glass to the party, which was still progressing nicely all around them. A footman swooped in and plucked the glass from Shipman's hand.

"Seems my cue to leave, doesn't it now? Don't worry, I'm not going anywhere. I'd like to have this out. And no need to tell your friends you've seen me yet. You have my word I'll head to them as soon as we've spoken."

Daniel nodded. "Then you've mine as well. I'll tell no other, um, parties you're here until after we've spoken."

"Good man," Shipman boomed. "Knew I could trust you. Miss Stewart." He nodded to Genevieve, then made his way toward Anna. Genevieve tensed, but Shipman only made a polite good-bye, then wound his way back into the house, presumably heading toward the front drive and his carriage home.

"What was that about?" Rupert asked in concern, drawing close to Daniel's shoulder.

Daniel hesitated, especially as Esmie drew near, her brow furrowed.

"Mr. Shipman had a relationship with two of the victims," Genevieve murmured. "One was his mistress, and he claimed to love another."

Rupert blanched. "Is he a suspect?" he hissed quietly. At her nod, he whipped his head in the direction Shipman had disappeared. "Matty Shipman, a murderer? I've known him for a decade, gone to all his parties—"

"Not anymore," Esmie cut in sharply, narrowing her eyes.

"No, of course not, darling," Rupert said, wrapping an arm around Esmie's waist and drawing her close. "But I was a wild bachelor for a very long time, and Matty always arranges for the best entertainment; he knew the most gorgeous . . . oh." Rupert, of all people, blushed as he realized what he was saying, casting a quick guilty look at Esmie, who stared at him steadily.

"He does know rather a lot of models and dancers and the like," Rupert finished faintly, his gaze trailing again to the spot where Shipman had recently stood, a horrified expression replacing his embarrassment.

Goose bumps now dotted her whole body, and Genevieve shook herself once, hard. The day had lost its pleasure. Even being surrounded by the familiar smiling faces of her mother's guests brought no comfort.

Shipman's presence, however brief, was a reminder that anyone could be the killer.

Anyone at all.

"I can tell that croquet isn't in the cards anymore," Rupert sighed. "I'll come to this talk with you, shall I?"

He raised his chin and snatched a drink from a passing tray.

"No," Daniel answered before Genevieve could. "He said nobody else."

"He meant no police," Genevieve clarified. She followed Rupert's lead and signaled for another glass of champagne to replace the one Suzanne had jostled, taking a large gulp.

"It wouldn't be smart," Daniel said. "Shipman's willing to talk to me and might not do so if someone else were there—even someone he may consider a friend."

Rupert appeared on the cusp of arguing but settled for another sigh instead. He sipped his drink and grimaced. "I appear to have taken some sherry by mistake. Wretched stuff. Well, I suppose you're right. But be careful, please. We just got you back, don't want to lose you again any sooner than we have to."

Daniel smiled faintly. "We will be careful, I promise."

"Come, Esmie," Rupert said, offering his wife his arm. "Charles said he was taking the *Anna Charlene* out; let's see if we can get a spot. We'll solve crimes with these two later." He sent Daniel and Genevieve a meaningful look as he and Esmie departed, making it clear he was not speaking metaphorically.

Suzanne hurried over to fill the space left by Rupert and Esmie. "I'm so sorry; I hadn't seen Mr. Shipman in town until just that moment, Genevieve, I promise," she said.

"I understand, Suzanne." Genevieve patted her arm. "Thank you for alerting me to his presence so quickly. Now, are you writing about the party for the paper?"

"I am. Mr. Horace specifically asked if I would." A line of worry creased Suzanne's forehead.

A very unladylike snort burst from Genevieve before she could help it. Sending the other society reporter—the one Genevieve had foisted upon her boss—to cover her own family's party was a trifle petty of Arthur. But she knew her editor was also making a point: Genevieve didn't get to pick and choose when she would cover society. If she didn't want the job, he would use someone who did.

"Well, as Mr. Horace likes to say, there's meat on those bones, if you'll find it," Genevieve responded mildly. Suzanne's brow smoothed as she sighed in relief.

And her editor was correct. The society pages sometimes yielded extraordinary stories despite themselves.

But today, she had a bigger story to catch.

★ ★ ★

"You're a surprise, Miss Stewart."

A surprise Shipman didn't seem happy about. He glowered at Genevieve's presence, stuffing his hands in his pockets and chomping ill-naturedly on a cigar.

The smell, one Daniel had so enjoyed while taking in the unusually tranquil Atlantic with Rupert, now turned Daniel's stomach.

"Miss Stewart is spearheading our investigations," Daniel said firmly. "If you want to speak with me, she will stay. You also noticed, no doubt, that she kept your name out of the newspaper."

Shipman frowned around his cigar but didn't argue further. He tilted his head toward down a long corridor that led deeper inside, signaling they should follow.

The exterior of the house was all pillars and buttery, cream-colored stone, orange light shining warmly through upper windows in the day's waning sun, a beacon of welcome. The interior, though, was the opposite; cold, pale-gray marble lined the floor and the walls of the long hallway, where niches inset at regular intervals featured sculpted busts of Shipman ancestors or sometimes a small bronze figurine. Genevieve gestured with her chin toward one as they passed and raised a brow; it was a miniature version of the *Clytie* sculpture, modeled after Bea, that they had seen in Callie's house. The echo of Daniel's heels resounded loudly, amplified in the sterile, empty space, accompanied only by the soft swishing of Genevieve's skirts.

"We can talk in here," Shipman said. He pushed on a panel of marble to their right, which turned out to be a door that swung inward. Daniel felt his brows rise despite himself; the door had been neatly hidden, and he wondered how many other rooms they had passed.

Genevieve gave him a quick look over her shoulder as they passed through the threshold, her amber eyes wide.

The atmosphere abruptly shifted again as they entered a large, oak-paneled study with spacious windows that faced the ocean. It was a wholly masculine space, one wall lined with books, the scent of good leather from the armchairs mingling with that of Shipman's cigar. The setting sun reflected brilliant colors across the water, deep pinks and oranges with splashes of yellow.

Due to the house's proximity to the edge of the bluff, Daniel couldn't quite see the narrow strip of sand he had run along all those weeks ago, looking for the two figures in the surf he'd spied from the Otts' veranda, but just knowing it was down there sent a frisson of unease through his chest.

Shipman carefully snuffed out his cigar, only half-finished, and gestured to the deep, cognac-colored armchairs, four arranged in front of a bare fireplace, before moving to a sideboard. He poured a splash of bourbon into a tumbler and wordlessly handed it to Daniel.

"I don't have any cordial," he said to Genevieve with what could only be described as a sneer.

"Some of that bourbon will do nicely, thank you, Mr. Shipman."

It was odd how much Shipman's demeanor had changed from earlier in the day. At the party, he had seemed a trifle subdued from his normal gregarious self, but now he was downright sullen and angry. Daniel didn't know Matt well enough to ascertain if either was the man's true nature.

Maybe they were both masks.

He also seemed quite drunk.

Whatever the abrupt change meant, Daniel didn't like it.

"What did you want to talk with us about?" he asked, inhaling the caramel and pepper scents of the bourbon.

Shipman cast a resentful eye at Genevieve, who sipped her drink calmly in response. "I wanted to explain to you about what I said," he said to Daniel, taking a seat by the cold fireplace and turning an equally cold shoulder to Genevieve. "At the birthday party. I know it alarmed you, and you told the police."

"You can speak freely in front of Miss Stewart. She has no feminine sensibilities you need worry over."

Genevieve sent a briefly affronted look his way.

"You know what I mean," he muttered.

"It's true I won't get the vapors if you speak plainly, Mr. Shipman," Genevieve declared.

Shipman twisted in his seat to take her in, his brow raised, then settled into his chair so that he faced them both. "Very well. It's true what I said at the party. I loved Violet. For two years." His voice turned mournful, and he stared past Genevieve toward the ocean.

"But we understand you had an arrangement with Beatrice Holler?" Genevieve pressed.

"Yes, Bea was my mistress. Prettiest bottom in all of New York." Shipman said this last in a blunt tone, looking directly at Genevieve, clearly wishing to shock her. "You're in a man's world now, honey."

Daniel felt rather than saw Genevieve stiffen slightly in her seat, surely more at the familiar moniker than the description of the deceased Bea's bottom. In response, she took a large mouthful of bourbon and tilted her head at Shipman.

"You loved Violet from afar, then?" she asked.

A short bark of laughter erupted at this suggestion. "Not from afar, no. Got as close to that woman as a man can get. We were lovers for several years."

Daniel and Genevieve exchanged a confused look.

"You kept two mistresses?" Daniel asked. It wasn't unheard of, but the uneasy feeling he'd had upon entering the room intensified.

The sun continued its inevitable descent, but the gas lamps installed above the fireplace remained unlit. Shadows previously confined to the corners of the study began to lengthen, swallowing details of the room.

Was it another woman they were looking for, rather than a man? Someone jealous?

"No, no." The leather squeaked slightly as Shipman shifted. "They wouldn't like that, now, would they? And it'd cost me more than double, appeasing all those hurt feelings. No, Violet ended things with me a few months ago. She had quit modeling, was going to study to be a nurse."

"So . . . you struck up the arrangement with Beatrice Holler after your affair ended with Violet?" Genevieve asked in a careful tone.

There was enough light to see Shipman nodding. "Yes." He sighed gustily and turned to face the water again, his florid face briefly illuminated and made redder by the light of the setting sun.

Daniel opened his mouth to speak, but Shipman continued.

"But we were never really done, not me and Violet. Couldn't stay away from each other. You know how that is sometimes, with women?" His head swung back toward Daniel, backlit by the sunset, his features hidden in the gloom. "There's that one you can't forsake?"

The formality of the old-fashioned word *forsake* struck Daniel deeply.

But he did know.

He knew quite well.

Daniel nodded back, not wanting to break Shipman's train of thought, carefully keeping his eyes off Genevieve.

"That's how it was with me and Violet." Shipman's voice floated in the darkness, disembodied, gravelly and grave. "I told her and told her, she didn't have to go to New Haven; hell, she didn't have to model if she didn't want to. I'd have paid for her to go to nursing school here. But Violet was raised by one of those dour fire-and-brimstone preachers from down south, and that kind of upbringing is hard to overcome. Worried constantly that she was going to hell. Her modeling, her relationship with me—she was sure it was all sending her to eternal damnation. She thought she could redeem her soul by becoming a nurse and helping people."

"Maybe she'd have felt better if the two of you had married." Genevieve's voice was like ice in the dark, sharp and cutting.

"I'm not the marrying kind," came Shipman's flinty response, but then his shadow slumped. "But to keep her, yes, maybe I should have."

"Did you not want to lose her badly enough that you'd ensure she couldn't leave?" Daniel kept his voice pitched low, but the air in the room turned tense regardless. Genevieve's sharp intake of breath punctuated the silence.

"Are you asking if I killed her?"

"Did you?"

A long pause followed Daniel's question. There was no movement in the room; he couldn't even hear the others' breath.

"No."

Daniel waited. Genevieve stayed quiet. Behind Shipman's head, a few stars blinked into existence.

All at once, Shipman heaved his bulky frame out of his chair. Daniel's muscles tensed, the soft leather of the chair's arms sinking beneath his fingers as he tightened his grip.

But all Shipman did was move toward the fireplace and turn on the lamps. The soft glow lit the room, chasing away most of the shadows.

"She moved out in early June," he said, turning to face them. "Said she had a place to stay, couldn't be with me anymore. Wouldn't listen to reason, wouldn't take any money. I've never made a woman stay with me who didn't want to be here; ask around. Granted, usually I end things first, but if any of them wants to go, we part ways, and I move on to the next."

"And in this instance, you moved on to Bea," Genevieve said softly.

"Exactly."

"But you and Violet weren't done, you said?" Daniel asked, fingers relaxing. "What did you mean by that?"

"She came back." Shipman resumed his seat and gulped the remainder of his bourbon. "Four weeks ago. Weeping. Said she couldn't stay away, even though she knew she was damning herself to eternal hellfire. And I couldn't say no." He shifted his gaze back to the window, watching the moon rise over the Atlantic.

Four weeks ago.

In the orange lamplight, Genevieve's startled gaze flew to his. He knew she must be thinking the exact same thing.

"Around that time, I saw something on the beach, from Clarence Ott's house," Daniel said, again being careful with his phrasing. "At night. A man and a woman who seemed to be struggling."

Surprise flashed across Shipman's face, then resignation.

"She was sobbing. Didn't want to stay, didn't want to go." Shipman stood and walked to the window, kept his back to them. "Ran to the beach and into the waves, praying and crying and carrying on. I convinced her to come back to the house, kissed away her tears, got her warm and dry. She fell asleep holding my hand."

The tenderness in his voice was heartbreaking.

Even killers, Daniel knew, could love.

Shipman faced them again. "But she was gone in the morning. That was the last time I saw her."

Daniel let the quiet that followed this statement stretch. Shipman turned his attention back to the sea.

It was Genevieve who finally broke the silence.

"None of Violet's friends seemed to have known about the two of you. Two years is a long time to keep a secret."

Shipman shook his head but didn't turn. "She was so ashamed. All the time. If I could find that father of hers, I'd strangle the life from him." He did turn, then, in time to catch their startled reactions. "Please. I didn't kill Violet. I didn't kill Bea. But because that man made my Violet ashamed, she ran from me. From safety. And then someone *did* kill her. I'll say the same to the police that I say to you now. Find him. Find the bastard that murdered my Violet."

CHAPTER 19

Boom. Another wave rolled onto the small slice of beach at the base of the bluff, then receded.

Boom. And another.

For a long time, that rhythmic noise was the only sound in the room. Shipman remained at the large picture window, his hands clasped behind his back as he watched the ocean. Daniel wondered if their host expected them to show themselves out.

Genevieve caught his eye and made a little head motion at the door with a querying look.

It was heartening that their thoughts seemed so often linked.

He had readied his muscles to stand, make his good-byes and leave, when Shipman's voice stopped him.

"I can show you her room, if you like."

All the earlier combativeness had leached from Shipman. He turned toward them then, and it was hard not to wince at the deep regret lining the man's face.

Genevieve, who had half risen in anticipation of leaving herself, paused in the act of standing. "Violet had a room here?"

"Yes. She lived here, on and off. Come with me."

They hurried after Shipman, who moved with surprising purpose, as if he wanted to complete an unpleasant task as soon as possible.

Back into the echoing marble hallway they went, then one flight up a grand curving staircase and down another corridor, this one lined with deep-blue carpet so plush nobody's footsteps made a sound.

"Here." Shipman paused at one of the polished wooden doors and turned an elegant brass handle.

Stepping into the dead girl's room was achingly similar to Daniel's experience in Bea's apartment in the city. The space was similarly trapped in time, even though it was cleaner, clearly less lived-in than Bea's rooms had been. It appeared Violet had taken most of her personal effects when she had decamped to Chase's studio, but there were still small, poignant signs of her existence everywhere: a half-used bottle of lily-of-the-valley scent resting on a dressing table, a pair of bright-red velvet evening slippers, which perhaps she had deemed too impractical for her new life as a nurse, partially shoved under the wardrobe.

A life she would never undertake now.

"She didn't have quarters in the city?" Genevieve asked, glancing over her shoulder from where she had been examining a framed print of pink roses on the wall.

"No. She stayed with friends, here and there, when she worked. All those durned painters keep rooms in their studios." Shipman spoke briskly. Undoubtedly the thought of where Violet had died—one of those artists' very studios—was painful.

Had Shipman been the cause of that pain, though? Had the possibility of losing Violet for good driven him to the brink?

Daniel still wasn't sure.

"Bea didn't mind that you kept a room for another woman in your house?" Daniel asked. He deliberately kept his voice mild.

"Bea never came here." Shipman had composed himself from his earlier sorrow and once again adopted a gruff demeanor. "We weren't together long before . . ." He turned to one of the windows in the room, presenting his back to them as he had downstairs.

"Speaking of Bea, I noticed you have a miniature of Walter Wilson's sculpture of her downstairs, the *Clytie*," Genevieve ventured.

"Yes. Nice piece, that. He captured her bottom perfectly."

Genevieve ignored the taunt. "Do you have works featuring Violet?" she asked instead.

Daniel had to stop himself from gaping. Why hadn't he thought of that?

"Of course," Shipman said. "She was a very popular model. Come, I'll show you my favorite."

Back in the blue carpeted hallway, Shipman led them to a double set of mahogany doors not far from Violet's room.

It was clearly his bedroom. A massive, four-poster bed monopolized the rectangular space, which Daniel realized was directly above the study, as the view from the terrace outside a set of French doors was the same.

"Here." Shipman gestured. Between two pilasters at the bed's headboard hung a large square canvas in a heavy gilded frame.

Genevieve gasped, and Daniel almost did the same, his breath catching in his throat on its way out.

"Can you blame me?" Shipman's voice had turned tender again as he regarded the painting. "Chase did this one.

The man can paint." He had retrieved his cigar on their way upstairs and now found a match in his pocket and relit it. The smoke gently drifted in front of the canvas but did nothing to obscure the view.

In the painting, Violet was seated, curled on a bench partially covered in pale-green Japanese floral silk. She was turned away from the viewer, her vibrant head bowed on her arms, which were folded on the back of the bench. Her legs were bent underneath her, one foot tucked in the fold of the other leg, toes pale as seashells peeking out.

She was posed in the exact same manner as she had been in death, only here she was seated rather than lying on her side on the floor of Chase's studio.

Even the fabric on which she had been arranged was the same.

"Beautiful, isn't it?" Shipman's voice had taken on a dreamy quality.

Genevieve's hand trembled slightly at the base of her throat, and she turned the color of new milk.

There was something about the painting that made Daniel unable to tear his eyes away, even though the scene itself wasn't macabre. He knew, however, that something about it had inspired a killer. How the flesh tones had been rendered, so different than they had been in death, the coy peekaboo of the toes, and the vibrancy of Violet's truly remarkable hair made the hair on his arms rise.

Much of the painting was so lifelike, it was almost as though Violet would uncurl and turn toward them.

Bile filed his throat with a sickening intensity, and he swallowed once, hard, his hands fists in his pockets.

"Mr. Shipman," he began. Why was his voice so scratchy and faint? He cleared his throat and tried again. "Matt."

There was more firmness to it this time, and Shipman forced his eyes away from the painting.

"We're going to have to call that other interested party now."

★   ★   ★

The Tombs was no place to which Daniel wanted to return, at least not willingly. But it was here, in one of the fetid, sweltering rooms that were part of the warren of police facilities, that Longstreet chose to interview Elbert Paxton, undoubtedly in an attempt to scare the elderly artist into confessing.

Daniel highly doubted Longstreet would achieve any such result. Paxton's hands shook as he lifted a tin cup of weak institutional tea to his mouth; he was so frail it was obvious he couldn't have overpowered and killed a young woman who, by all accounts, was in the peak of health.

Paxton appeared exhausted but was answering all of Longstreet's questions as best he could. Sweat trickled between Daniel's shoulder blades. He longed to scratch at it but didn't dare move, not while Longstreet was in the thick of his interview.

His attention wandered briefly, his mind replacing the close, sweating walls of the Tombs with the open green spaces and cool breezes of Newport. The heat had still not broken in the city; if anything, the temperatures felt more suffocating than ever.

"You expect me to believe it is mere coincidence that Beatrice Holler's corpse was posed exactly the same as your painting of her?" Longstreet asked, snapping Daniel's attention back to the present moment. The detective had not raised his voice, but it was filled with threat regardless. "A painting which remained in your possession, correct?"

Paxton blinked his rheumy eyes several times, flinching slightly at Longstreet's tone. "Yes, yes. I never did sell that painting."

"So you were the only person who conceived the deceased in that pose, picturing her as"—Longstreet checked his notes—"Ariadne?"

More blinks. "Well, it's a long-standing trope. Durand did it fifty years ago," Paxton said defensively.

"But nobody else knew of your painting?" Longstreet pressed, ignoring Paxton's reference to another painter. Of whom, Daniel guessed, the detective had never heard. "You kept it private, hidden for your own pleasure?"

"No, not exactly. It was exhibited at the National Academy. Twice."

Longstreet shot an accusing look at Daniel, as if this were information he had withheld.

"It's in their records; you can check—1886 and '87. Plenty of people saw the piece," Paxton continued. His trembling hands picked up the tin cup, but then he seemed to think better of it and set it down again.

"Nudes can be a hard sell," Paxton offered in his thin voice. "Not every person wants one hanging in their home, despite the long history and dignity of depicting the human form. That's why I still had the painting."

"You were obsessed with Beatrice Holler, though," Longstreet drawled, leaning back in his chair and crossing his arms over his chest. "There are hundreds of sketches, paintings, all manner of art created with her image on it in your studio."

Paxton sighed, observing his own shaking hands resting on the battered table's surface. "She was something of an inspiration for me, I suppose. After my Gertie died. But there was nothing untoward in our arrangement. She posed for me, I paid her."

"Forgive me for not understanding how looking at a girl young enough to be your granddaughter with no clothes on is not untoward," Longstreet snapped. "And you didn't approve of her relationship with Matthew Shipman, did you?"

Paxton stiffened. "Bea was a beautiful, kind girl. She was proper. I simply cannot believe she would consort with rabble like him."

"And yet she did. More than consort. They were lovers." Paxton winced at the word. "Did that enrage you, Mr. Paxton? That your muse had taken another man to her bed?"

Tears filled the painter's eyes but didn't fall, and Paxton straightened in his chair. "I was unaware of her relationship with Mr. Shipman until after her death," he said in a prim tone. "And had I known, I would have been saddened, not enraged. I suppose I should have paid her more." He sighed.

"What about your other paintings where she was the model?" Daniel asked, earning a sharp look from Longstreet. "Ones that *were* sold? Would you know their whereabouts?"

"Yes, yes." Paxton seemed eager to change the topic from Bea's status as Shipman's mistress. "Gertie kept the records of my sales; it's all in the office at our home. I can get those for you. I remember which featured Bea. Oh, that poor girl." The painter slumped in his chair, pressing his hands over his eyes. Longstreet's lips thinned beneath his moustache, but he seemed to accept that the frail man had nothing more to offer.

After sending Paxton home with an officer who would collect the painter's records, Longstreet tuned to Daniel.

"I appreciate your assistance," he said stiffly. "Though I'm not sure it will be much further needed. The painter Chase is on his way from Long Island as we speak. Between him and Mr. Shipman, I'm sure we have our man. The papers can let go of this ridiculous Jack the Ripper theory now," Longstreet concluded with some relish.

Daniel raised a brow but didn't reply.

"I know you think it was irresponsible to withhold information from the public," Longstreet said, clasping his hands behind his back and expanding his chest. "But we averted an unnecessary public crisis."

Perhaps. And perhaps additional young women had died because they weren't told to be more on guard. Daniel couldn't shake the thought Genevieve had planted, that there might be unknown bodies out there not yet linked to this killer's spree.

Longstreet dismissed Daniel in the same perfunctory way he had Paxton, and within minutes Daniel found himself in the torrid air of Centre Street, his perspiration instantly doubling.

He shoved his hands into his pockets and kept his back to the Tombs, searching in vain for a cab to carry him uptown. Finding none, Daniel turned in that direction and began to walk, though he doubted he'd make it the full distance in this heat.

Thick gray clouds hung low in the sky, obscuring the sun but doing nothing to lessen the stifling heat. If anything, the intense humidity made things worse, as if he were breathing through a damp towel. Daniel tried to distract himself from how his shirt now stuck to his body by pondering the recent turns of event in their investigation.

Longstreet was convinced they were closing in on the murderer, but Daniel wasn't so sure. It was interesting, but not surprising, that Chase was on his way from Long Island to be questioned by the police. The painter was now doubly suspicious—not only had Violet been found in his studio, but she had been posed in death after *his* painting of her. But as far as Daniel knew, Chase's whereabouts on the night of Violet's murder were well accounted for and solid.

Then there was Matthew Shipman, who had been involved with two of the dead women. He also seemed a likely candidate, but what of Ida? There was no evidence, thus far, that she had any connection to the financier. Longstreet seemed to be ignoring her death entirely in the hopes of pinning the murders on one of these two men.

Daniel squinted at the sky, assessing the likelihood of the clouds breaking open, sending some much-needed rain to their city. It didn't look promising, and his mood was as low and troubled as the barometric pressure. He didn't share Longstreet's optimism; in fact, he was slightly suspicious of it. They had gone from having no suspects to having too many, neither of whom seemed to entirely fit the bill.

He stopped on the corner of Grand Street. His cousin Kathleen's brothel was nearby, and Daniel was heartily tempted to take refuge from the heat there, sip something cold in her darkened front room under the gently whirling ceiling fans and try to forget about the lifeless eyes of dead models and the shaking hands of painters and the cold sneer in Longstreet's face, even for a little.

But the thought of Genevieve, who was waiting at home for a report on the interview, was equally—in all frankness, doubly—compelling. Daniel twisted south again, watching the oncoming traffic, and was soon rewarded for his efforts at the sight of a cab. Hailing the driver, he climbed in and gave Genevieve's Washington Square address, knowing that oblivion wouldn't be possible even if he were to try.

He had to see this through. For the sake of the dead, and the living.

CHAPTER 20

Tiredness seemed to pervade Daniel's entire form. He leaned against the doorway of the sitting room where Genevieve had been waiting, hands buried deep in his pockets, his head resting on the jamb. She had been fighting her own exhaustion with coffee and a novel Esmie had recommended; the novel wasn't helping, but the coffee was, especially once it had cooled slightly and been enhanced with a generous helping of sugar.

At the sight of Daniel, though, a current of alertness jolted her into sitting upright.

"How was the interview?" she asked eagerly, tossing the novel onto the settee next to her. It had stung that Longstreet would not allow her to attend.

Daniel peeled himself off the doorframe with a deep sigh, plopping into one of the room's matching armchairs. He had already surrendered his hat at the door, and his sweat-dried hair, rarely neat in the best of circumstances, was starting to spring from his head in unruly coils. He folded his hands on his stomach and stretched his long legs out in front of him, tilting his head back as if he were ready for a nap.

"Would you like some coffee?" she asked with sympathy. Genevieve wasn't sleeping well herself and guessed it was the same for him. "It's lukewarm now, but good and strong."

He raised his head and allowed one corner of his mouth to raise in his signature lazy half smile, a look that never failed to cause a small flutter in her chest.

"That would be divine," he said, then tilted his head to one side as she poured from a pot on the low table at her knees. "It was a nice break while it lasted, in Newport, wasn't it?" Daniel accepted his tepid coffee but drank it with what appeared to be real pleasure.

"It was," she said quietly.

"The interview." Daniel sighed again and set down his cup, rubbing his hand across his face once. "I believe Elbert Paxton is genuinely horror-struck at Beatrice's death. He was also none too pleased to learn about her affair with Shipman, but I do not think he is capable of murder."

Though she had not been at the interview, Genevieve wasn't so sure. Men who felt women didn't behave in the narrowly prescribed ways they wanted were often unpredictable and dangerous.

"You said it was hot; you didn't explain it was *beyond* tropical." Rupert had taken Daniel's place in the doorway and stood, fanning his face with his hat. Nellie hovered behind him, gesturing helplessly to Genevieve that she had a guest before snatching Rupert's hat out of his hand.

"This is outrageous," Rupert continued. "How is one supposed to *think* in such temperatures?"

"They manage it just fine in southern climes, dear," Esmie opined, sliding past Rupert and accepting Genevieve's embrace. Despite her gentle chiding of her husband, moist heat from Esmie's slim back radiated under Genevieve's palm. She sent Nellie for some iced water.

"Perhaps," Rupert allowed, moving to an armchair of his own and fanning his face with his hand, now that he was deprived of his hat. "Surely those who grew up in inferno-like conditions are well used to this. But I am a product of cool mists and constant drizzle and am positively wilting."

"We did warn you," Genevieve noted, motioning for Nellie to put the pitcher of water and glasses on the table and to take the now-cold coffee away.

"Never mind Rupert's harping; we have come to help," Esmie said, moving the discarded novel aside and settling herself on the settee with Genevieve, sending a stern glance at her husband. "As promised. Now, how is the investigation going? What can we do?"

Genevieve exchanged a look with Daniel. They had discussed in advance how Rupert and Esmie might be of help.

"Track down art?" Rupert's brow furrowed at Genevieve's explanation, and he took a long, thoughtful drink of iced water.

"We need to know which other pieces feature any of the deceased models," Daniel elaborated. "Particularly any by Chase or Paxton. As Paxton is handing his records over to the police today, you may not see them for some time." The police had generally been cooperative in sharing their materials as Longstreet had ordered, but sometimes they did take their time in complying with a request.

"But if you speak with him, he may recall quite a lot," Genevieve added. "He remembered which painting my parents owned, and his major figural works are quite rare. He's mostly a landscape painter, one whom, I'm afraid, has rather gone out of fashion in recent years. And Chase has already done the work for us, with Eliza's help, so even if he gives his accounts to the authorities, we have our own copy. I have it here."

"And when is Longstreet interviewing Chase?" Rupert asked.

"Tomorrow, I think. I am not invited to the interview," Daniel admitted.

Rupert raised a brow at him.

"Yes, you were correct, he is not to be trusted," Daniel muttered in response.

"Is this really the best course of action?" Rupert asked, finishing his water in one hearty gulp and setting the glass down with a flourish. "You said Boyle seemed to think Jack the Ripper may indeed be in town. Perhaps you and I . . ." he began, with a speculative look in Daniel's direction.

"No." Esmie's interjection was so firm that Rupert started. She sat ramrod straight, her mouth a thin line. "Absolutely not. You shall not go picking the locks of gangsters' taverns, or getting into fistfights with former prize-fighters, or prowling through the gasworks with a loaded weapon, endangering the entirety of downtown."

"I know my way around a firearm," Rupert protested. "I wouldn't have blown the place up. But Genevieve almost did."

"I most certainly did not," Genevieve interjected with indignation. "That was a crack shot, and you know it."

"I'll not have it, Rupert," Esmie warned, color blooming in her pale cheeks. "All three of you were very nearly killed earlier this summer, despite Genevieve's skill with a gun. It was a very near thing, *too* near. If the task needed to solve this crime is to write letters to purchasers of art and pay society calls to see this art, then that is what we shall do."

Rupert slouched in his chair like a chastened schoolboy. "Nobody's even in town."

"Nonsense. The *wives* are away; the husbands, those in industry at least, are here during the week. Besides, a servant could always let us in to see a piece if her employer writes from Newport and requests it."

Rupert huffed a breath but didn't protest further.

"Longstreet is ready to let the Jack the Ripper theory go, regardless," Daniel informed them all.

"Really?" Genevieve asked. She rattled her ice in her empty glass thoughtfully and then stopped, somehow discomfited by the sound. "To be honest, I don't think he ever thought it was a real possibility. He just didn't want the papers to report it."

"Perhaps," Daniel said. He had removed his jacket but had once again sprawled in his armchair.

"You don't believe Jack the Ripper hopped a boat and is prowling New York, do you?" Rupert asked Daniel.

"No," he said slowly. "But I do wonder if whoever is killing these models was inspired by those actions."

The room stilled. Genevieve thought, again, of the violence men could enact when a woman didn't conform to their wishes. She thought of how Violet had wanted to leave and start a new life and how, conversely, Bea had wanted to stay, entrenching herself deeper into the world of modeling. Of Ida, who had been getting married. Of how Callie had chosen to become someone's mistress rather than enter a loveless marriage for security. Of her own former fiancé, Ted Beekman, who had looked at her with disgust after her mother—a rebellious woman if there ever was one—had been arrested for participating in a rally for women's contraception, as if Genevieve were now tainted by association.

In a different man, Ted's disgusted look might easily have translated into something physical and dangerous.

Had Bea, Violet, and Ida angered the wrong man? Was it even the same man? What was the link, the thread she was missing?

With the mood turning somber, Esmie and Rupert took their leave, Rupert tucking Eliza's list safely into his inner breast pocket. Rupert announced he was going to compose letters to art owners from the comfort of the swimming pool in the basement of Esmie's father's house.

"It's so warm it's akin to taking a bath, but if I'm going to sweat anyway, I might as well do it in water," he said, offering Gavin, who entered the room as they were leaving, a quick handshake.

"I've had a letter from Charles. He is coming home for a few days," Gavin announced, helping himself to water, which still looked cold even though the ice had melted. He cast an askance look at Daniel's outstretched form. "Making yourself at home, McCaffrey?"

Embarrassment washed though Genevieve, though not at Gavin's snipe toward Daniel, who simply raised a brow in response, but at the unsettling moment she had witnessed late the night before.

Genevieve had spent the evening at her office, once again poring over Paxton's, Chase's and Shipman's files, searching for some connection between the three she had missed, working late into the night. She finally took a cab home close to midnight and quietly let herself in so as not to wake Gavin or the servants.

It had been near impossible to sleep in her room since the peeper incident. She had tried, but every time she closed her eyes, the feel of the stranger's moustache tickling her cheek manifested, as if it were happening at that exact moment, and she would jolt upright. After two nearly sleepless nights, she had begun using one of the guest rooms instead.

Last night—or early that morning, she supposed—she had been tiptoeing down the hall to her chosen guest chamber, her shoes hooked in one hand, when the telltale creak of

Gavin's door sounded. She turned, ready to whisper a greeting, when to her shock she saw not Gavin emerge, but Callie.

Moonlight shone through one window at the end of the second-story corridor, illuminating Callie's dark hair and accentuating the pert roundness of her chin. Genevieve's bedroom was close to that window, on the far end, and it was in that direction Callie peered before lightly traversing a few steps and slipping down the stairs. She, like Genevieve, had her shoes in one hand and her skirts slightly hitched in the other. The top few buttons of Callie's fashionable, separate shirt were unbuttoned, though, even as it was neatly tucked into her pale summer skirt.

Callie didn't check the far end of the hall, where Genevieve stood, before making her escape. Having grown up across the Square from the Stewart household, Callie knew the layout of the house intimately, including the fact that two guest rooms occupied this end, which she likely assumed would be empty at present.

Genevieve blinked at the spot where Callie had stood, seeing an afterimage of her friend poised and testing the air like a deer, and for a split second wondered if she had imagined the entire thing. Then, *creeeeaak* came Gavin's door again, and she scurried into her room as fast as she could, pressing her back to her own door and a hand to her pounding heart.

It shouldn't be shocking. She had interrupted Callie and Gavin kissing in the elephant at Coney Island, after all, and knew that feelings had been developing between them. Even so, Callie sneaking out of Gavin's bedroom after midnight could only mean one thing.

Despite her attempts at worldliness and her knowledge of Callie's current life, Genevieve was rather shocked all the same.

Her brother and one of her best friends. Making love, here in her house.

Now Gavin glowered at her. He must have heard the guest room door snap shut and realized she knew what had transpired.

"Why is Charles coming home? Doesn't he have a big race soon?" she asked, keeping her eye on her empty water glass.

"The New York Yacht Club's New London to Newport Cruise is next week, so he will travel to New London from here." Genevieve risked a glance up, relieved to see that, after his initial glare, Gavin seemed equally intent on avoiding her eyes.

She wrinkled her nose at his answer. "That doesn't make any sense," she said. "He'd be doubling his journey."

"I don't know, Genevieve. It's something to do with Walter," Gavin said in a cross tone.

Walter. That went a long way to explaining her brother's ill temper.

"Apparently Walter is returning to town too and wants our brother's opinion on some new project," Gavin continued.

"That is . . . generous," she said carefully. "I know Walter was so disappointed to lose the bank commission."

Gavin shrugged, as if trying to twitch something off his shoulder.

"I'm sure Callie will be pleased at his return," Daniel said cheerfully. His face fell into confusion at the look of extreme displeasure Gavin threw his direction.

"What was that about?" Daniel asked, after Gavin stomped away.

Genevieve hesitated, her own modesty battling with a deep need to unburden herself of her newfound knowledge.

Her anxiousness to confide in somebody won, but beyond that, she truly felt Daniel might be able to help her unpack her complex feelings around the situation.

"Oh," Daniel said, once she had finished explaining what she had witnessed in the early hours of the day.

Annoyance filled her chest. "Oh? That's all you have to say, *oh*?"

"It's a lot to take in."

Genevieve crossed her arms over her chest and immediately uncrossed them.

It was too hot to sit with crossed arms.

"Callie was with Walter at Mother's party," Genevieve said, using the toe of her shoe to trace a pattern on the carpet at her feet. "That was just last week. She hasn't told me she's broken it off with him yet."

Daniel tilted his head in the other direction.

"She probably hasn't."

"And yet she and Gavin . . ." Genevieve couldn't bring herself to say the words out loud, not in front of Daniel. A blush heated her cheeks.

Daniel simply nodded. "That is the logical conclusion, yes."

"I understand what is going on. My brother very likely hasn't offered anything formal yet. And he's going to Chicago. What if Callie were to end things with Walter and then Gavin left town, with no proposal? What would become of Callie?" A sigh wrestled itself out of her. It seemed her worry over Callie would never end; it simply shifted from one challenging situation to the other. She wished her friend would let her help more.

"It does sound as though what she and Walter have is a business arrangement—from her perspective, at least," Daniel said in a gentle tone. He had shifted position and was sitting up a bit straighter, one ankle crossed over the opposite knee. "She has said so, has she not?"

Genevieve nodded, well aware the blush was still staining her cheeks. "I am frustrated with my brother for even embarking on such an affair. He knows all about Callie's arrangement with Walter. I don't like to think he may be taking advantage of her."

A small smile played at the corners of Daniel's mouth. "I cannot imagine Callie would allow herself to be taken advantage of. She has proven herself to be quite resilient. My guess, based on what I know of both parties—and I'll admit I know neither as well as you—is that this is a mutually beneficial arrangement. Women have desires too."

Her gaze caught on his like a sleeve on a thorn, hooked and insistent. Her color deepened, but she couldn't tear her eyes away, transfixed by the intensity and rising heat in his.

Daniel shifted his body forward in his chair, and Genevieve's breath caught in her throat. She found herself leaning toward him, pulled in Daniel's direction as the moon dictates the tide. They might have met in the middle, eventually, had Gavin not entered the room again, flung himself into an empty armchair, and nosily rattled the evening's newspaper.

CHAPTER 21

Laughter exploded into the air as she opened the front door. Genevieve paused awkwardly on her own stoop, unable to see anyone from the foyer, a sudden and bizarre uncertainty welling.

Had Gavin arranged a party and not informed her?

Peering cautiously into the front drawing room, she found her answer.

Everyone was here.

Rupert and Emsie were gathered around the low table in the drawing room, with Callie and Daniel seated across from them, all four still chuckling, Rupert actually wiping tears of mirth from his eyes. Through the door to the dining room, Walter and Charles had papers spread on the table but were looking into the drawing room as well, laughing heartily. Only Gavin, standing by the window that offered a view of the front garden, appeared unmoved by whatever had set off the others, his mouth a thin, set line.

"What is happening here?" Genevieve asked cautiously. Frankly, she was a little nonplussed to find the house so full; despite frequent visits from Daniel, she had become used to only her and Gavin rattling around.

"Ah, you're back," Rupert cried gaily, gallantly rising and gesturing for her to take his seat. "Esmie and Callie were meant to meet for tea this afternoon, but then Walter said he was coming here to meet Charles, so we decided to come along, and Daniel heard of the plan and thought he would join as well. So here we all are!"

"Here you all are," she agreed, a bit dazed at the sight of so many bodies in her house after weeks of quiet.

"There's sandwiches and cold drinks on the sideboard in the dining room, if you're hungry," Gavin said. He looked as disoriented by the commotion as Genevieve felt, but with an additional, barely noticeable anger hovering around his eyes.

Of course. Having to play host to Walter and Callie must be unbearable for him. As it was, the sight of all three of them within a few feet of each other sent a frisson of anxiety skittering around Genevieve's skull, and she wasn't the one engaged in infidelity.

Genevieve took Rupert's seat, shaking her head slightly at Daniel, who had also risen to offer his. She found herself avoiding Daniel's eyes as she sat, arranging her skirts around her, handing her satchel and hat off to Nellie, who had popped in to see if she could bring anyone a drink, and busying herself with removing her gloves.

"Rupert was just telling us the most outrageous story about trying to view Nicholas Fuller's Chase painting," Callie said. Genevieve was relieved to have someone to fix her eyes upon, but frowned slightly when she got a closer look at her friend. Callie's own eyes were bright, nearly feverish, and she was highly flushed.

She was also anxious about being in a social setting with both men, it seemed.

"I would expect nothing less from Rupert," Genevieve said.

He smiled with false modesty.

"But this one is true," Esmie insisted.

"All my stories are true," Rupert said. "I happen to live a somewhat outrageous life. Or outrageous things tend to happen to me, I'm not sure which."

"A bit of both, no?" Daniel asked with his familiar half smile.

"Well, this one happened to me too," Esmie said, waving her hands a little as if to remind everyone she was present. "We had an appointment to see Fuller's painting, another nude where Violet was the model and Chase was the painter."

Genevieve sat a little straighter. "Oh?"

"Yes, we've much to tell you. Mrs. Fuller sent a cable from Newport with her permission and instructions."

"The most proper butler you've ever met answered the door," Rupert said. "I shouldn't disparage my own countrymen, but there is a certain class of British butler who manages to make even the most highly vaunted peer feel like a boy in short pants. This man certainly learned from the best of that ilk."

"Precisely," Esmie agreed. "He gave Rupert's card the most withering look I've ever seen. But he knew we were coming, and we had a copy of Mrs. Fuller's telegram, so he did admit us."

"With some reluctance, of course," Rupert interjected. A smile rose to Genevieve's face unbidden; it was nice to see the pair finishing each other's sentences. Callie and Daniel grinned in anticipation, having already head the outcome of the story. "He led us toward the parlor, which he explained wasn't in use currently, with the family mostly being away."

"Except Mr. Fuller, of course," intoned Emsie in a British accent, presumably in imitation of the butler.

"His words were hanging in the air like in a political cartoon, in a bubble over his head," Rupert said, "'Except Mr. Fuller, of course,' with the most haughty sneer you've ever seen,"

"When the parlor door opened and the man himself came out, saying, 'Yes, Potts?'" Esmie broke in, trying and failing to control fits of laughter as she spoke. "'What is it?'"

"In his undergarments," Rupert finished triumphantly.

Genevieve clapped a hand to her mouth, and the others pealed with renewed laughter.

"His undershorts and shirt," Esmie gasped, blushing at the memory. "In his stockings, held up by garters."

"It was hard to say who was more shocked," Rupert broke in, "poor Mr. Fuller, who gasped and dropped his drink before darting back into the parlor—"

"Or poor Potts, who turned the shade of red typically only seen on a cooked lobster."

"Or us. Esmie uttered a small shriek."

"Well, I was very surprised," Esmie said indignantly. "Even my father, whose manners are nonexistent by polite society's standards, wouldn't roam the house in his undergarments."

"'Please pardon me, it is very hot! I am so sorry, ma'am!' Fuller was yelling from behind the closed door," Rupert said.

Daniel was now nearly doubled over in his chair, he was laughing so hard, and Callie wiped away tears of amusement.

Genevieve was so shocked she simply gaped, her hand still attached to her mouth, though she, too, felt her shoulders shake with humor at the ridiculous picture they were painting.

"Potts stammered and stuttered, trying to explain he'd been in the root cellar overseeing some storage, Mr. Fuller wasn't expected until six, he hadn't realized the gentleman was home . . . I believe at some point he recalled we were an earl and countess," Esmie continued.

"Oh, he turned pale as a sheet. I did think he was about to swoon." Rupert said, explaining they'd agreed to return a different day, when all parties would know the whereabouts of all others.

Walter was now leaning in the doorway of the dining room, grinning at the tale and shaking his head in disbelief. Genevieve realized she hadn't spoken with him in some weeks, even though she had seen him at her mother's party in Newport. He was dressed in his typical unstructured jacket and shirt, his loose tie a bright red, hair unfashionably long. He gazed at Callie with a besotted expression, and a small pang resonated in her chest. Genevieve had no loyalty to Walter, but he had treated Callie well, and she hoped he wouldn't be too bruised by the inevitable parting of ways.

"I hear you've a new commission, Mr. Wilson," Genevieve said politely, also hoping to alert the others, especially Callie, whose back was to the dining room entrance, of his presence.

Callie flushed and twisted in her seat, Walter coming forward to clasp her hand over the back of the chair.

"Yes, in the Thousand Islands," Walter said. "The Adirondacks have been lovely, but it will be even lovelier to travel farther north. Perhaps I can finally convince Callie to accompany me upstate; I don't think I've ever experienced a summer as wretched as it is here."

"Bea was my friend," Callie said, giving Walter a tight smile. "I want to help, and am willing to sweat for it."

Genevieve wasn't sure if she was the only one who caught the swift, charged look between Callie and Gavin, there and gone so fast she would have missed it had she not already been looking directly at her brother.

Walter smiled, then circled around the chair to deposit a small kiss on Callie's cheek, causing her to blush even harder.

"You've done more for Bea than the inept police could," he said firmly as Gavin quietly slipped from the room, "bringing Genevieve and Daniel in to investigate. I can't help but wonder if perhaps, though, the authorities are correct and Shipman did kill those unfortunate girls, much as it pains me to say it," Walter continued. "I had no idea Matt had also been lovers with Violet Templeton."

Nobody had anything to say to that, the previously merry atmosphere of the room dissipating instantly. *And what of Ida?* Genevieve thought. They had no evidence linking the third murder victim to Shipman, and while she had modeled for Chase, it had been years prior, and she didn't appear to have ever sat for Paxton. The beginnings of a headache began to press on her right temple. Figuring out who was murdering these women was akin to riding a carousel, only one that circled too fast and never seemed to end. Round and round they went, back over the same well-trodden territory, theories and suspects rising and falling but the truth remaining as elusive and distant as it had seemed the first day they heard of Beatrice Holler.

"We have compiled a list of Paxton's and Chase's paintings that may feature the victims, based on those artists' records," Esmie said tentatively in the silence that followed Walter's statement. She opened a folder on the table containing a short stack of paper. "And started our visits to see the paintings, as with Mr. Fuller's."

The sight of the paper made Genevieve's head throb more.

"Go ahead and get started without me," she said, standing abruptly. "I think I need some food." She left the room and headed to her father's study, where she knew Nellie would have stored her satchel. More than food, what she really wanted was quiet.

Genevieve sighed as she shut the door behind her and arranged her notes on the desk, reveling in being alone again. Sometimes it helped to parse things out with the group, but tonight, silence seemed essential.

"I brought you this."

The voice startled her out of her deep concentration. A small brass clock that perched on the edge of the desk informed her thirty minutes had passed since she'd retreated to the office, and Genevieve swallowed guiltily. Her friends would be wondering why she hadn't returned.

Or perhaps they understood her need for solitude at the moment.

It wasn't a friend who had gently opened the study door bearing refreshment, though. It was Charles.

Calm suffused her at the sight of her brother, though her headache did not abate. Charles had always had this soothing effect on her; like the yachts he so loved, there was something inherently serene about his presence, all sleek lines and unruffled brow, so unlike Gavin, who was darker, broader chested, and prone to outbursts of extreme temper or joy.

"Thank you," she said, accepting the iced tea he proffered. "How are they getting on in there?"

He shrugged with one shoulder. "I'm not paying all that much attention. Walter and I have been busy."

The tea was good and cold, the sharp tang of lemon hitting the back of her throat with a pleasant sting.

"A better question is, how are *you* getting on in here?" he asked.

Genevieve shifted her attention back to the photographs and documents spread on what was normally her father's desk. Like her thoughts, they seemed jumbled and scattered, nonsensical even, no matter how hard she tried to order them into something coherent.

"Not well," she admitted.

Charles's harsh intake of breath made her turn in her seat in alarm.

"I know that photograph," he said.

Trepidation mixed with hope shot up her spine. Charles was pointing a shaking finger at the photograph of Ida.

"You've seen a painting of a model in that pose?" she breathed. Finally, this could be the missing link. Perhaps whoever owned the painting, or had painted it . . .

But Charles was shaking his head. His eyes remained transfixed on the image, even as his hand now covered his mouth.

"Not a painting. It's from another photograph. I saw it at the last Camera Club exhibition, I'm sure of it. But I don't know that group well, don't know who the artist would be." His head snapped up. "Walter might, though. Let me get him."

Genevieve waited, her heart in her mouth, her breath suddenly fast and shallow.

Charles led Walter into the study, Daniel close on their heels.

"Rupert and Esmie left," Daniel told her quietly as Charles showed Walter the photograph. "They took Callie as well but left the findings with me. We'll discuss them later."

"What do you think?" Charles was asking Walter. "You attended the Camera Club's last exhibition; wasn't there a photograph where the model was posed just like this? But she was in a shallow creek, reaching for an orb of some kind, yes? It was the most striking work in the show, I thought; that's why I remember it so well. I'm right, aren't I?" His finger was indicating the spots he mentioned, but he didn't quite touch the image's glossy surface.

Genevieve looked at the image, the camera's exacting process having caught the most mundane, heart-wrenching details of Ida's death: the pile of hastily discarded clothing, her slack mouth and staring, glassy eyes. The picture was horrible to look at, but it couldn't capture the other details of finding Ida's body in that shed. How there had been so much blood that the entire floor seemed to shimmer a deep, rich red; how its coppery scent had been omniscient, overwhelming to the point of nausea; how Maude's screams had resonated through the night.

She tried to reenvision the scene (with a creek? an orb?) as an artful photograph, and failed utterly.

Walter had not responded yet to Charles's queries but stared intently at the photograph, his face drained of color. Genevieve watched his eyes travel to images of the other women lying faceup on her desk, and she quickly gathered them into a small pile and turned them over.

"I'm so sorry, Walter. I'm sure these are upsetting to see."

He shook himself slightly, as if emerging from a dream, and visibly swallowed. "It's fine," he said with dignity. "I just . . . hadn't seen anything like that before. It's a little unsettling. As to this one . . ." He peered more closely at the image of Ida in Charles's hand. "Yes, I suppose. If the orb were there, it could be the same one you mention. I'm afraid it didn't strike me as much as it did you; I don't recall the details as well."

"But do you recall the photographer?" Genevieve pressed. "If we could find the original work, we could determine if the pose is the same."

Walter shook his head. "I'm afraid not." His tone was apologetic.

"It was a woman, wasn't it? I think that's why I recall the photograph so well. I was deeply impressed at the photographer's ability to capture such mood and presence, and I was—apologies, Genevieve—pleasantly surprised a woman had made the picture."

She gave her brother a sisterly eye roll but then frowned at the photograph consideringly.

"Well, surely that will narrow it down at least a little, yes? Only members of the New York Camera Club can participate in the exhibition, so if we can access the membership roster, we'll at least have somewhere to start."

"It was recently renamed; it had been the Society for Amateur Photographers before last year, I recall," Walter said. He had turned away from the photograph and was leaning against a bookshelf. His normally loose tie was even more open at the neck than usual, and a sheen of sweat glistened on his forehead.

She sympathized. It was quite warm in the small room, with four people crowded in.

"Are you saying more women are involved because the club is for amateurs?"

Walter shrugged. "Many women have taken up photography in recent years. It doesn't require quite the same level as training and talent as painting or sculpture."

Genevieve narrowed her eyes. "I'm sure the photographers themselves would disagree with that assertion."

"It's a machine," Walter said stubbornly. "Quite different from using one's own hands to make art."

"Now isn't the time for a philosophical debate on art," Daniel interjected. "It might be best if we can get a list of what was exhibited in the show last spring. We can go to the Camera Club headquarters; there will be some kind of published record."

Genevieve let the matter of the skill level needed for photography drop, unsure why Walter's comment nettled her so. After all, despite having been gifted a Kodak camera last Christmas from her parents, she didn't consider herself a photographer. "Good idea," she said to Daniel's suggestion.

Having something, someone, new to ponder in this investigation invigorated Genevieve so completely that she began restacking photographs and documents and placing them back in their slim paper sleeve, eager to begin.

"They won't be open now," Daniel said, watching her. "We'll go tomorrow, first thing."

"Tomorrow is Saturday," she replied with frustration. "Will anyone be there?"

"Excuse me, miss." Nellie was at the doorway. If she was confused as to why all four of them were crammed into Mr. Stewart's study, she didn't show it. "You have a visitor."

"A visitor?" Genevieve paused in her tidying, glancing again at the clock. Six in the evening; who would be calling at this hour?

The answer loomed behind Nellie's left shoulder, causing the maid to utter a small involuntary yelp of surprise.

Asher, Daniel's secretary and friend, could only be described as massive. His nose was slightly crooked in his scarred, rough-hewn face, a remnant of his days as a professional boxer. Genevieve didn't blame Nellie for her reaction, but she knew Daniel considered Asher to be family. She was fond of the giant man, even though they had barely exchanged twenty words.

He had helped save her life, and Daniel's, more than once.

Daniel was at his side in an instant, worry furrowing his brow, and Genevieve rose in concern.

"This came for you," Asher said in a voice as coarse as his face, handing a note to Daniel. "Thought you'd want it right away."

Genevieve crowded behind Daniel to read the note as he opened it. He held it higher so she could see, and she gave a small gasp at its content.

"What?" Charles demanded. "What has happened?"

It was Daniel who replied.

"Matthew Shipman has been arrested for the murders of Beatrice Holler and Violet Templeton."

CHAPTER 22

Longstreet's message sent the crowded room into turmoil. Charles uttered a soft curse, while Walter let out a short, stunned yell: *No.* Even though he had suggested his friend might be guilty a mere thirty minutes prior, he was visibly shaken. Gavin reappeared, pressing around Asher's solid form and scowling at the news.

Genevieve caught his eye and shook her head, once.

He's not the killer, the look said.

Daniel inclined his head toward the door an inch. *Let's get out of here.*

"There's far too many of us in this room," Gavin said in an authoritative tone. "Come out and let's reassemble in the dining room—there's more food."

"But Matt was at the Carson stag party the night Bea died. At Sherry's. I was there, I saw him. As did over a dozen other men," Walter said to no one in particular as they dutifully trailed after Gavin. "I was only trying to placate Callie when I said he might be guilty; I don't really think Matt could be a killer." He sent an anguished look around the room, as if his comment had somehow caused his friend's arrest.

"There is a good deal of evidence against Shipman," Daniel said slowly, though he remembered how the man had seemed to vanish the night of the birthday party he and Gavin had attended, from the same private room at Sherry's that Walter mentioned.

Something wasn't adding up. Or several things, for that matter. Had Shipman been able to slip out of Sherry's somehow, unseen by Walter, and commit Bea's murder? Would he really have killed Violet, the woman he professed to love deeply?

And what of Ida?

Daniel stared at the array of food Genevieve's staff had left on the sideboard, at the architectural renderings Charles and Walter had spread over the table, at the others starting to pile their plates while pondering the implications of Matthew Shipman's arrest in low tones.

An urgency tugged, as if it were physically pulling his sleeve toward the door. He didn't want to discuss the possibilities of what might have occurred in front of the others. He wanted—no, he *needed*—to do so with Genevieve. Alone.

Once again, Daniel caught her eye and gestured that they should leave, not bothering to hide his impatience, not caring if he was being rude. Her amber gaze swept the room, seeming to see what he did: Walter's anxiety, Charles's somewhat detached concern, Gavin's glowering. She nodded her firm agreement and wrapped several cold chicken sandwiches in sky-blue linen napkins before unobtrusively slipping out of the dining room behind him.

Once in the hallway, he summoned Asher as well. "Can you give us a lift?"

Genevieve gave a sandwich to Asher and, once they were settled in Daniel's carriage, one to him. He hadn't realized how ravenous he was, and the perfectly roasted chicken between slices of thick, chewy bread slathered with a biting mustard were exactly what he needed.

"Where are we going?" Genevieve asked, taking a large bite of her own sandwich.

"I have an idea," he said between mouthfuls, wiping his lips with the napkin. The food was good but making him thirsty; he would get Asher to stop at a grocer's for some bottles of beer.

After they had procured drinks, Daniel had Asher take them into Five Points, his childhood neighborhood. Genevieve's eyes widened in surprise when they pulled over on a rough-looking Orange Street block.

"What are we doing here?" Genevieve asked, looking out the window cautiously. "I didn't think the murders had much connection to this neighborhood."

"I don't think so, either," Daniel said. "But I believe there's someone here who can help us. Would you rather wait in the carriage?"

In response, Genevieve climbed out after him, as he'd assumed she would, and followed him around the corner and into Mulberry Bend.

"Daniel," she began in a soft voice, but didn't finish. He knew she, like him, must be thinking of the night they'd met. The night she had followed him, Paddy, and Billy into this alley, trying to find information about a jewel thief.

The night he had watched her from one of the fire escapes above, appalled and impressed in equal measure by her bravery.

Without thinking too hard about it, Daniel reached down and clasped Genevieve's hand. It was ungloved, as they'd left the house so quickly, and her palm was dry and warm as her long fingers wrapped around his.

Keeping their hands intact, he gently pulled her toward a closed door that seemed unremarkable, no different from the several others in the darkening alley, and knocked.

A small panel within the door opened and a hostile face peered out. Beside him, Genevieve stiffened in surprise, her hand tightening slightly on his.

"He here tonight?" Daniel asked, his voice automatically slipping into the rougher cadences of his youth.

There was a grunt from the other side of the door before the panel slid shut, though whether the sound signaled assent or negation, Daniel wasn't quite sure. He took a step back and waited, subtly keeping Genevieve at his back, their palms still clasped. After a few moments, the door opened.

"Ah, Mr. McCaffrey. I thought it might be you. And with Miss Stewart. Nice to see you again."

Dagmar Hansen stepped into the waning light of the alley, wiping his hands on a rag, which he shoved into his jacket pocket before extending his palm to shake.

Genevieve dropped Daniel's hand to meet Dagmar's outstretched one.

His palm tingled at the loss, inexplicably cold.

She glanced between their faces, obviously confused as to how and why they were here.

"There is a tavern in the basement, Miss Stewart," Dagmar explained. "In my hours off, I've been taking photographs of various parts of this neighborhood and some others to offer pictorial proof of the wretchedness of how the deeply impoverished live. Our thought is, perhaps if those in charge really see these conditions, they will become serious about reform."

"Our?" she asked.

"I've been aware of Dagmar's project for some time," Daniel explained, "and am now one of his funders. He told me he would be here tonight. You didn't leave your equipment down there, did you?"

"No, no, it is far too early to take any pictures. I will return later, in the middle of the night. Now is for recognizance only."

Daniel asked Genevieve for the picture of Ida's corpse, the very one Dagmar had taken. She pulled it out of her satchel, realization dawning on her face as to the purpose of their visit.

"I am sorry to disturb your important work, but we need urgent answers, and I thought you might have them. You recall this photograph you took, yes?" Daniel asked.

Dagmar blinked solemnly at the image. "Of course. The young lady at Coney Island, in the shed. Even in my line of work, a most horrific scene."

Genevieve picked up Daniel's questioning. "My brother Charles and another friend both believed the pose of the body to match that of a photograph taken by a member of the Camera Club. You are a member, are you not?" She cast a swift, quizzical look to Daniel, who nodded slightly, confirming, his whole body starting to hum with anticipation. It was happening again, that conjunction between them where they almost seemed to read each other's thoughts. He could feel it in the air between them as it became charged, nearly electric.

"Did you see something like this at the last exhibition?" she continued. "Charles said there was a stream and the woman was reaching for a glowing orb."

The sun was setting, but there was enough light left to make out the main feature of the photograph—the shape of Ida's body—even if some of the details were lost. Dagmar squinted at it. "I was away this spring, visiting my home country, Denmark," he said apologetically. "I missed the exhibition."

"The figure was probably a nude," Daniel pressed. The man was a very active member of the Camera Club; surely *something* they said would ring a bell. "And we believe the photographer is a woman."

Relief poured through him as Dagmar's face lit up. "Ah, *ja*. Dorothy Flender makes pictures very close to what you describe. Almost always a nude, in a mystical landscape; this is what she is known for. Her work is very good, very modern." He grimaced at the photograph, as if he could not reconcile what was printed there with the art he could envision.

"Do you know where we might find her?" Genevieve asked. She lightly touched Dagmar's sleeve. "She's not in trouble or danger, but it is important."

"She lives on a farm on Staten Island," Dagmar said with a small shrug. "I have not been there; I only know as she has said how long it takes her to get to our monthly meetings. She is a very private person, I think."

They thanked Dagmar profusely and made their way back to the carriage.

"I've never been to Staten Island," Genevieve said. She too was thrumming with excitement, obviously ready to chase their new lead.

"We should wait until tomorrow," Daniel said, looking out the window as the carriage wove its way through Five Points' filthy streets. Even as he said it, he knew they would go tonight, indeed had already directed Asher to take them downtown to the ferry. It was part of that symmetry they were sharing; he knew in his bones, as Genevieve did, exactly what their next step would be.

Even though it was ill-conceived. So much so, he felt compelled to make a token protest. "It's nearly eight o'clock and will be dark in an hour. We don't even know where this woman lives."

"Someone will probably know, don't you think? We'll ask for the Flenders' farm. Surely there are cabs?"

"I've only been twice, on legal business early in my career, before I left for Europe," Daniel said. They moved away from the narrow, cramped tenements, so like the one he had grown up in, toward the stately, stern buildings of the financial district, shuttered and quiet at this time on a Friday. "I took a cab one of those times, but it was during business hours. Another time, the client sent a carriage to meet me at the ferry."

Genevieve twisted in her seat to peer out the window and into the sky. "I think we've enough time to at least try," she insisted, turning back to him. "This is the first lead we've had in ages, and I have a feeling it could be significant. I'm also afraid if we don't find answers soon, more women will die."

Daniel looked back out his own window, the movement of the carriage creating a slight breeze from the still, fetid air trapped among the downtown streets. His knee jangled a restless rhythm of its own accord.

Unease mixed with fervor gnawed at his gut.

Genevieve was right on both counts. They were getting closer.

They were also running out of time.

He could feel it too.

Twenty minutes later, a far better breeze lifted his hair and ruffled it, offering his sweaty brow much-needed relief.

Moonlight skittered across the dark, gently roiling waters of the Upper New York Bay. He and Genevieve leaned against the ferry railing, watching the water ripple and curl. Their shoulders didn't quite touch, but they were close enough the warmth from her torso radiated, heating Daniel's left side.

They were on their way to Staten Island.

Salty air filled his lungs, fresh and satisfying. The rising moon was portentous and fat, a stark contrast to the thin, sinister crescent it had been the night he and Genevieve had climbed the howdah at Coney Island. Daniel remained doubtful of the entire endeavor but kept those thoughts to himself. They were inextricably bound to the course they were now on, sure as if they'd been strapped into the Channel Chute on that fateful night. It would take an extreme amount of luck to find this Dorothy Flender and make it back in time for the ten o'clock ferry to Manhattan, the last one of the night. Asher would wait for them in case they caught the boat, but Daniel reminded himself to keep an eye out for potential lodgings as soon as they disembarked.

Just in case.

Another deep breath. He could feel Genevieve following suit next to him, her entire upper body expanding on her inhale.

Maybe they would find the photographer quickly and make the ferry home after all. That was an awfully lucky-looking moon.

The shoreline approached, the lights of the dock shining. The ferry groaned and clanked as it slowed and maneuvered into place, its workers deftly throwing and securing lines. Daniel and Genevieve lined up to disembark with a handful of other passengers; at this time of night, most of the island's residents who worked in the city had already gone home, and it was still too early for those enjoying Manhattan's nightlife to be making their way across the water. He guessed the later ferries, those leaving New York at nine thirty or ten, would be far more crowded.

They entered a bustling downtown filled with restaurants and dwellings and, Daniel noted, a large, handsome hotel. Cabs were plentiful, though the first driver Daniel inquired had not heard of a Dorothy Flender, or her farm.

"Daniel," Genevieve called, waving him to a different vehicle.

"The Flender place isn't that far," the man at the cab said, tilting his hat back. Now that they were off the ferry, the refreshing breeze had disappeared, but the buildings were neither as close nor as crowded here in St. George, and the air didn't feel nearly as oppressive as it had in the city. "Bright Haven, it's called. I can take you there, sure."

Daniel's pulse quickened as the cab wended its way out of the town's streets and onto a dark country lane. The bay remained in sight to their left, still visible by the light of that heavy moon. As he watched, though, a cloud passed over it, momentarily darkening the landscape. Craning his neck, Daniel saw other clouds gathering to the south, crowding against the moon-bright sky.

Would they break? Would the city, at long last, have the rain it so sorely needed?

The ride wasn't long. Within twenty minutes, the carriage stopped at a fence at the end of a lane. The driver leaned over and gestured down the lane. "Bright Haven is there. Not sure if anyone's home."

As the cab rattled its way back to town, Daniel surveyed their surroundings. The smell of the sea was strong and pungent. A few other houses dotted the nearby landscape, a light or two gleaming through their windows, but for the most part, the Flender land, as far as he could tell, sat in glorious semi-isolation, right on the tip of where the bay emptied into the Atlantic.

"Bright Haven is a nice name," Genevieve said. She sounded cautious. "Let's see if anyone is home." She began to walk down the lane, peeking behind her shoulder to make sure Daniel was following.

He jogged a few steps to catch up, his stomach twinging with unease at the sight of her walking into darkness alone. Down the dark lane, the moonlight played hide-and-seek behind those clouds, first brightening their path, then obscuring it. Genevieve clapped her hands on her skirt as it fluttered in an unexpected strong gust of wind.

"That feels delicious," she said in a delighted low voice.

Daniel agreed; the wind did feel delicious. Its sudden appearance added to his unease, though, and he sent another worried look toward the ever-increasing clouds.

Once they were over a slight bend, the pointed gables of dormer windows rose into view. A few more steps and the rest of the house followed: a neat, trim white structure with a sloping roof, the dormers lining the upper story. The surrounding front gardens were lush, filled with drooping hydrangeas and late-blooming roses, the flowers hanging heavily on their stalks. Even in the intermittent light, it was obvious the garden and home were well cared for.

The house, though, was dark and shuttered.

Genevieve made a little hiss of frustration. "Shall we knock anyway?"

Daniel tilted his head and considered the house. It sat on a slight rise, facing the water. The sound of gentle lapping must be soothing at night.

Bright Haven was dark, true. But it didn't feel empty.

It felt like they were being watched.

"Hello?" He kept his voice pitched low, but loud enough for anyone within to hear. "Is anybody home?"

Only the chorus of night insects answered.

The wind blew again, unnerving in its strength. He frowned as he checked the sky again.

There did not seem to be any doubt now. A storm was coming.

Daniel jutted his chin toward the back, then made his way around the house on quiet feet. Genevieve followed, once again having to hold down her unruly skirt in the face of another strong gust. The back garden was as well kept as the front, precisely arranged with big, luscious flowers. An empty hammock strung between two trees swayed gently next to a small well, and in the far corner stood a little shack, perhaps for gardening equipment.

It did seem a haven, this quiet slice of Staten Island, and it was obviously meant to be a calming place, offering respite.

So why was he so unsettled?

The back door was only a few cautious steps away. He took them, Genevieve close at his heels.

Daniel stood at the back door, his fist raised to knock, but something gave him pause. Some sense of movement in the stillness.

The unmistakable sound of a shotgun being cocked rang though the night.

Daniel froze.

"I don't know who you are or what you want, but get off my property."

CHAPTER 23

Daniel raised his hands in the air, anxious to demonstrate he was unarmed. He turned, slowly, and stepped in front of Genevieve as he faced the silhouette of the shotgun-wielding woman behind them.

She must have emerged from the shed he'd noticed earlier.

"I said, get off my property." The shotgun made an arc to the right, a shooing motion.

"Dorothy Flender?" Daniel asked.

"I won't ask again," the woman growled.

"We want to talk to you about Ida Gouse," Genevieve said.

"I know why you're here," the woman, presumably Dorothy, snapped. "You're that journalist, aren't you? I was warned you would come. I've got nothing to say, and for the last time, you are trespassing on private property." The silhouette advanced three quick steps, and Daniel retreated as far as he could go, stumbling a little as he shoved Genevieve backward.

Dammit. Genevieve was pressed against the back door of the house, Daniel shielding her with his body. There was deep shrubbery on either side of the doorway, blocking any exit.

"We're leaving," he yelled. "Lower the gun and let us pass; we'll be on our way."

In response, the figure stepped closer. His heartbeat ratcheted up and the back of his neck tingled in alarm.

"Mrs. Flender, please," Genevieve called. She sounded frightened but determined. "We just want to find out who killed her."

The figure stilled, and Daniel held his breath.

"Ida deserves justice." Genevieve's voice floated from behind him, softer now, pleading.

They remained there, suspended, for what couldn't have been more than thirty seconds but felt like hours.

Finally, the shotgun lowered a few inches. A sigh of pure relief wrested itself from the innermost depths of his chest, and muscles he hadn't realized he'd been clenching relaxed.

A muffled noise rose in the darkness. It took a few moments to realize it was coming from Dorothy.

She was crying as quietly as she could, her shoulders shaking with the effort of suppressing her emotion.

Genevieve stepped around him before he could stop her and approached Dorothy cautiously, like one might a wild animal. "Mrs. Flender? Dorothy?"

A break in the clouds allowed a shaft of moonlight to illuminate Dorothy's face. She was younger than Daniel had expected, though he wasn't sure why he had envisioned her as elderly. But she was perhaps his age, in her midthirties, not as tall as Genevieve but taller than most women, wearing a simple dark blouse and striped skirt.

"Miss," she finally said. "Not missus."

"Miss Flender, then." Genevieve reached a hand toward the woman in a gesture of consolation but then dropped it. Daniel had to stop himself from rushing forward, mindful of that cocked gun. It was lowered but would be easy enough to swing upward again. "You're right, I'm Genevieve Stewart. Polly Palmer. How did you know I might be coming?"

It was an excellent question, one Daniel very much wanted the answer to as well. The wind gusted again, making his jacket flap.

Dorothy scrubbed at her face with the back of her hand, seeming angry at her tears. "So you want to find Ida's killer." Her voice was unbearably weary. "What else do you want to know?"

Daniel caught Genevieve's confused look in the moonlight. "I don't understand what you mean. Someone has killed three women, all artist's models, including Ida. An arrest has been made, but we don't think the authorities have the right person. We believe the real murderer is still out there. You knew Ida, it seems?" Genevieve took another cautious step toward Dorothy. "Cared for her?"

Dorothy raised her head, a flash of defiance plain on her face.

"Of course I knew her. Ida was the love of my life."

★   ★   ★

Dorothy lit several gas lamps in what seemed to be the main sitting room of Bright Haven, casting the space in a warm, golden glow. Genevieve was grateful for the invitation to come inside. The wind had begun to pick up quite a lot, and the temperature was dropping.

"Thank you for letting us in," she said.

Dorothy looked over her shoulder at Genevieve briefly, then lit a final lamp.

"Storm's coming," was her only response.

Daniel remained close to the door, arms crossed in front of his chest, keeping a wary eye on the gun still dangling from Dorothy's right hand.

The house was cozy, with red-and-pink wallpaper, gleaming wood floors, and vases of fresh flowers on multiple surfaces. Framed photographs were everywhere: hanging on walls, cluttering tabletops, lined across the mantel. Genevieve's eyes swept across them, trying to take in as much information as she could.

Dorothy herself was an elegant-looking woman, with a sharp jaw and a long, regal nose, her soft brown hair loosely bundled at the nape of her beck. She had the type of countenance Genevieve associated with Parisians, and she could picture Dorothy in a terribly fashionable black dress, striding across one of that city's wide boulevards, not deigning to meet anyone's eye.

"Did Ida have any connection to Matthew Shipman?" Daniel asked.

Dorothy finally put the gun down, laying it across a flowered settee. Her mouth twisted.

"I know who he is. No. Ida danced at one or two of his parties years ago, she told me, but she hadn't had to do that kind of work for a long time."

Genevieve wondered if there were parts of Ida's life Dorothy didn't know about.

"How did you meet?" Daniel asked. He had uncrossed his arms and was taking in a series of three photographs hung vertically near the doorway. Dorothy and Ida, their arms around each other's waists, the water behind them. In the first, they were looking over their shoulders at the camera, smiling, Dorothy's impish grin making her look like a young girl. In the second, they stared into each other's eyes, arms still linked. In the final, their backs were toward the photographer as they gazed at the sea, each with an arm wrapped around the other's back.

Dorothy looked surprised at Daniel's question, and so was Genevieve. Rather than answering him, though, Dorothy looked to Genevieve, her earlier defiance now mixed with melancholy.

"You don't want to write about us? About me and Ida? I won't have her memory tarnished. Or her fiancé Mike knowing; it would ruin him. She never wanted that."

"You have my word," Genevieve said, and meant it. She had no interest in besmirching Ida's name or in exposing what was clearly a private matter. "We are hunting for the murderer, nothing else."

Dorothy nodded once. She didn't invite them to sit, but Genevieve didn't mind. She was grateful Dorothy didn't kick them out.

"We met at a party," Dorothy said, smiling slightly at the memory. "A fancy-dress one. It was a little wild, but fun. Ida was costumed as Boudica. It made quite an impression."

Something tickled Genevieve's memory, but she couldn't put her finger on what.

"And you?" Daniel asked. "What was your costume?" Genevieve followed his gaze to another series of photographs, these hung on the other side of the door. They resembled what Charles and Dagmar had described: nude women in various mythical-looking landscapes, here at one with a tree, in the next rising seamlessly from the ocean. Genevieve didn't know much about photography but assumed Dorothy had augmented the prints somehow to obtain the effects she had gotten. They were quite dream-like, a cross between a painting and a photograph.

Ida was the model in every one.

"I was a cowpoke," Dorothy replied. "Ten-gallon hat, boots, and spurs. I carried a child's toy horse. Ida said it was the funniest thing she'd ever seen."

Genevieve's heart contracted as Dorothy relayed the rest of her tale. They'd begun seeing each other at art-related events, openings, and parties, and soon fallen in love.

"We had a beautiful life here," Dorothy said in a voice tinged with sadness, running her finger along the mantel-piece. "Peaceful. I grew up here, and renamed the place Bright Haven once my parents passed and it was mine. It was our home, for a time." She sighed. "But after a few years, Ida couldn't stand the secrecy. She wanted a conventional life. Children. I couldn't deny her anything she wanted."

"Even if it meant losing her?" Genevieve asked quietly.

Dorothy offered a melancholy smile. "Even then. Her happiness was the most important thing, you see. I'd rather she was happy without me than always wanting with me."

Genevieve flitted her gaze to Daniel, quickly, and caught the small furrow in his brow in return. He was thinking the same thing she was, she would bet anything. That Dorothy's sentiments were almost the same as what Matt Shipman had said about Violet.

"So you didn't mind she was marrying another?" Daniel asked.

A harsh laugh rose from their hostess. "What an odd thing to ask, Mr . . . ?"

"McCaffrey."

Dorothy's mouth twisted again, but this time into a wry smile. "It's clear to me you've never truly been in love, Mr. McCaffrey."

Daniel's eyes flew to Genevieve's and caught them, a shocked expression on his face. Genevieve felt heat flush her cheeks, and she turned abruptly, unwilling to attempt to unravel whatever his look signified. She swallowed, staring at but not quite seeing the photographs on the wall she was facing.

"Of course I minded." Dorothy's voice was the embodiment of regret, of sorrow itself. "But she wanted things I could not give her. I had to let her go."

"And what of this project?" Genevieve didn't have to turn to know Daniel was speaking of the remarkable series of Ida, posed as if one with nature itself.

"We finished it before she left. I would have made more, but it wouldn't have been proper, once she was a wife."

Daniel drew in breath to speak; even across the room, it was audible. But Genevieve raised a hand to still him.

She had finally registered what the photograph on the wall contained.

It made her blood run cold. So cold, in fact, that for a moment she was unable to speak, utterly gripped with terror.

"Miss Flender," she finally rasped. "Was this taken at the fancy-dress party where you and Ida met?" She turned to find Daniel looking concerned.

"It was." Dorothy joined her, brushing her fingertips over the glass covering the image.

"And was that party at the Tenth Street Studio Building, by chance?" Genevieve had trouble getting the words out.

Images and snippets of conversation flashed through her mind, flipping faster and faster.

"Yes." Dorothy sounded surprised. "A photographer keeps a studio there, George Collins Cox. He set up his equipment that night, created a makeshift studio so he could capture our costumes. Like they do for society parties. He took that."

Daniel was at Genevieve's shoulder now, his harsh intake of breath at the photograph loud in her ear.

The photograph showed exactly what Dorothy had described: herself as a cowboy, in a large hat paired with a plaid shirt and trousers, a kerchief around her neck, a small toy horse tucked under her arm. A cigarette dangled from one corner of her mouth as she affected a tough expression. On her left stood Ida, tall and willowy in a long, pleated Roman-style gown, cinched in under her bodice, with an armored helmet atop her loose hair. Unlike Dorothy, Ida was smiling broadly, holding a cigarette up between two fingers, the other hand on her hip.

To Dorothy's right was a man costumed as a court jester in a patchwork shirt and trousers. The man's face was covered in a half mask, and a jester's belled hat sat on his head, under which flowed long, almost shoulder-length hair.

Like a magic lantern slide show gone berserk, memories and thoughts piled atop each other.

Ida on the train to Coney Island: *You know I was Walter's* Columbia, *the one he did for the Centennial.*

Columbia, so similar in costume to Boudica.

Elbert Paxton, sighing: *Ah, my Beatrice. My angel, my muse . . . When I returned from the mountains last fall, she told me she was too busy with other projects, other commitments.*

Matthew Shipman, his visage a picture of anguish: *Violet ended things with me a few months ago. She had quit modeling, was going to study to be a nurse.*

William Chase, speaking of Violet: *She was my favorite model, you see.*

And back to the beginning, Walter saying of Bea and Paxton: *She truly was his muse, if she was anyone's; he created some of his best work with her as his model. His heart was breaking that she wouldn't sit for him any longer.*

Click, click, click. In Genevieve's mind, the puzzle pieces pulled themselves together as though magnetized, finding their homes with a sickening, insectile sound.

"It was Walter Wilson who told you a journalist called Polly Palmer might come to speak to you about Ida, wasn't it?" Daniel asked. His voice sounded very far away.

"It was," Dorothy confirmed. "That's him, there." One of her long, elegant fingers traced the photograph's surface again, indicating the man in the court jester outfit. "He's a good friend, Walter."

The floor was suddenly unsteady beneath her feet, and Genevieve grasped Daniel's arm for support.

Click, click, click. Pictures and words kept rotating and rearranging in her mind.

Callie. *He's so sentimental, he's taken to calling me his muse.*

"But Walter's been upstate," Daniel was saying, frowning at the photograph.

Why did he still sound so far away? He was standing right next to her.

"Walter? No, he's been in the city all summer." Dorothy sounded as confused as Daniel and equally distant.

"We were told he had an important commission on a chalet in the Adirondacks. And now one in the Thousand Islands. I saw the plans."

The world snapped back into place, Daniel and Dorothy no longer receding but next to her, solid.

"He was lying, Daniel." Genevieve was surprised at how strong her own voice sounded. "He lied."

"Dammit," Daniel swore, rushing to the window. Trees lashed back and forth in the wind.

"What is going on?" Dorothy asked. Her voice, too, was strong, her jaw set firmly. "What do you mean, Walter lied? About being in town? He's been here all summer," she repeated. "Finishing his *Persephone*. He hasn't had any new architectural work for months, not since he lost that bank commission in the spring. Though honestly, it's been drying up since the disaster of his post office building a decade ago, the one with the controversial *Athena* statue."

Genevieve sank into a nearby rocking chair, heedless of propriety. She buried her head in her hands, and for a brief moment, the world went gray. She took a deep breath and raised her head, the room swimming back into focus.

"It was Walter," Daniel said. "We bought his lies so easily." Pain and self-recrimination were etched on his face, a portrait of stunned regret.

"How were we to know?" Genevieve responded in a wooden tone, more for form's sake than because she believed it.

They should have known. Somehow, they should have.

A small wooden cuckoo clock ticked away on the mantelpiece.

Click, click, click.

Nausea rose at the back of her throat at the steady beat of those hands, at what their constant, relentless progress signified.

They had missed the last ferry back to New York.

They were trapped on Staten Island until the morning.

A killer was just across the bay. He knew they had come to find Dorothy. He knew he was about to be exposed.

And he had Callie.

CHAPTER 24

The rising wind had kicked up the water, turning the normally calm bay into something churning, its waves lapping at Bright Haven's small shore. Daniel paced its length, furious with himself.

There had to be a way back to the city.

Genevieve stood motionless, staring at the distant lights of Manhattan.

"We could swim for it," she said.

"It's much too far."

"We did so before." The big, round moon was fully obscured by clouds now, but there was enough light shining from Dorothy's white house that he could clearly see as she began to unbutton the top of her dress.

"Genevieve, no. That was life-or-death." They were both referring to when they had swum across the East River earlier that summer.

"And this isn't?" she snapped. She kept going, her fingers trembling at the buttons.

He stepped forward and caught her hands, stilling her motions. "Of course it is. But the water is far too rough. If we die, Walter gets away with this."

"And if we don't try, Callie may not live to see the morning." Tears were bright in her eyes, but her face was furious.

Daniel knew they were thinking the same thing: Callie might already be dead.

His gut twisted. How had they not seen it?

Walter had somehow slipped away from Sherry's, taken Callie's key to Bea's apartment and killed her there, then slipped back in, providing an alibi for Matthew Shipman, even after killing the man's mistress.

Because Walter had provided the alibi, nobody had thought to question *his* whereabouts.

He had known Violet was staying in Chase's studio, as he had been in the Tenth Street Studio Building the whole summer, hiding out. Perhaps he had knocked on the door, bearing a bottle that had left those empty glasses. And she knew him, trusted him, allowed him inside.

Ida had trusted Walter also, when he approached her at the bar in the elephantine colossus, and followed him easily, eager to engage in one last, seemingly harmless adventure, sliding down the trunk to her death.

He had followed them, somehow, all the way to Coney Island.

Had Walter been following Callie, or Ida? Daniel didn't know, but the results had been disastrous all the same.

And Walter might have seen what he and Genevieve saw. He might have seen Callie and Gavin together, might have surmised Callie was planning to end her relationship with Walter.

Which put Callie in terrible danger.

"We can walk back to town, find a telegraph, and send a cable to Longstreet." But he knew this could take hours, if they could even find an establishment with a telegraph office open at this hour.

"You think he did it?" Dorothy's voice cut across the wind. She strode over the lawn, stopping at the shoreline where they stood. "You think it was Walter?"

They had rushed from the house, barely even acknowledging Dorothy in their haste to find some way, any way, to return to the city.

"I'm sorry, Miss Flender," Genevieve said. "But yes, we are quite certain."

In the dim light, Dorothy paled.

"How do we get back?" Daniel asked, pointing across the water. "Is there any way?"

Their hostess eyed the churning waves with a steely gaze, even as evident grief drooped her features.

"Follow me."

Less than fifteen minutes later, they were in a neat sailboat, far too small for the current water conditions. The little boat repeatedly jerked up, then splashed back down, washing them with fine, salty spray. Daniel's fingers ached from gripping the craft's edges, and he kept an eye on Genevieve, making sure she held on just as tightly.

"I've sailed these waters my entire life," Dorothy said, casting a gimlet eye their way. "Bit of chop tonight, but she can take it."

Daniel had no choice but to believe her.

His stomach swooped up along with the boat, then sank as they descended from the swell.

"Why?" Dorothy asked. She kept her eye on the water, on their destination.

She didn't need to articulate any further. *Why Ida? Why the others?*

"I don't know exactly," Daniel admitted. That wasn't entirely true. He had ideas; he just wasn't sure how to articulate them yet.

"Muses," Genevieve said. Dorothy's eyes briefly slid to Genevieve, then forward again. "He is obsessed with the idea of muses."

"Yes," Daniel added. As often happened, Genevieve knew exactly how to voice what he was thinking. "The why of his obsession, we don't know. But the pattern is there. The women were all models. They all worked with artists who considered them their muse, their favorite model, someone who inspired them to create their best work. And when, for various reasons, the woman chose to end that relationship, to move on, Walter . . . retaliated."

At the tiller, Dorothy flinched at little, even though Daniel took pains not to say any of the actual words that more aptly described what happened to the victims: *killed, murdered, throats cut.*

"Your friend," Dorothy said instead. "The one posing for *Persephone.* You believe her to be in danger?"

Genevieve closed her eyes briefly.

"We do," Daniel said. "She has begun a relationship with someone else."

The lights were getting closer. *Swoosh, drop.* Another spray of water coated him, dampening his shirt, his collar gone limp.

Across the stern, Genevieve was shivering.

"There." Dorothy pointed. Daniel couldn't see anything specific in the wild spray and the dark, just the lights, a mix of warm gas and cold electric, gleaming from buildings dotting the southernmost tip of the city.

Dorothy had brought them up the East River a short ways, though not quite as far as the East River Bridge.

"There's a few docks here boats like mine can use," she said. "I won't be able to join you; I can't leave her or she'll get impounded. I'll have to make my way back tonight."

"Is that safe?" he asked. "Those clouds will surely break soon."

Dorothy didn't answer, focusing all her attention on maneuvering the small craft toward the dock, which appeared out of the night like an apparition, something from a pirate story.

As they approached the dock, Daniel readied himself, crouching on the edge of the boat. Dorothy raised a brow at him but stayed silent, only nodding to herself as he leapt onto the slippery dock and grabbed the line she threw, pulling it taut around a barnacle-encrusted cleat.

Genevieve's hand in his was slick with salt water, but she climbed steadily from the rocking boat.

"You said you wanted justice for Ida," Dorothy said, watching Genevieve disembark.

"We do. And we'll find it, I promise," Daniel said, leaning down to uncoil the line. He held it tight, waiting for Dorothy to give the signal she was ready to leave.

"You know what that means," Dorothy said, meeting his eye squarely. "You know what he did. And you know what he deserves."

A disquiet that had nothing to do with the sudden gust of wind that made the boat rock harder settled over him.

He did know.

★ ★ ★

"Fifty-One West Tenth Street," Genevieve told the driver.

She and Daniel hadn't discussed their destination, but Dorothy had said Walter had spent the summer finishing his *Persephone* sculpture, and that meant only one place.

The Tenth Street Studio Building.

The interior of the hansom cab was hot and stuffy following the sharp winds that now whipped between the buildings of lower Manhattan. Pedestrians hurried along the streets, hunched against the wind as they glanced nervously at the sky, eager to find shelter.

Tap, tap, tap. The first hard clicks of rain batted against the carriage, but Genevieve still longed to crack the window next to her to let in some fresh air. The walls of the cab, Daniel's warm form pressing against her left side, the heavy dampness of her clothes from the boat ride all conspired against her.

Couldn't this cab go any faster?

Genevieve hurled herself from the vehicle the moment it slowed in front of the stately, Italianate brick building. The rain was picking up now, its sharp and pungent scent filling her nostrils. Thunder rumbled ominously in the distance as she tugged on the handle of the front door to no avail.

"It's locked," she cried to Daniel as the cab clattered away, it too being in a hurry to find shelter from the impending storm.

Daniel frowned, grasping the handle and yanking hard. The giant wooden door shifted but hesitated. "It's not locked, just swollen," he muttered and pulled again, harder. With a groan, the door gave way, creaking open.

The silent building seemed empty, dark with the lack of sunlight, the pleasant scent of rain instantly replaced with the musty odor of a seldom-used building. The shadow of the large staircase loomed directly ahead of them, and Daniel led the way, slowly moving on quiet feet.

They didn't speak during their ascent. When they reached the second floor landing, enough light pooled in through the windows from the exterior streetlights for Daniel to cast her an inquiring look. She pointed up, then held up three fingers.

Third floor.

That's where Callie had said Walter's studio was located. Up they went.

Daniel stumbled suddenly in front of her, clasping the banister hard, a soft curse escaping his mouth. Something warm and sinuous slid across her ankles. Genevieve yelped uncontrollably and was fighting for balance, her arms wheeling, certain for a sickening moment that she was about to tumble down the wide, dark stairs, when a strong arm wrapped around her waist and pulled her close, steadying her.

They stood for a moment, pressed hard against each other and gripping the banister, panting in the shadows.

"Keep a firm grip," Daniel said, keeping his voice low, even though, other than the cat that had almost sent them tumbling, there was no sign of life in the place: no light shining beneath closed, locked studio doors, no sound of chatter, no acrid tang of turpentine in the air.

The third floor was like the rest of the building, still and shuttered.

"Here." Daniel had advanced farther down the dark hall. Genevieve followed the sound of his voice, the shapes of doors on either side emerging as her eyes continued to adjust to the dim hallway.

One door was slightly cracked, and the plaintive sound of a meow rose from the other side.

Genevieve kept her hand on Daniel's damp sleeve as he slowly opened the door.

A cat shot past their feet, its color indeterminable in the dark.

"Callie?" Daniel called. His voice echoed slightly; it must be a big space. "Walter?"

Quiet answered.

"Can you find a light?" Genevieve whispered. She wanted to rush into the studio, to scream, to tear the place apart until she found her friend. She had her favorite gun in her pocket, the small derringer. She'd begun carrying it everywhere after the peeper had appeared in her room.

But she hadn't fired it, or any weapon, since she'd killed Tommy Meade.

She wasn't sure she could.

Her fingers curled around the derringer's slight, familiar weight in the warmth of her pocket, just as Daniel turned up a gas lamp next to the door.

Glowing light illuminated a big, rectangular, wood-paneled room. It was filthy: scraps of balled-up paper and plates of moldy, half-eaten meals littered the floor; empty wine and whiskey bottles crowded the corners. A few spindled wooden chairs had been shoved against one wall, but otherwise the space was devoid of furniture, with no hangings or bric-a-brac, so unlike the cluttered, crammed studios of Chase and Paxton.

Daniel pulled a face, and Genevieve understood. It smelled in here, of unwashed bodies and rotten food, overlaid with a scent of chalky earthiness.

In the center of the room, in glorious isolation, stood the gleaming, pristine sculpture of Callie as Persephone.

Walter had chosen the moment of Persephone's abduction by Hades. Callie-as-Persephone was twisting, pure anguish on her face, desperate to escape the god of the underworld's clutches. The figure of Hades was a monster, with cloven feet and deep, curling horns on either side of his head, clawed hands firmly wrapped around Persephone's waist as she writhed in his grasp. His head was thrown back, fangs bared in a fearsome snarl, long locks of hair falling to his shoulders.

Artistically, the work was a marvel. Walter had achieved a level of technical virtuosity, as the figure of Persephone seemed weightless, her reaching arms and revolved torso appearing to hover realistically, the heavy marble somehow so perfectly balanced it was nearly suspended. Similarly, the way Walter had crafted Hades's cruel, pointed claws digging into the soft sides of Persephone's middle was astonishing, the hard stone carved to look pliant and soft.

Sudden nausea racked Genevieve's body at the sight of it, artistic merit or not.

That was her friend's face contorted in agony. Even if hewn from marble and not flesh, the sight of it turned her stomach.

Fine white dust from where the stone had been chiseled rested on everything: the plates, the old food, filmy on half-drunk cups of wine, all across the floors. Cats' paw prints crisscrossed the powder in a dizzying pattern.

It was the room of a man who had descended into madness.

"Genevieve, look." She tore her gaze away from Callie-as-Persephone's writhing form and followed the direction of Daniel's finger.

Near a door on the right wall, the thick dust was disturbed, patches shoved aside, some areas long and thin, some thick and oblong, the stained wooden floor beneath laid bare.

Shoe prints, some muddled, some clear, surrounded this area.

Her eyes flew to the closed door.

"Someone's been here." The words were tight in her throat.

Daniel nodded. He produced a gun from beneath his jacket and crept toward the door on silent feet, pausing just outside before glancing at her for affirmation.

Genevieve withdrew her own firearm. One of Daniel's brows rose slightly, but more in acknowledgment than surprise.

She wished her hands would stop shaking.

Daniel kept to the left of the door as he reached over and slowly turned the knob.

Genevieve steadied her right hand with her left, holding it firm, aiming her gun squarely at whatever lay within.

A low groan sounded as the door opened, and she dropped her arm, racing into the blackness.

CHAPTER 25

"Genevieve."

Daniel's heart spiked as Genevieve dashed past him, heedlessly thrusting herself into the room and whatever unknown danger lay within.

Dammit, dammit, dammit.

He kept his gun drawn as he quickly followed, unsure what he would discover.

It was Gavin. His eyes were closed but fluttered once as he gave another low moan. The left side of his face and neck were covered in blood, and even in the dim light, it was obvious his arm was bent at an unnatural angle.

Genevieve knelt by her brother's side, and he joined her, assessing the damage. A large gash was present on the left side of Gavin's head, but it seemed to have stopped bleeding. Daniel pressed his handkerchief there all the same.

"Daniel." Genevieve whispered his name, pointing to the nasty, inch-long cut on the left side of Gavin's neck, also thick with just-congealing blood. Daniel swallowed with relief.

Whatever had happened, Walter hadn't been able to finish what he started.

"Callie." Gavin's eyes partially opened, his voice a low croak.

"Don't try to talk, Gavin. You're hurt." Genevieve had retrieved her own handkerchief and was gently wiping blood from her brother's face, her voice gentle but her eyes large, worried pools, her shoulders a tense line.

"No, please. We have to find Callie." Gavin pressed his forearms into the floor, trying to push himself upright.

"Gavin, your sister is right. You've got a nasty head wound, and you've lost a lot of blood. Lie still, and we'll fetch a doctor," Daniel said.

Genevieve slipped a palm under Gavin's head as he collapsed to the floor again, his arms giving way.

"No. I'll be fine," he gasped. "You must find Callie."

Daniel caught Genevieve's eye. She returned his gaze wildly, her breath hitching. He understood: leave her brother in a fragile condition to chase her best friend, or stay with Gavin and possibly let Callie die?

"Gavin, can you say what happened? Do you know where Callie might be?" he asked, hoping against hope Gavin could help.

Haltingly, Gavin told his tale.

He had received a note from Walter earlier that evening, in which Walter claimed to know about him and Callie and asked if they could meet to discuss the matter.

"Like men," Gavin said, leaning his head back and closing his eyes. He was pale as a sheet. At his insistence, and with Genevieve and Daniel's help, he had managed to sit, and was now propped against a wall in the side room of the studio, which Walter was using as a bedroom.

There had clearly been a struggle. A side table was overturned, a blue ceramic pitcher smashed, tiny shards littering the floor. Pooling water from the pitcher mixed with

Gavin's blood, splashing the walls in a dizzying pattern, puddling on the floor.

Otherwise, the room was inexplicably much tidier than the main studio, devoid of rotting food, empty bottles, and that fine, eerie sheen of marble dust.

Gavin was cradling his right arm and had gasped sharply in pain as they shifted him. There were no protruding bones, but Daniel was certain it was broken.

"I want to marry Callie," Gavin said. His voice was a trifle stronger now that he was seated. Or perhaps his depth of feeling added force to his words. "I want her to come to Chicago with me. I think she wants the same. It was foolish, wrong of me to speak to Walter before Callie, but I couldn't share her anymore. I wanted to be done with it, wanted Walter out of our lives, so I said yes."

Genevieve's lips thinned, but she said nothing as she continued to wipe blood from Gavin's face.

"He asked me to come here," Gavin continued. "I should have known right away. That sculpture, the mess. Something wasn't right."

Walter had leaned out of the bedroom and called to Gavin, apologizing for the state of the studio and asking Gavin to join him for something to drink.

"I felt I owed it to Callie to have this out with him," Gavin said. His voice was losing strength again, and his eyelids were drooping. "As I entered, Callie yelled for me to run. And then it all happened so fast. Walter had my arm behind my back, a knife at my throat. Callie was there, on the bed; her hands were tied, but she was trying to stand. We struggled, Walter and I. My arm snapped. I heard it almost before I felt it. I don't know what happened next. I woke up to you."

"It looks as though you hit your head on this side table," Daniel said, indicating the broken pottery, the overturned table. He was crouching next to Gavin and could envision the grim scene clearly. "It's lucky you weren't killed."

"We have to get you help," Genevieve said. Desperation laced her words. "Your arm," she began, but Gavin cut her off.

"You have to find Callie."

"I'm not leaving you."

"I've stopped bleeding. Haven't I, McCaffrey? I'm lucid. It's Friday. Benjamin Harrison is president. You're my sister. And you need to find your friend, the woman I love."

Genevieve took a breath to speak, but Gavin kept talking. If anything, he paled further as he spoke, and his words were becoming more labored. Talking was obviously costing him extraordinary effort.

"I'll be okay. They'll set my arm; it will be okay. But Callie might not be. Two of you is better than one. McCaffrey here doesn't have time for his usual hooligan backups. There's no *time*, Genevieve. Please, go."

Tears ran down her cheeks as Gavin closed his eyes, his breath shallow.

"I was wrong, Genevieve. So wrong." Gavin's eyes opened again, mere slits, but they slid between Daniel and Genevieve. "You'll do better together. Find her."

* * *

Genevieve barely had time to process Gavin's words as she and Daniel moved, as quickly as they could, back down the wide staircase in the dark, gripping the banister to avoid being tripped by a stray feline. Leaving her brother broken and bloody in that horrible place, with that obscene sculpture, was one of the hardest things she had ever had to do.

"He will be fine. We will get him the help he needs," Daniel promised as they finally descended. Genevieve grasped the front door handle, eager to leave this wretched building, but Daniel's hand on her arm stayed her.

"Wait, Genevieve. There's a major storm happening. Let's take a moment to think."

She opened the door a few inches anyway. Wind howled, blowing the hard rain nearly sideways, incongruous after weeks of debilitating heat.

"We don't have a moment," she snapped. *Blast* the storm. Her brother was barely conscious; Callie was somewhere in the city with a murderous madman. The fierce urge to be out there searching, even in the thunder and pouring rain, pulled at her incessantly.

"All we'll do is waste time if we don't have a plan. Let's think of where they might be before running pell-mell in the middle of a raging thunderstorm."

Her frustration mounted, but Genevieve knew Daniel was right. She kept her hand on the door handle, kept the door open, and looked into the wild night.

Where could they be?

"Maybe back at his house, on Stuyvesant Park?" she said. "Where Callie lives? That's what he did to Bea . . . at her own apartment." She swallowed hard.

Daniel shook his head. "I don't think so. He knows we'll have found Dorothy Flender by now, knows we'll have pieced it together. He's getting reckless, luring Gavin to the studio with a note, a note the police could find later. You saw that sculpture, how he depicted himself as a beast. He doesn't expect to come back from this."

The rain pounded and a flare of lighting lit the sky, illuminating Daniel's face, determination rendering his handsome features harsh.

"What, then?" Her stomach clenched, and her fingers gripped the door handle tightly. It was taking all her self-control to not fling the door open the rest of the way and dash into the street, screaming Callie's name.

"He'll want to do something big. Callie is his muse, after all. The one he doesn't want to get away."

It hit her, all at once.

Something big. *Somewhere* big.

"The Bridge," she breathed. "He's taken her to the Bridge, hasn't he?" The East River Bridge that connected New York to Brooklyn, the structure Walter most admired in the city.

"That's my best guess."

Gavin's words leapt into her brain: *You'll do better together.*

There wasn't time to debate it or second-guess themselves.

"We'll never get a cab," Genevieve said, staring through the door again. If anything, the rain was coming down harder. "But my house is only a few blocks away. We can take my family's carriage. Come on."

The temperature had dropped so sharply Genevieve gasped, her already-damp clothes instantly soaked through. They ran through the empty streets, kicking up sprays of water, heads bowed against the downpour. She winced at a particularly loud clap of thunder but kept running, mentally cursing her heavy, rain-soaked skirts and the inconveniences of women's fashion.

"Here," she called over the wind, rounding the corner of the Mews behind Washington Square North and pointing Daniel to her family's carriage house.

Being in the Mews instantly recalled to mind the peeper, who had escaped this way from her bedroom and still not been caught. She shuddered, from the memory and the cold equally, and wrapped her arms around her chest. The narrowness of the lane between the back of the row homes and the carriage houses, the familiar silhouette of the rooflines, including her own, all took on a sinister cast in the dark, raging storm. The same suffocating feeling she'd experienced in the cab closed in again, but she climbed into the carriage regardless once Daniel had finished hitching their horse, Junie. Genevieve hated bringing her out in this weather, but there was no helping it.

Junie was well used to the city streets, though, and while she snorted her displeasure, she followed Daniel's instructions, pulling the carriage steadily down Broadway. They passed few other vehicles on their way, most of the city's populace having had the sense to have taken shelter. Genevieve shivered, her teeth chattering, the shelter of the closed carriage providing little relief from the cold as her clothes lay sodden and chilly against her body. Daniel, sitting outside to drive, must be even colder.

It didn't matter.

Nothing mattered, except getting to the Bridge on time.

They clattered down Newspaper Row, past her office, and suddenly there it was, its unmistakable Gothic arches and graceful span dominating the skyline. Even at night, only half-visible in the storm, the Bridge was breathtaking in its elegance.

And also in its height.

The span itself was at least 125 feet above the East River, she recalled, and the towers more than twice that.

What if you guessed wrong, and Callie isn't here at all?

She shoved the thought away, as it would do no good now.

Callie was up there, somewhere.

She had to be.

The rain continued to pound, bouncing off the carriage roof with force. They had stopped at the foot of the approach, and Daniel climbed back in after securing Junie to a post.

He was as soaked as if he had jumped into the East River.

"There isn't any way I can convince you to stay in the carriage, is there?"

Genevieve didn't bother answering or even slanting him a look.

"You're shivering," she said instead, watching rivulets of water run down his face from his sodden hat.

"Your teeth are chattering."

"We should walk, though, rather than drive up the approach."

"I agree."

They stared at each other for a beat, the interior of the carriage humid with their commingled breath. The feeling that they were savoring a final moment, the barest amount of time as every second ticked closer to Callie's potential demise, hung between them. Genevieve felt, somehow in her very bones, that once they left the carriage and ascended the bridge, they would be embarking on a journey that could have disastrous, potentially fatal, consequences.

Daniel blinked and swallowed, shifting his attention to the rain outside, the fragile moment broken.

"Let's go," he said.

Once again, the briny scent of the river assailed her senses, forcibly reminding her how close they were to the ocean. She glanced in the direction of Staten Island, hoping Dorothy's sturdy little boat had recrossed the bay safely. The rain slowed as they walked, not stopping but lessening in intensity. Genevieve breathed a sigh of relief, able to see the stretch of walkway ahead of them more clearly. The bridge was normally busy with traffic, thronged with pedestrians on the upper walkway and carriages on the lower roadway, but now, past midnight during the worst weather the city had seen in months, it was preternaturally empty.

"Isn't there a night watchman?" she said as they progressed, speaking as quietly as she could. The only sound was the steady thrum of rain, beating on the wooden planks of the walkway and on the asphalt of the roadway below. In a city usually so vibrant, so busy, the quiet was eerie.

"There is," Daniel affirmed, glancing back once over his shoulder. Genevieve glanced back too.

There was nothing, just the empty stretch of walkway leading back to the city, the river on either side of them.

"The guard house looked empty when we passed it," he continued, looking forward again, also keeping his voice just above a whisper.

Genevieve's skin prickled under her soaked clothing. Empty by chance, or by design? There was no way to know. They were approaching the first of the Bridge's two towers, its twin pointed arches a dark silhouette against the low clouds.

Could Callie be atop the tower?

A low huff of laughter came from her left.

She turned to Daniel in astonishment.

"What on earth could be funny?" she hissed.

He pointed as a slim gray cat, its fur wet and matted, trotted past them, seeming to not mind the rain in the least.

"What in the world?" she asked, turning again to watch the cat's descent.

"There's a band of strays that roam the Bridge," Daniel said. "Left from when they demolished the tenements to make way for the approach."

"I've had quite my share of felines," she muttered, frowning after the cat. She didn't find the animal's presence amusing. If anything, it disquieted her further.

Genevieve placed her hand in her pocket, reassured that her derringer still rested within. She hoped it hadn't become too wet to fire.

Once on the other side of the tower, she stopped in frustration. The rain had slowed even more, but she still had to wipe it from her face to see very far. They were almost at the apex of the span, high above the water.

There was nothing. Nobody. Just a few spare, distant lights on both shores.

"What if we're wrong?" she asked. Her chest contracted, and unwanted tears crowded her eyes. "What if we guessed wrong?" Genevieve picked up her skirt and twisted it fiercely, trying to wring out some of the water.

Daniel stopped with her. "I don't think we are," he said, but his features were troubled.

Genevieve released her skirts, letting them damply fall. It was no use; they would simply be soaked. She turned in a slow circle, straining her eyes to see something, anything, through the low, shrouding mists.

As she completed her turn, facing Brooklyn once more, a flash of white caught her eye.

She grabbed Daniel's sleeve and pointed.

"There. What is that?"

The white smear seemed to hover above the water, not moving, about a hundred yards ahead and to the right of them.

"Stay close to me," Daniel whispered, his eyes never leaving the spot. "And be careful."

Genevieve did as requested, hovering close to Daniel's broad back. The bright patch was still there, growing bigger and starker as they moved close, vibrant against the shifting grays of sky and water.

A gasp rent itself from her chest, louder than she wished, but she was unable to control herself.

The white smudge had coalesced, forming into the unmistakable shape of a person.

A woman, clad only in her undergarments, somehow resting on one of the steel beams that secured the outermost network of the bridge's suspension cables.

It was Callie, dangling above the East River, one hundred feet in the air.

CHAPTER 26

Horror filled Daniel at the sight.

The pedestrian walkway, where he and Genevieve stood, ran down the middle of the length of the bridge. About twenty feet below them was the roadway for vehicular traffic, which was wider than the walkway by around thirty feet on both sides. The astonishing web of suspension cables for which the bridge was so famous connected from each tower to both the girders that made up the walkway, and those of the wider roadway.

Callie was laid on the outermost girder of the bridge. She was partially undressed, in her knickers, chemise unbuttoned, her dress and petticoats nowhere to be seen. Daniel suspected they had been cast over the bridge's edge and had fluttered, wraith-like, into the water far below.

A fate that could easily befall their wearer, only her descent would be less graceful, and far more horrific.

Surely Callie was secured to the girder somehow. It was impossibly narrow, and it would take the skill of a Barnum acrobat to maintain one's balance on it, especially in the rain. Squinting, he leaned far over the walkway's railing, desperate to ascertain if she was still alive. She wasn't moving, but there was no sign of blood, no telltale gash on her pale, exposed neck. Perhaps she was simply unconscious, for which Daniel was grateful. The precariousness of her position would be utterly terrifying were she awake. Daniel wasn't particularly afraid of heights, but the idea of shimmying across one of the beams above the roadway to get to where Callie was, where there was nothing but air between one and the churning East River far below, still turned his stomach.

And where is Walter? He could see nothing in the shadows of the tower, nothing and nobody on what he could make out of the span toward Brooklyn.

Genevieve already had a leg over the walkway's railing, clearly intending to undertake the journey across a beam to Callie herself. His heart plunged to his stomach in alarm.

"Genevieve, no," he ordered, swinging his own legs over, one, then the other. "I'm going. You stay here."

"I can do this," she said, fury and anguish evident in each word.

"This isn't about your athleticism, Genevieve. Your skirts are full of rainwater; they must weigh twenty pounds. It's not safe for you to traverse that beam. Let me go. Let me do it."

She hesitated, looking with longing at her friend. They were both on the other side of the railing now, above the roadway, feet jammed into the metal lattice of the barrier, holding on to the handrail with both arms.

The road was almost twenty feet down. One could survive a fall that distance, though asphalt was hardly a forgiving surface. Survive, yes, but the probability of breaking bones—legs, arms, neck, spine—was high.

"I'll get her," he promised. "I won't let her fall."

Genevieve bit her lip, then nodded once. "I'm staying here, though. You may need help." She inched her way slightly to her right, where she was able to rest one foot on one of the beams that crossed the roadway.

Daniel nodded back. He would have far preferred for her to wait on the safety of the walkway, on the other side of the railing, but knew this was as good as it was going to get.

Frankly, he wasn't sure his promise was one he could keep. He could get to Callie, but how would he carry her inert form back over the beam to the safety of the walkway?

There was nothing to do but try. There were no other options. Neither of them should stay on the bridge alone with Callie while the other went for help. If Walter were to return . . .

Daniel stopped that line of thought in its tracks. Even though he was sure Walter was nearby, watching them from the shadows somewhere, he couldn't dwell on that now. He needed to focus.

The steel was slippery and uncomfortable between his legs as he straddled the beam, soaking through his already-wet trousers instantly. Swallowing hard, he wrapped his fingers tightly around the beam's heft and scooched forward a few inches.

Daniel paused, looking back to Genevieve. It was on the tip of his tongue to ask her to have her gun at the ready, but it was already in her hand.

Their eyes locked.

"Keep an eye out for Walter," he said in a low voice.

Her jaw visibly tightened as her gaze darted up and down the bridge. Genevieve nodded again, wrapping her arm more firmly around the top of the railing.

"And be careful," he added, desperation and fear turning his voice rough. The sight of her, bedraggled and soaked, derringer in hand, balancing precariously above the roadway of the bridge, was almost too much to bear. "Genevieve," he began, but she cut him off.

"You be careful too." Her eyes blazed in the night.

Daniel drank in the sight of her one last time, then turned his attention back to his task.

Rain was still falling, though blessedly it had slowed to a drizzle, so his vision wasn't compromised. The beam was slick under his hands. He inhaled deeply, then blew the air out all at once before beginning to shift himself across the beam, moving slowly, taking his time. Callie's still form grew closer with every slight motion forward, and he found himself settling into a rhythm, clenching his thighs to grip the beam, placing his hands forward, then inching his seat up to his hands.

It was slow but steady. The kind of maneuver he wouldn't have thought twice about as a child, when he'd scampered through the city's construction sites like a monkey with his friends, scaling scaffoldings and clambering up half-built offices and homes, stealing whatever valuable materials they could find.

Finally, he reached the end of the beam, where it connected to the long, outermost band of steel to which the bridge's suspension cables were secured. He was on the very edge of the bridge. The East River spread before him, his view unimpeded, yawning its way toward the bay and eventually the ocean. Small, twinkling lights scattered across downtown to his right, fewer than there had been earlier, and even less to his left in Brooklyn. The rain had all but stopped, but a breeze gusted, sticking his wet clothes to his body, chilling his skin.

The sudden noise of a carriage rattling below sent a start through his body, and Daniel gripped one of the vertical suspenders to maintain his balance. He cast a quick look back to Genevieve, who hadn't moved, and then to Callie.

He had been right. Callie was tied to the girder in three places with a pale, slim rope: at her waist, around her rib cage, and at the tops of her thighs. Her body was twisted, half on its side, in an impossible position, her arms carefully placed over her head as though she were reaching for something, or someone, to save her.

Another chill racked his body. Walter had been attempting to pose Callie as Persephone before he stripped her bare and cut her throat as he had done to the others.

"Callie," Daniel whispered. He inched closer, studying the ropes as closely as he could. Another breeze blew, tossing Callie's long, unbound hair over the empty expanse beyond the bridge. "Callie," he said again, placing a hand gently on her ribs.

She was ice cold.

He felt for a pulse at her neck. It was there, faint and reedy, but there.

"She's alive," he called back to Genevieve. She sagged in relief.

How had Walter gotten her out here? Daniel suspected chloroform, as if Callie had struggled, they both would have surely fallen. Perhaps he could use the ropes, lower her unconscious form to the relative safety of the roadway below, if Genevieve was waiting there. If a vehicle passed, all the better; they could be sent for help.

He turned to call his plan to Genevieve just as her scream ripped through the night.

For the barest of seconds, Daniel was frozen with terror, unable to move his limbs, as Genevieve, shoved hard by Walter, lost her grip on the vertical suspender cable and fell, her expression of shock and panic acute and clear, before she grabbed the beam she had been standing on and hung, suspended, over the road below.

"*No.*" The word ripped from his chest as his limbs became unglued. Daniel turned fast on the beam and crawled its length, tapping into that dexterity he'd known as a boy, grasping the steel with sure fingers.

Rage laced with fear propelled him.

Walter nimbly climbed over the railing and, staring directly at Daniel, raised his foot before smashing it upon Genevieve's forearm, trying to dislodge her from the beam. Daniel's heart spiked in response to her scream of pain. She was holding fast to the beam that ran parallel to his.

"Come get her, McCaffrey," Walter taunted. He was jacketless, his thin linen shirt stuck to his body with rainwater, his long hair hanging in his face as his eyes glittered with a deranged intensity. He held a cable and leaned as far forward as his arm would allow, raising his foot for another strike. Somehow, Genevieve managed to shift her arms farther back, hauling her own dangling body more toward the center of where the beam crossed the road, away from Walter. Daniel couldn't imagine the strength it was costing her.

An evil smile danced across Walter's face as his foot made contact with Genevieve's arms again. One arm gave way and Genevieve screamed, for a second hanging by one arm alone, before wrapping both back around the security of the beam.

The moonlight, shining through a swift parting of clouds, glinted off the knife in Walter's hand as he lowered his body and began to inch on the beam toward Genevieve.

The same knife, he was sure, that had cut three women's throats. That had tried to cut Gavin's.

"Hang on, Genevieve," Daniel yelled, praying she could. He could see the next horrifying steps, clearly, in his mind: Walter sitting on the beam, lifting the knife high and plunging it wherever he could reach: Genevieve's arms, shoulders, skull.

No. His brain rejected the image forcibly, expelling it as quickly as it had come.

He couldn't allow that to happen.

Almost there.

"That's right, McCaffrey." Walter seemed delighted by Daniel's approach and abandoned his beam, climbing over the railing, readying himself for Daniel. "Come get her. Save her. Give your all for her. I've seen you two together; she's your muse, you're hers, you can't deny it."

Daniel reached the end of the beam and hauled himself up and over the railing ten seconds after Walter, but they were a costly ten seconds. He reached for his gun as soon as one leg was safely over the railing, but Walter was ready and slammed into him, knocking him to the ground, the gun skittering from his hand and across the walkway.

Pain erupted in his jaw as Walter, holding him by the collar, smashed his fist into Daniel's face.

"Muses aren't just for art, McCaffrey." A second fist, a second blast of pain, followed. "They're for *life*. You are your best with her, as she is with you. But you're too much of a coward to embrace that connection. The two of you, dancing around each other, it's absurd." Another smash, and Daniel's vision blurred. "At least I admit it, my need for my muse. I celebrate it! And I'm man enough to not let her get away. None of them should be able to get away."

A growl ripped from Daniel as he gained the fraction of space he needed to shove Walter off his chest, reversing their positions so he was on top of the other man and it was his fist pounding into Walter's face.

An ache shot up Daniel's left arm, where he had been shot earlier that summer, from the force of pressing Walter into the walkway, suddenly joined by a sharp pain lancing his belly. He flung himself off of Walter, barely having time to register the bright flower of blood staining his shirt at the abdomen before Walter lunged at him again.

The damn knife.

Daniel whirled to his left, evading Walter's grasp and the winking knife, now stained with his own blood, then lunged himself, trying to grasp the other man's legs to tackle him to the ground.

He succeeded, but barely. Walter wrenched himself free with a fierce kick, then rounded on Daniel again, lifting the knife and thrusting it down in an arc toward Daniel's chest. Daniel rolled away in time, hearing the blade hit the wooden walkway with a dull thud. He was on his feet in seconds, ignoring the pain in his arm, the searing in his stomach, and launched his body at Walter's once more. Even in the midst of the struggle, with his own blood roaring in his ears and knowing Genevieve could lose her grip and drop to the asphalt below at any moment, Daniel felt surprise at Walter's strength. But the man had spent the summer hammering marble and had the physical prowess to prove it.

Also, Walter was a madman. He had no reason for caution, no reason to hold back. He had nothing left to lose.

Daniel had everything to lose.

"Come on, McCaffrey," Walter gasped as they struggled. Daniel had Walter's right wrist in his grasp, trying to force Walter to drop the knife.

"Admit it." Their faces were inches apart. Spittle from Walter's mouth rained on Daniel's face, but he didn't dare let go of Walter's wrist. He twisted harder. "Admit you do all this for her."

The knife made a clattering noise as it fell from Walter's hand and hit the walkway, spinning away into the darkness.

"Of course I do," Daniel roared, shoving Walter away from him, hard. "Of course."

The other man stumbled, falling back on the wet surface, and Daniel wasted no time. He ran to the railing, relieved joy overwhelming him at the sight of Genevieve, still hanging fiercely to the beam.

"I'm coming, Genevieve," he yelled. He'd started to bring his leg over the railing when he was hauled back, quickly turned, and slammed against the railing.

Walter's body pressed against his, his hands wrapped around Daniel's throat, squeezing hard. Daniel pushed with all his might, trying to force Walter off of him, but the pain in his stomach was excruciating.

"Then die for her." Walter's voice was soft, almost seductive, in his ear. "Die for your muse, as she shall die for you."

Daniel gripped Walter's arms forcefully, trying to wrench the man's hands off his neck, but his strength was beginning to ebb, blackness creeping into the edges of his vision. Somewhere, in the far distance of his senses, he could hear Genevieve screaming and calling his name.

NO.

Ever since that fateful night in the gasworks, with Tommy Meade's gun pointed at his head and the indifferent stars coldly keeping vigil, Daniel had known. Known he loved Genevieve enough to die for her. That it would be his honor, his privilege, to give his life to keep hers safe.

But not like this.

NO.

He didn't want to die for Genevieve.

He wanted to *live* for her.

Genevieve was not his muse. She didn't exist to inspire him, though she did. She was her own living, radiant being, who existed to inspire herself. He only wanted to be lucky enough to live in the sphere of that light.

And the thought of that, of the preciousness of the life they could have, *should* have, drew a reserve a strength from deep within him.

With a harsh cry, Daniel forced Walter's arms apart and pushed him back.

The clouds had been steadily clearing, and out of the corner of his eye, Daniel caught moonlight twinkling off the barrel of a gun near the tower. He didn't have time to stop and consider whose gun it might be; didn't, frankly, have the wherewithal to care.

It was time to finish this.

He was charging at Walter, ignoring the screaming in his middle, a low rumbling noise ripping from his chest unbidden, when the unmistakable sound of a shot rang, shattering the night.

Daniel stopped short, his hands instinctively flying to his chest, once again expecting to see the bloom of red on his shirt.

His mind insisted, for a moment, that it was June, and the sound of the gun was the sound of his death, as he had thought it was then, not realizing at the time it had been Genevieve who pulled the trigger. That the sound of the shot didn't signify his death but his life.

He wasn't shot. It was Walter, instead, who clutched his chest. He gave Daniel one final, disbelieving look before crumpling to the ground.

It wasn't June, it was August. The stars were barely visible behind the lingering storm clouds, and he was not dead. He hadn't died. He was gloriously, wonderfully alive, as was Genevieve.

Genevieve.

Daniel hurled himself over the railing as fast as he could, the pain in his midsection forgotten, hanging on to the handrail as he reached for her hands.

He was six inches shy.

"Here, boss."

Asher's firm hand held Daniel's wrist, and satisfaction soared within him. He clasped Asher's hand and made his way farther onto the beam, anchoring himself to Asher, until he grabbed Genevieve's arm.

"Swing your leg up. I've got you."

With a grunt of effort, Genevieve swung her body up to the beam. He could feel her arms slip, having held their difficult position for minutes on end already.

"Come on," he urged. "You can do it."

She swung again, this time managing to hook a leg over the beam. His middle howled in protest as he helped haul Genevieve up until she was lying on the beam, clutching it with all her might. Asher held him steady as they both slowly drew Genevieve across the precarious beam, over the railing, and onto the safety of the walkway, where they tumbled together.

Daniel barely registered Asher, turning and yelling at someone, gesturing for help, or Rupert, holding a gun and rushing to join them, or Billy, climbing over the railing himself, shimmying across the beam with ease toward Callie, or Paddy barking orders from the walkway.

All of his attention, his senses, his entire world, had shrunk to Genevieve.

She was sobbing. Great, heaving cries that racked her whole body, and they tore Daniel apart. He heard himself whispering her name, over and over like an incantation, as he ran his fingers over her face, across her hair, down her arms, somehow unable to believe she was truly unscathed, that they had truly been blessed with such good fortune as to be alive.

When her mouth pressed to his, the shock and pleasure of it was so great, a wave of dizziness nearly caused him to black out. Instead, he grounded himself in her, in the firm reality of her body, burying his hands in her hair.

It felt exactly like coming home.

"I thought I'd lost you," she said, wrenching her mouth from him and pressing her face against his shoulder before tilting it back to his. "Again. And I couldn't bear it. I can't bear it, Daniel. I can't bear losing you."

Daniel shuddered a breath, nearly a sob, at how close, once more, they had come to death. At the precariousness of life, and at their own extreme luck.

"You didn't. You won't. I'm not going anywhere, and neither are you." Daniel pulled her into his arms and held her tight, reveling in the feel of it, breathing her in.

"Boss. Danny. You're hurt," said Asher, kneeling at his side. "We gotta get you to a doctor, and quick."

"You're bleeding, Daniel," Rupert added. He darted his eyes between the two of them, an expression of delighted tenderness gracing his features. "Can you stand?"

Genevieve scrambled up to help, gasping as she saw the blood soaking Daniel's shirt, staining her own dress.

He tried to stand but stopped short, wary of the figure who suddenly appeared behind Rupert.

It was Boyle's man, the rat-faced fellow who herded show girls at private parties, who tended bar at the Suicide Tavern. The one called Dickie.

Daniel stared at him, his mind stupefied, but his injured body instantly tensed, readying itself for another fight.

"Boyle says you're even now," Dickie said, before turning and disappearing into the low mists beginning to blanket the bridge.

CHAPTER 27

Two weeks later

"Well, you've gone and done it. Wasted the entire summer, sweating in the hot city, and now going and getting yourself stabbed. The Newport season is quite done, you know. Everyone is packing up and leaving." Rupert helped himself to a cinnamon scone as Mrs. Rafferty, Daniel's cook, offered him one from a laden tray. "We never even got to play tennis."

"You're right," Daniel said in a deadpan voice. "I should have endeavored not to injure myself so you could enjoy tennis."

"It would have been the gentlemanly thing to do." Rupert took a massive bite of his scone, his eyes rolling into the back of his head in appreciation. "Mrs. Rafferty, don't offer any of these to my lovely wife, for they will be gone in an instant and I want at least three more."

"Hush, you rascal," Mrs. Rafferty said placidly, piling Emsie's plate high. "Your missus can have as many as she wants."

"I'd like to see him try to stop me," Esmie said, nibbling one of her own scones with pleasure.

"Darling, I'd never deny you sweets, you know that. I'm merely being greedy. You know I'm incorrigible, and your appetite is one of my favorite qualities you possess." He accompanied this statement with a roguish grin and salacious wink as he demolished the remainder of his scone. Esmie blushed fiercely, hastily turning her attention to her teacup.

Genevieve caught Daniel's eye and smiled. He returned her smile with a look so charged heat rose to her face as well.

"It is a shame you can't get out and enjoy the cooler weather, though," Rupert said, moving on to his second scone. "It's nearly proper fall now."

The large, graceful windows on the front of Daniel's house showed the still bright-green leaves of the trees in Gramercy Park rustling in a soft breeze, but Genevieve understood what Rupert meant. The early September air held an undercurrent of crispness, a promise of cooler temperatures to come.

The oppressive heat had broken with the thunderstorm the night they had rescued Callie, and the temperatures since had been glorious, sunny, cooler and temperate.

"I'll be up and about more in a few weeks, the doctors say," Daniel replied, sipping his own tea. Mrs. Rafferty urged a scone on him.

It had taken over ten days following the incident on the bridge before Daniel was released from the hospital and allowed to recuperate at home. Miraculously, Walter's knife had missed his major organs, but it was going to take some months of healing before he could resume regular physical activity. He was resting in a large, comfortable armchair, clad only in his shirt sleeves and loose trousers, a woolen blanket tucked around his legs by his housekeeper, Mrs. Kelly.

"What is on your agenda while you're abroad?" Genevieve asked Esmie, sipping her tea. Rupert and Esmie were finally going on their honeymoon, a delayed trip to Europe, but they would also take time to visit Rupert's ancestral home and check the progress being made on the estate—repairs made possible by Esmie's fortune.

"Italy and France, and then we'll travel to England. I'm quite nervous to meet Rupert's mother and sisters."

"They will love you like I do," Rupert declared stoutly, but Genevieve could see some doubt in his eyes. She grimaced internally, hoping her friend had an easy visit. Rupert had claimed his family were notoriously snobbish.

"And your return?" Daniel asked quietly, refusing the offer of a third scone. Mrs. Rafferty harumphed before bustling out of the room.

The staff was committed to Daniel's recovery, including trying to help him regain some of the weight he'd lost while in hospital.

"By mid-November," Esmie said firmly. "In time for the Season."

"So you won't settle in England, then?" Genevieve asked, delighted. At one time, that had been Esmie's fondest hope, but Genevieve would miss her friend terribly were she to move abroad.

"The British countryside is frightfully dull," Rupert said, spooning more sugar into his tea. "Besides, you two can't stay out of trouble for more than a fortnight, and somebody has to make sure you don't succeed in dying." He favored them both with a gaze of mock severity before he too glanced at the trees in Gramercy Park, his expression softening. "We love New York. We want to make our home here. On our return, we'll find our own house rather than continue to live with Esmie's father. Perhaps we'll even commission Charles to design one for us."

Genevieve's eyes were drawn to Daniel again, and once more her color rose as she found him looking at her as well, a small smile playing at the corners of his mouth. They too had discussed asking Charles to design a house for them.

She and Daniel didn't have a formal agreement, not yet, but she knew it was coming. Genevieve had rarely left his bedside at the hospital, and they had spent long hours together, in his bedridden days, discussing everything under the sun and more. She knew he wanted to leave this house, Jacob Van Joost's house.

And she knew, though the question had not yet been voiced, that they would marry.

There was no going back, not now. Not ever.

She loved him, and he loved her. And they would be together.

Once he healed.

"And the accolades keep pouring in for you, Miss Palmer," Esmie teased her, tapping the folded newspaper that rested on a small mahogany side table.

Genevieve's story on Walter and the dead models had been published in the *Globe* a week prior. Esmie was right: Genevieve was receiving an inordinate amount of praise for her reporting.

But oh, there had been so much she had been forced to leave out.

She couldn't, for example, write about the gangster John Boyle's involvement in the solving of the crime. How it was he who had become suspicious that Walter was the city's version of Jack the Ripper, had thought so even when Daniel and Genevieve visited him on that sticky early August day.

"Show girls talk," he'd said, when Genevieve had gone to visit him a second time, while Daniel was still in the hospital. She had sent a note first, asking if they could meet and fully expecting to be refused, and frankly had been quite shocked when he agreed.

Asher had insisted upon accompanying her.

When Genevieve raised a gentle brow at Boyle's assertion, seated across his wide banker's desk in his windowless office, he'd raised one back.

"I wasn't lying, what I said before. Dead girls are bad for business. They're a mouthy bunch too. Some of them had suspicions about this Wilson fellow, talked about how intense he was. Too intense. They didn't like to pose for him."

"I didn't think you'd pay attention to the gossip of show girls," Genevieve said, struggling to keep the surprise from her face. She refrained from mentioning that the last time they'd talked, Boyle had referred to show girls as meat.

"You don't get far in my business unless you pay attention, Miss Stewart. To everything and anything."

Boyle had asked his thug Dickie to keep an eye on Walter, especially after Daniel and Genevieve's visit. Dickie had, even following Walter to Coney Island as Walter followed Genevieve and her group.

"Lost the bastard in the crowd." Boyle frowned. "But when I heard about that next dead girl, I knew. Didn't take a genius to put two and two together." He fixed Genevieve with a cold, wry look, clearing implying she and Daniel should have figured out Walter was dangerous much sooner.

"Why didn't you kill him right away?" Genevieve asked softly.

Boyle regarded her impassively. "Not my job. Figured I'd let you lot do it for me. And you did." After Dickie had seen Walter emerging from the Tenth Street Studio Building under the cover of the storm, carrying Callie's limp body, which had indeed been chloroformed, as Daniel suspected, he'd followed their carriage to the foot of the bridge. Dickie had raced to tell Daniel, but when he had arrived at Daniel's house, he'd found it empty, and had told Asher instead. Not knowing where Daniel was, Asher had gathered Rupert, Billy, and Paddy.

"My job was to protect my girls, however I needed to. Dead girls is bad for business," Boyle repeated. His shoulders rolled in what could generously be described as a shrug. "That Violet did have the most beautiful hair." For a moment, Boyle's expression softened.

"Everyone loved Violet, it seems," Genevieve murmured.

Boyle leaned forward suddenly, all softness gone as quickly as it had appeared, the motion so abrupt and menacing that Genevieve had to actively not shrink back in her chair.

"This," he said in voice like steel, flicking a finger between the two of them across his desk. "This meeting, that night. It was for her, and those others. And for Danny. And," he said, as he leaned back and eyed her with a predator's gaze, causing her palms to sweat, "for you."

"Me?"

"You killed Meade. My territory expanded. Like it or not, I owed you."

Genevieve started to shake her head.

"I know you didn't do it for me," Boyle continued. "But that's what happened, and I pay my debts, intended or not."

She let that sit for a moment, shaken to realize a notorious gangster like John Boyle had felt he was indebted to her.

There was only one other thing she wanted to know, a question that had burned at her for weeks now.

"Have you heard anything of Nora Westwood?" she asked. Nora, whom she and Daniel had been hired to find earlier this summer. Nora, whose betrayal had nearly caused Daniel's death. Nora, who had disappeared that night and hadn't been seen since.

As far as she knew.

Boyle's face could have been carved from stone. "Don't ask questions you don't want the answers to."

No, she couldn't write about any of that for the *Globe*'s readers.

Nor could she tell Detective Longstreet, who had stared at her long and hard when he'd questioned her in her living room, her brothers glowering at the detective from their seats.

"Who shot Walter Wilson?" Longstreet asked. "I know your skill with a firearm, Miss Stewart, and I have forgiven it once before. I don't know that I can do so a second time."

"As my sister told you, she was busy trying not to plunge to her death when the shooting occurred," Gavin said acerbically, his arm wrapped in a sling. Rupert had brought medical assistance to Gavin once it was clear Daniel was safely on the way to the hospital. His arm was broken in two places, but it would heal, as would the cuts on his head and neck.

"So you are telling me you have no idea who killed Mr. Wilson?" The detective's moustache bristled with disbelief.

"That's right," Genevieve said. She had no qualms about lying, not to protect the people she loved. She knew Rupert had pulled the trigger.

"We have recovered your derringer from the roadway, Miss Stewart."

"Then you'll know it was not my gun that fired the shot."

"Mr. McCaffrey claims it was an unknown man, a gang member, he believes."

Genevieve nodded slowly. "I would trust his account, as I witnessed nothing."

Longstreet sucked in a breath through his teeth. "He says he also witnessed nothing, having been stabbed in the abdomen by Mr. Wilson."

Genevieve nodded again.

"I think it is time for this interview to end," Charles interjected, his voice soft but stern. He stood up, forcing Longstreet to follow suit. "Our sister has endured a terrible ordeal. One which, I might add, could have been prevented had the police handled the matter properly from the beginning."

The detective's eyes blazed, but he swept them back toward Genevieve as he was handed his hat by Nellie. "I am sure I will see all of this in the papers soon, won't I, Miss Stewart?"

"Some version of it, Detective, yes. One which shall remain favorable to your department, which was indeed very helpful in this matter." She shot Charles a quelling look. "And I shall give you full credit for catching the peeper, which was ably accomplished." The police had actually had very little to do with the capture of Jack the Peeper, who, as it turned out, was a man named Norbert Ellington, a Brooklyn native whose penchant for breaking into people's homes and watching women sleep was entirely unrelated to Walter Wilson. At the next house Ellington chose, only a few blocks from the Stewart home on Washington Square, he had been tackled by the adult son of the widowed woman who lived there and nearly beaten to death before the police could arrive.

"Driven crazy by the heat, that one," Longstreet said under his breath as he left. Whether the detective meant Ellington or the man who'd almost killed him was unclear, but Genevieve held her tongue. She had a feeling she might need Longstreet's assistance again in the future.

Genevieve had kept her promise. She made sure to mention how the police department had been thorough, highlighting the role of police photographer Dagmar Hansen in particular.

But mostly she had written about the victims, about Bea and Violet and Ida. She had fully identified them, and rather than focusing on their deaths, she had fleshed out their lives. She had honored Dorothy's wishes and had not referred to her relationship with Ida, instead detailing Ida's engagement to Mikey. She wrote about their childhoods, about their ambitions and aspirations, their dreams and hopes, interests and hobbies, and how their promising young lives had been cut short by a demented man they thought they could trust—but also by a system that offered limited choices to women without means.

She had written that they were more than muses, more than empty vessels into which the desires of men could be placed, that they were fully realized women whose identities did not deserve to be reduced to their somewhat salacious profession.

She did not write about Callie.

Callie had been quieter in recent weeks, more subdued, but also glowing. She and Gavin were planning a simple wedding for next week, just immediate family and a few close friends in the Stewart front parlor, before they left for Chicago.

She wrote as little as she could about Walter, not wanting his name to become synonymous with Jack the Ripper's, not wanting the murderer to have more fame than the murdered. She'd had to relay some of it, of course. That Longstreet had found no trace of Priscilla Langston in Pittsburgh, or any-where. That Priscilla, too, was feared dead. Walter's career had been skyrocketing until the scandal with the post office building and the *Athena* sculpture, after which it went into steady decline, with fewer and fewer commissions each year. Genevieve suspected Walter had blamed his waning success on Priscilla's refusal to model for him any further, suspected Priscilla had wanted to return home against Walter's wishes, suspected she had never made it there.

Who knew how many other victims there had been, between Priscilla and Bea? How many women had already slipped through the cracks of society, dismissed, after Walter recognized them as easy prey?

Genevieve wondered if their bodies would ever be found. She figured Walter had started tentatively, hiding his victims, and had only grown bolder and more determined as the years passed and he hadn't been caught. The fact that he encouraged Callie's idea to have Genevieve and Daniel investigate Bea's murder, even, supported her theory. He had gotten away with killing for so long, preying on a vulner-able population, he must have thought himself invincible.

Plus, she suspected he had grown to enjoy it, the killing.

Genevieve shivered once, then set down her empty teacup and forced herself to relax further in her chair, allowing the patch of sun that shone through a nearby window to warm her. The ebb and flow of the others' conversation swirled around her, and she took in each precious face in turn.

All the pieces of her life were clicking into place. Not with that horrible, insectile sound she had heard in her head the night at Bright Haven, when she had figured out Walter was the killer. This was a gentle merging, like one lantern slide seamlessly transforming to the next, until the story each told became a unified, continuous whole.

Arthur had confirmed she could work on feature stories now, be a true investigative journalist.

"You've earned it," he had said, dropping the issue with her latest article onto his desk, where it displaced several loose telegrams and sheets of paper scribbled with notes, sending them fluttering to the floor. He eyed her over the rims of his spectacles. "Miss Anwyll can take over the society pages. She's better at it anyway. People want to hear what Polly Palmer has to say, Miss Stewart. Don't disappoint them. Or me."

The possibility of what this meant for her career left her nearly breathless. Her mind was already spinning with what to turn to next, where to best focus her energies.

Of the good she could do.

Across the room, Daniel caught her eye. He didn't smile this time, but held her gaze with such warmth, she promptly forgot all about her next story.

What a miracle she hadn't lost him. It made her giddy, astonished with relief and delight nearly every time she looked at him. The world was brighter now, despite its very real dangers, dangers she knew all too well. That darkness would always exist, no matter what she did—what *they*, she and Daniel together—did to try to erase it. But it coexisted with the brightest of light, one filled with luck and wonder and love.

She was brimming with all three.

"I'm relieved you'll be back for the holidays," Daniel was saying to Rupert and Esmie. "I'd be pleased to host Christmas dinner."

"Delightful," Rupert said, his eyes lighting up at the thought. "And the New Year. We don't want to miss the turning of 1890 without you. Just think, a new decade. The last of this century."

They all marveled at the idea.

"But that is months away," Esmie said. "We have a whole lovely autumn to enjoy first. One with no more adventures, if you please. Can you promise? I'm not sure I can bear another."

"I can't engage in any adventure in my condition," said Daniel. "So you can count on me to keep that promise."

"Well, Genevieve?" Esmie said. "And what about you? Do you promise?"

Genevieve took a breath to reply, but thought of all the stories she wanted to write, of the wrongs she wanted to help make right.

Of Dagmar Hansen, taking photographs of slums and tenements and bars and opium dens, trying to raise awareness about poverty.

Of the impoverished shoved onto Blackwell's Island, trapped there, criminalized for merely trying to survive.

Of the Priscillas and Beas and Violets and Idas, girls who had also been merely trying to survive, of their limited options.

Of Nora Westwood.

Of the fate that had nearly befallen Callie.

"I shall try," she said, smiling at Daniel. He smiled back, a knowing smile, as though he knew exactly what she was thinking.

As if he knew, and understood. And loved her for it.

"But no, I can't make any promises."

ACKNOWLEDGMENTS

While I draw on my academic research and knowledge of nineteenth-century New York for all of the Gilded Gotham Mystery books, *Treachery on Tenth Street* is first instance in which my two professional worlds—art history and fiction—have so neatly intersected. I am grateful to my many colleagues in the field who have supported and encouraged my segue from academia into the world of writing. For this book, I enjoyed a long conversation with art historian and longtime friend Bruce Weber about the lives of artists' models in this period, and he pointed me to some very helpful sources.

The Tenth Street Studio building was a real place, located at 51 West 10th Street, between 5th and 6th avenues. It was designed by Richard Morris Hunt, opened in 1857, and was among the first structures in the city specifically designed to address the needs of artists. William Merritt Chase was a real artist who did have a famous studio within the building, though to the best of my knowledge nobody was ever murdered there. I relied heavily on both period descriptions and contemporary scholarship of the Tenth Street Studio Building to make it come to life, including a delightful 1966 article by Garnett McCoy in *The Archives of American Art Journal,* which detailed both the gangs of cats that roamed the place and the impromptu fancy-dress party I describe. No work on the subject would be complete without consulting the essential research of art historian Annette Blaugrund. As for Chase, it was my pleasure to work on an exhibition on the artist with Bruce Weber many years ago, and our catalogue from that show served me well in the writing of this book, as did multiple other sources. Chase's art colony at Shinnecock was also a real place, becoming a proper school of art in 1891. Among others, Cynthia V. A. Schaffner and Lori Zabar's 2010 article in *Winterthur Portfolio,* "The Founding and Design of William Merritt Chase's Shinnecock Hills Summer School of Art and the Art Village," is a wonderful resource on this topic.

Several other artists that appear in the book are fictionalized versions of real people. Dagmar Hansen in based on the late nineteenth century police reporter, reformer and photographer Jacob Riis (it is one of Riis's most well-known photographs, *Bandit's Roost* of 1888, that inspired the opening scene in *Deception by Gaslight,* where Genevieve and Daniel first meet), and Dorothy Flender is based on the photographer Alice Austen, whose Staten Island home Clear Comfort is now a wonderful museum devoted to the artist's life. I took some liberties with the timing of Austen's work, as she was more active as a photographer a few years after *Treachery on Tenth Street* takes place, and the photographic series Dorothy creates of Ida is based on the work of photographer Anne Brigman.

The wild dinner hosted by Matthew Shipman at Sherry's in the book is based on the description of such dinners in M. H. Dunlop's book *Gilded City: Scandal and Sensation in*

Turn-of-the-Century New York, in particular the 1896 stag party Herbert Seeley threw for his brother Clinton Seeley (both nephews of P. T. Barnum). Also real, of course, is the indominable Coney Island. It has changed significantly since 1889, but is still a locus of pleasure and entertainment for all New Yorkers. The Elephantine Colossus was a short-lived but fascinating structure at the amusement park, in existence from 1885 to 1896, when it burned down. At some point the phrase "seeing the elephant" came to be a euphemism for visiting a sex worker, due to the use of the upstairs rooms for such purposes. In 1885, a woman named Eliza Hemerman really did slide down the inside of the elephant's trunk and became trapped in the shed at its base, though to less deadly results. The plague of "Jack the Peeper" was also real, based on a person of that nickname who broke into homes during the hot summer of 1889 to spy on women while they slept.

As always, I am indebted to the suggestions, enthusiasm, and careful editing of Faith Black Ross, and to the entire team at Crooked Lane Press. Also as always, my continued writing of this series is only possible with the support, encouragement and business savvy of my agent Danielle Egan-Miller. Enormous thanks to her and to her entire team at Browne & Miller Literary Associates, in particular Eleanor Imbody.

I am wildly lucky to be surrounded by wonderful friends and family, and extend a general blanket of gratitude to them all, especially Chrissy Gillespie, Celeste Donovan, and of course my husband Marc. Lastly, I want to thank each and every reader who has taken a chance on any of the Gilded Gotham Mysteries. I am truly humbled and grateful that you take time out of your lives to inhabit Genevieve and Daniel's world with me.